SO-CUI-611

OXFORD WORLD'S CLASSICS

DAISY MILLER

AND

AN INTERNATIONAL EPISODE

HENRY JAMES was born in New York in 1843 of ancestry both Irish and Scottish. He received a remarkably cosmopolitan education in New York, London, Paris, and Geneva, and entered law school at Harvard in 1862. After 1869 he lived mostly in Europe, at first writing critical articles, reviews, and short stories for American periodicals. He lived in London for more than twenty years, and in 1898 moved to Rye, where his later novels were written. Under the influence of an ardent sympathy for the British cause in the First World War, Henry James was in 1915 naturalized a British subject. He died in 1916.

In his early novels, which include *Roderick Hudson* (1875), *The American* (1877), and *The Portrait of a Lady* (1881), he was chiefly concerned with the impact of the older civilization of Europe upon American life. He analysed English character with extreme subtlety in such novels as *What Maisie Knew* (1897) and *The Awkward Age* (1899). In his last three great novels, *The Wings of the Dove* (1902), *The Ambassadors* (1903), and *The Golden Bowl* (1904), he returned to the 'international' theme of the contrast of American and European character.

ADRIAN POOLE is Professor of English Literature and Fellow of Trinity College, Cambridge. He has written extensively on Henry James and has edited *What Maisie Knew*, *The American*, *Washington Square*, and *The Aspern Papers and Other Stories* for Oxford World's Classics.

OXFORD WORLD'S CLASSICS

*For over 100 years Oxford World's Classics have brought
readers closer to the world's great literature. Now with over 700
titles—from the 4,000-year-old myths of Mesopotamia to the
twentieth century's greatest novels—the series makes available
lesser-known as well as celebrated writing.*

*The pocket-sized hardbacks of the early years contained
introductions by Virginia Woolf, T. S. Eliot, Graham Greene,
and other literary figures which enriched the experience of reading.
Today the series is recognized for its fine scholarship and
reliability in texts that span world literature, drama and poetry,
religion, philosophy, and politics. Each edition includes perceptive
commentary and essential background information to meet the
changing needs of readers.*

OXFORD WORLD'S CLASSICS

HENRY JAMES

Daisy Miller

and

An International Episode

Edited with an Introduction and Notes by
ADRIAN POOLE

OXFORD
UNIVERSITY PRESS

OXFORD

UNIVERSITY PRESS

Great Clarendon Street, Oxford OX2 6DP
United Kingdom

Oxford University Press is a department of the University of Oxford.
It furthers the University's objective of excellence in research, scholarship,
and education by publishing worldwide. Oxford is a registered trade mark of
Oxford University Press in the UK and in certain other countries

First published as an Oxford World's Classics paperback 2013

Impression: 9

British Library Cataloguing in Publication Data

Data available

ISBN 978-0-19-963988-5

Printed in Great Britain by
Clays Ltd, Elcograf S.p.A.

CONTENTS

CONTENTS

INTRODUCTION

In Daisy Miller James created, or recognized, a new kind of American princess. She is beautiful, bold, wealthy, and extraordinarily well dressed. She is also ill-mannered, reckless, vulgar, ignorant, and in some sense 'innocent'. In what sense, exactly? Is she truly, in the root sense of the word 'innocent', harmless? What harm could she inflict or incur? To her fellow characters this is not a theoretical question but a practical or even a pragmatic one. How are you supposed to behave towards this person? What do you say? What do you *do*? For Daisy puts everyone on the spot, not least the serious and cautious young man with the ill-omened name of Winterbourne, who is attracted and repelled in unpredictably varying measure.

'Daisy Miller: A Study' (as it was first known)[1] provided her author with a popular success he never repeated. It remains the fiction by which James is best known to readers who know little else of him. Why? Like his other most resonant fictions, it draws on a myth of beauty, innocence, grace, and promise menaced by predatory worldliness. This fable goes back to the Garden of Eden and popular folk tale, but it was particularly congenial to the imagination that produced Milton's *Comus* and winged Puritans to America in the seventeenth century. Two centuries later its vitality had become troubled, both for Nathaniel Hawthorne before the American Civil War and his successor Henry James after it, by modern forms of scepticism, resistance, and outright hostility towards such hoary anachronisms. What did such ancient superstitions about 'virtue' and 'vice' have to do with a contemporary world? And yet, for better or worse, they still exerted a pressure and answered a need requiring new kinds of explanation, such as Freud and others would shortly provide. James does not disown the force of a fable in which a young American woman embodies values that the Old World threatens to maim, distort,

---

[1] James reflects on his decision to drop the subtitle in his Preface to the New York edition: see Appendix 1, p. 150.

degrade, and destroy. But he does hold it up for inspection and
subject it to 'complication'.

'Complication' is a word that becomes important in the second
tale reprinted here, 'An International Episode'. James conceived it
as a 'counterpart' to 'Daisy Miller', and wrote it while 'Daisy' was
enjoying its first serial run in the *Cornhill Magazine*, June–July
1878. The two tales owe much to the moment of their first writing, both for their author, in his mid-30s, establishing himself in
London as more than a promising young man of letters, and also
for the wider Anglo-American audience he was addressing on
both sides of the Atlantic, in the wake of the centenary of American
independence in 1876.[2] Both tales are deeply interested in what it
means to generalize—about Americans, Englishmen, Italians,
young women, young men, the Old World, the New World, class,
money, and status. In his non-fictional writings James enters with
zest into the adventure of categorizing and typing, a popular activ-
ity in the later nineteenth century as older forms of collective
identity broke down, became blurred and indeed complicated by
social mobility, migration, and intermarriage.[3]

In October 1878, between the first appearance of 'Daisy Miller'
and 'An International Episode', an American journal published an
essay of James's entitled 'Americans Abroad'.[4] 'Americans in
Europe are *outsiders*,' James insisted; 'to be known in Europe as
an American is to enjoy an imperfect reciprocity. . . . The great
innocence of the usual American tourist is perhaps his most general quality'. Americans have little idea of the impression they
make on sophisticated Europeans, to whom they simply appear
'very vulgar'. Nevertheless there were distinctions to be drawn
between 'the conscious and the unconscious' American, between
the expatriate resident and the tourist. There were different
forms and degrees of being an 'outsider'. What is more, and this is

---

[2] See Millicent Bell, *Meaning in Henry James*, and Adeline R. Tintner, ' "An
International Episode" '. Unless noted otherwise, full details of references in this
Introduction may be found in the Select Bibliography.

[3] See Sara Blair, *Henry James and the Writing of Race and Nation*, esp. ch. 1, 'First
Impressions: "Questions of Ethnography" and the Art of Travel', and Kendall Johnson,
Henry James and the Visual.

[4] 'Appendix III', in *The Tales of Henry James*, iii, ed. Aziz, 518–22.

typical of the way James's mind turns from one 'point of view' to its opposite, the ignorance of Americans about Europe was nothing in comparison to the ignorance of Europeans about America:

it is hardly too much to say that as a general thing, as regards this subject, the European mind is a perfect blank. A great many Americans are very ignorant of Europe, but in default of knowledge it may be said that they have a certain amount of imagination. In respect to the United States the European imagination is motionless; . . .

Not only do Americans exercise their imagination about Europe, they actually come in some numbers, for better or worse, to see for themselves.

The same month that 'Americans Abroad' appeared, another tale of James's was finishing its serial run. In *The Europeans* James imagined what might have happened, back in the innocence of pre-war New England, if a brother and sister had travelled west across the Atlantic. Two months later 'An International Episode' sent two upper-class Englishmen on a first visit to New York and Newport, and exposed their motionless imagination to modern American manners. The more eligible of the two, Lord Lambeth, is bewildered by the generalizations his attractive talkative hostess, Mrs Westgate, brandishes with such confidence.

Lord Lambeth listened to her with, it must be confessed, a rather ineffectual attention, though he summoned to his aid such a show as he might of discriminating motions and murmurs. He had no great faculty for apprehending generalisations. There were some three or four indeed which, in the play of his own intelligence, he had originated and which had sometimes appeared to meet the case—any case; yet he felt he had never known such a case as Mrs Westgate or as her presentation of *her* cases. But at the present time he could hardly have been said to follow this exponent as she darted fish-like through the sea of speculation. (p. 90)

Her more available sister asks him if he has come to study American manners. But alas he hasn't yet risen, and never will, to such a level of curiosity. No wonder he's at the mercy of American hyperbole, when she extols her brother-in-law as a perfect husband.

' "But all Americans are that," she confidently continued. "Really!" Lord Lambeth exclaimed again; and wondered whether all American ladies had such a passion for generalising as these two' (p. 91). This is innocence indeed, to match Daisy Miller's.

'Daisy Miller' also rebukes the inertness of the European imagination about the fluidity, diversity, and potential of the new 'America', but it does so less directly by exposing the negotiations between Americans themselves about individual and collective identity. In 'Americans Abroad' James noticed the urgency of this debate in the wake of the centennial, a debate that at the time—for history has dramatically intervened since then—James claims would have been inconceivable for the English, the French, or the Germans, confident in their boundaries and sense of national identity.

But travel essays or critical reviews are one thing and novels and tales are another. Fiction provided James with the chance to test and contest the generalizations in which his non-fictional writings indulge through the uniqueness of a particular 'case'. This is the word associated with Mrs Westgate and Lord Lambeth's perplexities. It is quietly important in the 'case' of Daisy Miller ('a terrible case of the *perniciosa*'), as it would be a few years later in the title of his friend Robert Louis Stevenson's 'Strange Case of Dr Jekyll and Mr Hyde'. Another significant word is the subtitle that qualified 'Daisy Miller' on its first appearances: 'A Study'. This promises a preparatory sketch rather than a finished portrait, such as Isabel Archer would enjoy two years later in *The Portrait of a Lady* (1880–1). But it also suggests the analytic attitude assumed by the main male character through whom we view Daisy, the studious Winterbourne. An affair of the head then, in the way the tale views her, rather than of the heart? For the head generalizes and abstracts, it perceives forms and invents formulae, while the heart seeks the particular.

Daisy Miller

Daisy Miller is a problematic princess, drifting across Europe with her wealth and her beauty, her ribbons and parasol, not to mention her helpless mother and resentful young brother. She is an easy target for scorn, a recalcitrant object of desire, a puzzling case of neediness. The scorn is readily supplied by the matriarchs in charge of the manners and morals of polite society in New York (Winterbourne's aunt, Mrs Costello) and in Rome (the resident hostess, Mrs Walker). Daisy breaks all the rules governing relations with the other sex, about whom you speak to, where you can go, under whose supervision. For good and ill Daisy has grown up entirely unchecked; so too has her brother, the 9-year-old Randolph, one of James's most incisive cameos. In a telling revision to the tale's ending, we are told that 'she did what she liked' (p. 65). This echoes a phrase made famous by Matthew Arnold in his time, epitomizing a deplorable idea of personal liberty (see note to p. 65). As for the desire, this is naturally excited in the men around her, her Europeanized compatriot Winterbourne and his rival, the flamboyant Italian Giovanelli. And then there is the question of Daisy's neediness.

One of the things she needs is to look and be looked at. The other women look at her 'hard', as we say, constantly appraising her looks, her dress, and her conduct; it is only susceptible men who look soft. One of the tale's subjects is all this looking, gazing, surveillance. Daisy's good looks come by nature, as do her good instincts for how best to dress them and frame them, but the clothes themselves and all her accessories, including the settings she chooses, are matters of money and art. And it's these that get everyone round her excited. How artful or artless is she? Everyone sees money in the way Daisy looks and behaves, the expensive clothes and the lifestyle. And yet what provokes and troubles above all else is the ease and directness with which Daisy looks at others and receives their gaze, her confidence.

A decade earlier James had reflected on the new American girl striding into view after the end of the Civil War in 1865. 'She has . . . great composure and impenetrability of aspect. She practises a sort of half-cynical indifference to the beholder (we speak of the extreme cases). Accustomed to walk alone in the streets of a great city, and to be looked at by all sorts of people, she has

acquired an unshrinking directness of gaze.'[5] Daisy doesn't shrink
from looking or being looked at. She does not appear to be artful
in the ways conventionally sanctioned for well-bred women, for
ladies. When she flirts with Winterbourne, if that is the right word
for it—he is always struggling to find the right words for her—she
does it so openly that it seems more natural than artful. She rarely
seems to stand still or sit in one place—except at the Colosseum,
fatally, the last time we see her. She prefers to be in constant
motion, walking out and about, taking trips, tripping up and down
stairways. Even when she stands in one spot, she's usually fiddling
with ribbons or twirling her parasol. And talking, talking, talking.
This is *not* the portrait of a 'lady'. Could she be more of a contrast
to the ideal of a still and silent maiden modestly averting her gaze
from spectators?

Daisy is surrounded by other more or less wealthy Americans
living lives of expensive leisure. Where does the money come
from? James is notoriously vague about how money gets made but
he is all the more precise about how it gets used and displayed,
how it 'shows'. Like many of the fathers and husbands in his tales
(Mr Westgate in 'An International Episode' is a partial exception),
Mr Miller remains invisible back in 'the better place' championed
by his instinctively patriotic son, the aggrieved young Randolph,
labouring to sustain the lifestyle to which his womenfolk have
become accustomed. Meanwhile the Millers drift round Europe,
with the vaguest sense of what they are looking at, let alone looking for. They typify the 'unconscious' Americans in Europe James
describes in 'Americans Abroad'. They have no idea why they're
in Europe at all, except that all that money has to get spent somehow. Mrs Miller would be happier back in Schenectady sharing
her ailments with Dr Davis; so too would Randolph, stuffing himself with American candy. The young James wrote that to be an
American was a great preparation for culture, but the culture of
old Europe holds no real appeal for the Millers.

Yet Daisy is curious about the *people*, and she has an obscure

---

[5] 'Modern Women', *Literary Criticism*, i. 23. In the early version of 'Daisy Miller' her
glance is described as 'perfectly direct and unshrinking' (for the revised text, see
Appendix 3, p. 160).

sense of mission. She says that she's in search of 'society'—something to replicate what she's known in New York: 'I'm very fond of society' (p. 12). There is none in Vevey, but she's happy enough in Rome, her mother affirms: 'It's on account of the society—the society's splendid' (p. 35). 'The society's extremely select', declares Daisy. She has a naïve but genuine idea of hospitality—'I never saw anything so hospitable' (p. 39). Her sad cautionary tale touches deep instinctual beliefs we all have about the mutual obligations of hosts and guests, the promise and danger of strangers, the welcome and rebuff accorded outsiders, topics to which anthropology, a discipline concerting itself at the time James was writing, has alerted us all. T. S. Eliot memorably described James as 'possessed by the vision of an ideal society'.[6] Poor Daisy is possessed by nothing so grand, nor does she readily minister to the idea of 'some eventual sublime consensus of the educated', to which James confesses in one of his Prefaces (reprinted here, Appendix 1, p. 153). Yet in her restless, impatient, innocuous way she does express the instinct and desire for sociability. Thinking of the 'manners' of James's own writing style—the little courtesies and qualifications and circumlocutions—Mary Ann O'Farrell writes suggestively of their 'meaning (sometimes) nothing, but speaking and bespeaking something really huge: the felt need for sociability itself'.[7] In her tenuous well-meaning way Daisy mimics her author in expressing 'the felt need for sociability itself'.

Daisy flouts the conventions with such abandon that someone needs to 'save' her. Otherwise, so the matriarchs contend, she will be 'ruined', an outcast, a social pariah. For Winterbourne's aunt, accustomed as she is to the 'minutely hierarchical' world of New York, Daisy is already beyond the pale. In Rome Mrs Walker initially tries to save her for the 'good society' over which she presides, to educate Daisy about the boundary lines she must not cross, such as walking unchaperoned in the Pincio gardens with

---

[6] 'A Prediction in Regard to Three English Authors', *Vanity Fair* (Feb. 1924); partially repr. in *Henry James: A Collection of Critical Essays*, ed. Leon Edel (Englewood Cliffs, NJ, 1963), 56.

[7] O'Farrell, 'Manners', 198.

an almost certainly unscrupulous Italian. But it is Winterbourne who has the best chance of proving her saviour, or at least her protector, and to whom she appeals. Could he be like one of George Eliot's upright 'monitors', like Daniel Deronda in the recently published novel of that name, who shows the vain Gwendolen Harleth how she might liberate herself from the prison of egoism? This is never going to work for Daisy. She does look to Winterbourne for something, but it is neither a stern moral lesson nor 'lawless passion'. These are precisely the black and white alternatives that Winterbourne's dichotomous personality has been trained to think in. And out of which Daisy might tempt him.

For there is another less obvious possible story in which Daisy rescues Winterbourne. In another context James writes of 'the possible other case',[8] and a possible other case for Daisy and Winterbourne can be found in the dramatic version James composed a few years later, *Daisy Miller: A Comedy* (1883: see Appendix 2). In the play the chains that enthrall young Winterbourne clank much more loudly. They partly take the form of the older worldly woman who remains a mere hint in the tale, the 'very clever foreign lady' in Geneva. On stage she materializes as a wealthy, weary, glamorous Russian princess named Madame de Katkoff. She is being blackmailed by the Millers' courier, Eugenio, who plans to get his hands on their money. When this villain suggests that Winterbourne's family may set out from America to rescue him from her clutches, we suddenly glimpse the premise of one of James's later masterpieces, *The Ambassadors*, in which Chad Newsome's apparent infatuation with a Parisian *femme fatale* excites just such a plot. Daisy's mission to save Winterbourne succeeds with assistance at a critical moment from Madame de Katkoff herself, and the play ends on a classic note of comedic resolution. The younger generation—there is a secondary couple, introduced to eke out the symmetries—triumph over their elders, both the obvious dangers represented by

---

[8] James is talking in the Preface to vol. xv of the New York Edition about 'operative irony. . . the possible other case, the case rich and edifying where the actuality is pretentious and vain' (*Literary Criticism*, ii. 1229).

Madame de Katkoff (sex) and Eugenio (money), and their puritanically repressive complements, the Mrs Costellos and Walkers (Mrs Miller herself never appears). Eugenio is probably the play's best role.[9]

James's tale is infinitely more subtle than this. But in its very overtness the play helps us recognize what in the tale is so largely repressed, especially by Winterbourne himself: the possibility that Daisy might save him, not so much from the erotic clutches of the Genevan charmer as from the whole imprisoning mindset to which he has largely surrendered. Winterbourne is almost but not quite a lost cause. If only he and Daisy could make *common* cause and unite several aspects of America's potential identity—the material wealth, the desire for culture, the instinct for sociability. If only they could 'confide' in each other, to use a word and its cognates that feature significantly in James's revisions to these two tales (as well as elsewhere in his writing, including the novella *Confidence* (1879)). This is how we first see her, as 'a pretty American girl coming to stand in front of you in a garden with all the confidence in life' (p. 7). Of course she can be irritating: 'Of all this Daisy delivered herself with the sweetest brightest loudest confidence, looking now at her hostess and now at all the room' (p. 48); and yet, as with her instinct for sociability, 'her impatient confiding step' (p. 27) expresses a trust in someone else. It is a sad moment in the final scene when one of her bereft admirers decides to 'confide' in the other.

The personal liberty so blatantly—and vulnerably—championed by Daisy can never stand on its own. It needs something more than the 'imperfect reciprocity' James thought Americans were bound to encounter in Europe, something more nearly if not perfectly reciprocal, such as another kind of American might conceivably supply. A slim chance for these two particular persons, yet imaginable enough to hurt when it fails. Quite how badly it hurts Winterbourne we shall never know. But we do know that Daisy dies of it.

[9] James had a particular actor in mind for the part, Charles Brookfield, to whom he made an interesting approach about the play in Nov. 1882 (*James Letters*, ed. Edel, ii. 389–90).

It is through the dialogue that we get the most promising glimpse of what might have developed. For much of the time we have to watch Daisy through Winterbourne's eyes or over his shoulder, so it is a relief when she meets him on equal terms as a speaking partner. Daisy can more than hold her own in quick-fire repartee. The effect of her racy colloquialisms on the reader, then or now, is uncertain. An old-fashioned ear might hear the contemporary idioms she shares with her mother and brother as horribly vulgar: 'She's always blowing at me', 'She's right down timid', 'Zürich's real lovely', 'I'm going to go it on the Pincio', and so on (pp. 6, 21, 35, 37). By contrast Winterbourne is constantly picking words up to inspect them for their credentials—ironically, quizzically, gingerly: 'an insinuation that she "picked up" acquaintances', ' "tremendous flirts" ', 'he should enjoy deucedly going "off" with her' (pp. 15, 18, 27). All the punctuation marks we have learned to call 'scare quotes' indicate his effort to hold words in a kind of quarantine. Yet one of the things that attracts him is exactly Daisy's exemption from the studied, finished verbal forms he's used to. If talking with her is so free and easy, what might more intimate intercourse be like? He's not used to being teased, and Daisy is good at it. When she rebukes him for not instantly coming to visit her in Rome, he declares: 'I've had the honour of telling you that I've only just stepped out of the train' (p. 39). Later she returns the compliment of this absurdly pompous courtesy: 'As I've had the pleasure of informing you, you're too stiff' (p. 50). Relax, she keeps trying to tell him: 'you've no more "give" than a ramrod' (p. 58). Or as one might say on her behalf, let your winter turn into spring.

Much of the tale's magic depends on its 'romantic' settings, in Switzerland and in Rome. The vocabulary of magic, charms, and spells is of great importance to James,[10] and Winterbourne struggles throughout the tale to work out whether Daisy's magic potion will kill him or cure him. But it is something more that works through her, something to do with the landscape and history invested in Switzerland and in Rome. Switzerland stands for the

[10] See my essay 'Henry James and Charm'.

struggle of liberty against oppression, both the Geneva of Calvin and the Vevey of Rousseau, whereas Rome stands for the weight of the past, of authority both papal and imperial. No wonder Mrs Miller prefers Zurich. Yet Switzerland is itself divided, so at least the guidebooks consumed by James's first readers assured them. Calvinist Geneva stood for spiritual probity against the libertinism of Rousseau, whose controversial best-seller *Julie, ou La Nouvelle Héloïse* (1761) had 'immortalized' Vevey and its environs. Baedeker sternly warned its readers that Rousseau had employed 'his transcendant [*sic*] powers of mind in disseminating principles, generally considered to conduce neither to the good nor the happiness of mankind'.[11] Winterbourne may have seen in Rousseau's story about the passionate love of St Preux for his pupil Julie a warning against taking on a similar role with Daisy (and her brother Randolph). As with Switzerland's contradictory models, so too with Rome, its Vatican and Colosseum, its multitudinous lessons about the possibilities of human history for good and ill, triumph and defeat, innocence and experience. Where else could an innocent American girl, 'a child of nature and of freedom', as James described her in his Preface (Appendix 1, p. 149), come face to face with a worldly old pope called—'Innocent'?

The magic of James's tale is that Daisy's 'case' is inseparable from its setting in time and place. Consider the reverberating word that describes the effect on Winterbourne when he comes across Daisy in one of Rome's most celebrated sites, 'that supreme seat of flowering desolation known as the Palace of the Caesars'.

The early Roman spring had filled the air with bloom and perfume, and the rugged surface of the Palatine was muffled with tender verdure. Daisy moved at her ease over the great mounds of ruin that are embanked with mossy marble and paved with monumental inscriptions. It seemed to him he had never known Rome so lovely as just then. He looked off at the enchanting harmony of line and colour that remotely encircles the city—he inhaled the softly humid odours and felt the freshness of the year and the antiquity of the place reaffirm themselves in deep interfusion. (p. 57)

[11] K. Baedeker, *Switzerland: Handbook for Travellers* (Leipzig, 1879), 193.

We know that the memory of this beautiful girl moving at her ease over the great mounds of ruin will live on after she is dead and gone. It is the word 'interfusion' that clinches it. 'Interfused' and 'interfusion' were not uncommon in nineteenth-century writing. They are readily found in George Eliot, Meredith, and Pater, and with some frequency in James: of Venice in 1882, for example, he declares that '[N]owhere . . . do art and life seem so interfused'.[12] Shortly after the first appearance of 'Daisy Miller', James wrote of Hawthorne's 'mixture of subtlety and simplicity, his interfusion of genius with what I have ventured to call the provincial quality'.[13] There is a fine passage describing the comfort that Isabel Archer takes in the Roman *campagna*, blending her personal sadness with thoughts of the longer continuity of the human lot: 'She had become deeply, tenderly acquainted with Rome; it interfused and moderated her passion' (ch. 49).[14] The Protestant cemetery too, had made James reflect that 'when funereal things are so interfused it seems ungrateful to call them sad'.[15]

To an ear attuned to English Romantic poetry, the word is bound to recall its appearance in Wordsworth's 'Lines Composed a Few Miles Above Tintern Abbey':

> And I have felt
> A presence that disturbs me with the joy
> Of elevated thoughts; a sense sublime
> Of something far more deeply interfused,
> Whose dwelling is the light of setting suns,
> And the round ocean and the living air,
> And the blue sky, and in the mind of man:
> A motion and a spirit, that impels
> All thinking things, all objects of all thoughts
> And rolls through all things.[16]

[12] *Collected Travel Writings: The Continent*, 303.

[13] *Literary Criticism*, i. 438.

[14] The text of 1881 is unchanged in the New York Edition, save that the semicolon becomes a colon.

[15] *Collected Travel Writings: The Continent*, 467.

[16] William Wordsworth, *The Poems*, ed. John O. Hayden (New Haven and London, 1977), i. 360.

And again in a memorable passage of *The Prelude* (Book II: School-Time), beginning 'Blest the infant Babe':

> No outcast he, bewildered and depressed:
> Along his infant veins are interfused
> The gravitation and the filial bond
> Of Nature that connect him with the world.[17]

Poor outcast Daisy, a memory of loss and painful regret, like Wordsworth's Lucy in her grave, rolled round with earth's diurnal course, with rocks and stones and trees. In his Preface James would call her a figure of 'pure poetry' (Appendix 1, p. 151).

The English Romantic poet officially invoked in 'Daisy Miller' is Byron, both at the Castle of Chillon and the Colosseum in Rome; all the guidebooks told you he was the one to read there. But here in the word 'interfusion' it is Wordsworth through whom James rebukes Winterbourne for failing to recognize Daisy for what she was, all too simply, in her mighty innocence and conceivable potential.

An International Episode

'An International Episode' inverts some leading features of 'Daisy Miller' by sending two representatives of the Old World to the New. In the earlier tale the focus was on differences within American 'society', whereas here it is on the differences between England and America. Lord Lambeth and his slightly wiser companion, Percy Beaumont, travel to New York on the pretext of some legal business but mainly as tourists. They make a familiar kind of comedic duo; Percy Beaumont is the elder 'Sense' to Lord Lambeth's 'Sensibility'. They take refuge from the summer heat in the resort of Newport, Rhode Island, where they are royally entertained by two sisters. The elder is married, a confident, loquacious hostess, Mrs Westgate, the younger a serious blue-eyed Bostonian, Bessie Alden, an antitype of Daisy Miller. Indeed, like

[17] *The Prelude: A Parallel Text*, ed. J. C. Maxwell (Harmondsworth, 1971), 87.

the Winterbourne who has lived too long in Geneva, Bessie may have lived 'rather too much in Boston', so her sister thinks. At the first sign of danger that Lord Lambeth might be getting too deeply involved with Bessie, he is summoned back by his anxious imperious mother, the Duchess of Bayswater. Not, however, before he's invited the Americans to renew their acquaintance on a visit to Europe next year. The dangerous relationship deepens in London, but just as it threatens to reach a crisis, there is a show-down between the Americans and Lord Lambeth's mother and sister. The spectre of a transatlantic union comes to nothing. It is Bessie who calls it off, anticipating Isabel Archer's rejection of Lord Warburton in *The Portrait of a Lady* (though spared the ter-rible alternative she opts for). Meanwhile her sister suffers some chagrin at the thought that the Englishwomen will suppose they have scared the interlopers off. Or no less seriously, that they won't have realized how well she is dressed. James called her 'a silly woman'.[18]

In his essay on 'The Art of Fiction' (1884) James used this tale to illustrate the range of what 'adventure' could mean for the novelist: 'for a Bostonian nymph to reject an English duke is an adventure only less stirring, I should say, than for an English duke to be rejected by a Bostonian nymph'.[19] Ian Bell suggests that James may well have been provoked to imagine his reciprocal adventure by Laurence Oliphant's *The Tender Recollections of Irene Macgillicuddy*, which he reviewed in May 1878. James noted its satirical portrait of New York manners, especially 'the eager-ness and energy displayed by marriageable maidens in what is vul-garly called "hooking" a member of the English aristocracy. The desire to connect itself by matrimony with the British nobility would seem to be, in the author's eyes, the leading characteristic of the New York "great world".'[20] It would make a good story, as would one about British nobility 'hooking' American heiresses to shore up their tottering fortunes. But English readers needed to know there was more than one kind of American woman.

---

[18] *James Letters*, ed. Edel, ii. 222.
[19] *Literary Criticism*, i. 61.
[20] Ibid. 1192.

They might even not realize the difference between New York and Boston.

If the literary sponsors of 'Daisy Miller' include Hawthorne, Turgenev,[21] and a particular tale of the now little-known Victor Cherbuliez (see note to p. 32), then 'An Episode' draws more on James's beloved Thackeray.[22] Bessie Alden is as replete with preconceptions about the Old World as poor Daisy Miller was devoid of them. She joins a series of Jamesian protagonists, sentimental tourists and passionate pilgrims, including James himself, who brim over with images of England and the English derived from their reading. In Bessie's case it is Thackeray and, more vaguely, poets and historians, some of whom she gets to meet in person. Like her author, who in later life pronounced Tennyson to be 'not Tennysonian',[23] Bessie is disappointed by the disparity between the ideas she arrives with and the realities she encounters—a very Thackerayan experience.

The comedy of these two tales is largely invested in their dialogue, in the endless possibilities for bewilderment, for half-understanding, for being surprised. When James's characters open their mouths, their words twist and turn. No wonder that James makes so much use of inverted commas, as we've seen with Winterbourne, even if it's not always clear whose eyebrows are being raised, the author-narrator's or the speaking character's. These marks on the page can also be thought of as tweezers holding up words for inspection with various kinds of amusement, amazement, and scorn. James portrays Americans as more generally hospitable than their English cousins, and they are certainly more welcoming to verbal innovation. James got into trouble with one reviewer for portraying his Englishmen as cockneyfied 'Arries' who went around saying 'I say', which of course no gentleman would. Some years later Alice James noted the kindly rebuke her brother had received for putting into an Englishman's mouth the

[21] Comparisons have been drawn with Hawthorne's tale 'Rapaccini's Daughter' (1844) and with Turgenev's 1858 novella *Asya* (I am grateful to Catherine Brown for bringing this latter to my attention).

[22] See Tintner, '"An International Episode"', 25, 32–3.

[23] *Notes of a Son and Brother*, ed. Collister, 457.

words 'Never, never', and 'Never in the World', which was inconceivable. Alice wickedly concurred:

This is undoubtedly true, for you *can* absolutely assert what an Englishman never has said, it satisfying his highest craving to crib, cabin and confine his fancies within a dozen or so locutions, as if there were a certain absence of decency in playing with verbal subtleties: 'very clever' for example, doing service for the infinite and delicate shades of subdivision to be noted upon the intellectual scale, . . .; but how could one deny that this or that had been said by a Yankee, for is *his* soul ever more rejoiced than when he has made the next man 'sit up' by some start into the open, linguistic or ideal?[24]

This gives a good sense of the receptive hearing brother Harry could rely on back home in Cambridge and Boston when he penned the portrait of Lord Lambeth and his restricted verbal resources.

James had an amused and curious ear for the colloquial, the slangy, the idiomatic, the fashionable. 'An International Episode' is rich in such diction: 'I call that "real mean" ', 'American girls are very "cute" ', 'boasting and "blowing" and waving the American flag', 'every one would want them to "visit round", as somebody called it', 'she's what they call in Boston "thoughtful" ', 'Mr Westgate, all this time, hadn't, as they said at Newport, "come on" ' (pp. 81, 82, 89, 92, 99, 105). Here is a typical exchange between Beaumont and his friend:

'I shouldn't think she'd be in your line.'
  'What do you call my "line"? You don't set her down, I suppose, as "fast"?' (p. 103)

Particularly noticeable is the way everyday speech turns slightly mysterious: 'when you take to visiting the sights of the metropolis with a little nobody of an American girl something may be supposed to be "up" '. Or:

'She'll go to the girl herself.'
  'How do you mean "go" to her?'
  'She'll try to get "at" her—to square her.' (p. 138)

The effect is unsettling, as if your own language were turning foreign. Little words you thought were innocuous turn difficult and contrary—'up', 'go', 'at'. Of course this is not all harmless fun; through such verbal skirmishes, serious duels can be fought:

'However, I don't believe in that.'
 'I like the way you say "however"!' (p. 141)

At the final showdown between the four women, the narrator intervenes to mark the resonance, for Bessie, of the Duchess's climactic assault on the young girl: 'Shall you be long at Branches?' she asks abruptly. Bessie wonders ever after, what the Duchess meant by 'long'. 'But', we are told, 'she might as well somehow have wondered what the occupants of the planet Mars would' (p. 145).

Though lighter than its predecessor, 'An International Episode' is no less seriously concerned with the anxious negotiations, the potential alliances and disappointments informing new collective and individual identities. Not the all-American cast of 'Daisy Miller' in this case, but the beginnings of a new Anglo-American pact, with which we are now all familiar, one based on marriage and money. It is one of James's great subjects. Though we do here get a glimpse of Mr Westgate, the father and husband who makes all the money, it's the women who hold centre stage, as they do in 'Daisy Miller'. They do the shopping and the hospitality, the performance of 'culture'. Mrs Westgate is as formidable a representative of the new American wife as poor Mrs Miller was feckless and hopeless. One can never imagine Daisy's mother saying this: 'An American woman who respects herself . . . must buy something every day of her life. If she can't do it herself she must send out some member of her family for the purpose' (p. 98). But then Kitty Westgate and her serious sister are as different from the Millers as their stylish Newport is from vulgar Saratoga (see note to p. 3 on Newport and Saratoga).

The main contrast here is between Newport and London, comparable to the one in 'Daisy Miller' between Vevey and Rome. In both cases we move from the light bright open air to the big old city, heavy with History and Society. Newport represents a kind of idyll, a pastoral refuge run by the matriarchs. It is almost too good to be true: 'it was all the book of life, of American life, at least; with the chapter of "complications" bodily omitted' (p. 100). But 'complications' is a euphemism, shorthand for what the Americans will encounter in London: 'in respect to this proposal as well Mrs Westgate had the cold sense of complications' (p. 111).

James brilliantly intimates the sense of unease that can be induced by the *absence* of 'complications', by having things too easy. If the English appear not hospitable enough, the Americans are almost too much so. There is something oppressive about the endless sherry-cobblers that Mr Westgate has mixed for a previous English visitor (six in about fifteen minutes in the New York text, slightly faster than the twenty minutes in the earlier version). Or the way he enjoins the two new ones to 'Open your mouth and shut your eyes!', and—a striking revision in 1909—'Just let them do what they want with you. Take it as it's meant. Renounce your own personality. I'll come down by and by and enjoy what's left of you' (p. 80). As for his wife, the narrator finds a surprisingly hostile metaphor to describe the 'mild merciless monotony' and 'impartial flatness' of her streaming discourse, 'that suggested a flowery mead scrupulously "done over" by a steam roller that had reduced its texture to that of a drawing-room carpet' (p. 90). (Mrs Westgate noticeably suffers in revision; she is demoted from being 'extremely pretty' to merely 'pretty'.) At least one of the Englishmen senses the sharp points that can lurk behind flowery meads, drawing-room carpets, and other smooth surfaces: 'if you go straight into it, if you hurl yourself bang upon the spears, you do so with your eyes open' (p. 102), he warns his companion. When the hosts and guests change places in London, Mrs Westgate starts to match Beaumont's suspicions and anxieties. She becomes quite sharp with her less wary sister, who is determined to visit the scene of Lady Jane Grey's execution: 'Oh go to the Tower and feel the axe if you like!' (p. 113). Kitty becomes increasingly abrasive to the point where she sounds almost, well, English in her wielding of the diplomatic insult: 'She smiled at the two gentlemen for a moment with terrible brightness, as if to toss at their feet—upon their native heath—the gauntlet of defiance. "For me there are only two social positions worth speaking of—that of an American lady and that of the Emperor of Russia"' (p. 126). Is it an accident that back in America she had passingly invoked some words of the Ghost in *Hamlet*, 'with all our imperfections on our heads'? She plots a kind of revenge on their English counterparts, Lord Lambeth's wife and mother—'Then I should like to frighten them!' (p. 126)—which only the generosity and rationality of her younger sister serve to thwart. One is reminded of the words with which James closed his essay 'Americans Abroad': 'On the whole, the American in Europe may be spoken of as a provincial who is terribly bent on taking, in the fullness of ages, his revenge'.[25] Or hers, of course.

Like 'Daisy Miller', this tale takes great interest not only in speech and dialogue but also in settings, structures, and scenery. It shows a particular interest in the massive new edifices that can hold large numbers of people together, blurring the boundaries between public and private space: the hotels in New York and Newport, 'the immense labyrinthine ship' that transports them from one to the other. The description of the Newport hotel is particularly revealing: 'It was perforated from end to end with immense bare corridors, through which a strong draught freely blew, bearing along wonderful figures of ladies in white morning-dresses and clouds of Valenciennes lace, who floated down the endless vistas on expanded furbelows very much as angels spread their wings' (p. 84). This heaven is also a stage set, or a catwalk for the display of the latest expensive fashion. To English or European eyes, everything in America appears so 'open'. Hence James's amused and sometimes aghast reaction to the bewildering proliferation of apertures that characterized modern American architecture (in the New York of 1904, for example, unforgettably recorded in *The American Scene* (1907), ch. 2 'New York Revisited'). In the Newport of 'An Episode' the note he strikes is mainly one of amused astonishment at the confidence of such

[25] 'Appendix III', in *Tales of Henry James*, ed. Aziz, 522.

a structure as the Westgates' 'cottage' or magnified chalet, an edifice that knows no fear or sense of threat from intruders, or strangers, or anyone at all. Space is simply not so heavily owned and
marked off as it is back in the Old World. Here, the visitors cannot
even work out which is 'the regular entrance'.

Should we be disappointed that the Bostonian nymph and the
English duke fail to hook up across the Atlantic? Bessie is initially
attracted to Lord Lambeth because he 'repaid contemplation' (the
passage is heavily revised):

tall straight and strong, he was handsome as certain young Englishmen,
and certain young Englishmen almost alone, are handsome; with a perfect finish of feature and a visible repose of mind, an inaccessibility to
questions, somehow stamped in by the same strong die and pressure
that nature, designing a precious medal, had selected and applied. It
was not that he looked stupid; it was only, we assume, that his perceptions didn't show in his face for restless or his imagination for irritable.
(p. 94)

'Stamped in': this is the equivalent of the coarser 'steam-roller'
applied by the narrator to Bessie's sister. Lord Lambeth may not
look stupid, but on his home turf Bessie discovers that to all intents
and purposes, certainly to hers, he is exactly that: 'He affected her
as on occasion, dreadful to say, almost *actively* stupid' (p. 133).
Above all, he is inaccessible to the questions she wants to ask. He
is as uneducated in his way as Daisy Miller was in hers. He is as
incurious as Daisy about history, politics, and art, but like her, he
is curious about this other particular person and what she might
do for him. He recognizes in Bessie a freedom from the fears,
taboos, and superstitions that afflict all the other young women
with whom he's so far had contact. There is something touching
about the reasons he gives for his attraction to her: 'She's not
afraid, and she says things out and thinks herself as good as any
one. She's the only girl I've ever seen,' Lord Lambeth explained,
'who hasn't seemed to me dying to marry me' (p. 139). It's a good
start, the absence of fearfulness, but it's not enough for their alli-
ance to flourish, certainly not in the teeth of their elders' resistance, or indeed their barely concealed hostility.

The contemporary responses to this tale are instructive.

James told one American friend that it had given offence to a number of his English acquaintances: 'So long as one serves up Americans for their entertainment it is all right—but hands off the sacred natives! They are really I think, thinner-skinned than we!'[26] A couple of weeks later he told his mother, he would 'keep off dangerous ground in future'; it was 'an entirely new sensation for them (the people here) to be (at all delicately) *ironized* or satirized, from the American point of view, and they don't at all relish it. Their conception of the normal in such a relation is that the satire should be all on their side against the Americans'.[27] But it was on a reviewer that James unleashed the full force of his indignation. Mrs Hill had complained about the portrayal of the two Englishmen, that they were presented as vulgar ''Arries'. James vigorously disputed this. He had spent six months at the St James's Club studying the slang freely employed by the 'racketing, pleasure-loving, "golden-youth" section of English society'. He had heard well-educated young men all around him talking in 'a very offhand, informal, irregular manner'. But James's biggest objection was to Mrs Hill's complaint that his portrayal of the two English ladies carried a general judgement on English manners. 'My dear Mrs Hill—the idea is fantastic! . . . One may make figures and figures without intending generalizations— generalizations of which I have a horror. I make a couple of English ladies doing a disagreeable thing . . . and forthwith I find myself responsible for a representation of English manners! Nothing is my *last word* about anything—I am interminably supersubtle and analytic—'.[28] The only hope of escaping the charge of generalization was to carry on making more and more figures and figures.

Light and Dark

A few years earlier the young James had declared to a friend: 'It's a complex fate, being an American, and one of the responsibilities

[26] Letter to Grace Norton, 4 Jan. 1879 (*James Letters*, ed. Edel, ii. 209–10).
[27] Ibid. 213.
[28] Ibid. 221.

it entails is fighting against a superstitious valuation of Europe.'[29] Valuing things and people aright is a challenge for all James's characters, and for his readers. But valuing 'Europe' justly is a predicament reserved for Americans confronting a past from which they have been partially but not wholly severed. What is more, it is a past with a continuing history, including a future that may involve them in new complications, as Daisy Miller finds in Rome and Bessie Alden discovers in London.

Though light by comparison with James's lengthier fictions, these tales nevertheless wield a remarkable amount of weighty matter. Behind Daisy's encounter with Rome there stands a long line of real and fictional travellers and their writings, including Goethe, Hawthorne, and George Eliot.[30] Only a few years earlier in *Middlemarch* Dorothea Brooke had been profoundly shocked by the accumulated weight of the past in Rome. This is partly a matter of history, in that Eliot's novel is set back in time, some forty years earlier in the 1830s. By the later decades of the century it would have been almost impossible to be so unprepared. Virtually all travellers and tourists would have been forearmed with their Baedekers and Murrays, let alone their *Marble Fauns*, and the innumerable other fictions with which their heads had been filled. James was recording the start of a whole new phase in the way the West experienced and valued its own past, at the same time as it was forging a future of concerted encounter with other pasts, histories, and cultures elsewhere on the globe, at far-flung borders and frontiers. James's subject is the confrontation of the West with itself, and for this his Americans serve an invaluable purpose in colliding, with all their newly formed values, ideas, and ideals, both shallow and gravid, against the evidence of their own past. It is vital that these Americans are so various. James teases his readers with their own preconceptions, with generalities; Daisy Miller is *one* type, by all means, but Bessie Alden is another. And his other tales of around this time—'Four Meetings', 'The Pension Beaurepas', 'A Bundle of Letters'—exult

[29] Letter to Charles Eliot Norton, 4 Feb. 1872 (ibid. i. 274).

[30] For the specifically American encounter with Rome, see William L. Vance, *America's Rome*, 2 vols. (New Haven and London, 1989).

in proliferating the 'points of view' adopted by Americans of all
kinds, some rabidly Europhile, others equally Anglophobe.

There's an instructive doubleness to a word that James applies
to Americans like Daisy but also to the cultural ambience they
carry with them: 'light'. There are as many virtues to being light
as to being heavy, to being free of baggage and proportionately
agile, volatile—why, one might even fly. But 'light' is not only the
contrary of heavy; it is also the opposite of dark. Hence this good
joke of Mrs Westgate's, complaining about a previous visit to
London: 'There was always the most frightful fog—I couldn't see
to try my things on. When I got over to America—into the light—
I usually found they were twice too big' (p. 88).

Light is to dark as white is to black. The lightness and brightness and whiteness of America is so powerful that it carries the
hint of oppression, so sharply does it demarcate white from black.
We might recall a phrase associated with Mrs Westgate: 'terrible
brightness'. No soft blurring of boundaries, no mist, no twilight.
The first half of 'An International Episode' insists on the pattern
of white and black to the point where it implies a subconscious
context, social and cultural: 'marble walks arranged in black and
white lozenges', 'a long negro in a white jacket', 'the intelligent
black', 'the huge white marble façades', 'white trousers', 'white
dresses', 'the huge white vessel', 'the great white decks', 'a hundred negroes in white jackets', and so on.[31] Such references almost
disappear when the scene shifts to London, save for this observation in Hyde Park, of one of the riders: ' "That's the Marquis of
Blackborough," the young man was able to contribute—"the one
in the queer white coat" ' (p. 117). How different from the great
black spots in 'Daisy Miller' that typify the ancient forms of tyr-
anny and violence, the Château de Chillon and the Colosseum.
And yet if these points of blackness in the American landscape strike the reader now as quietly ominous, the predominant

---

[31] Clair Hughes notes the way James dresses his girls and young women in white,
from Pansy Osmond in *The Portrait of a Lady* to Milly Theale in *The Wings of the Dove*;
she also reflects on its ambiguous associations with mourning as well as with virginal
purity. In *The Ambassadors* Jim Pocock's preference for white hats prompts Hughes to
remark that 'white seems to be a colour James returns to when he wants to suggest
Americanness' (*Henry James and the Art of Dress*, 121).

emphasis in this tale is on a light so bright that it dazzles. Newport is full of brilliant, scintillating colour. The idea that America boasts *too much* light may be one to conjure with (and the revisions to the New York edition slightly increase the 'glare' and the 'blaze'), but here in the main such a notion just glimmers. For in these two tales at least, the connotations of American light are primarily positive and liberating.

In 1909 James gives Bessie Alden a fine riposte when Lord Lambeth accuses her of 'Yankee prejudice'. She is disappointed at the low expectations he has of himself and the use he could make of his privileged position.

'Well, if your own people are content with you,' Bessie laughed, 'it's not for me to complain. But I shall always think that properly you should have a great mind—a great character.'

'Ah that's very theoretic!' the young man promptly brought out. 'Depend upon it, that's a Yankee prejudice.'

'Happy the country then,' she as eagerly declared, 'where people's prejudices make so for light.' (p. 130)

In his Preface James confesses to an 'incurable prejudice in favour of grace' (Appendix 1, p. 151). These tales are designed to work on our prejudices and alert us to how they might best make for light and for grace. We might go so far as to say that—in all senses of a colloquialism at which James would have smiled—they urge us to 'lighten up'.

NOTE ON THE TEXTS

LIKE most of James's shorter fictions, these two tales were first published in magazines and soon after in book form. Both were among the fifty-five tales revised for inclusion in the 'definitive' New York Edition of 1907–9, published by Scribner's in New York and Macmillan in London; these are the versions reprinted here. In the present edition spaced contractions have been normalized; single quotation marks are substituted for double, and positioned according to English conventions instead of American.

'Daisy Miller: A Study' and 'An International Episode' both first appeared in the *Cornhill*, the prestigious British magazine for fiction first edited by Thackeray, and in the late 1870s by Leslie Stephen, the former tale in June–July 1878, the latter in December 1878–January 1879, both in two instalments. Publication in the *Cornhill* was James's big breakthrough into the English market for fiction, a welcome variation on his more established outlets in North America, such as the *Atlantic Monthly* (which published *The Europeans*, for example, in July–October 1878) and *Scribner's Monthly* (which published *Confidence* in August–October 1879). Stephen's magazine went on to serialize *Washington Square* in June–November 1880 (simultaneously with *Harper's New Monthly*) and 'The Siege of London', January–February 1883.

As James describes in the Preface reprinted here (Appendix 1, p. 149), he had first offered 'Daisy Miller' to the Philadelphian magazine, *Lippincott's*, who had previously taken some of his short pieces, most recently the tale 'Théodolinde', which came out in May 1878 (later retitled 'Rose-Agathe', it is not one of James's strongest). When *Lippincott's* rejected 'Daisy Miller' without comment, Leslie Stephen accepted it with enthusiasm for the *Cornhill*. Its popularity meant that it was promptly pirated in America before James could arrange for serial publication there, as he had hoped. He did however sell the book rights to Harper & Brothers who brought it out as an independent volume in a cheap format on 1 November 1878. They sold 20,000 copies within weeks but the 10 per-cent royalty for which James had settled meant that this, the 'most prosperous child' of his invention as he called it in his New York Edition Preface, initially yielded the modest figure of $200. Nevertheless, its popular success on both sides of the Atlantic made 'Daisy Miller' a turning point in James's career. 'From this point on', writes Michael Anesko, 'he would work as a professional man of letters in both England and America.'[1] In Britain the tale was issued in book form in two volumes by Macmillan and Co. on 15 February 1879, accompanied by 'An International Episode' and 'Four Meetings'. It was subsequently reprinted several times in new formats by Macmillan and Harper. James included it in his Collective Edition of 1883 (published by Macmillan in 14 volumes); it headed vol. xiii, where it was partnered by 'Four Meetings', 'Longstaff's Marriage', and 'Benvolio'. It was similarly given pride of place, now shorn of its subtitle, 'A Study', as the lead story for one of the volumes in the New York edition, vol. xviii (1909), followed by 'Pandora', 'The Patagonia', 'The Marriages', 'The Real Thing', 'Brooksmith', 'The Beldonald Holbein', 'The Story in It', 'Flickerbridge', and 'Mrs Medwin'.

The first appearances of 'An International Episode' followed a similar pattern, though the piracy of 'Daisy Miller' prompted the author to sell the later tale outright to the *Cornhill* and *Harper's* for simultaneous publication, for which he received the apparently handsome sum of £95 ($460). Serial issue in the *Cornhill* (December 1878–January 1879) effectively coincided with book publication in America by Harper & Brothers on 24 January 1879, as an individual tale in the same cheap Half-Hour Series as 'Daisy Miller'. A few weeks later it came out in the two-volume set by Macmillan, shared with 'Daisy Miller' and 'Four Meetings', straddling volumes i and ii. By June of that year it dawned on the author that he had made after all 'a very poor bargain', so he told his brother William, with no percentage on sales. Not that the

---

[1] Michael Anesko, *'Friction with the Market': Henry James and the Profession of Authorship* (New York and Oxford, 1986), 44. Anesko's whole account of James's dealings with publishers is of great interest; for these two tales in particular, see 'An International Episode: The Man of Letters in England and America', 33–51.

royalty returns on 'Daisy Miller' had been much to write home about. He moaned to his friend (and editor at the *Atlantic*), W. D. Howells, that he was 'born to be victimized by the pitiless race of publishers'. In future he would need to be cannier.[2] 'An International Episode' was included in the Collective Edition of 1883, heading vol. xii, in an attractive pairing with 'The Pension Beaurepas' and 'The Point of View'. Like 'Daisy Miller', it was extensively revised for the volume of tales devoted to the 'international theme', vol. xiv of the New York Edition (1908), alongside 'Lady Barbarina', 'The Siege of London', 'The Pension Beaurepas', 'A Bundle of Letters', and 'The Point of View'.

[2] See ibid. 48–9; for the letters of June 1879 to William James and W. D. Howells from which quotations are taken, describing James's reactions to the fate of these two tales and the lessons he was learning, see *Henry James: A Life in Letters*, ed. Philip Horne (London, 1999), 108, 111.

ACKNOWLEDGEMENTS

I owe a warm debt of thanks to Lili Sarnyai for her assistance with the Explanatory Notes and her work on Appendix 3: Variant Readings.

SELECT BIBLIOGRAPHY

James's Writings

NOVELS AND TALES

IN his Preface to the volume headed by his short novel *The Reverberator*, James is led by reflection on its leading figure, the young American woman, Francie Dosson, to declare: 'In the heavy light of "Europe" thirty or forty years ago, there were more of the Francie Dossons and of the Daisy Millers and the Bessie Aldens and the Pandora Days than of all the other attested American objects put together' (*Literary Criticism*, ii. 1202). He also recalls that after settling in London at the end of 1876, 'the "international" light, lay, in those days, to my sense, thick and rich upon the scene' (*Literary Criticism*, ii. 1085). The following is a selection of tales and novels featuring young Americans, mainly women, facing the prospect or actuality of marriage, viewed in the 'international' light for which James became celebrated. The dates given in parenthesis are those of first publication, which was usually in magazine form. The version of the tales first published in book form may be found in *The Complete Tales of Henry James*, 12 vols, ed. Leon Edel (London, 1962–4), and in the 5 volumes of *Complete Stories*, Library of America (New York, 1996–9). Many though not all were revised for the New York Edition, 1907–9 (NYE).

'Travelling Companions' (1870).
'The Last of the Valerii' (1874).
'Madame de Mauves' (1874). NYE, vol. xiii.
'Four Meetings' (1877). NYE, vol. xvi.
The Europeans (1878).
'The Pension Beaurepas' (1879). NYE, vol. xiv.
'A Bundle of Letters' (1879). NYE, vol. xiv.
The Portrait of a Lady (1880–1). NYE, vols. iii–iv.
'The Point of View' (1882). NYE, vol. xiv.
'The Siege of London' (1883). NYE, vol. xiv.
'Lady Barberina' (1884). NYE, vol. xiv (where it is 'Lady Barbarina').
'Pandora' (1884). NYE, vol. xviii.
The Reverberator (1888). NYE, vol. xiii.
'A London Life' (1888). NYE, vol. x.
'The Patagonia' (1888). NYE, vol. xviii.

OTHER WRITINGS

'Americans Abroad', *Nation*, 3 Oct. 1878; repr. in 'Appendix III', *The Tales of Henry James*, iii. *1875–1879*, ed. Maqbool Aziz (Oxford, 1984), 518–22.

A Small Boy and Others: A Critical Edition, ed. Peter Collister (Charlottesville, Va., and London, 2011).

Notes of a Son and Brother and *The Middle Years*, ed. Peter Collister (Charlottesville, Va., and London, 2011).

The Complete Notebooks of Henry James, ed. with introd. and notes by Leon Edel and Lyall H. Powers (New York, 1987).

The Complete Plays of Henry James, ed. Leon Edel (New York and Oxford, 1990).

Henry James: Collected Travel Writings: Great Britain and America, ed. Richard Howard, Library of America (New York, 1993).

Henry James: Collected Travel Writings: The Continent, ed. Richard Howard, Library of America (New York, 1993).

Henry James Letters, 4 vols., ed. Leon Edel (Cambridge, Mass., and London, 1974–84).

Henry James: A Life in Letters, ed. Philip Horne (London, 1999).

The Complete Letters of Henry James, ed. Pierre A. Walker and Greg W. Zacharias (Lincoln, Nebr., 2006–).

Literary Criticism, i. *Essays on Literature, American Writers, English Writers*, and ii. *French Writers, Other European Writers, The Prefaces to the New York Edition*, ed. Leon Edel with the assistance of Mark Wilson, Library of America (New York, 1984).

Biography

Edel, Leon, *The Life of Henry James*, 2 vols. (London, 1977).

Fisher, Paul, *House of Wits: An Intimate Portrait of the James Family* (New York, 2008).

Gordon, Lyndall, *A Private Life of Henry James: Two Women and His Art* (London, 1998).

Kaplan, Fred, *Henry James: The Imagination of Genius* (New York, 1992).

Lewis, R. W. B., *The Jameses: A Family Narrative* (London, 1991).

Bibliography

Edel, Leon, and Laurence, Dan H. (eds.), *A Bibliography of Henry James*, 3rd edn., revised with the assistance of James Rambeau (Oxford, 1982).

Supino, David, *Henry James: A Bibliographical Catalogue of a Collection of Editions to 1921* (Liverpool, 2006).

Selected Criticism

Allen, Elizabeth, *A Woman's Place in the Novels of Henry James* (London, 1984).

Anesko, Michael, *'Friction with the Market': Henry James and the Profession of Authorship* (New York and Oxford, 1986).

Aziz, Maqbool, 'Introduction' to *The Tales of Henry James*, iii. *1875–1879*, ed. Maqbool Aziz (Oxford, 1984), 1–21.

Bell, Ian F. A., 'Displays of the Female: Formula and Flirtation in "Daisy Miller"', in Neil Reeve (ed.), *Henry James: The Shorter Fiction* (Basingstoke, 1997), 17–40.

Bell, Millicent, *Meaning in Henry James* (Cambridge, Mass., and London, 1991).

Bentley, Nancy, *The Ethnography of Manners: Hawthorne, James, Wharton* (Cambridge, 1995).

Berland, Alwyn, *Culture and Conduct in the Novels of Henry James* (Cambridge, 1981).

Blair, Sara, *Henry James and the Writing of Race and Nation* (Cambridge, 1996).

Buzard, James, *The Beaten Track: European Tourism, Literature, and the Ways to 'Culture' 1900–1918* (Oxford, 1993).

Cross, David, 'Framing the "Sketch": Bogdanovich's *Daisy Miller*', in John R. Bradley (ed.), *Henry James on Stage and Screen* (Basingstoke, 2000), 127–42.

Deakin, Motley F., 'Two Studies of Daisy Miller', *Henry James Review*, 5/1 (1983), 2–28.

Fogel, Daniel Mark, *Daisy Miller: A Dark Comedy of Manners* (Boston, 1990).

Fowler, Virginia, *Henry James's American Girl: The Embroidery on the Canvas* (Madison, 1984).

Graham, Kenneth, *Henry James: A Literary Life* (London, 1995).

Habegger, Alfred, *Henry James and the 'Woman Business'* (Cambridge, 1989).

Hocks, Richard A., *Henry James: A Study of the Short Fiction* (New York, 1990).

——'Daisy Miller, Backward into the Past: A Centennial Essay', *Henry James Review*, 1/2 (1980), 164–78.

Horne, Philip, *Henry James and Revision: The New York Edition* (Oxford, 1990).

Hughes, Clair, *Henry James and the Art of Dress* (Basingstoke, 2001).

Jolly, Roslyn, 'Travel and Tourism', in McWhirter (ed.), *Henry James in Context*, 343–53.

Johnson, Kendall, *Henry James and the Visual* (Cambridge, 2007).

McCormack, Peggy, 'Reexamining Bogdanovich's *Daisy Miller*', in Susan M. Griffin (ed.), *Henry James Goes to the Movies* (Lexington, Ky., 2002), 34–59.

McWhirter, David (ed.), *Henry James in Context* (Cambridge, 2010).

O'Farrell, Mary Ann, 'Manners', in McWhirter (ed.), *Henry James in Context*, 192–202.

Oltean, Roxana, 'From Grand Tour to a Space of Detour: Henry James's Europe', *Henry James Review*, 31/1 (2010), 46–53.

Pahl, Dennis, '"Going Down" with Henry James's Uptown Girl: Genteel Anxiety and the Promiscuous World of *Daisy Miller*', *LIT: Literature, Interpretation, Theory*, 12/2 (2001), 129–64.

Pippin, Robert B., *Henry James and Modern Moral Life* (Cambridge and New York, 2000).

Pollack, Vivian R. (ed.), *New Essays on 'Daisy Miller' and 'The Turn of the Screw'* (Cambridge, 1993).

Poole, Adrian, 'Henry James and Charm', *Essays in Criticism*, 61/2 (Apr. 2011), 115–36.

Stone, Edward, *The Battle and the Books: Some Aspects of Henry James* (Athens, O., 1964).

Tintner, Adeline R., '"An International Episode": A Centennial Review of a Centennial Story', *Henry James Review*, 1/1 (1979), 24–56.

Wadsworth, Sarah, 'What Daisy Knew: Reading Against Type in *Daisy Miller: A Study*', in Greg W. Zacharias (ed.), *A Companion to Henry James* (Chichester, 2008), 32–50.

Walker, Pierre A., *Reading Henry James in French Cultural Contexts* (DeKalb, Ill., 1995).

Wardley, Lynn, 'Reassembling Daisy Miller', *American Literary History*, 3/2 (Summer 1991), 232–55.

Wortman, William A., 'The "Interminable Dramatic Daisy Miller"', *Henry James Review*, 28/3 (2007), 281–91.

Wrenn, Angus, *Henry James and the Second Empire* (London, 2009).

Zacharias, Greg W. (ed.), *A Companion to Henry James* (Chichester, 2008).

Further Reading in Oxford World's Classics

James, Henry, *The Ambassadors*, ed. Christopher Butler.
—— *The American*, ed. Adrian Poole.
—— *The Aspern Papers and Other Stories*, ed. Adrian Poole.
—— *The Awkward Age*, ed. Vivien Jones.
—— *The Bostonians*, ed. R. D. Gooder.
—— *The Europeans*, ed. Ian Campbell Ross.
—— *The Golden Bowl*, ed. Virginia Llewellyn Smith.
—— *The Portrait of a Lady*, ed. Roger Luckhurst.
—— *The Spoils of Poynton*, ed. Bernard Richards.
—— *The Turn of the Screw and Other Stories*, ed. Tim Lustig.
—— *What Maisie Knew*, ed. Adrian Poole.
—— *Washington Square*, ed. Adrian Poole.
—— *The Wings of the Dove*, ed. Peter Brooks.

A CHRONOLOGY OF HENRY JAMES
COMPILED BY LEON EDEL

1843   Born 15 April at No. 21 Washington Place, New York City.

1843–4 Taken abroad by parents to Paris and London: period of residence at Windsor.

1845–55 Childhood in Albany and New York.

1855–8 Attends schools in Geneva, London, Paris, and Boulogne-sur-mer and is privately tutored.

1858   James family settles in Newport, Rhode Island.

1859   At scientific school in Geneva. Studies German in Bonn.

1860   At school in Newport. Receives back injury on eve of Civil War while serving as volunteer fireman. Studies art briefly. Friendship with John La Farge.

1862–3 Spends term in Harvard Law School.

1864   Family settles in Boston and then in Cambridge. Early anonymous story and unsigned reviews published.

1865   First signed story published in *Atlantic Monthly*.

1869–70 Travels in England, France, and Italy. Death of his beloved cousin Minny Temple.

1870   Back in Cambridge, publishes first novel in *Atlantic*, *Watch and Ward*.

1872–4 Travels with sister Alice and aunt in Europe; writes impressionistic travel sketches for the *Nation*. Spends autumn in Paris and goes to Italy to write first large novel.

1874–5 On completion of *Roderick Hudson* tests New York City as residence; writes much literary journalism for *Nation*. First three books published: *Transatlantic Sketches*, *A Passionate Pilgrim* (tales), and *Roderick Hudson*.

1875–6 Goes to live in Paris. Meets Ivan Turgenev and through him Flaubert, Zola, Daudet, Maupassant, and Edmond de Goncourt. Writes *The American*.

1876–7 Moves to London and settles in 3 Bolton Street, Piccadilly. Revisits Paris, Florence, Rome.

1878   'Daisy Miller', published in London, establishes fame on both sides of the Atlantic. Publishes first volume of essays, *French Poets and Novelists*.

1879–82   *The Europeans, Washington Square, Confidence, The Portrait of a Lady*.

1882–3   Revisits Boston: first visit to Washington. Death of parents.

1884–6   Returns to London. Sister Alice comes to live near him. Fourteen-volume collection of novels and tales published. Writes *The Bostonians* and *The Princess Casamassima*, published in the following year.

1886   Moves to flat at 34 De Vere Gardens West.

1887   Sojourn in Italy, mainly Florence and Venice. 'The Aspern Papers', *The Reverberator*, 'A London Life'. Friendship with grand-niece of Fenimore Cooper—Constance Fenimore Woolson.

1888   *Partial Portraits* and several collections of tales.

1889–90   *The Tragic Muse*.

1890–1   Dramatizes *The American*, which has a short run. Writes four comedies, rejected by producers.

1892   Alice James dies in London.

1894   Miss Woolson commits suicide in Venice. James journeys to Italy and visits her grave in Rome.

1895   He is booed at first night of his play *Guy Domville*. Deeply depressed, he abandons the theatre.

1896–7   *The Spoils of Poynton, What Maisie Knew*.

1898   Takes long lease of Lamb House, in Rye, Sussex. *The Turn of the Screw* published.

1899–1900 *The Awkward Age, The Sacred Fount*. Friendship with Conrad and Wells.

1902–4   *The Ambassadors, The Wings of the Dove*, and *The Golden Bowl*. Friendships with H. C. Andersen and Jocelyn Persse.

1905   Revisits USA after 20-year absence, lectures on Balzac and the speech of Americans.

1906–10   *The American Scene*. Edits selective and revised 'New York Edition' of his works in 24 volumes. Friendship with Hugh Walpole.

1910 Death of brother, William James.

1913 Sargent paints his portrait as 70th birthday gift from some 300 friends and admirers. Writes autobiographies, *A Small Boy and Others*, and *Notes of a Son and Brother*.

1914 *Notes on Novelists*. Visits wounded in hospitals.

1915 Becomes a British subject.

1916 Given Order of Merit. Dies 28 February in Chelsea, aged 72. Funeral in Chelsea Old Church. Ashes buried in Cambridge, Mass., family plot.

1976 Commemorative tablet unveiled in Poets' Corner of Westminster Abbey, 17 June.

DAISY MILLER

I

AT the little town of Vevey,* in Switzerland, there is a particularly comfortable hotel; there are indeed many hotels, since the
entertainment of tourists is the business of the place, which, as
many travellers will remember, is seated upon the edge of a
remarkably blue lake—a lake that it behoves every tourist to visit.
The shore of the lake presents an unbroken array of establish-
ments of this order, of every category, from the 'grand hotel' of
the newest fashion, with a chalk-white front, a hundred balconies,
and a dozen flags flying from its roof, to the small Swiss pension
of an elder day, with its name inscribed in German-looking lettering upon a pink or yellow wall and an awkward summer-house in
the angle of the garden. One of the hotels at Vevey, however, is
famous, even classical, being distinguished from many of its
upstart neighbours by an air both of luxury and of maturity. In
this region, through the month of June, American travellers are
extremely numerous; it may be said indeed that Vevey assumes at
that time some of the characteristics of an American watering-
place. There are sights and sounds that evoke a vision, an echo,
of Newport and Saratoga.* There is a flitting hither and thither of
'stylish' young girls, a rustling of muslin flounces, a rattle of
dance-music in the morning hours, a sound of high-pitched voices
at all times. You receive an impression of these things at the excellent inn of the 'Trois Couronnes', and are transported in fancy to
the Ocean House or to Congress Hall.* But at the 'Trois
Couronnes', it must be added, there are other features much at
variance with these suggestions: neat German waiters who look
like secretaries of legation; Russian princesses sitting in the
garden; little Polish boys walking about, held by the hand, with
their governors; a view of the snowy crest of the Dent du Midi and
the picturesque towers of the Castle of Chillon.*

I hardly know whether it was the analogies or the differences
that were uppermost in the mind of a young American, who, two
or three years ago, sat in the garden of the 'Trois Couronnes',

looking about him rather idly at some of the graceful objects
I have mentioned. It was a beautiful summer morning, and in
whatever fashion the young American looked at things they must
have seemed to him charming. He had come from Geneva the
day before, by the little steamer, to see his aunt, who was staying
at the hotel—Geneva having been for a long time his place of
residence. But his aunt had a headache—his aunt had almost
always a headache—and she was now shut up in her room smell-
ing camphor, so that he was at liberty to wander about. He was
some seven-and-twenty years of age; when his friends spoke of
him they usually said that he was at Geneva 'studying'. When his
enemies spoke of him they said—but after all he had no enemies:
he was extremely amiable and generally liked. What I should say
is simply that when certain persons spoke of him they conveyed
that the reason of his spending so much time at Geneva was that
he was extremely devoted to a lady who lived there—a foreign
lady, a person older than himself. Very few Americans—truly
I think none—had ever seen this lady, about whom there were
some singular stories. But Winterbourne had an old attachment
for the little capital of Calvinism;* he had been put to school there
as a boy and had afterwards even gone, on trial—trial of the grey
old 'Academy'* on the steep and stony hillside—to college there;
circumstances which had led to his forming a great many youthful
friendships. Many of these he had kept, and they were a source of
great satisfaction to him.

After knocking at his aunt's door and learning that she was
indisposed he had taken a walk about the town and then he had
come in to his breakfast. He had now finished that repast, but was
enjoying a small cup of coffee which had been served him on a
little table in the garden by one of the waiters who looked like
attachés. At last he finished his coffee and lit a cigarette. Presently
a small boy came walking along the path—an urchin of nine or
ten. The child, who was diminutive for his years, had an aged
expression of countenance, a pale complexion and sharp little features. He was dressed in knickerbockers and had red stockings
that displayed his poor little spindle-shanks; he also wore a brilliant red cravat. He carried in his hand a long alpenstock, the

sharp point of which he thrust into everything he approached—the flower-beds, the garden-benches, the trains of the ladies' dresses. In front of Winterbourne he paused, looking at him with a pair of bright and penetrating little eyes.

'Will you give me a lump of sugar?' he asked in a small sharp hard voice—a voice immature and yet somehow not young.

Winterbourne glanced at the light table near him, on which his coffee-service rested, and saw that several morsels of sugar remained. 'Yes, you may take one,' he answered; 'but I don't think too much sugar good for little boys.'

This little boy stepped forward and carefully selected three of the coveted fragments, two of which he buried in the pocket of his knickerbockers, depositing the other as promptly in another place. He poked his alpenstock, lance-fashion, into Winterbourne's bench and tried to crack the lump of sugar with his teeth.

'Oh blazes; it's har-r-d!' he exclaimed, divesting vowel and consonants, pertinently enough, of any taint of softness.

Winterbourne had immediately gathered that he might have the honour of claiming him as a countryman. 'Take care you don't hurt your teeth,' he said paternally.

'I haven't got any teeth to hurt. They've all come out. I've only got seven teeth. Mother counted them last night, and one came out right afterwards. She said she'd slap me if any more came out. I can't help it. It's this old Europe. It's the climate that makes them come out. In America they didn't come out. It's these hotels.'

Winterbourne was much amused. 'If you eat three lumps of sugar your mother will certainly slap you,' he ventured.

'She's got to give me some candy then,' rejoined his young interlocutor. 'I can't get any candy here—any American candy. American candy's the best candy.'

'And are American little boys the best little boys?' Winterbourne asked.

'I don't know. *I'm* an American boy,' said the child.

'I see you're one of the best!' the young man laughed.

'Are you an American man?' pursued this vivacious infant. And then on his friend's affirmative reply, 'American men are the best,' he declared with assurance.

His companion thanked him for the compliment, and the child, who had now got astride of his alpenstock, stood looking about him while he attacked another lump of sugar. Winterbourne wondered if he himself had been like this in his infancy, for he had been brought to Europe at about the same age.

'Here comes my sister!' cried his young compatriot. 'She's an American girl, you bet!'

Winterbourne looked along the path and saw a beautiful young lady advancing. 'American girls are the best girls,' he thereupon cheerfully remarked to his visitor.

'My sister ain't the best!' the child promptly returned. 'She's always blowing at me.'

'I imagine that's your fault, not hers,' said Winterbourne. The young lady meanwhile had drawn near. She was dressed in white muslin, with a hundred frills and flounces* and knots of pale-coloured ribbon. Bareheaded, she balanced in her hand a large parasol with a deep border of embroidery; and she was strikingly, admirably pretty. 'How pretty they are!' thought our friend, who straightened himself in his seat as if he were ready to rise.

The young lady paused in front of his bench, near the parapet of the garden, which overlooked the lake. The small boy had now converted his alpenstock into a vaulting-pole, by the aid of which he was springing about in the gravel and kicking it up not a little. 'Why Randolph,' she freely began, 'what *are* you doing?'

'I'm going up the Alps!' cried Randolph. 'This is the way!' And he gave another extravagant jump, scattering the pebbles about Winterbourne's ears.

'That's the way they come down,' said Winterbourne.

'He's an American man!' proclaimed Randolph in his harsh little voice.

The young lady gave no heed to this circumstance, but looked straight at her brother. 'Well, I guess you'd better be quiet,' she simply observed.

It seemed to Winterbourne that he had been in a manner presented. He got up and stepped slowly toward the charming creature, throwing away his cigarette. 'This little boy and I have made acquaintance,' he said with great civility. In Geneva, as he had been perfectly aware, a young man wasn't at liberty to speak to a young unmarried lady save under certain rarely-occurring conditions; but here at Vevey what conditions could be better than these?—a pretty American girl coming to stand in front of you in a garden with all the confidence in life. This pretty American girl, whatever that might prove, on hearing Winterbourne's observation simply glanced at him; she then turned her head and looked over the parapet, at the lake and the opposite mountains. He wondered whether he had gone too far, but decided that he must gallantly advance rather than retreat. While he was thinking of something else to say the young lady turned again to the little boy, whom she addressed quite as if they were alone together. 'I should like to know where you got that pole.'

'I bought it!' Randolph shouted.

'You don't mean to say you're going to take it to Italy!'

'Yes, I'm going to take it t' Italy!' the child rang out.

She glanced over the front of her dress and smoothed out a knot or two of ribbon. Then she gave her sweet eyes to the prospect again. 'Well, I guess you'd better leave it somewhere,' she dropped after a moment.

'Are you going to Italy?' Winterbourne now decided very respectfully to inquire.

She glanced at him with lovely remoteness. 'Yes, sir,' she then replied. And she said nothing more.

'And are you—a—thinking of the Simplon?'* he pursued with a slight drop of assurance.

'I don't know,' she said. 'I suppose it's some mountain. Randolph, what mountain are we thinking of?'

'Thinking of?'—the boy stared.

'Why going right over.'

'Going to where?' he demanded.

'Why right down to Italy'—Winterbourne felt vague emulations.

'I don't know,' said Randolph. 'I don't want to go t' Italy. I want to go to America.'

'Oh Italy's a beautiful place!' the young man laughed.

'Can you get candy there?' Randolph asked of all the echoes.

'I hope not,' said his sister. 'I guess you've had enough candy, and mother thinks so too.'

'I haven't had any for ever so long—for a hundred weeks!' cried the boy, still jumping about.

The young lady inspected her flounces and smoothed her ribbons again; and Winterbourne presently risked an observation on the beauty of the view. He was ceasing to be in doubt, for he had begun to perceive that she was really not in the least embarrassed. She might be cold, she might be austere, she might even be prim; for that was apparently—he had already so generalised—what the most 'distant' American girls did: they came and planted themselves straight in front of you to show how rigidly unapproachable they were. There hadn't been the slightest flush in her fresh fairness however; so that she was clearly neither offended nor fluttered. Only she was composed—he had seen that before too—of charming little parts that didn't match and that made no *ensemble*; and if she looked another way when he spoke to her, and seemed not particularly to hear him, this was simply her habit, her manner, the result of her having no idea whatever of 'form' (with such a tell-tale appendage as Randolph where in the world would she have got it?) in any such connexion. As he talked a little more and pointed out some of the objects of interest in the view, with which she appeared wholly unacquainted, she gradually, none the less, gave him more of the benefit of her attention; and then he saw that act unqualified by the faintest shadow of reserve. It wasn't however what would have been called a 'bold' front that she presented, for her expression was as decently limpid as the very cleanest water. Her eyes were the very prettiest conceivable, and indeed Winterbourne hadn't for a long time seen anything prettier than his fair countrywoman's various features—her complexion, her nose, her ears, her teeth. He took a great interest generally in that range of effects and was addicted to noting and, as it were, recording them; so that in regard to this young lady's face he made several observations. It wasn't at all insipid, yet at the same time wasn't pointedly—what point, on earth, could she ever make?—expressive; and though it offered such a collection of small finenesses and neatnesses he mentally accused it—very forgivingly—of a want of finish. He thought nothing more likely than that its wearer would have had her own experience of the action of her charms, as she would certainly have acquired a resulting confidence; but even should she depend on this for her main amusement her bright sweet superficial little visage gave out neither mockery nor irony. Before long it became clear that, however these things might be, she was much disposed to conversation. She remarked to Winterbourne that they were going to Rome for the winter—she and her mother and Randolph. She asked him if he was a 'real American'; she wouldn't have taken him for one; he seemed more like a German—this flower was gathered as from a large field of comparison—especially when he spoke. Winterbourne, laughing, answered that he had met Germans who spoke like Americans, but not, so far as he remembered, any American with the resemblance she noted. Then he asked her if she mightn't be more at ease should she occupy the bench he had just quitted. She answered that she liked hanging round, but she none the less resignedly, after a little, dropped to the bench. She told him she was from New York State—'if you know where that is'; but our friend really quickened this current by catching hold of her small slippery brother and making him stand a few minutes by his side.

'Tell me your honest name, my boy.' So he artfully proceeded.

In response to which the child was indeed unvarnished truth. 'Randolph C. Miller. And I'll tell you hers.' With which he levelled his alpenstock at his sister.

'You had better wait till you're asked!' said this young lady quite at her leisure.

'I should like very much to know *your* name,' Winterbourne made free to reply.

'Her name's Daisy Miller!' cried the urchin. 'But that ain't her real name; that ain't her name on her cards.'

'It's a pity you haven't got one of my cards!' Miss Miller quite as naturally remarked.

'Her real name's Annie P. Miller,' the boy went on.

It seemed, all amazingly, to do her good. 'Ask him *his* now'—and she indicated their friend.

But to this point Randolph seemed perfectly indifferent; he continued to supply information with regard to his own family. 'My father's name is Ezra B. Miller. My father ain't in Europe—he's in a better place than Europe.' Winterbourne for a moment supposed this the manner in which the child had been taught to intimate that Mr Miller had been removed to the sphere of celestial rewards. But Randolph immediately added: 'My father's in Schenectady.* He's got a big business. My father's rich, you bet.'

'Well!' ejaculated Miss Miller, lowering her parasol and looking at the embroidered border. Winterbourne presently released the child, who departed, dragging his alpenstock along the path. 'He don't like Europe,' said the girl as with an artless instinct for historic truth. 'He wants to go back.'

'To Schenectady, you mean?'

'Yes, he wants to go right home. He hasn't got any boys here. There's one boy here, but he always goes round with a teacher. They won't let him play.'

'And your brother hasn't any teacher?' Winterbourne inquired.

It tapped, at a touch, the spring of confidence. 'Mother thought of getting him one—to travel round with us. There was a lady told her of a very good teacher; an American lady—perhaps you know her—Mrs Sanders. I think she came from Boston. She told her of this teacher, and we thought of getting him to travel round with us. But Randolph said he didn't want a teacher travelling round with us. He said he wouldn't have lessons when he was in the cars.* And we *are* in the cars about half the time. There was an English lady we met in the cars—I think her name was Miss Featherstone; perhaps you know her. She wanted to know why I didn't give Randolph lessons—give him "instruction", she called it. I guess he could give me more instruction than I could give him. He's very smart.'

'Yes,' said Winterbourne; 'he seems very smart.'

'Mother's going to get a teacher for him as soon as we get t' Italy. Can you get good teachers in Italy?'

'Very good, I should think,' Winterbourne hastened to reply.

'Or else she's going to find some school. He ought to learn some more. He's only nine. He's going to college.' And in this way

Miss Miller continued to converse upon the affairs of her family and upon other topics. She sat there with her extremely pretty hands, ornamented with very brilliant rings, folded in her lap, and with her pretty eyes now resting upon those of Winterbourne, now wandering over the garden, the people who passed before her and the beautiful view. She addressed her new acquaintance as if she had known him a long time. He found it very pleasant. It was many years since he had heard a young girl talk so much. It might have been said of this wandering maiden who had come and sat down beside him upon a bench that she chattered. She was very quiet, she sat in a charming tranquil attitude; but her lips and her eyes were constantly moving. She had a soft slender agreeable voice, and her tone was distinctly sociable. She gave Winterbourne a report of her movements and intentions, and those of her mother and brother, in Europe, and enumerated in particular the various hotels at which they had stopped. 'That English lady in the cars,' she said—'Miss Featherstone—asked me if we didn't all live in hotels in America. I told her I had never been in so many hotels in my life as since I came to Europe. I've never seen so many—it's nothing but hotels.' But Miss Miller made this remark with no querulous accent; she appeared to be in the best humour with everything. She declared that the hotels were very good when once you got used to their ways and that Europe was perfectly entrancing. She wasn't disappointed—not a bit. Perhaps it was because she had heard so much about it before. She had ever so many intimate friends who had been there ever so many times, and that way she had got thoroughly posted. And then she had had ever so many dresses and things from Paris. Whenever she put on a Paris dress she felt as if she were in Europe.

'It was a kind of a wishing-cap,' Winterbourne smiled.

'Yes,' said Miss Miller at once and without examining this analogy; 'it always made me wish I was here. But I needn't have done that for dresses. I'm sure they send all the pretty ones to America, you see the most frightful things here. The only thing I don't like,' she proceeded, 'is the society. There ain't any society—or if there is I don't know where it keeps itself. Do you? I suppose there's some society somewhere, but I haven't seen

anything of it. I'm very fond of society and I've always had plenty
of it. I don't mean only in Schenectady, but in New York. I used
to go to New York every winter. In New York I had lots of society.
Last winter I had seventeen dinners given me, and three of them
were by gentlemen,' added Daisy Miller. 'I've more friends in
New York than in Schenectady—more gentlemen friends; and
more young lady friends too,' she resumed in a moment. She
paused again for an instant; she was looking at Winterbourne with
all her prettiness in her frank grey eyes and in her clear rather
uniform smile. 'I've always had', she said, 'a great deal of gentlemen's society.'

Poor Winterbourne was amused and perplexed—above all he
was charmed. He had never yet heard a young girl express herself
in just this fashion; never at least save in cases where to say such
things was to have at the same time some rather complicated consciousness about them. And yet was he to accuse Miss Daisy
Miller of an actual or a potential *arrière-pensée*,* as they said at
Geneva? He felt he had lived at Geneva so long as to have got
morally muddled; he had lost the right sense for the young
American tone. Never indeed since he had grown old enough to
appreciate things had he encountered a young compatriot of so
'strong' a type as this. Certainly she was very charming, but how
extraordinarily communicative and how tremendously easy! Was
she simply a pretty girl from New York State—were they all like
that, the pretty girls who had had a good deal of gentlemen's
society? Or was she also a designing, an audacious, in short an
expert young person? Yes, his instinct for such a question had
ceased to serve him, and his reason could but mislead. Miss Daisy
Miller looked extremely innocent. Some people had told him that
after all American girls *were* exceedingly innocent, and others
had told him that after all they weren't. He must on the whole
take Miss Daisy Miller for a flirt—a pretty American flirt. He had
never as yet had relations with representatives of that class. He
had known here in Europe two or three women—persons older
than Miss Daisy Miller and provided, for respectability's sake,
with husbands—who were great coquettes; dangerous terrible women with whom one's light commerce might indeed take

a serious turn. But this charming apparition wasn't a coquette in that sense; she was very unsophisticated; she was only a pretty American flirt. Winterbourne was almost grateful for having found the formula that applied to Miss Daisy Miller. He leaned back in his seat; he remarked to himself that she had the finest little nose he had ever seen; he wondered what were the regular conditions and limitations of one's intercourse with a pretty American flirt. It presently became apparent that he was on the way to learn.

'Have you been to that old castle?' the girl soon asked, pointing with her parasol to the far-shining walls of the Château de Chillon.

'Yes, formerly, more than once,' said Winterbourne. 'You too, I suppose, have seen it?'

'No, we haven't been there. I want to go there dreadfully. Of course I mean to go there. I wouldn't go away from here without having seen that old castle.'

'It's a very pretty excursion,' the young man returned, 'and very easy to make. You can drive, you know, or you can go by the little steamer.'

'You can go in the cars,' said Miss Miller.

'Yes, you can go in the cars,' Winterbourne assented.

'Our courier says they take you right up to the castle,' she continued. 'We were going last week, but mother gave out. She suffers dreadfully from dyspepsia. She said she couldn't any more go——!' But this sketch of Mrs Miller's plea remained unfinished. 'Randolph wouldn't go either; he says he don't think much of old castles. But I guess we'll go this week if we can get Randolph.'

'Your brother isn't interested in ancient monuments?' Winterbourne indulgently asked.

He now drew her, as he guessed she would herself have said, every time. 'Why no, he says he don't care much about old castles. He's only nine. He wants to stay at the hotel. Mother's afraid to leave him alone, and the courier won't stay with him; so we haven't been to many places. But it will be too bad if we don't go up there.' And Miss Miller pointed again at the Château de Chillon.

'I should think it might be arranged,' Winterbourne was thus emboldened to reply. 'Couldn't you get some one to stay—for the afternoon—with Randolph?'

Miss Miller looked at him a moment, and then with all serenity, 'I wish *you'd* stay with him!' she said.

He pretended to consider it. 'I'd much rather go to Chillon with you.'

'With me?' she asked without a shadow of emotion.

She didn't rise blushing, as a young person at Geneva would have done; and yet, conscious that he had gone very far, he thought it possible she had drawn back. 'And with your mother,' he answered very respectfully.

But it seemed that both his audacity and his respect were lost on Miss Daisy Miller. 'I guess mother wouldn't go—for *you*,' she smiled. 'And she ain't much *bent* on going, anyway. She don't like to ride round in the afternoon.' After which she familiarly proceeded: 'But did you really mean what you said just now—that you'd like to go up there?'

'Most earnestly I meant it,' Winterbourne declared.

'Then we may arrange it. If mother will stay with Randolph I guess Eugenio will.'

'Eugenio?' the young man echoed.

'Eugenio's our courier. He doesn't like to stay with Randolph—he's the most fastidious man I ever saw. But he's a splendid courier. I guess he'll stay at home with Randolph if mother does, and then we can go to the castle.'

Winterbourne reflected for an instant as lucidly as possible: 'we' could only mean Miss Miller and himself. This prospect seemed almost too good to believe; he felt as if he ought to kiss the young lady's hand. Possibly he would have done so,—and quite spoiled his chance; but at this moment another person—presumably Eugenio—appeared. A tall handsome man, with superb whiskers and wearing a velvet morning-coat and a voluminous watch-guard, approached the young lady, looking sharply at her companion. 'Oh Eugenio!' she said with the friendliest accent.

Eugenio had eyed Winterbourne from head to foot; he now bowed gravely to Miss Miller. 'I have the honour to inform Mademoiselle that luncheon's on table.'

Mademoiselle slowly rose. 'See here, Eugenio, I'm going to that old castle anyway.'

'To the Château de Chillon, Mademoiselle?' the courier inquired. 'Mademoiselle has made arrangements?' he added in a tone that struck Winterbourne as impertinent.

Eugenio's tone apparently threw, even to Miss Miller's own apprehension, a slightly ironical light on her position. She turned to Winterbourne with the slightest blush. 'You won't back out?'

'I shall not be happy till we go!' he protested.

'And you're staying in this hotel?' she went on. 'And you're really American?'

The courier still stood there with an effect of offence for the young man so far as the latter saw in it a tacit reflexion on Miss Miller's behaviour and an insinuation that she 'picked up' acquaintances. 'I shall have the honour of presenting to you a person who'll tell you all about me,' he said, smiling, and referring to his aunt.

'Oh well, we'll go some day,' she beautifully answered; with which she gave him a smile and turned away. She put up her parasol and walked back to the inn beside Eugenio. Winterbourne stood watching her, and as she moved away, drawing her muslin furbelows* over the walk, he spoke to himself of her natural elegance.

II

HE had, however, engaged to do more than proved feasible in promising to present his aunt, Mrs Costello, to Miss Daisy Miller. As soon as that lady had got better of her headache he waited on her in her apartment and, after a show of the proper solicitude about her health, asked if she had noticed in the hotel an American family—a mamma, a daughter and an obstreperous little boy.

'An obstreperous little boy and a preposterous big courier?' said Mrs Costello. 'Oh yes, I've noticed them. Seen them, heard them and kept out of their way.' Mrs Costello was a widow of fortune, a person of much distinction and who frequently intimated that if she hadn't been so dreadfully liable to sick-headaches she would probably have left a deeper impress on her time. She had a long pale face, a high nose and a great deal of very striking white hair, which she wore in large puffs and over the top of her head. She had two sons married in New York and another who was now in Europe. This young man was amusing himself at Homburg and, though guided by his taste, was rarely observed to visit any particular city at the moment selected by his mother for her appearance there. Her nephew, who had come to Vevey expressly to see her, was therefore more attentive than, as she said, her very own. He had imbibed at Geneva the idea that one must be irreproachable in all such forms. Mrs Costello hadn't seen him for many years and was now greatly pleased with him, manifesting her approbation by initiating him into many of the secrets of that social sway which, as he could see she would like him to think, she exerted from her stronghold in Forty-Second Street.* She admitted that she was very exclusive, but if he had been better acquainted with New York he would see that one had to be. And her picture of the minutely hierarchical constitution of the society of that city, which she presented to him in many different lights, was, to Winterbourne's imagination, almost oppressively striking.

He at once recognised from her tone that Miss Daisy Miller's place in the social scale was low. 'I'm afraid you don't approve of them,' he pursued in reference to his new friends.

'They're horribly common'—it was perfectly simple. 'They're the sort of Americans that one does one's duty by just ignoring.'

'Ah you just ignore them?'—the young man took it in.

'I can't *not*, my dear Frederick. I wouldn't if I hadn't to, but I have to.'

'The little girl's very pretty,' he went on in a moment.

'Of course she's very pretty. But she's of the last crudity.'

'I see what you mean of course,' he allowed after another pause.

'She has that charming look they all have,' his aunt resumed. 'I can't think where they pick it up; and she dresses in perfection—no, you don't know how well she dresses. I can't think where they get their taste.'

'But, my dear aunt, she's not, after all, a Comanche savage.'*

'She is a young lady,' said Mrs Costello, 'who has an intimacy with her mamma's courier!'

'An "intimacy" with him?' Ah there it was!

'There's no other name for such a relation. But the skinny little mother's just as bad! They treat the courier as a familiar friend—as a gentleman and a scholar. I shouldn't wonder if he dines with them. Very likely they've never seen a man with such good manners, such fine clothes, so *like* a gentleman—or a scholar. He probably corresponds to the young lady's idea of a count. He sits with them in the garden of an evening. I think he smokes in their faces.'

Winterbourne listened with interest to these disclosures; they helped him to make up his mind about Miss Daisy. Evidently she was rather wild. 'Well,' he said, 'I'm not a courier and I didn't smoke in her face, and yet she was very charming to me.'

'You had better have mentioned at first,' Mrs Costello returned with dignity, 'that you had made her valuable acquaintance.'

'We simply met in the garden and talked a bit.'

'By appointment—no? Ah that's still to come! Pray what did you say?'

'I said I should take the liberty of introducing her to my admirable aunt.'

'Your admirable aunt's a thousand times obliged to you.'

'It was to guarantee my respectability.'

'And pray who's to guarantee hers?'

'Ah you're cruel!' said the young man. 'She's a very innocent girl.'

'You don't say that as if you believed it,' Mrs Costello returned.

'She's completely uneducated,' Winterbourne acknowledged, 'but she's wonderfully pretty, and in short she's very nice. To prove I believe it I'm going to take her to the Château de Chillon.'

Mrs Costello made a wondrous face. 'You two are going off there together? I should say it proved just the contrary. How long had you known her, may I ask, when this interesting project was formed? You haven't been twenty-four hours in the house.'

'I had known her half an hour!' Winterbourne smiled.

'Then she's just what I supposed.'

'And what do you suppose?'

'Why that she's a horror.'

Our youth was silent for some moments. 'You really think then,' he presently began, and with a desire for trustworthy information, 'you really think that——' But he paused again while his aunt waited.

'Think what, sir?'

'That she's the sort of young lady who expects a man sooner or later to—well, we'll call it carry her off?'

'I haven't the least idea what such young ladies expect a man to do. But I really consider you had better not meddle with little American girls who are uneducated, as you mildly put it. You've lived too long out of the country. You'll be sure to make some great mistake. You're too innocent.'

'My dear aunt, not so much as that comes to!' he protested with a laugh and a curl of his moustache.

'You're too guilty then!'

He continued all thoughtfully to finger the ornament in question. 'You won't let the poor girl know you then?' he asked at last.

'Is it literally true that she's going to the Château de Chillon with you?'

'I've no doubt she fully intends it.'

'Then, my dear Frederick,' said Mrs Costello, 'I must decline the honour of her acquaintance. I'm an old woman, but I'm not too old—thank heaven—to be honestly shocked!'

'But don't they all do these things—the little American girls at home?' Winterbourne inquired.

Mrs Costello stared a moment. 'I should like to see my granddaughters do them!' she then grimly returned.

This seemed to throw some light on the matter, for Winterbourne remembered to have heard his pretty cousins in New York, the daughters of this lady's two daughters, called 'tremendous flirts.' If therefore Miss Daisy Miller exceeded the liberal license allowed to these young women it was probable she did go even by the American allowance rather far. Winterbourne was impatient to see her again, and it vexed, it even a little humiliated him, that he shouldn't by instinct appreciate her justly.

Though so impatient to see her again he hardly knew what ground he should give for his aunt's refusal to become acquainted with her; but he discovered promptly enough that with Miss Daisy Miller there was no great need of walking on tiptoe. He found her that evening in the garden, wandering about in the warm starlight after the manner of an indolent sylph and swinging to and fro the largest fan he had ever beheld. It was ten o'clock. He had dined with his aunt, had been sitting with her since dinner, and had just taken leave of her till the morrow. His young friend frankly rejoiced to renew their intercourse; she pronounced it the stupidest evening she had ever passed.

'Have you been all alone?' he asked with no intention of an epigram and no effect of her perceiving one.

'I've been walking round with mother. But mother gets tired walking round,' Miss Miller explained.

'Has she gone to bed?'

'No, she doesn't like to go to bed. She doesn't sleep scarcely any—not three hours. She says she doesn't know how she lives. She's dreadfully nervous. I guess she sleeps more than she thinks. She's gone somewhere after Randolph; she wants to try to get him to go to bed. He doesn't like to go to bed.'

The soft impartiality of her *constatations*,* as Winterbourne would have termed them, was a thing by itself—exquisite little fatalist as they seemed to make her. 'Let us hope she'll persuade him,' he encouragingly said.

'Well, she'll talk to him all she can—but he doesn't like her to talk to him': with which Miss Daisy opened and closed her fan. 'She's going to try to get Eugenio to talk to him. But Randolph ain't afraid of Eugenio. Eugenio's a splendid courier, but he can't make much impression on Randolph! I don't believe he'll go to bed before eleven.' Her detachment from any invidious judgement of this was, to her companion's sense, inimitable; and it appeared that Randolph's vigil was in fact triumphantly prolonged, for Winterbourne attended her in her stroll for some time without meeting her mother. 'I've been looking round for that lady you want to introduce me to,' she resumed—'I guess she's your aunt.' Then on his admitting the fact and expressing some curiosity as to how she had learned it, she said she had heard all about Mrs Costello from the chambermaid. She was very quiet and very *comme il faut*;* she wore white puffs;* she spoke to no one and she never dined at the common table. Every two days she had a headache. 'I think that's a lovely description, headache and all!' said Miss Daisy, chattering along in her thin gay voice. 'I want to know her ever so much. I know just what *your* aunt would be; I know I'd like her. She'd be very exclusive. I like a lady to be exclusive; I'm dying to be exclusive myself. Well, I guess we *are* exclusive, mother and I. We don't speak to any one—or they don't speak to us. I suppose it's about the same thing. Anyway, I shall be ever so glad to meet your aunt.'

Winterbourne was embarrassed—he could but trump up some evasion. 'She'd be most happy, but I'm afraid those tiresome headaches are always to be reckoned with.'

The girl looked at him through the fine dusk. 'Well, I suppose she doesn't have a headache every day.'

He had to make the best of it. 'She tells me she wonderfully does.' He didn't know what else to say.

Miss Miller stopped and stood looking at him. Her prettiness was still visible in the darkness; she kept flapping to and fro her enormous fan. 'She doesn't want to know me!' she then lightly broke out. 'Why don't you say so? You needn't be afraid. *I'm* not afraid!' And she quite crowed for the fun of it.

Winterbourne distinguished however a wee false note in this: he was touched, shocked, mortified by it. 'My dear young lady, she knows no one. She goes through life immured. It's her wretched health.'

The young girl walked on a few steps in the glee of the thing. 'You needn't be afraid,' she repeated. 'Why should she want to know me?' Then she paused again; she was close to the parapet of the garden, and in front of her was the starlit lake. There was a vague sheen on its surface, and in the distance were dimly-seen mountain forms. Daisy Miller looked out at these great lights and shades and again proclaimed a gay indifference—'Gracious! she *is* exclusive!' Winterbourne wondered if she were seriously wounded and for a moment almost wished her sense of injury might be such as to make it becoming in him to reassure and comfort her. He had a pleasant sense that she would be all accessible to a respectful tenderness at that moment. He felt quite ready to sacrifice his aunt—conversationally; to acknowledge she was a proud rude woman and to make the point that they needn't mind her. But before he had time to commit himself to this questionable mixture of gallantry and impiety, the young lady, resuming her walk, gave an exclamation in quite another tone. 'Well, here's mother! I guess she *hasn't* got Randolph to go to bed.' The figure of a lady appeared, at a distance, very indistinct in the darkness; it advanced with a slow and wavering step and then suddenly seemed to pause.

'Are you sure it's your mother? Can you make her out in this thick dusk?' Winterbourne asked.

'Well,' the girl laughed, 'I guess I know my own mother! And when she has got on my shawl too. She's always wearing my things.'

The lady in question, ceasing now to approach, hovered vaguely about the spot at which she had checked her steps.

'I'm afraid your mother doesn't see you,' said Winterbourne. 'Or perhaps,' he added—thinking, with Miss Miller, the joke permissible—'perhaps she feels guilty about your shawl.'

'Oh it's a fearful old thing!' his companion placidly answered. 'I told her she could wear it if she didn't mind looking like a fright. She won't come here because she sees you.'

'Ah then,' said Winterbourne, 'I had better leave you.'

'Oh no—come on!' the girl insisted.

'I'm afraid your mother doesn't approve of my walking with you.'

She gave him, he thought, the oddest glance. 'It isn't for me; it's for you—that is it's for *her*. Well, I don't know who it's for! But mother doesn't like any of my gentlemen friends. She's right down timid. She always makes a fuss if I introduce a gentleman. But I *do* introduce them—almost always. If I didn't introduce my gentlemen friends to mother,' Miss Miller added, in her small flat monotone, 'I shouldn't think I was natural.'

'Well, to introduce me,' Winterbourne remarked, 'you must know my name.' And he proceeded to pronounce it.

'Oh my—I can't say all that!' cried his companion, much amused. But by this time they had come up to Mrs Miller, who, as they drew near, walked to the parapet of the garden and leaned on it, looking intently at the lake and presenting her back to them. 'Mother!' said the girl in a tone of decision—upon which the elder lady turned round. 'Mr Frederick Forsyth Winterbourne,' said the latter's young friend, repeating his lesson of a moment before and introducing him very frankly and prettily. 'Common' she might be, as Mrs Costello had pronounced her; yet what provision was made by that epithet for her queer little native grace?

Her mother was a small spare light person, with a wandering eye, a scarce perceptible nose, and, as to make up for it, an unmistakable forehead, decorated—but too far back, as Winterbourne mentally described it—with thin much-frizzled hair. Like her daughter Mrs Miller was dressed with extreme elegance; she had enormous diamonds in her ears. So far as the young man could observe, she gave him no greeting—she certainly wasn't looking at him. Daisy was near her, pulling her shawl straight. 'What are you doing, poking round here?' this young lady inquired—yet by no means with the harshness of accent her choice of words might have implied.

'Well, I don't know'—and the new-comer turned to the lake again.

'I shouldn't think you'd want that shawl!' Daisy familiarly proceeded.

'Well—I do!' her mother answered with a sound that partook for Winterbourne of an odd strain between mirth and woe.

'Did you get Randolph to go to bed?' Daisy asked.

'No, I couldn't induce him'—and Mrs Miller seemed to confess to the same mild fatalism as her daughter. 'He wants to talk to the waiter. He *likes* to talk to that waiter.'

'I was just telling Mr Winterbourne,' the girl went on; and to the young man's ear her tone might have indicated that she had been uttering his name all her life.

'Oh yes!' he concurred—'I've the pleasure of knowing your son.'

Randolph's mamma was silent; she kept her attention on

the lake. But at last a sigh broke from her. 'Well, I don't see how he lives!'

'Anyhow, it isn't so bad as it was at Dover,' Daisy at least opined.

'And what occurred at Dover?' Winterbourne desired to know.

'He wouldn't go to bed at all. I guess he sat up all night—in the public parlour. He wasn't in bed at twelve o'clock: it seemed as if he couldn't budge.'

'It was half-past twelve when *I* gave up,' Mrs Miller recorded with passionless accuracy.

It was of great interest to Winterbourne. 'Does he sleep much during the day?'

'I guess he doesn't sleep *very* much,' Daisy rejoined.

'I wish he just *would*!' said her mother. 'It seems as if he *must* make it up somehow.'

'Well, I guess it's we that make it up. I think he's real tiresome,' Daisy pursued.

After which, for some moments, there was silence. 'Well, Daisy Miller,' the elder lady then unexpectedly broke out, 'I shouldn't think you'd want to talk against your own brother!'

'Well, he *is* tiresome, mother,' said the girl, but with no sharpness of insistence.

'Well, he's only nine,' Mrs Miller lucidly urged.

'Well, he wouldn't go up to that castle, anyway,' her daughter replied as for accommodation. 'I'm going up there with Mr Winterbourne.'

To this announcement, very placidly made, Daisy's parent offered no response. Winterbourne took for granted on this that she opposed such a course; but he said to himself at the same time that she was a simple easily-managed person and that a few deferential protestations would modify her attitude. 'Yes,' he therefore interposed, 'your daughter has kindly allowed me the honour of being her guide.'

Mrs Miller's wandering eyes attached themselves with an appealing air to her other companion, who, however, strolled a few steps further, gently humming to herself. 'I presume you'll go in the cars,' she then quite colourlessly remarked.

'Yes, or in the boat,' said Winterbourne.

'Well, of course I don't know,' Mrs Miller returned. 'I've never been up to that castle.'

'It is a pity you shouldn't go,' he observed, beginning to feel reassured as to her opposition. And yet he was quite prepared to find that as a matter of course she meant to accompany her daughter.

It was on this view accordingly that light was projected for him. 'We've been thinking ever so much about going, but it seems as if we couldn't. Of course Daisy—she wants to go round everywhere. But there's a lady here—I don't know her name—she says she shouldn't think we'd want to go to see castles *here*; she should think we'd want to wait till we got t' Italy. It seems as if there would be so many there,' continued Mrs Miller with an air of increasing confidence. 'Of course we only want to see the principal ones. We visited several in England,' she presently added.

'Ah yes, in England there are beautiful castles,' said Winterbourne. 'But Chillon here is very well worth seeing.'

'Well, if Daisy feels up to it——' said Mrs Miller in a tone that seemed to break under the burden of such conceptions. 'It seems as if there's nothing she won't undertake.'

'Oh I'm pretty sure she'll enjoy it!' Winterbourne declared. And he desired more and more to make it a certainty that he was to have the privilege of a *tête-à-tête* with the young lady who was still strolling along in front of them and softly vocalising. 'You're not disposed, madam,' he inquired, 'to make the so interesting excursion yourself?'

So addressed Daisy's mother looked at him an instant with a certain scared obliquity and then walked forward in silence. Then, 'I guess she had better go alone,' she said simply.

It gave him occasion to note that this was a very different type of maternity from that of the vigilant matrons who massed themselves in the forefront of social intercourse in the dark old city at the other end of the lake. But his meditations were interrupted by hearing his name very distinctly pronounced by Mrs Miller's unprotected daughter. 'Mr Winterbourne!' she piped from a considerable distance.

'Mademoiselle!' said the young man.

'Don't you want to take me out in a boat?'

'At present?' he asked.

'Why of course!' she gaily returned.

'Well, Annie Miller!' exclaimed her mother.

'I beg you, madam, to let her go,' he hereupon eagerly pleaded; so instantly had he been struck with the romantic side of this chance to guide through the summer starlight a skiff freighted with a fresh and beautiful young girl.

'I shouldn't think she'd want to,' said her mother. 'I should think she'd rather go indoors.'

'I'm sure Mr Winterbourne wants to *take* me,' Daisy declared. 'He's so awfully devoted!'

'I'll row you over to Chillon under the stars.'

'I don't believe it!' Daisy laughed.

'Well!' the elder lady again gasped, as in rebuke of this freedom.

'You haven't spoken to me for half an hour,' her daughter went on.

'I've been having some very pleasant conversation with your mother,' Winterbourne replied.

'Oh pshaw! I want you to take me out in a boat!' Daisy went on as if nothing else had been said. They had all stopped and she had turned round and was looking at her friend. Her face wore a charming smile, her pretty eyes gleamed in the darkness, she swung her great fan about. No, he felt, it was impossible to be prettier than that.

'There are half a dozen boats moored at that landing-place,' and he pointed to a range of steps that descended from the garden to the lake. 'If you'll do me the honour to accept my arm we'll go and select one of them.'

She stood there smiling; she threw back her head; she laughed as for the drollery of this. 'I like a gentleman to be formal!'

'I assure you it's a formal offer.'

'I was bound I'd make you say something,' Daisy agreeably mocked.

'You see it's not very difficult,' said Winterbourne. 'But I'm afraid you're chaffing me.'

'I think not, sir,' Mrs Miller shyly pleaded.

'Do then let me give you a row,' he persisted to Daisy.

'It's quite lovely, the way you say that!' she cried in reward.

'It will be still more lovely to do it.'

'Yes, it would be lovely!' But she made no movement to accompany him; she only remained an elegant image of free light irony.

'I guess you'd better find out what time it is,' her mother impartially contributed.

'It's eleven o'clock, Madam,' said a voice with a foreign accent out of the neighbouring darkness; and Winterbourne, turning, recognised the florid personage he had already seen in attendance. He had apparently just approached.

'Oh Eugenio,' said Daisy, 'I'm going out with Mr Winterbourne in a boat!'

Eugenio bowed. 'At this hour of the night, Mademoiselle?'

'I'm going with Mr Winterbourne,' she repeated with her shining smile. 'I'm going this very minute.'

'Do tell her she can't, Eugenio,' Mrs Miller said to the courier.

'I think you had better not go out in a boat, Mademoiselle,' the man declared.

Winterbourne wished to goodness this pretty girl were not on such familiar terms with her courier; but he said nothing, and she meanwhile added to his ground. 'I suppose you don't think it's proper! My!' she wailed; 'Eugenio doesn't think anything's proper.'

'I'm nevertheless quite at your service,' Winterbourne hastened to remark.

'Does Mademoiselle propose to go alone?' Eugenio asked of Mrs Miller.

'Oh no, with this gentleman!' cried Daisy's mamma for reassurance.

'I *meant* alone with the gentleman.' The courier looked for a moment at Winterbourne—the latter seemed to make out in his face a vague presumptuous intelligence as at the expense of their companions—and then solemnly and with a bow, 'As Mademoiselle pleases!' he said.

But Daisy broke off at this. 'Oh I hoped you'd make a fuss! I don't care to go now.'

'Ah but I myself shall make a fuss if you don't go,' Winterbourne declared with spirit.

'That's all I want—a little fuss!' With which she began to laugh again.

'Mr Randolph has retired for the night!' the courier hereupon importantly announced.

'Oh Daisy, now we can go then!' cried Mrs Miller.

Her daughter turned away from their friend, all lighted with her odd perversity. 'Good-night—I hope you're disappointed or disgusted or something!'

He looked at her gravely, taking her by the hand she offered. 'I'm puzzled, if you want to know!' he answered.

'Well, I hope it won't keep you awake!' she said very smartly; and, under the escort of the privileged Eugenio, the two ladies passed toward the house.

Winterbourne's eyes followed them; he was indeed quite mystified. He lingered beside the lake a quarter of an hour, baffled by the question of the girl's sudden familiarities and caprices. But the only very definite conclusion he came to was that he should enjoy deucedly 'going off' with her somewhere.

Two days later he went off with her to the Castle of Chillon. He waited for her in the large hall of the hotel, where the couriers, the servants, the foreign tourists were lounging about and staring. It wasn't the place he would have chosen for a tryst, but she had placidly appointed it. She came tripping downstairs, buttoning her long gloves, squeezing her folded parasol against her pretty figure, dressed exactly in the way that consorted best, to his fancy, with their adventure. He was a man of imagination and, as our ancestors used to say, of sensibility;* as he took in her charming air and caught from the great staircase her impatient confiding step the note of some small sweet strain of romance, not intense but clear and sweet, seemed to sound for their start. He could have believed he was *really* going 'off' with her. He led her out through all the idle people assembled—they all looked at her straight and hard: she had begun to chatter as soon as she joined him. His preference had been that they should be conveyed to Chillon in a carriage, but she expressed a lively wish to go in the little steamer—there would be such a lovely breeze upon the water and they should see such lots of people. The sail wasn't long, but Winterbourne's companion found time for many characteristic remarks and other demonstrations, not a few of which were, from the extremity of their candour, slightly disconcerting. To the young man himself their small excursion showed so far delightfully irregular and incongruously intimate that, even allowing for her habitual sense of freedom, he had some expectation of seeing her appear to find in it the same savour. But it must be confessed that he was in this particular rather disappointed. Miss Miller was highly animated, she was in the brightest spirits; but she was clearly not at all in a nervous flutter—as she should have been to match *his* tension; she avoided neither his eyes nor those of any one else; she neither coloured from an awkward consciousness when she looked at him nor when she saw that people were looking at herself. People continued to look at her a great deal, and Winterbourne could at least take pleasure in his pretty companion's distinguished air. He had been privately afraid she would talk loud, laugh overmuch, and even perhaps desire to move extravagantly about the boat. But he quite forgot his fears; he sat smiling with his eyes on her face while, without stirring from her place, she delivered herself of a great number of original reflexions. It was the most charming innocent prattle he had ever heard, for, by his own experience hitherto, when young persons were so ingenuous they were less articulate and when they were so confident were more sophisticated. If he had assented to the idea that she was 'common', at any rate, *was* she proving so, after all, or was he simply getting used to her commonness? Her discourse was for the most part of what immediately and superficially surrounded them, but there were moments when it threw out a longer look or took a sudden straight plunge.

'What on *earth* are you so solemn about?' she suddenly demanded, fixing her agreeable eyes on her friend's.

'*Am* I solemn?' he asked. 'I had an idea I was grinning from ear to ear.'

'You look as if you were taking me to a prayer-meeting or a funeral. If that's a grin your ears are very near together.'

'Should you like me to dance a hornpipe on the deck?'

'Pray do, and I'll carry round your hat. It will pay the expenses of our journey.'

'I never was better pleased in my life,' Winterbourne returned.

She looked at him a moment, then let it renew her amusement. 'I like to make you say those things. You're a queer mixture!'

In the castle, after they had landed, nothing could exceed the light independence of her humour. She tripped about the vaulted chambers, rustled her skirts in the corkscrew staircases, flirted back with a pretty little cry and a shudder from the edge of the oubliettes* and turned a singularly well-shaped ear to everything Winterbourne told her about the place. But he saw she cared little for medieval history and that the grim ghosts of Chillon loomed but faintly before her. They had the good fortune to have been able to wander without other society than that of their guide;* and Winterbourne arranged with this companion that they shouldn't be hurried—that they should linger and pause wherever they chose. He interpreted the bargain generously—Winterbourne on his side had been generous—and ended by leaving them quite to themselves. Miss Miller's observations were marked by no logical consistency; for anything she wanted to say she was sure to find a pretext. She found a great many, in the tortuous passages and rugged embrasures of the place, for asking her young man sudden questions about himself, his family, his previous history, his tastes, his habits, his designs, and for supplying information on corresponding points in her own situation. Of her own tastes, habits and designs the charming creature was prepared to give the most definite and indeed the most favourable account.

'Well, I hope you know enough!' she exclaimed after Winterbourne had sketched for her something of the story of the unhappy Bonnivard.* 'I never saw a man that knew so much!' The history of Bonnivard had evidently, as they say, gone into one ear and out of the other. But this easy erudition struck her none the less as wonderful, and she was soon quite sure she wished Winterbourne would travel with them and 'go round' with them: they too in that case might learn something about something. 'Don't you want to come and teach Randolph?' she asked; 'I guess he'd improve with a gentleman teacher.' Winterbourne was certain that nothing could possibly please him so much, but that he had unfortunately other occupations. 'Other occupations? I don't believe a speck of it!' she protested. 'What do you mean now? You're not in business.' The young man allowed that he was not in business, but he had engagements which even within a day or two would necessitate his return to Geneva. 'Oh bother!' she panted, 'I don't believe it!' and she began to talk about something else. But a few moments later, when he was pointing out to her the interesting design of an antique fireplace, she broke out irrelevantly: 'You don't mean to say you're going back to Geneva?'

'It is a melancholy fact that I shall have to report myself there to-morrow.'

She met it with a vivacity that could only flatter him. 'Well, Mr Winterbourne, I think you're horrid!'

'Oh don't say such dreadful things!' he quite sincerely pleaded—'just at the last.'

'The last?' the girl cried; 'I call it the very first! I've half a mind to leave you here and go straight back to the hotel alone.' And for the next ten minutes she did nothing but call him horrid. Poor Winterbourne was fairly bewildered; no young lady had as yet done him the honour to be so agitated by the mention of his personal plans. His companion, after this, ceased to pay any attention to the curiosities of Chillon or the beauties of the lake; she opened fire on the special charmer in Geneva whom she appeared to have instantly taken it for granted that he was hurrying back to see. How did Miss Daisy Miller know of that agent of his fate in Geneva? Winterbourne, who denied the existence of such a person, was quite unable to discover; and he was divided between amazement at the rapidity of her induction and amusement at the directness of her criticism. She struck him afresh, in all this, as an extraordinary mixture of innocence and crudity. 'Does she never allow you more than three days at a time?' Miss Miller wished ironically to know. 'Doesn't she give you a vacation in summer? there's no one so hard-worked but they can get leave to go off somewhere at this season. I suppose if you stay another day she'll come right after you in the boat. Do wait over till Friday and I'll go down to the landing to see her arrive!' He began at last even to feel he had been wrong to be disappointed in the temper in which his lady had embarked. If he had missed the personal accent, the personal accent was now making its appearance. It sounded very distinctly, toward the end, in her telling him she'd stop 'teasing' him if he'd promise her solemnly to come down to Rome that winter.

'That's not a difficult promise to make,' he hastened to acknowledge. 'My aunt has taken an apartment in Rome from January and has already asked me to come and see her.'

'I don't want you to come for your aunt,' said Daisy; 'I want you just to come for me.' And this was the only allusion he was ever to hear her make again to his invidious kinswoman. He promised her that at any rate he would certainly come, and after this she forbore from teasing. Winterbourne took a carriage and they drove back to Vevey in the dusk; the girl at his side, her animation a little spent, was now quite distractingly passive.

In the evening he mentioned to Mrs Costello that he had spent the afternoon at Chillon with Miss Daisy Miller.

'The Americans—of the courier?' asked this lady.

'Ah happily the courier stayed at home.'

'She went with you all alone?'

'All alone.'

Mrs Costello sniffed a little at her smelling-bottle. 'And that,' she exclaimed, 'is the little abomination you wanted me to know!'

III

WINTERBOURNE, who had returned to Geneva the day after his excursion to Chillon, went to Rome toward the end of January.* His aunt had been established there a considerable time and he had received from her a couple of characteristic letters. 'Those people you were so devoted to last summer at Vevey have turned up here, courier and all,' she wrote. 'They seem to have made several acquaintances, but the courier continues to be the most *intime*. The young lady, however, is also very intimate with various third-rate Italians, with whom she rackets about in a way that makes much talk. Bring me that pretty novel of Cherbuliez's*— "Paule Méré"—and don't come later than the 23rd.'

Our friend would in the natural course of events, on arriving in Rome, have presently ascertained Mrs Miller's address at the American banker's* and gone to pay his compliments to Miss Daisy. 'After what happened at Vevey I certainly think I may call upon them,' he said to Mrs Costello.

'If after what happens—at Vevey and everywhere—you desire to keep up the acquaintance, you're very welcome. Of course you're not squeamish—a man may know every one. Men are welcome to the privilege!'

'Pray what is it then that "happens"—here for instance?' Winterbourne asked.

'Well, the girl tears about alone with her unmistakably low foreigners. As to what happens further you must apply elsewhere for information. She has picked up half a dozen of the regular Roman fortune-hunters of the inferior sort and she takes them about to such houses as she may put *her* nose into. When she comes to a party—such a party as she can come to—she brings with her a gentleman with a good deal of manner and a wonderful moustache.'

'And where's the mother?'

'I haven't the least idea. They're very dreadful people.'

Winterbourne thought them over in these new lights. 'They're very ignorant—very innocent only, and utterly uncivilised. Depend on it they're not "bad".'

'They're hopelessly vulgar,' said Mrs Costello. 'Whether or no being hopelessly vulgar is being "bad" is a question for the metaphysicians. They're bad enough to blush for, at any rate; and for this short life that's quite enough.'

The news that his little friend the child of nature of the Swiss lakeside was now surrounded by half a dozen wonderful moustaches checked Winterbourne's impulse to go straightway to see her. He had perhaps not definitely flattered himself that he had made an ineffaceable impression upon her heart, but he was annoyed at hearing of a state of affairs so little in harmony with an image that had lately flitted in and out of his own meditations; the image of a very pretty girl looking out of an old Roman window and asking herself urgently when Mr Winterbourne would arrive. If, however, he determined to wait a little before reminding this young lady of his claim to her faithful remembrance, he called with more promptitude on two or three other friends. One of these friends was an American lady who had spent several winters at Geneva, where she had placed her children at school. She was a very accomplished woman and she lived in Via Gregoriana.* Winterbourne found her in a little crimson drawing-room on a third floor; the room was filled with southern sunshine. He hadn't been there ten minutes when the servant, appearing in the door-way, announced complacently 'Madame Mila!' This announce-ment was presently followed by the entrance of little Randolph Miller, who stopped in the middle of the room and stood staring at Winterbourne. An instant later his pretty sister crossed the threshold; and then, after a considerable interval, the parent of the pair slowly advanced.

'I guess I know you!' Randolph broke ground without delay.

'I'm sure you know a great many things'—and his old friend clutched him all interestedly by the arm. 'How's your education coming on?'

Daisy was engaged in some pretty babble with her hostess, but when she heard Winterbourne's voice she quickly turned her head with a 'Well, I declare!' which he met smiling. 'I told you I should come, you know.'

'Well, I didn't believe it,' she answered.

'I'm much obliged to you for that,' laughed the young man.

'You might have come to see me then,' Daisy went on as if they had parted the week before.

'I arrived only yesterday.'

'I don't believe any such thing!' the girl declared afresh.

Winterbourne turned with a protesting smile to her mother, but this lady evaded his glance and, seating herself, fixed her eyes on her son. 'We've got a bigger place than this,' Randolph here-upon broke out. 'It's all gold on the walls.'

Mrs Miller, more of a fatalist apparently than ever, turned uneasily in her chair. 'I told you if I was to bring you you'd say something!' she stated as for the benefit of such of the company as might hear it.

'I told *you*!' Randolph retorted. 'I tell *you*, sir!' he added jocosely, giving Winterbourne a thump on the knee. 'It *is* bigger too!'

As Daisy's conversation with her hostess still occupied her Winterbourne judged it becoming to address a few words to her mother—such as 'I hope you've been well since we parted at Vevey.'

Mrs Miller now certainly looked at him—at his chin. 'Not very well, sir,' she answered.

'She's got the dyspepsia,' said Randolph. 'I've got it too. Father's got it bad. But I've got it worst!'

This proclamation, instead of embarrassing Mrs Miller, seemed to soothe her by reconstituting the environment to which she was most accustomed. 'I suffer from the liver,' she amiably whined to Winterbourne. 'I think it's this climate; it's less bracing than Schenectady, especially in the winter season. I don't know whether you know we reside at Schenectady. I was saying to Daisy that I certainly hadn't found any one like Dr Davis and I didn't believe I *would*. Oh up in Schenectady, he stands first; they think everything of Dr Davis. He has so much to do, and yet there was nothing he wouldn't do for *me*. He said he never saw anything like my dyspepsia, but he was bound to get at it. I'm sure there was nothing he wouldn't try, and I didn't care what he did to me if he only brought me relief. He was just going to try something new, and I just longed for it, when we came right off. Mr Miller felt as if he wanted Daisy to see Europe for herself. But I couldn't help writing the other day that I supposed it was all right for Daisy, but that I didn't know as I *could* get on much longer without Dr Davis. At Schenectady he stands at the very top; and there's a great deal of sickness there too. It affects my sleep.'

Winterbourne had a good deal of pathological gossip with Dr Davis's patient, during which Daisy chattered unremittingly to her own companion. The young man asked Mrs Miller how she was pleased with Rome. 'Well, I must say I'm disappointed,' she confessed. 'We had heard so much about it—I suppose we had heard too much. But we couldn't help that. We had been led to expect something different.'

Winterbourne, however, abounded in reassurance. 'Ah wait a little, and you'll grow very fond of it.'

'I hate it worse and worse every day!' cried Randolph.

'You're like the infant Hannibal,'* his friend laughed.

'No I ain't—like any infant!' Randolph declared at a venture.

'Well, that's so—and you never *were!*' his mother concurred. 'But we've seen places,' she resumed, 'that I'd put a long way ahead of Rome.' And in reply to Winterbourne's interrogation, 'There's Zürich—up there in the mountains,' she instanced; 'I think Zürich's real lovely, and we hadn't heard half so much about it.'

'The best place we've seen's the *City of Richmond!*'* said Randolph.

'He means the ship,' Mrs Miller explained. 'We crossed in that ship. Randolph had a good time on the *City of Richmond.*'

'It's the best place *I've* struck,' the child repeated. 'Only it was turned the wrong way.'

'Well, we've got to turn the right way sometime,' said Mrs Miller with strained but weak optimism. Winterbourne expressed the hope that her daughter at least appreciated the so various interest of Rome, and she declared with some spirit that Daisy was quite carried away. 'It's on account of the society—the society's splendid. She goes round everywhere; she has made a great number of acquaintances. Of course she goes round more than I do. I must say they've all been very sweet—they've taken her right in. And then she knows a great many gentlemen. Oh she thinks there's nothing like Rome. Of course it's a great deal pleasanter for a young lady if she knows plenty of gentlemen.'

By this time Daisy had turned her attention again to Winterbourne, but in quite the same free form. 'I've been telling Mrs Walker how mean you were!'

'And what's the evidence you've offered?' he asked, a trifle disconcerted, for all his superior gallantry, by her inadequate measure of the zeal of an admirer who on his way down to Rome had stopped neither at Bologna nor at Florence, simply because of a certain sweet appeal to his fond fancy, not to say to his finest curiosity. He remembered how a cynical compatriot had once told him that American women—the pretty ones, and this gave a largeness to the axiom—were at once the most exacting in the world and the least endowed with a sense of indebtedness.

'Why, you were awfully mean up at Vevey,' Daisy said. 'You wouldn't do most anything. You wouldn't stay there when I asked you.'

'Dearest young lady,' cried Winterbourne, with generous passion, 'have I come all the way to Rome only to be riddled by your silver shafts?'

'Just hear him say that!'—and she gave an affectionate twist to a bow on her hostess's dress. 'Did you ever hear anything so quaint?'

'So "quaint", my dear?' echoed Mrs Walker more critically— quite in the tone of a partisan of Winterbourne.

'Well, I don't know'—and the girl continued to finger her ribbons. 'Mrs Walker, I want to tell you something.'

'Say, mother-r,' broke in Randolph with his rough ends to his words, 'I tell you you've got to go. Eugenio'll raise something!'

'I'm not afraid of Eugenio,' said Daisy with a toss of her head. 'Look here, Mrs Walker,' she went on, 'you know I'm coming to your party.'

'I'm delighted to hear it.'

'I've got a lovely dress.'

'I'm very sure of that.'

'But I want to ask a favour—permission to bring a friend.'

'I shall be happy to see any of your friends,' said Mrs Walker, who turned with a smile to Mrs Miller.

'Oh they're not my friends,' cried that lady, squirming in shy repudiation. 'It seems as if they didn't take to *me*—I never spoke to one of them!'

'It's an intimate friend of mine, Mr Giovanelli,' Daisy pursued without a tremor in her young clearness or a shadow on her shining bloom.

Mrs Walker had a pause and gave a rapid glance at Winterbourne. 'I shall be glad to see Mr Giovanelli,' she then returned.

'He's just the finest kind of Italian,' Daisy pursued with the prettiest serenity. 'He's a great friend of mine and the handsomest man in the world—except Mr Winterbourne! He knows plenty of Italians, but he wants to know some Americans. It seems as if he was crazy about Americans. He's tremendously bright. He's perfectly lovely!'

It was settled that this paragon should be brought to Mrs Walker's party, and then Mrs Miller prepared to take her leave. 'I guess we'll go right back to the hotel,'* she remarked with a confessed failure of the larger imagination.

'You may go back to the hotel, mother,' Daisy replied, 'but I'm just going to walk round.'

'She's going to go it with Mr Giovanelli,' Randolph unscrupulously commented.

'I'm going to go it on the Pincio,'* Daisy peaceably smiled, while the way that she 'condoned'* these things almost melted Winterbourne's heart.

'Alone, my dear—at this hour?' Mrs Walker asked. The afternoon was drawing to a close—it was the hour for the throng of carriages and of contemplative pedestrians. 'I don't consider it's safe, Daisy,' her hostess firmly asserted.

'Neither do I then,' Mrs Miller thus borrowed confidence to add. 'You'll catch the fever as sure as you live. Remember what Dr Davis told you!'

'Give her some of that medicine before she starts in,' Randolph suggested.

The company had risen to its feet; Daisy, still showing her pretty teeth, bent over and kissed her hostess. 'Mrs Walker, you're too perfect,' she simply said. 'I'm not going alone; I'm going to meet a friend.'

'Your friend won't keep you from catching the fever even if it *is* his own second nature,' Mrs Miller observed.

'Is it Mr Giovanelli that's the dangerous attraction?' Mrs Walker asked without mercy.

Winterbourne was watching the challenged girl; at this

question his attention quickened. She stood there smiling and smoothing her bonnet-ribbons; she glanced at Winterbourne. Then, while she glanced and smiled, she brought out all affirmatively and without a shade of hesitation: 'Mr Giovanelli—the beautiful Giovanelli.'

'My dear young friend'—and, taking her hand, Mrs Walker turned to pleading—'don't prowl off to the Pincio at this hour to meet a beautiful Italian.'

'Well, he speaks first-rate English,' Mrs Miller incoherently mentioned.

'Gracious me,' Daisy piped up, 'I don't want to do anything that's going to affect my health—or my character either! There's an easy way to settle it.' Her eyes continued to play over Winterbourne. 'The Pincio's only a hundred yards off, and if Mr Winterbourne were as polite as he pretends he'd offer to walk right in with me!'

Winterbourne's politeness hastened to proclaim itself, and the girl gave him gracious leave to accompany her. They passed downstairs before her mother, and at the door he saw Mrs Miller's carriage drawn up, with the ornamental courier whose acquaintance he had made at Vevey seated within. 'Good-bye, Eugenio,' cried Daisy; 'I'm going to take a walk!' The distance from Via Gregoriana to the beautiful garden at the other end of the Pincian Hill is in fact rapidly traversed. As the day was splendid, however, and the concourse of vehicles, walkers and loungers numerous, the young Americans found their progress much delayed. This fact was highly agreeable to Winterbourne, in spite of his consciousness of his singular situation. The slow-moving, idly-gazing Roman crowd bestowed much attention on the extremely pretty young woman of English race who passed through it, with some difficulty, on his arm; and he wondered what on earth had been in Daisy's mind when she proposed to exhibit herself unattended to its appreciation. His own mission, to her sense, was apparently to consign her to the hands of Mr Giovanelli; but, at once annoyed and gratified, he resolved that he would do no such thing.

'Why haven't you been to see me?' she meanwhile asked. 'You can't get out of that.'

'I've had the honour of telling you that I've only just stepped out of the train.'

'You must have stayed in the train a good while after it stopped!' she derisively cried. 'I suppose you were asleep. You've had time to go to see Mrs Walker.'

'I knew Mrs Walker——' Winterbourne began to explain.

'I know where you knew her. You knew her at Geneva. She told me so. Well, you knew me at Vevey. That's just as good. So you ought to have come.' She asked him no other question than this; she began to prattle about her own affairs. 'We've got splendid rooms at the hotel; Eugenio says they're the best rooms in Rome. We're going to stay all winter—if we don't die of the fever; and I guess we'll stay then! It's a great deal nicer than I thought; I thought it would be fearfully quiet—in fact I was sure it would be deadly pokey. I foresaw we should be going round all the time with one of those dreadful old men who explain about the pictures and things. But we only had about a week of that, and now I'm enjoying myself. I know ever so many people, and they're all so charming. The society's extremely select. There are all kinds— English and Germans and Italians. I think I like the English best. I like their style of conversation. But there are some lovely Americans. I never saw anything so hospitable. There's something or other every day. There's not much dancing—but I must say I never thought dancing was everything. I was always fond of conversation. I guess I'll have plenty at Mrs Walker's—her rooms are so small.' When they had passed the gate of the Pincian Gardens Miss Miller began to wonder where Mr Giovanelli might be. 'We had better go straight to that place in front, where you look at the view.'

Winterbourne at this took a stand. 'I certainly shan't help you to find him.'

'Then I shall find him without you,' Daisy said with spirit.

'You certainly won't leave me!' he protested.

She burst into her familiar little laugh. 'Are you afraid you'll get lost—or run over? But there's Giovanelli leaning against that tree. He's staring at the women in the carriages: did you ever see anything so cool?'

Winterbourne descried hereupon at some distance a little figure
that stood with folded arms and nursing its cane. It had a handsome face, a hat artfully poised, a glass in one eye and a nosegay in
its buttonhole. Daisy's friend looked at it a moment and then said:
'Do you mean to speak to that thing?'

'Do I mean to speak to him? Why, you don't suppose I mean to
communicate by signs!'

'Pray understand then,' the young man returned, 'that I intend
to remain with you.'

Daisy stopped and looked at him without a sign of troubled
consciousness, with nothing in her face but her charming eyes,
her charming teeth and her happy dimples. 'Well, she's a cool
one!' he thought.

'I don't like the way you say that,' she declared. 'It's too imperious.'

'I beg your pardon if I say it wrong. The main point's to give
you an idea of my meaning.'

The girl looked at him more gravely, but with eyes that were
prettier than ever. 'I've never allowed a gentleman to dictate to me
or to interfere with anything I do.'

'I think that's just where your mistake has come in,' he retorted.
'You should sometimes listen to a gentleman—the right one.'

At this she began to laugh again. 'I do nothing but listen to
gentlemen! Tell me if Mr Giovanelli is the right one.'

The gentleman with the nosegay in his bosom had now
made out our two friends and was approaching Miss Miller with
obsequious rapidity. He bowed to Winterbourne as well as to the
latter's compatriot; he seemed to shine, in his coxcombical way,
with the desire to please and the fact of his own intelligent joy,
though Winterbourne thought him not a bad-looking fellow. But
he nevertheless said to Daisy: 'No, he's not the right one.'

She had clearly a natural turn for free introductions; she mentioned with the easiest grace the name of each of her companions
to the other. She strolled forward with one of them on either hand;
Mr Giovanelli, who spoke English very cleverly—Winterbourne
afterwards learned that he had practised the idiom upon a great
many American heiresses—addressed her a great deal of very
polite nonsense. He had the best possible manners, and the young

American, who said nothing, reflected on that depth of Italian subtlety, so strangely opposed to Anglo-Saxon simplicity, which enables people to show a smoother surface in proportion as they're more acutely displeased. Giovanelli of course had counted upon something more intimate—he had not bargained for a party of three; but he kept his temper in a manner that suggested far-stretching intentions. Winterbourne flattered himself he had taken his measure. 'He's anything but a gentleman,' said the young American; 'he isn't even a very plausible imitation of one. He's a music-master or a penny-a-liner* or a third-rate artist. He's awfully on his good behaviour, but damn his fine eyes!' Mr Giovanelli had indeed great advantages; but it was deeply disgusting to Daisy's other friend that something in her shouldn't have instinctively discriminated against such a type. Giovanelli chattered and jested and made himself agreeable according to his honest Roman lights. It was true that if he was an imitation the imitation was studied. 'Nevertheless,' Winterbourne said to himself, 'a nice girl ought to know!' And then he came back to the dreadful question of whether this *was* in fact a nice girl. Would a nice girl—even allowing for her being a little American flirt—make a rendezvous with a presumably low-lived foreigner? The rendezvous in this case indeed had been in broad daylight and in the most crowded corner of Rome; but wasn't it possible to regard the choice of these very circumstances as a proof more of vulgarity than of anything else? Singular though it may seem, Winterbourne was vexed that the girl, in joining her *amoroso,** shouldn't appear more impatient of his own company, and he was vexed precisely because of his inclination. It was impossible to regard her as a wholly unspotted flower—she lacked a certain indispensable fineness; and it would therefore much simplify the situation to be able to treat her as the subject of one of the visitations known to romancers as 'lawless passions'. That she should seem to wish to get rid of him would have helped him to think more lightly of her, just as to be able to think more lightly of her would have made her less perplexing. Daisy at any rate continued on this occasion to present herself as an inscrutable combination of audacity and innocence.

She had been walking some quarter of an hour, attended by her two cavaliers and responding in a tone of very childish gaiety, as it after all struck one of them, to the pretty speeches of the other, when a carriage that had detached itself from the revolving train drew up beside the path. At the same moment Winterbourne noticed that his friend Mrs Walker—the lady whose house he had lately left—was seated in the vehicle and was beckoning to him. Leaving Miss Miller's side, he hastened to obey her summons— and all to find her flushed, excited, scandalised. 'It's really too dreadful'—she earnestly appealed to him. 'That crazy girl mustn't do this sort of thing. She mustn't walk here with you two men. Fifty people have remarked her.'

Winterbourne—suddenly and rather oddly rubbed the wrong way by this—raised his grave eyebrows. 'I think it's a pity to make too much fuss about it.'

'It's a pity to let the girl ruin herself!'

'She's very innocent,' he reasoned in his own troubled interest.

'She's very reckless,' cried Mrs Walker, 'and goodness knows how far—left to itself—it may go. Did you ever', she proceeded to inquire, 'see anything so blatantly imbecile as the mother? After you had all left me just now I couldn't sit still for thinking of it. It seemed too pitiful not even to attempt to save them. I ordered the carriage and put on my bonnet and came here as quickly as possible. Thank heaven I've found you!'

'What do you propose to do with us?' Winterbourne uncomfortably smiled.

'To ask her to get in, to drive her about here for half an hour— so that the world may see she's not running absolutely wild— and then take her safely home.'

'I don't think it's a very happy thought,' he said after reflexion, 'but you're at liberty to try.'

Mrs Walker accordingly tried. The young man went in pursuit of their young lady who had simply nodded and smiled, from her distance, at her recent patroness in the carriage and then had gone her way with her own companion. On learning, in the event, that Mrs Walker had followed her, she retraced her steps, however, with a perfect good grace and with Mr Giovanelli at her side.

She professed herself 'enchanted' to have a chance to present this gentleman to her good friend, and immediately achieved the introduction; declaring with it, and as if it were of as little import- ance, that she had never in her life seen anything so lovely as that lady's carriage-rug.

'I'm glad you admire it,' said her poor pursuer, smiling sweetly. 'Will you get in and let me put it over you!'

'Oh no, thank you!'—Daisy knew her mind. 'I'll admire it ever so much more as I see you driving round with it.'

'Do get in and drive round *with* me,' Mrs Walker pleaded.

'That would be charming, but it's so fascinating just as I am!'—with which the girl radiantly took in the gentlemen on either side of her.

'It may be fascinating, dear child, but it's not the custom here,' urged the lady of the victoria,* leaning forward in this vehicle with her hands devoutly clasped.

'Well, it ought to be then!' Daisy imperturbably laughed. 'If I didn't walk I'd expire.'

'You should walk with your mother, dear,' cried Mrs Walker with a loss of patience.

'With my mother dear?' the girl amusedly echoed. Winterbourne saw she scented interference. 'My mother never walked ten steps in her life. And then, you know,' she blandly added, 'I'm more than five years old.'

'You're old enough to be more reasonable. You're old enough, dear Miss Miller, to be talked about.'

Daisy wondered to extravagance. 'Talked about? What do you mean?'

'Come into my carriage and I'll tell you.'

Daisy turned shining eyes again from one of the gentlemen beside her to the other. Mr Giovanelli was bowing to and fro, rub- bing down his gloves and laughing irresponsibly; Winterbourne thought the scene the most unpleasant possible. 'I don't think I want to know what you mean,' the girl presently said. 'I don't think I should like it.'

Winterbourne only wished Mrs Walker would tuck up her carriage-rug and drive away; but this lady, as she afterwards told him, didn't feel she could 'rest there'. 'Should you prefer being thought a very reckless girl?' she accordingly asked.

'Gracious me!' exclaimed Daisy. She looked again at Mr Giovanelli, then she turned to her other companion. There was a small pink flush in her cheek; she was tremendously pretty. 'Does Mr Winterbourne think', she put to him with a wonderful bright intensity of appeal, 'that—to save my reputation—I ought to get into the carriage?'

It really embarrassed him; for an instant he cast about—so strange was it to hear her speak that way of her 'reputation'. But he himself in fact had to speak in accordance with gallantry. The finest gallantry here was surely just to tell her the truth; and the truth, for our young man, as the few indications I have been able to give have made him known to the reader, was that his charming friend should listen to the voice of civilised society. He took in again her exquisite prettiness and then said the more distinctly: 'I think you should get into the carriage.'

Daisy gave the rein to her amusement. 'I never heard anything so stiff! If this is improper, Mrs Walker,' she pursued, 'then I'm *all* improper, and you had better give me right up. Good-bye; I hope you'll have a lovely ride!'—and with Mr Giovanelli, who made a triumphantly obsequious salute, she turned away.

Mrs Walker sat looking after her, and there were tears in Mrs Walker's eyes. 'Get in here, sir,' she said to Winterbourne, indicating the place beside her. The young man answered that he felt bound to accompany Miss Miller; whereupon the lady of the victoria declared that if he refused her this favour she would never speak to him again. She was evidently wound up. He accordingly hastened to overtake Daisy and her more faithful ally, and, offering her his hand, told her that Mrs Walker had made a stringent claim on his presence. He had expected her to answer with something rather free, something still more significant of the perversity from which the voice of society, through the lips of their distressed friend, had so earnestly endeavoured to dissuade her. But she only let her hand slip, as she scarce looked at him, through his slightly awkward grasp; while Mr Giovanelli, to make it worse, bade him farewell with too emphatic a flourish of the hat.

Winterbourne was not in the best possible humour as he took his seat beside the author of his sacrifice. 'That was not clever of you,' he said candidly, as the vehicle mingled again with the throng of carriages.

'In such a case,' his companion answered, 'I don't want to be clever—I only want to be *true*!'

'Well, your truth has only offended the strange little creature—it has only put her off.'

'It has happened very well'—Mrs Walker accepted her work. 'If she's so perfectly determined to compromise herself the sooner one knows it the better—one can act accordingly.'

'I suspect she meant no great harm, you know,' Winterbourne maturely opined.

'So I thought a month ago. But she has been going too far.'

'What has she been doing?'

'Everything that's not done here. Flirting with any man she can pick up; sitting in corners with mysterious Italians; dancing all the evening with the same partners; receiving visits at eleven o'clock at night. Her mother melts away when the visitors come.'

'But her brother', laughed Winterbourne, 'sits up till two in the morning.'

'He must be edified by what he sees. I'm told that at their hotel every one's talking about her and that a smile goes round among the servants when a gentleman comes and asks for Miss Miller.'

'Ah we needn't mind the servants!' Winterbourne compassionately signified. 'The poor girl's only fault', he presently added, 'is her complete lack of education.'

'She's naturally indelicate,' Mrs Walker, on her side, reasoned. 'Take that example this morning. How long had you known her at Vevey?'

'A couple of days.'

'Imagine then the taste of her making it a personal matter that you should have left the place!'

He agreed that taste wasn't the strong point of the Millers—after which he was silent for some moments; but only at last to add: 'I suspect, Mrs Walker, that you and I have lived too long at Geneva!' And he further noted that he should be glad to learn with what particular design she had made him enter her carriage.

'I wanted to enjoin on you the importance of your ceasing your relations with Miss Miller; that of your not appearing to flirt with her; that of your giving her no further opportunity to expose herself; that of your in short letting her alone.'

'I'm afraid I can't do anything quite so enlightened as *that*,' he returned. 'I like her awfully, you know.'

'All the more reason you shouldn't help her to make a scandal.'

'Well, there shall be nothing scandalous in my attentions to her,' he was willing to promise.

'There certainly will be in the way she takes them. But I've said what I had on my conscience,' Mrs Walker pursued. 'If you wish to rejoin the young lady I'll put you down. Here, by the way, you have a chance.'

The carriage was engaged in that part of the Pincian drive which overhangs the wall of Rome and overlooks the beautiful Villa Borghese.* It is bordered by a large parapet, near which are several seats. One of these, at a distance, was occupied by a gentleman and a lady, toward whom Mrs Walker gave a toss of her head. At the same moment these persons rose and walked to the parapet. Winterbourne had asked the coachman to stop; he now descended from the carriage. His companion looked at him a moment in silence and then, while he raised his hat, drove majestically away. He stood where he had alighted; he had turned his eyes toward Daisy and her cavalier. They evidently saw no one; they were too deeply occupied with each other. When they reached the low garden-wall they remained a little looking off at the great flat-topped pine-clusters of Villa Borghese; then the girl's attendant admirer seated himself familiarly on the broad ledge of the wall. The western sun in the opposite sky sent out a brilliant shaft through a couple of cloud-bars; whereupon the gallant Giovanelli took her parasol out of her hands and opened it. She came a little nearer and he held the parasol over her; then, still holding it, he let it so rest on her shoulder that both of their heads were hidden from Winterbourne. This young man stayed but a moment longer; then he began to walk. But he walked—not toward the couple united beneath the parasol, rather toward the residence of his aunt Mrs Costello.

IV

HE flattered himself on the following day that there was no smiling among the servants when he at least asked for Mrs Miller at her hotel. This lady and her daughter, however, were not at home; and on the next day after, repeating his visit, Winterbourne again was met by a denial. Mrs Walker's party took place on the evening of the third day, and in spite of the final reserves that had marked his last interview with that social critic our young man was among the guests. Mrs Walker was one of those pilgrims from the younger world who, while in contact with the elder, make a point, in their own phrase, of studying European society; and she had on this occasion collected several specimens of diversely-born humanity to serve, as might be, for text-books. When Winterbourne arrived the little person he desired most to find wasn't there; but in a few moments he saw Mrs Miller come in alone, very shyly and ruefully. This lady's hair, above the dead waste of her temples, was more frizzled than ever. As she approached their hostess Winterbourne also drew near.

'You see I've come all alone,' said Daisy's unsupported parent. 'I'm so frightened I don't know what to do; it's the first time I've ever been to a party alone—especially in this country. I wanted to bring Randolph or Eugenio or some one, but Daisy just pushed me off by myself. I ain't used to going round alone.'

'And doesn't your daughter intend to favour us with her society?' Mrs Walker impressively inquired.

'Well, Daisy's all dressed,' Mrs Miller testified with that accent of the dispassionate, if not of the philosophic, historian with which she always recorded the current incidents of her daughter's career. 'She got dressed on purpose before dinner. But she has a friend of hers there; that gentleman—the handsomest of the Italians—that she wanted to bring. They've got going at the piano—it seems as if they couldn't leave off. Mr Giovanelli does sing splendidly. But I guess they'll come before very long,' Mrs Miller hopefully concluded.

'I'm sorry she should come—in that particular way,' Mrs Walker permitted herself to observe.

'Well, I told her there was no use in her getting dressed before dinner if she was going to wait three hours,' returned Daisy's mamma. 'I didn't see the use of her putting on such a dress as that to sit round with Mr Giovanelli.'

'This is most horrible!' said Mrs Walker, turning away and addressing herself to Winterbourne. '*Elle s'affiche, la malheureuse.** It's her revenge for my having ventured to remonstrate with her. When she comes I shan't speak to her.'

Daisy came after eleven o'clock, but she wasn't, on such an occasion, a young lady to wait to be spoken to. She rustled forward in radiant loveliness, smiling and chattering, carrying a large bouquet and attended by Mr Giovanelli. Every one stopped talking and turned and looked at her while she floated up to Mrs Walker. 'I'm afraid you thought I never was coming, so I sent mother off to tell you. I wanted to make Mr Giovanelli practise some things before he came; you know he sings beautifully, and I want you to ask him to sing. This is Mr Giovanelli; you know I introduced him to you; he's got the most lovely voice and he knows the most charming set of songs. I made him go over them this evening on purpose; we had the greatest time at the hotel.' Of all this Daisy delivered herself with the sweetest brightest loudest confidence, looking now at her hostess and now at all the room, while she gave a series of little pats, round her very white shoulders, to the edges of her dress. 'Is there any one I know?' she as undiscourageably asked.

'I think every one knows you!' said Mrs Walker as with a grand intention; and she gave a very cursory greeting to Mr Giovanelli. This gentleman bore himself gallantly; he smiled and bowed and showed his white teeth, he curled his moustaches and rolled his eyes and performed all the proper functions of a handsome Italian at an evening party. He sang, very prettily, half a dozen songs, though Mrs Walker afterwards declared that she had been quite unable to find out who asked him. It was apparently not Daisy who had set him in motion—this young lady being seated a distance from the piano and though she had publicly, as it were, professed herself his musical patroness or guarantor, giving herself to gay and audible discourse while he warbled.

'It's a pity these rooms are so small; we can't dance,' she remarked to Winterbourne as if she had seen him five minutes before.

'I'm not sorry we can't dance,' he candidly returned. 'I'm incapable of a step.'

'Of course you're incapable of a step,' the girl assented. 'I should think your legs *would* be stiff cooped in there so much of the time in that victoria.'

'Well, they were very restless there three days ago,' he amicably laughed; 'all they really wanted was to dance attendance on you.'

'Oh my other friend—my friend in need—stuck to me; he seems more at one with his limbs than you are—I'll say that for him. But did you ever hear anything so cool,' Daisy demanded, 'as Mrs Walker's wanting me to get into her carriage and drop poor Mr Giovanelli, and under the pretext that it was proper? People have different ideas! It would have been most unkind; he had been talking about that walk for ten days.'

'He shouldn't have talked about it at all,' Winterbourne decided to make answer on this: 'he would never have proposed to a young lady of this country to walk about the streets of Rome with him.'

'About the streets?' she cried with her pretty stare. 'Where then would he have proposed to her to walk? The Pincio ain't the streets either, I guess; and I besides, thank goodness, am not a young lady of this country. The young ladies of this country have a dreadfully pokey time of it, by what I can discover; I don't see why I should change my habits for *such* stupids.'

'I'm afraid your habits are those of a ruthless flirt,' said Winterbourne with studied severity.

'Of course they are!'—and she hoped, evidently, by the manner of it, to take his breath away. 'I'm a fearful frightful flirt! Did you ever hear of a nice girl that wasn't? But I suppose you'll tell me now I'm not a nice girl.'

He remained grave indeed under the shock of her cynical profession. 'You're a very nice girl, but I wish you'd flirt with me, and me only.'

'Ah thank you, thank you very much: you're the last man I should think of flirting with. As I've had the pleasure of informing you, you're too stiff.'

'You say that too often,' he resentfully remarked.

Daisy gave a delighted laugh. 'If I could have the sweet hope of making you angry I'd say it again.'

'Don't do that—when I'm angry I'm stiffer than ever. But if you won't flirt with me do cease at least to flirt with your friend at the piano. They don't', he declared as in full sympathy with 'them', 'understand that sort of thing here.'

'I thought they understood nothing else!' Daisy cried with startling world-knowledge.

'Not in young unmarried women.'

'It seems to me much more proper in young unmarried than in old married ones,' she retorted.

'Well,' said Winterbourne, 'when you deal with natives you must go by the custom of the country. American flirting is a purely American silliness; it has—in its ineptitude of innocence— no place in *this* system. So when you show yourself in public with Mr Giovanelli and without your mother——'

'Gracious, poor mother!'—and she made it beautifully unspeakable.

Winterbourne had a touched sense for this, but it didn't alter his attitude. 'Though *you* may be flirting, Mr Giovanelli isn't— he means something else.'

'He isn't preaching at any rate,' she returned. 'And if you want very much to know, we're neither of us flirting—not a little speck. We're too good friends for that. We're real intimate friends.'

He was to continue to find her thus at moments inimitable. 'Ah,' he then judged, 'if you're in love with each other it's another affair altogether!'

She had allowed him up to this point to speak so frankly that he had no thought of shocking her by the force of his logic; yet she now none the less immediately rose, blushing visibly and leaving him mentally to exclaim that the name of little American flirts was incoherence. 'Mr Giovanelli at least,' she answered, sparing but a single small queer glance for it, a queerer small glance, he felt, than he had ever yet had from her—'Mr Giovanelli never says to me such very disagreeable things.'

It had an effect on him—he stood staring. The subject of their contention had finished singing; he left the piano, and his recognition of what—a little awkwardly—didn't take place in celebration of this might nevertheless have been an acclaimed operatic tenor's series of repeated ducks before the curtain. So he bowed himself over to Daisy. 'Won't you come to the other room and have some tea?' he asked—offering Mrs Walker's slightly thin refreshment as he might have done all the kingdoms of the earth.

Daisy at last turned on Winterbourne a more natural and calculable light. He was but the more muddled by it, however, since so inconsequent a smile made nothing clear—it seemed at the most to prove in her a sweetness and softness that reverted instinctively to the pardon of offences. 'It has never occurred to Mr Winterbourne to offer me any tea,' she said with her finest little intention of torment and triumph.

'I've offered you excellent advice,' the young man permitted himself to growl.

'I prefer weak tea!' cried Daisy, and she went off with the brilliant Giovanelli. She sat with him in the adjoining room, in the embrasure of the window, for the rest of the evening. There was an interesting performance at the piano, but neither of these conversers gave heed to it. When Daisy came to take leave of Mrs Walker this lady conscientiously repaired the weakness of which she had been guilty at the moment of the girl's arrival—she turned her back straight on Miss Miller and left her to depart with what grace she might. Winterbourne happened to be near the door; he saw it all. Daisy turned very pale and looked at her mother, but Mrs Miller was humbly unconscious of any rupture of any law or of any deviation from any custom. She appeared indeed to have felt an incongruous impulse to draw attention to her own striking conformity. 'Good-night, Mrs Walker,' she said; 'we've had a beautiful evening. You see if I let Daisy come to parties without me I don't want her to go away without me.' Daisy turned away, looking with a small white prettiness, a blighted grace, at the circle near the door: Winterbourne saw that for the first moment she was too much shocked and puzzled even for indignation. He on his side was greatly touched.

'That was very cruel,' he promptly remarked to Mrs Walker.

But this lady's face was also as a stone. 'She never enters my drawing-room again.'

Since Winterbourne then, hereupon, was not to meet her in Mrs Walker's drawing-room he went as often as possible to Mrs Miller's hotel. The ladies were rarely at home, but when he found them the devoted Giovanelli was always present. Very often the glossy little Roman, serene in success, but not unduly presumptuous, occupied with Daisy alone the florid salon enjoyed by Eugenio's care, Mrs Miller being apparently ever of the opinion that discretion is the better part of solicitude.* Winterbourne noted, at first with surprise, that Daisy on these occasions was neither embarrassed nor annoyed by his own entrance; but he presently began to feel that she had no more surprises for him and that he really liked, after all, not making out what she was 'up to'. She showed no displeasure for the interruption of her *tête-à-tête* with Giovanelli; she could chatter as freshly and freely with two gentlemen as with one, and this easy flow had ever the same anomaly for her earlier friend that it was so free without availing itself of its freedom. Winterbourne reflected that if she was seriously interested in the Italian it was odd she shouldn't take more trouble to preserve the sanctity of their interviews, and he liked her the better for her innocent-looking indifference and her inexhaustible gaiety. He could hardly have said why, but she struck him as a young person not formed for a troublesome jealousy. Smile at such a betrayal though the reader may, it was a fact with regard to the women who had hitherto interested him that, given certain contingencies, Winterbourne could see himself afraid—literally afraid—of these ladies. It pleased him to believe that even were twenty other things different and Daisy should love him and he should know it and like it, he would still never be afraid of Daisy. It must be added that this conviction was not altogether flattering to her: it represented that she was nothing every way if not light.

But she was evidently very much interested in Giovanelli. She looked at him whenever he spoke; she was perpetually telling him to do this and to do that; she was constantly chaffing and abusing him. She appeared completely to have forgotten that her other friend had said anything to displease her at Mrs Walker's entertainment. One Sunday afternoon, having gone to Saint Peter's* with his aunt, Winterbourne became aware that the young woman held in horror by that lady was strolling about the great church under escort of her coxcomb of the Corso.* It amused him, after a debate, to point out the exemplary pair—even at the cost, as it proved, of Mrs Costello's saying when she had taken them in through her eye-glass: 'That's what makes you so pensive in these days, eh?'

'I hadn't the least idea I was pensive,' he pleaded.

'You're very much preoccupied; you're always thinking of something.'

'And what is it', he asked, 'that you accuse me of thinking of?'

'Of that young lady's, Miss Baker's, Miss Chandler's—what's her name?—Miss Miller's intrigue with that little barber's block.'

'Do you call it an intrigue,' he asked—'an affair that goes on with such peculiar publicity?'

'That's their folly,' said Mrs Costello, 'it's not their merit.'

'No,' he insisted with a hint perhaps of the preoccupation to which his aunt had alluded—'I don't believe there's anything to be called an intrigue.'

'Well'—and Mrs Costello dropped her glass—'I've heard a dozen people speak of it: they say she's quite carried away by him.'

'They're certainly as thick as thieves,' our embarrassed young man allowed.

Mrs Costello came back to them, however, after a little; and Winterbourne recognised in this a further illustration—than that supplied by his own condition—of the spell projected by the case. 'He's certainly very handsome. One easily sees how it is. She thinks him the most elegant man in the world, the finest gentleman possible. She has never seen anything like him—he's better even than the courier. It was the courier probably who introduced him, and if he succeeds in marrying the young lady the courier will come in for a magnificent commission.'

'I don't believe she thinks of marrying him,' Winterbourne reasoned, 'and I don't believe he hopes to marry her.'

'You may be very sure she thinks of nothing at all. She romps on from day to day, from hour to hour, as they did in the Golden Age. I can imagine nothing more vulgar,' said Mrs Costello, whose figure of speech scarcely went on all fours.* 'And at the same time,' she added, 'depend upon it she may tell you any moment that she is "engaged".'

'I think that's more than Giovanelli really expects,' said Winterbourne.

'And who is Giovanelli?'

'The shiny—but, to do him justice, not greasy—little Roman. I've asked questions about him and learned something. He's apparently a perfectly respectable little man. I believe he's in a small way a *cavaliere avvocato*.* But he doesn't move in what are called the first circles. I think it really not absolutely impossible the courier introduced him. He's evidently immensely charmed with Miss Miller. If she thinks him the finest gentleman in the world, he, on his side, has never found himself in personal contact with such splendour, such opulence, such personal daintiness, as this young lady's. And then she must seem to him wonderfully pretty and interesting. Yes, he can't really hope to pull it off. That must appear to him too impossible a piece of luck. He has nothing but his handsome face to offer, and there's a substantial, a possibly explosive Mr Miller in that mysterious land of dollars and six-shooters. Giovanelli's but too conscious that he hasn't a title to offer. If he were only a count or a *marchese*!* What on earth can he make of the way they've taken him up?'

'He accounts for it by his handsome face and thinks Miss Miller a young lady *qui se passe ses fantaisies!*'*

'It's very true', Winterbourne pursued, 'that Daisy and her mamma haven't yet risen to that stage of—what shall I call it?—of culture, at which the idea of catching a count or a *marchese* begins. I believe them intellectually incapable of that conception.'

'Ah but the *cavaliere avvocato* doesn't believe them!' cried Mrs Costello.

Of the observation excited by Daisy's 'intrigue' Winterbourne gathered that day at Saint Peter's sufficient evidence. A dozen of the American colonists in Rome came to talk with his relative, who sat on a small portable stool at the base of one of the great pilasters. The vesper-service was going forward in splendid chants and organ-tones in the adjacent choir, and meanwhile, between Mrs Costello and her friends, much was said about poor little Miss Miller's going really 'too far'. Winterbourne was not pleased with what he heard; but when, coming out upon the great steps of the church, he saw Daisy, who had emerged before him, get into an open cab with her accomplice and roll away through the cynical streets of Rome, the measure of her course struck him as simply there to take. He felt very sorry for her—not exactly that he believed she had completely lost her wits, but because it was painful to see so much that was pretty and undefended and natural sink so low in human estimation. He made an attempt after this to give a hint to Mrs Miller. He met one day in the Corso a friend—a tourist like himself—who had just come out of the Doria Palace,* where he had been walking through the beautiful gallery. His friend 'went on' for some moments about the great portrait of Innocent X, by Velasquez,* suspended in one of the cabinets of the palace, and then said: 'And in the same cabinet, by the way, I enjoyed sight of an image of a different kind; that little American who's so much more a work of nature than of art and whom you pointed out to me last week.' In answer to Winterbourne's inquiries his friend narrated that the little American—prettier now than ever—was seated with a companion in the secluded nook in which the papal presence is enshrined.

'All alone?' the young man heard himself disingenuously ask.

'Alone with a little Italian who sports in his button-hole a stack of flowers. The girl's a charming beauty, but I thought I understood from you the other day that she's a young lady *du meilleur monde*.'*

'So she is!' said Winterbourne; and having assured himself that his informant had seen the interesting pair but ten minutes before, he jumped into a cab and went to call on Mrs Miller.

She was at home, but she apologised for receiving him in Daisy's absence.

'She's gone out somewhere with Mr Giovanelli. She's always going round with Mr Giovanelli.'

'I've noticed they're intimate indeed,' Winterbourne concurred.

'Oh it seems as if they couldn't live without each other!' said Mrs Miller. 'Well, he's a real gentleman anyhow. I guess I have the joke on Daisy—that she *must* be engaged!'

'And how does your daughter *take* the joke?'

'Oh she just says she ain't. But she might as *well* be!' this philosophic parent resumed. 'She goes on as if she was. But I've made Mr Giovanelli promise to tell me if Daisy don't. I'd want to write to Mr Miller about it—wouldn't you?'

Winterbourne replied that he certainly should; and the state of mind of Daisy's mamma struck him as so unprecedented in the annals of parental vigilance that he recoiled before the attempt to educate at a single interview either her conscience or her wit.

After this Daisy was never at home and he ceased to meet her at the houses of their common acquaintance, because, as he perceived, these shrewd people had quite made up their minds as to the length she must have gone. They ceased to invite her, intimating that they wished to make, and make strongly, for the benefit of observant Europeans, the point that though Miss Daisy Miller was a pretty American girl all right, her behaviour wasn't pretty at all—was in fact regarded by her compatriots as quite monstrous. Winterbourne wondered how she felt about all the cold shoulders that were turned upon her, and sometimes found himself suspecting with impatience that she simply didn't feel and didn't know. He set her down as hopelessly childish and shallow, as such mere giddiness and ignorance incarnate as was powerless either to heed or to suffer. Then at other moments he couldn't doubt that she carried about in her elegant and irresponsible little organism a defiant, passionate, perfectly observant consciousness of the impression she produced. He asked himself whether the defiance would come from the consciousness of innocence or from her being essentially a young person of the reckless class. Then it had to be admitted, he felt, that holding fast to a belief in her 'innocence' was more and more but a matter of gallantry too fine-spun for use. As I have already had occasion to relate, he was reduced without pleasure to this chopping of logic and vexed at his poor fallibility, his want of instinctive certitude as to how far her extravagance was generic and national and how far it was crudely personal. Whatever it was he had helplessly missed her, and now it was too late. She was 'carried away' by Mr Giovanelli.

A few days after his brief interview with her mother he came across her at that supreme seat of flowering desolation known as the Palace of the Caesars.* The early Roman spring had filled the air with bloom and perfume, and the rugged surface of the Palatine was muffled with tender verdure. Daisy moved at her ease over the great mounds of ruin that are embanked with mossy marble and paved with monumental inscriptions. It seemed to him he had never known Rome so lovely as just then. He looked off at the enchanting harmony of line and colour that remotely encircles the city—he inhaled the softly humid odours and felt the freshness of the year and the antiquity of the place reaffirm themselves in deep interfusion.* It struck him also that Daisy had never showed to the eye for so utterly charming; but this had been his conviction on every occasion of their meeting. Giovanelli was of course at her side, and Giovanelli too glowed as never before with something of the glory of his race.

'Well,' she broke out upon the friend it would have been such mockery to designate as the latter's rival, 'I should think you'd be quite lonesome!'

'Lonesome?' Winterbourne resignedly echoed.

'You're always going round by yourself. Can't you get any one to walk with you?'

'I'm not so fortunate', he answered, 'as your gallant companion.'

Giovanelli had from the first treated him with distinguished politeness; he listened with a deferential air to his remarks; he laughed punctiliously at his pleasantries; he attached such import-ance as he could find terms for to Miss Miller's cold compatriot. He carried himself in no degree like a jealous wooer; he had obviously a great deal of tact; he had no objection to any one's expecting a little humility of him. It even struck Winterbourne that he almost yearned at times for some private communication in the interest of his character for common sense; a chance to remark to him as another intelligent man that, bless him, *he* knew how extraordinary was their young lady and didn't flatter himself with confident—at least *too* confident and too delusive—hopes of matrimony and dollars. On this occasion he strolled away from his charming charge to pluck a sprig of almond-blossom which he carefully arranged in his button-hole.

'I know why you say that,' Daisy meanwhile observed. 'Because you think I go round too much with *him*!' And she nodded at her discreet attendant.

'Every one thinks so—if you care to know,' was all Winterbourne found to reply.

'Of course I care to know!'—she made this point with much expression. 'But I don't believe a word of it. They're only pretending to be shocked. They don't really care a straw what I do. Besides, I don't go round so much.'

'I think you'll find they do care. They'll show it—disagreeably,' he took on himself to state.

Daisy weighed the importance of that idea. 'How—disagreeably?'

'Haven't you noticed anything?' he compassionately asked.

'I've noticed *you*. But I noticed you've no more "give" than a ramrod the first time ever I saw you.'

'You'll find at least that I've more "give" than several others,' he patiently smiled.

'How shall I find it?'

'By going to see the others.'

'What will they do to me?'

'They'll show you the cold shoulder. Do you know what that means?'

Daisy was looking at him intently; she began to colour. 'Do you mean as Mrs Walker did the other night?'

'Exactly as Mrs Walker did the other night.'

She looked away at Giovanelli, still titivating with his almond-blossom. Then with her attention again on the important subject: 'I shouldn't think you'd let people be so unkind!'

'How can I help it?'

'I should think you'd want to say something.'

'I do want to say something'—and Winterbourne paused a moment. 'I want to say that your mother tells me she believes you engaged.'

'Well, I guess she does,' said Daisy very simply.

The young man began to laugh. 'And does Randolph believe it?'

'I guess Randolph doesn't believe anything.' This testimony to Randolph's scepticism excited Winterbourne to further mirth, and he noticed that Giovanelli was coming back to them. Daisy, observing it as well, addressed herself again to her countryman. 'Since you've mentioned it,' she said, 'I *am* engaged.' He looked at her hard—he had stopped laughing. 'You don't believe it!' she added.

He asked himself, and it was for a moment like testing a heartbeat; after which, 'Yes, I believe it!' he said.

'Oh no, you don't,' she answered. 'But *if* you possibly do,' she still more perversely pursued—'well, I ain't!'

Miss Miller and her constant guide were on their way to the gate of the enclosure, so that Winterbourne, who had but lately entered, presently took leave of them. A week later on he went to dine at a beautiful villa on the Cælian Hill, and, on arriving, dismissed his hired vehicle. The evening was perfect and he promised himself the satisfaction of walking home beneath the Arch of Constantine and past the vaguely-lighted monuments of the Forum.* Above was a moon half-developed, whose radiance was not brilliant but veiled in a thin cloud-curtain that seemed to diffuse and equalise it. When on his return from the villa at eleven o'clock he approached the dusky circle of the Colosseum* the sense of the romantic in him easily suggested that the interior, in such an atmosphere, would well repay a glance. He turned aside and walked to one of the empty arches, near which, as he observed, an open carriage—one of the little Roman street cabs—was stationed. Then he passed in among the cavernous shadows of the great structure and emerged upon the clear and silent arena. The place had never seemed to him more impressive. One half of the gigantic circus was in deep shade while the other slept in the luminous dusk. As he stood there he began to murmur Byron's famous lines out of 'Manfred';* but before he had finished his quotation he remembered that if nocturnal meditation thereabouts was the fruit of a rich literary culture it was none the less deprecated by medical science. The air of other ages surrounded one; but the air of other ages, coldly analysed, was no better than a villainous miasma. Winterbourne sought, however, toward the middle of the arena, a further reach of vision, intending the next moment a hasty retreat. The great cross in the centre was almost obscured; only as he drew near did he make it out distinctly. He thus also distinguished two persons stationed on the low steps that formed its base. One of these was a woman seated; her companion hovered before her.

Presently the sound of the woman's voice came to him distinctly in the warm night-air. 'Well, he looks at us as one of the old lions or tigers may have looked at the Christian martyrs!' These words were winged with their accent, so that they fluttered and settled about him in the darkness like vague white doves.* It was Miss Daisy Miller who had released them for flight.

'Let us hope he's not very hungry'—the bland Giovanelli fell in with her humour. 'He'll have to take *me* first; you'll serve for dessert.'

Winterbourne felt himself pulled up with final horror now—and, it must be added, with final relief. It was as if a sudden clearance had taken place in the ambiguity of the poor girl's appearances and the whole riddle of her contradictions had grown easy to read. She was a young lady about the *shades* of whose perversity a foolish puzzled gentleman need no longer trouble his head or his heart. That once questionable quantity *had* no shades—it was a mere black little blot. He stood there looking at her, looking at her companion too, and not reflecting that though he saw them vaguely he himself must have been more brightly presented. He felt angry at all his shiftings of view—he felt ashamed of all his tender little scruples and all his witless little mercies. He was about to advance again, and then again checked himself; not from the fear of doing her injustice, but from a sense of the danger of showing undue exhilaration for this disburdenment of cautious criticism. He turned away toward the entrance of the place; but as he did so he heard Daisy speak again.

'Why it was Mr Winterbourne! He saw me and he cuts me dead!'

What a clever little reprobate she was, he was amply able to reflect at this, and how smartly she feigned, how promptly she sought to play off on him, a surprised and injured innocence! But nothing would induce him to cut her either 'dead' or to within any measurable distance even of the famous 'inch' of her life. He came forward again and went toward the great cross. Daisy had got up and Giovanelli lifted his hat. Winterbourne had now begun to think simply of the madness, on the ground of exposure and infection, of a frail young creature's lounging away such hours in a nest of malaria. What if she *were* the most plausible of little reprobates? That was no reason for her dying of the *perniciosa*.* 'How long have you been "fooling round" here?' he asked with conscious roughness.

Daisy, lovely in the sinister silver radiance, appraised him a moment, roughness and all. 'Well, I guess all the evening.' She answered with spirit and, he could see even then, with exaggeration. 'I never saw anything so quaint.'

'I'm afraid', he returned, 'you'll not think a bad attack of Roman fever very quaint. This is the way people catch it. I wonder', he added to Giovanelli, 'that you, a native Roman, should countenance such extraordinary rashness.'

'Ah,' said this seasoned subject, 'for myself I have no fear.'

'Neither have I—for you!' Winterbourne retorted in French. 'I'm speaking for this young lady.'

Giovanelli raised his well-shaped eyebrows and showed his shining teeth, but took his critic's rebuke with docility. 'I assured Mademoiselle it was a grave indiscretion, but when was Mademoiselle ever prudent?'

'I never was sick, and I don't mean to be!' Mademoiselle declared. 'I don't look like much, but I'm healthy! I was bound to see the Colosseum by moonlight—I wouldn't have wanted to go home without *that*; and we've had the most beautiful time, haven't we, Mr Giovanelli? If there has been any danger Eugenio can give me some pills. Eugenio has got some splendid pills.'

'*I* should advise you then,' said Winterbourne, 'to drive home as fast as possible and take one!'

Giovanelli smiled as for the striking happy thought. 'What you say is very wise. I'll go and make sure the carriage is at hand.' And he went forward rapidly.

Daisy followed with Winterbourne. He tried to deny himself the small fine anguish of looking at her, but his eyes themselves refused to spare him, and she seemed moreover not in the least embarrassed. He spoke no word; Daisy chattered over the beauty of the place: 'Well, I *have* seen the Colosseum by moonlight—that's one thing I can rave about!' Then noticing her companion's silence she asked him why he was so stiff—it had always been her great word. He made no answer, but he felt his laugh an immense negation of stiffness. They passed under one of the dark archways; Giovanelli was in front with the carriage. Here Daisy stopped a moment, looking at her compatriot. '*Did* you believe I was engaged the other day?'

'It doesn't matter now what I believed the other day!' he replied with infinite point.

It was a wonder how she didn't wince for it. 'Well, what do you believe now?'

'I believe it makes very little difference whether you're engaged or not!'

He felt her lighted eyes fairly penetrate the thick gloom of the vaulted passage—as if to seek some access to him she hadn't yet compassed.* But Giovanelli, with a graceful inconsequence, was at present all for retreat. 'Quick, quick; if we get in by midnight we're quite safe!'

Daisy took her seat in the carriage and the fortunate Italian placed himself beside her. 'Don't forget Eugenio's pills!' said Winterbourne as he lifted his hat.

'I don't care', she unexpectedly cried out for this, 'whether I have Roman fever or not!' On which the cab-driver cracked his whip and they rolled across the desultory patches of antique pavement.

Winterbourne—to do him justice, as it were—mentioned to no one that he had encountered Miss Miller at midnight in the

Colosseum with a gentleman; in spite of which deep discretion, however, the fact of the scandalous adventure was known a couple of days later, with a dozen vivid details, to every member of the little American circle, and was commented accordingly. Winterbourne judged thus that the people about the hotel had been thoroughly empowered to testify, and that after Daisy's return there would have been an exchange of jokes between the porter and the cab-driver. But the young man became aware at the same moment of how thoroughly it had ceased to ruffle him that the little American flirt should be 'talked about' by low-minded menials. These sources of current criticism a day or two later abounded still further: the little American flirt was alarmingly ill and the doctors now in possession of the scene. Winterbourne, when the rumour came to him, immediately went to the hotel for more news. He found that two or three charitable friends had preceded him and that they were being entertained in Mrs Miller's salon by the all-efficient Randolph.

'It's going round at night that way, you bet—that's what has made her so sick. She's always going round at night. I shouldn't think she'd want to—it's so plaguey dark over here. You can't see anything over here without the moon's right up. In America they don't go round by the moon!' Mrs Miller meanwhile wholly surrendered to her genius for unapparent uses; her salon knew her less than ever, and she was presumably now at least giving her daughter the advantage of her society. It was clear that Daisy was dangerously ill.

Winterbourne constantly attended for news from the sick-room, which reached him, however, but with worrying indirectness, though he once had speech, for a moment, of the poor girl's physician and once saw Mrs Miller, who, sharply alarmed, struck him as thereby more happily inspired than he could have conceived and indeed as the most noiseless and light-handed of nurses. She invoked a good deal the remote shade of Dr Davis, but Winterbourne paid her the compliment of taking her after all for less monstrous a goose. To this indulgence indeed something she further said perhaps even more insidiously disposed him. 'Daisy spoke of you the other day quite pleasantly. Half the time she doesn't know what she's saying, but that time I think she did. She gave me a message—she told me to tell you. She wanted you to know she never was engaged to that handsome Italian who was always round. I'm sure I'm very glad; Mr Giovanelli hasn't been near us since she was taken ill. I thought he was so much of a gentleman, but I don't call that very polite! A lady told me he was afraid I hadn't approved of his being round with her so much evenings. Of course it ain't as if their evenings were as pleasant as ours—since *we* don't seem to feel that way about the poison. I guess I *don't* see the point now; but I suppose he knows I'm a lady and I'd scorn to raise a fuss. Anyway, she wants you to real-ise she ain't engaged. I don't know why she makes so much of it, but she said to me three times "Mind you tell Mr Winterbourne." And then she told me to ask if you remembered the time you went up to that castle in Switzerland. But I said I wouldn't give any such messages as *that*. Only if she ain't engaged I guess I'm glad to realise it too.'

But, as Winterbourne had originally judged, the truth on this question had small actual relevance. A week after this the poor girl died; it had been indeed a terrible case of the *perniciosa*. A grave was found for her in the little Protestant cemetery,* by an angle of the wall of imperial Rome, beneath the cypresses and the thick spring-flowers. Winterbourne stood there beside it with a number of other mourners; a number larger than the scandal excited by the young lady's career might have made probable. Near him stood Giovanelli, who came nearer still before Winterbourne turned away. Giovanelli, in decorous mourning, showed but a whiter face; his button-hole lacked its nosegay and he had visibly something urgent—and even to distress—to say, which he scarce knew how to 'place'. He decided at last to confide it with a pale convulsion to Winterbourne. 'She was the most beautiful young lady I ever saw, and the most amiable.' To which he added in a moment: 'Also—naturally!—the most innocent.'

Winterbourne sounded him with hard dry eyes, but presently repeated his words, 'The most innocent?'

'The most innocent!'

It came somehow so much too late that our friend could only

glare at its having come at all. 'Why the devil', he asked, 'did you take her to that fatal place?'

Giovanelli raised his neat shoulders and eyebrows to within suspicion of a shrug. 'For myself I had no fear; and *she*—she did what she liked.'

Winterbourne's eyes attached themselves to the ground. 'She did what she liked!'*

It determined on the part of poor Giovanelli a further pious, a further candid, confidence. 'If she had lived I should have got nothing. She never would have married me.'

It had been spoken as if to attest, in all sincerity, his disinterestedness, but Winterbourne scarce knew what welcome to give it. He said, however, with a grace inferior to his friend's: 'I daresay not.'

The latter was even by this not discouraged. 'For a moment I hoped so. But no. I'm convinced.'

Winterbourne took it in; he stood staring at the raw protuberance among the April daisies. When he turned round again his fellow-mourner had stepped back.

He almost immediately left Rome, but the following summer he again met his aunt Mrs Costello at Vevey. Mrs Costello extracted from the charming old hotel there a value that the Miller family hadn't mastered the secret of. In the interval Winterbourne had often thought of the most interesting member of that trio—of her mystifying manners and her queer adventure. One day he spoke of her to his aunt—said it was on his conscience he had done her injustice.

'I'm sure I don't know'—that lady showed caution. 'How did your injustice affect her?'

'She sent me a message before her death which I didn't understand at the time. But I've understood it since. She would have appreciated one's esteem.'

'She took an odd way to gain it! But do you mean by what you say', Mrs Costello asked, 'that she would have reciprocated one's affection?'

As he made no answer to this she after a little looked round at him—he hadn't been directly within sight; but the effect of that wasn't to make her repeat her question. He spoke, however, after a while. 'You were right in that remark that you made last summer. I was booked to make a mistake. I've lived too long in foreign parts.' And this time she herself said nothing.

Nevertheless he soon went back to live at Geneva, whence there continue to come the most contradictory accounts of his motives of sojourn: a report that he's 'studying' hard—an intimation that he's much interested in a very clever foreign lady.

AN INTERNATIONAL EPISODE

Four years ago—in 1874*—two young Englishmen had occasion to go to the United States. They crossed the ocean at midsummer and, arriving in New York on the first day of August, were much struck with the high, the torrid temperature. Disembarking upon the wharf they climbed into one of the huge high-hung coaches that convey passengers to the hotels, and with a great deal of bouncing and bumping they took their course through Broadway.* The midsummer aspect of New York is doubtless not the most engaging, though nothing perhaps could well more solicit an alarmed attention. Of quite other sense and sound from those of any typical English street was the endless rude channel, rich in incongruities, through which our two travellers advanced—looking out on either side at the rough animation of the sidewalks, at the high-coloured heterogeneous architecture, at the huge white marble façades that, bedizened with gilded lettering, seemed to glare in the strong crude light, at the multifarious awnings, banners and streamers, at the extraordinary number of omnibuses, horse-cars and other democratic vehicles, at the vendors of cooling fluids, the white trousers and big straw hats of the policemen, the tripping gait of the modish young persons on the pavement, the general brightness, newness, juvenility, both of people and things. The young men had exchanged few observations, but in crossing Union Square,* in front of the monument to Washington*—in the very shadow indeed projected by the image of the *pater patriae*—one of them remarked to the other: 'Awfully rum place.'

'Ah very odd, very odd,' said the other, who was the clever man of the two.

'Pity it's so beastly hot,' resumed the first speaker after a pause.

'You know we're in a low latitude,' said the clever man.

'I dare say,' remarked his friend.

'I wonder', said the second speaker presently, 'if they can give one a bath.'

'I dare say not,' the other returned.

'Oh I say!' cried his comrade.

This animated discussion dropped on their arrival at the hotel, recommended to them by an American gentleman whose acquaintance they had made—with whom, indeed, they had become very intimate—on the steamer and who had proposed to accompany them to the inn and introduce them in a friendly way to the proprietor. This plan, however, had been defeated by their friend's finding his 'partner' in earnest attendance on the wharf, with urgent claims on his immediate presence of mind. But the two Englishmen, with nothing beyond their national prestige and personal graces to recommend them, were very well received at the hotel, which had an air of capacious hospitality.* They found a bath not unattainable and were indeed struck with the facilities for prolonged and reiterated immersion with which their apartment was supplied. After bathing a good deal—more indeed than they had ever done before on a single occasion—they made their way to the dining-room of the hotel, which was a spacious restaurant with a fountain in the middle, a great many tall plants in ornamental tubs and an array of French waiters. The first dinner on land, after a sea-voyage, is in any connexion a delightful hour, and there was much that ministered to ease in the general situation of our young men. They were formed for good spirits and addicted and appointed to hilarity: they were more observant than they appeared; they were, in an inarticulate accidentally dissimulative fashion, capable of high appreciation. This was perhaps especially the case with the elder, who was also, as I have said, the man of talent. They sat down at a little table which was a very different affair from the great clattering see-saw in the saloon of the steamer. The wide doors and windows of the restaurant stood open, beneath large awnings, to a wide expanse studded with other plants in tubs and rows of spreading trees—beyond which appeared a large shady square without palings and with marble-paved walks. And above the vivid verdure rose other façades of white marble and of pale chocolate-coloured stone, squaring themselves against the deep blue sky. Here, outside, in the light and the shade and the heat, was a great tinkling of the bells of innumerable street-cars and a constant strolling and shuffling and rustling of many pedestrians, extremely frequent among whom were young women in Pompadour-looking dresses.* The place within was cool and vaguely-lighted; with the plash of water, the odour of flowers and the flitting of French waiters, as I have said, on soundless carpets.

'It's rather like Paris, you know,' said the younger of our two travellers.

'It's like Paris—only more so,' his companion returned.

'I suppose it's the French waiters,' said the first speaker. 'Why don't they have French waiters in London?'

'Ah but fancy a French waiter at a London club!' said his friend.

The elder man stared as if he couldn't fancy it. 'In Paris I'm very apt to dine at a place where there's an English waiter. Don't you know, what's-his-name's, close to the thingumbob?* They always set an English waiter at me. I suppose they think I can't speak French.'

'No more you can!' And this candid critic unfolded his napkin.

The other paid no heed whatever to his candour. 'I say,' the latter resumed in a moment, 'I suppose we must learn to speak American. I suppose we must take lessons.'

'I can't make them out, you know,' said the clever man.

'What the deuce is *he* saying?' asked his comrade, appealing from the French waiter.

'He's recommending some soft-shell crabs,' said the clever man.

And so, in a desultory view of the mysteries of the new world bristling about them, the young Englishmen proceeded to dine—going in largely, as the phrase is, for cooling draughts and dishes, as to which their attendant submitted to them a hundred alternatives. After dinner they went out and slowly walked about the neighbouring streets. The early dusk of waning summer was at hand, but the heat still very great. The pavements were hot even to the stout boot-soles of the British travellers, and the trees along the kerb-stone emitted strange exotic odours. The young men wandered through the adjoining square—that queer place without palings and with marble walks arranged in black and white lozenges. There were a great many benches crowded with shabby-looking people, and the visitors remarked very justly that it wasn't much like Grosvenor Square.* On one side was an enormous hotel, lifting up into the hot darkness an immense array of open and brightly-lighted windows. At the base of this populous structure was an eternal jangle of horse-cars, and all round it, in the upper dusk, a sinister hum of mosquitoes. The ground-floor of the hotel, figuring a huge transparent cage, flung a wide glare of gaslight into the street, of which it formed a public adjunct, absorbing and emitting the passers-by promiscuously. The young Englishmen went in with every one else, from curiosity, and saw a couple of hundred men sitting on divans along a great marble-paved corridor, their legs variously stretched out, together with several dozen more standing in a cue, as at the ticket-office of a railway-station, before a vast marble altar of sacrifice, a thing shaped like the counter of a huge shop. These latter persons, who carried portmanteaux in their hands, had a dejected exhausted look; their garments were not fresh, as if telling of some rush, or some fight, for life, and they seemed to render mystic tribute to a magnificent young man with a waxed moustache and a shirt front adorned with diamond buttons, who every now and then dropped a cold glance over their multitudinous patience. They were American citizens doing homage to an hotel-clerk.

'I'm glad he didn't tell us to go there,' said one of our Englishmen, alluding to their friend on the steamer, who had told them so many things. They walked up the Fifth Avenue,* where he had for instance told them all the first families lived. But the first families were out of town, and our friends had but the satisfaction of seeing some of the second—or perhaps even the third—taking the evening air on balconies and high flights of doorsteps in streets at right angles to the main straight channel. They went a little way down one of these side-streets and there saw young ladies in white dresses—charming-looking persons—seated in graceful attitudes on the chocolate-coloured steps. In one or two places these young ladies were conversing across the street with other young ladies seated in similar postures and costumes in front of the opposite houses, and in the warm night air their colloquial tones sounded strangely in the ears of the young Englishmen. One of the latter, nevertheless—the younger—betrayed a disposition to intercept some stray item of this interchange and see what it would lead to; but his companion observed pertinently enough that he had better be careful. They mustn't begin by making mistakes.

'But he told us, you know—he told us,' urged the young man, alluding again to the friend on the steamer.

'Never mind what he told us!' answered his elder, who, if he had more years and a more developed wit, was also apparently more of a moralist.

By bedtime—in their impatience to taste of a terrestrial couch again our seafarers went to bed early—it was still insufferably hot, and the buzz of the mosquitoes at the open windows might have passed for an audible crepitation of the temperature. 'We can't stand this, you know,' the young Englishmen said to each other; and they tossed about all night more boisterously than they had been tossed by Atlantic billows. On the morrow their first thought was that they would re-embark that day for England, but it then occurred to them they might find an asylum nearer at hand. The cave of Æolus* became their ideal of comfort, and they wondered where the Americans went when wishing to cool off. They hadn't the least idea, and resolved to apply for information to Mr J. L. Westgate. This was the name inscribed in a bold hand on the back of a letter carefully preserved in the pocket-book of our younger gentleman. Beneath the address, in the left-hand corner of the envelope, were the words 'Introducing Lord Lambeth and Percy Beaumont Esq.'* The letter had been given to the two Englishmen by a good friend of theirs in London, who had been in America two years previously and had singled out Mr J. L. Westgate from the many friends he had left there as the consignee, as it were, of his compatriots. 'He's really very decent,' the Englishman in London had said, 'and he has an awfully pretty wife. He's tremendously hospitable—he'll do everything in the world for you, and as he knows every one over there it's quite needless I should give you any other introduction. He'll make you see every one—trust him for the right kick-off. He has a

tremendously pretty wife.' It was natural that in the hour of tribu-
lation Lord Lambeth and Mr Percy Beaumont should have
bethought themselves of so possible a benefactor; all the more so
that he lived in the Fifth Avenue and that the Fifth Avenue, as
they had ascertained the night before, was contiguous to their
hotel. 'Ten to one he'll be out of town,' said Percy Beaumont; 'but
we can at least find out where he has gone and can at once give
chase. He can't possibly have gone to a hotter place, you know.'

'Oh there's only one hotter place,' said Lord Lambeth, 'and
I hope he hasn't gone there.'

They strolled along the shady side of the street to the number
indicated by the precious letter. The house presented an imposing
chocolate-coloured expanse, relieved by facings and window-
cornices of florid sculpture and by a couple of dusty rose-trees
which clambered over the balconies and the portico. This last-
mentioned feature was approached by a monumental flight of steps.

'Rather better than a dirty London thing,' said Lord Lambeth,
looking down from this altitude after they had rung the bell.

'It depends upon what London thing you mean,' replied his
companion. 'You've a tremendous chance to get wet between the
house-door and your carriage.'

'Well,' said Lord Lambeth, glancing at the blaze of the sky,
'I "guess" it doesn't rain so much here!'

The door was opened by a long negro in a white jacket, who
grinned familiarly when Lord Lambeth asked for Mr Westgate.
'He ain't at home, sir; he's down town at his o'fice.'

'Oh at his office?' said the visitors. 'And when will he be at
home?'

'Well, when he goes out dis way in de mo'ning he ain't liable to
come home all day.'

This was discouraging; but the address of Mr Westgate's office
was freely imparted by the intelligent black and was taken down
by Percy Beaumont in his pocket-book. The comrades then
returned, languidly enough, to their hotel and sent for a hackney-
coach;* and in this commodious vehicle they rolled comfortably
down town. They measured the whole length of Broadway again
and found it a path of fire; and then, deflecting to the left, were

deposited by their conductor before a fresh light ornamental structure, ten stories high, in a street crowded with keen-faced light-limbed young men who were running about very nimbly and stopping each other eagerly at corners and in doorways. Passing under portals that were as the course of a twofold torrent, they were introduced by one of the keen-faced young men—he was a charming fellow in wonderful cream-coloured garments and a hat with a blue ribbon, who had evidently recognised them as aliens and helpless—to a very snug hydraulic elevator,* in which they took their place with many other persons and which, shooting upward in its vertical socket, presently projected them into the seventh heaven, as it were, of the edifice. Here, after brief delay, they found themselves face to face with the friend of their friend in London. His office was composed of several conjoined rooms, and they waited very silently in one of these after they had sent in their letter and their cards. The letter was not one it would take Mr Westgate very long to read, but he came out to speak to them more instantly than they could have expected; he had evidently jumped up from work. He was a tall lean personage and was dressed all in fresh white linen; he had a thin sharp familiar face, a face suggesting one of the ingenious modern objects with alternative uses, good as a blade or as a hammer, good for the deeps and for the shallows. His forehead was high but expressive, his eyes sharp but amused, and a large brown moustache, which concealed his mouth, made his chin, beneath it, look small. Relaxed though he was at this moment Lord Lambeth judged him on the spot tremendously clever.

'How do you do, Lord Lambeth, how do you do, sir?'—he held the open letter in his hand. 'I'm very glad to meet you—I hope you're very well. You had better come in here—I think it's cooler'; and he led the way into another room, where there were law-books and papers and where windows opened wide under striped awnings. Just opposite one of the windows, on a line with his eyes, Lord Lambeth observed the weather-vane of a church-steeple. The uproar of the street sounded infinitely far below, and his lordship felt high indeed in the air. 'I say it's cooler,' pursued their host, 'but everything's relative. How do you stand the heat?'

'I can't say we like it,' said Lord Lambeth; 'but Beaumont likes it better than I.'

'Well, I guess it will break,' Mr Westgate cheerfully declared; 'there's never anything bad over here but it does break. It was very hot when Captain Littledale was here; he did nothing but drink sherry-cobblers.* He expresses some doubt in his letter whether I shall remember him—as if I don't remember once mixing six sherry-cobblers for him in about fifteen minutes. I hope you left him well. I'd be glad to mix him some more.'

'Oh yes, he's all right—and without *them*,' said Lord Lambeth.

'I'm always very glad to see your countrymen,' Mr Westgate pursued. 'I thought it would be time some of you should be coming along. A friend of mine was saying to me only a day or two ago "It's time for the water-melons and the Englishmen."'

'The Englishmen and the water-melons just now are about the same thing,' Percy Beaumont observed with a wipe of his dripping forehead.

'Ah well, we'll put you on ice as we do the melons. You must go down to Newport.'*

'We'll go anywhere!' said Lord Lambeth.

'Yes, you want to go to Newport; that's what you want to do.' Mr Westgate was very positive. 'But let's see—when did you get here?'

'Only yesterday,' said Percy Beaumont.

'Ah yes, by the *Russia*.* Where are you staying?'

'At the Hanover, I think they call it.'

'Pretty comfortable?' enquired Mr Westgate.

'It seems a capital place, but I can't say we like the gnats,' said Lord Lambeth.

Mr Westgate stared and laughed. 'Oh no, of course you don't like the gnats. We shall expect you to like a good many things over here, but we shan't insist on your liking the gnats; though certainly you'll admit that, as gnats, they're big things, eh? But you oughtn't to remain in the city.'

'So we think,' said Lord Lambeth. 'If you'd kindly suggest something—'

'Suggest something, my dear sir?'—and Mr Westgate looked

him over with narrowed eyelids. 'Open your mouth and shut your eyes! Leave it to me and I'll fix you all right. It's a matter of national pride with me that all Englishmen should have a good time, and as I've been through a good deal with them I've learned to minister to their wants. I find they generally want the true thing. So just please consider yourselves my property; and if any one should try to appropriate you please say "Hands off— too late for the market." But let's see,' continued the American with his face of toil, his voice of leisure and his general intention, apparently, of everything; 'let's see: are you going to make something of a stay, Lord Lambeth?'

'Oh dear no,' said the young Englishman; 'my cousin was to make this little visit, so I just came with him, at an hour's notice, for the lark.'

'Is it your first time over here?'

'Oh dear yes.'

'I was obliged to come on some business,' Percy Beaumont explained, 'and I brought Lambeth along for company.'

'And *you* have been here before, sir?'

'Never, never!'

'I thought from your referring to business—' Mr Westgate threw off.

'Oh you see I'm just acting for some English shareholders by way of legal advice. Some of my friends—well, if the truth must be told,' Mr Beaumont laughed—'have a grievance against one of your confounded railways, and they've asked me to come and judge, if possible, on the spot, what they can hope.'

Mr Westgate's amused eyes grew almost tender. 'What's your railroad?' he asked.

'The Tennessee Central.'*

The American tilted back his chair and poised it an instant. 'Well, I'm sorry you want to attack one of our institutions. But I guess you had better enjoy yourself *first!*'

'I'm certainly rather afraid I can't work in this weather,' the young emissary confessed.

'Leave that to the natives,' said Mr Westgate. 'Leave the Tennessee Central to me, Mr Beaumont. I guess I can tell you more about it than most any one. But I didn't know you Englishmen ever did any work—in the upper classes.'

'Oh we do a lot of work, don't we, Lambeth?' Percy Beaumont appealed.

'I must certainly be back early for *my* engagements,' said his companion irrelevantly but gently.

'For the shooting, eh? or is it the yachting or the hunting or the fishing?' enquired his entertainer.

'Oh I must be in Scotland,'—and Lord Lambeth just amiably blushed.

'Well then,' Mr Westgate returned, 'you had better amuse yourself first also. You must go right down and see Mrs Westgate.'

'We should be so happy—if you'd kindly tell us the train,' said Percy Beaumont.

'You don't take any train. You take a boat.'

'Oh I see. And what is the name of—a—the—a—town?'

'It's a regular old city—don't you let them hear you call it a village or a hamlet or anything of that kind. They'd half-kill you. Only it's a city of pleasure—of lawns and gardens and verandahs and views and, above all, of good Samaritans,' Mr Westgate developed. 'But you'll see what Newport is. It's cool. That's the principal thing. You'll greatly oblige me by going down there and putting yourself in the hands of Mrs Westgate. It isn't perhaps for me to say it, but you couldn't be in better ones. Also in those of her sister, who's staying with her. She's half-crazy about Englishmen. She thinks there's nothing like them.'

'Mrs Westgate or—a—her sister?' asked Percy Beaumont modestly, yet in the tone of a collector of characteristic facts.

'Oh I mean my wife,' said Mr Westgate. 'I don't suppose my sister-in-law knows much about them yet. You'll show her anyhow. She has always led a very quiet life. She has lived in Boston.'*

Percy Beaumont listened with interest. 'That, I believe, is the most intellectual centre.'

'Well, yes—Boston knows it's central and feels it's intellectual. I don't go there much—I stay round here,' Mr Westgate more loosely pursued.

'I say, you know, *we* ought to go there,' Lord Lambeth broke out to his companion.

'Oh Lord Lambeth, wait till the great heat's over!' Mr Westgate interposed. 'Boston in this weather would be very trying; it's not the temperature for intellectual exertion. At Boston, you know, you have to pass an examination at the city limits, and when you come away they give you a kind of degree.'

Lord Lambeth flushed himself, in his charming way, with wonder, though his friend glanced to make sure he wasn't looking too credulous—they had heard so much about American practices. He decided in time, at any rate, to take a safe middle course. 'I dare say it's very jolly.'

'I dare say it is,' Mr Westgate returned. 'Only I must impress on you that at present—to-morrow morning at an early hour— you'll be expected at Newport. We have a house there—many of our most prominent citizens and society leaders go there for the summer. I'm not sure that at this very moment my wife can take you in—she has a lot of people staying with her. I don't know who they all are—only she may have no room. But you can begin with the hotel and meanwhile you can live at my house. In that way—simply sleeping at the hotel—you'll find it tolerable. For the rest you must make yourself at home at my place. You mustn't be shy, you know; if you're only here for a month that will be a great waste of time. Mrs Westgate won't neglect you, and you had better not undertake to resist her. I know something about that. I guess you'll find some pretty girls on the premises. I shall write to my wife by this afternoon's mail, and to-morrow she and Miss Alden will look out for you. Just walk right in and get into touch. Your steamer leaves from this part of the city, and I'll send right out and get you a cabin. Then at half-past four o'clock just call for me here, and I'll go with you and put you on board. It's a big boat; you might get lost. A few days hence, at the end of the week, I don't know but I'll come down myself and see how you are.'

The two young Englishmen inaugurated the policy of not resisting Mrs Westgate by submitting, with great docility and thankfulness, to her husband. He was evidently a clear thinker, and he made an impression on his visitors; his hospitality seemed

to recommend itself consciously—with a friendly wink, as might
be, hinting judicially that you couldn't make a better bargain.
Lord Lambeth and his cousin left their entertainer to his labours
and returned to their hotel, where they spent three or four hours
in their respective shower-baths. Percy Beaumont had suggested
that they ought to see something of the town, but 'Oh damn
the town!' his noble kinsman had rejoined. They returned to
Mr Westgate's office in a carriage, with their luggage, very punc-
tually; but it must be reluctantly recorded that this time he so kept
them waiting that they felt themselves miss their previous escape
and were deterred only by an amiable modesty from dispensing
with his attendance and starting on a hasty scramble to embark.
But when at last he appeared and the carriage plunged into the
purlieus of Broadway they jolted and jostled to such good purpose
that they reached the huge white vessel while the bell for departure was still ringing and the absorption of passengers still active.
It was indeed, as Mr Westgate had said, a big boat,* and his
leadership in the innumerable and interminable corridors and
cabins, with which he seemed perfectly acquainted and of which
any one and every one appeared to have the *entrée*, was very grateful to the slightly bewildered voyagers. He showed them their
state-room—a luxurious retreat embellished with gas-lamps,
mirrors *en pied** and florid furniture—and then, long after they
had been intimately convinced that the steamer was in motion and
launched upon the unknown stream they were about to navigate,
he bade them a sociable farewell.

'Well good-bye, Lord Lambeth,' he said. 'Goodbye, Mr Percy
Beaumont. I hope you'll have a good time. Just let them do what
they want with you. Take it as it's meant. Renounce your own
personality. I'll come down by and by and enjoy what's left of you.'

II

THE young Englishmen emerged from their cabin and amused
themselves with wandering about the immense labyrinthine
ship, which struck them as a monstrous floating hotel or even as

a semi-submerged kindergarten. It was densely crowded with passengers, the larger number of whom appeared to be ladies and very young children; and in the big saloons, ornamented in white and gold, which followed each other in surprising succession, beneath the swinging gas-lights and among the small side-passages where the negro domestics of both sexes assembled with an air of amused criticism, every one was moving to and fro and exchanging loud and familiar observations. Eventually, at the instance of a blackamoor more closely related to the scene than his companions, our friends went and had 'supper' in a wonderful place arranged like a theatre, where, from a gilded gallery upon which little boxes appeared to open, a large orchestra played operatic selections and, below, people handed about bills of fare in the manner of programmes. All this was sufficiently curious; but the agreeable thing, later, was to sit out on one of the great white decks in the warm breezy darkness and, the vague starlight aiding, make out the line of low mysterious coast. Our travellers tried American cigars—those of Mr Westgate—and conversed, as they usually conversed, with many odd silences, lapses of logic and incongruities of transition; like a pair who have grown old together and learned to guess each other's sense; or, more especially, like persons so conscious of a common point of view that missing links and broken lights and loose ends, the unexpressed and the understood, could do the office of talk.

'We really seem to be going out to sea,' Percy Beaumont observed. 'Upon my honour we're going back to England. He has shipped us off again. I call that "real mean".'

'I dare say it's all right,' said Lord Lambeth. 'I want to see those pretty girls at Newport. You know he told us the place was an island, and aren't all islands in the sea?'

'Well,' resumed the elder traveller after a while, 'if his house is as good as his cigars I guess we shall muddle through.'

'I fancy he's awfully "prominent", you know, and I rather liked him,' Lord Lambeth pursued as if this appreciation of Mr Westgate had but just glimmered on him.

His comrade, however, engaged in another thought, didn't so much as appear to catch it. 'I say, I guess we had better remain at

the inn. I don't think I like the way he spoke of his house. I rather
object to turning in with such a tremendous lot of women.'

'Oh I don't mind,' said Lord Lambeth. And then they smoked
a while in silence. 'Fancy his thinking we do no work in England!'
the young man resumed.

But it didn't rouse his friend, who only replied: 'I dare say he
didn't really a bit think so.'

'Well, I guess they don't know much about England over here!'
his lordship humorously sighed. After which there was another
long pause. 'He *has* got us out of a hole,' observed the young
nobleman.

Percy Beaumont genially assented. 'Nobody certainly could
have been more civil.'

'Littledale said his wife was great fun,' Lord Lambeth then
contributed.

'Whose wife—Littledale's?'

'Our benefactor's. Mrs Westgate. What's his name? J. L. It
"kind of" sounds like a number. But I guess it's a high number,'
he continued with freshened gaiety.

The same influences appeared, however, with Mr Beaumont to
make rather for anxiety. 'What was fun to Littledale,' he said at
last a little sententiously, 'may be death to us.'

'What do you mean by that?' his companion asked. 'I'm as good
a man as Littledale.'

'My dear boy, I hope you won't begin to flirt,' said the elder
man.

His friend smoked acutely. 'Well, I dare say I shan't *begin*.'

'With a married woman, if she's bent upon it, it's all very well,'
Mr Beaumont allowed. 'But our friend mentioned a young
lady—a sister, a sister-in-law. For God's sake keep free of her.'

'How do you mean, "free"?'

'Depend upon it she'll try to land you.'

'Oh rot!' said Lord Lambeth.

'American girls are very "cute",' the other urged.

'So much the better,' said the young man.

'I fancy they're always up to some wily game,' Mr Beaumont
developed.

'They can't be worse than they are in England,' said Lord Lambeth judicially.

'Ah but in England you've got your natural protectors. You've got your mother and sisters.'

'My mother and sisters—!' the youth began with a certain energy. But he stopped in time, puffing at his cigar.

'Your mother spoke to me about it with tears in her eyes,' said his monitor. 'She said she felt very nervous. I promised to keep you out of mischief.'

'You had better take care of yourself!' cried Mr Beaumont's charge.

'Ah,' the responsible party returned, 'I haven't the expectation of—whatever it is you expect. Not to mention other attractions.'

'Well,' said Lord Lambeth, 'don't cry out before you're hurt!'

It was certainly very much cooler at Newport, where the travellers found themselves assigned to a couple of diminutive bedrooms in a far-away angle of an immense hotel. They had gone ashore in the early summer twilight and had very promptly put themselves to bed; thanks to which circumstance and to their having, during the previous hours, in their commodious cabin, slept the sleep of youth and health, they began to feel, towards eleven o'clock, very alert and inquisitive. They looked out of their windows across a row of small green fields, bordered with low stone dykes of rude construction, and saw a deep blue ocean lying beneath a deep blue sky and flecked now and then with scintillating patches of foam. A strong fresh breeze came in through the curtainless apertures and prompted our young men to observe generously that it didn't seem half a bad climate. They made other observations after they had emerged from their rooms in pursuit of breakfast—a meal of which they partook in a huge bare hall where a hundred negroes in white jackets shuffled about on an uncarpeted floor; where the flies were superabundant and the tables and dishes covered over with a strange voluminous integument of coarse blue gauze; and where several little boys and girls, who had risen late, were seated in fastidious solitude at the morning repast. These young persons had not the morning paper before them, but were engaged in languid perusal of the bill of fare.

This latter document was a great puzzle to our friends, who, on reflecting that its bewildering categories took account of breakfast alone, had the uneasy prevision of an encyclopædic dinner-list. They found copious diversion at their inn, an enormous wooden structure for the erection of which it struck them the virgin forests of the West must have been quite laid waste. It was perforated from end to end with immense bare corridors, through which a strong draught freely blew, bearing along wonderful figures of ladies in white morning-dresses and clouds of Valenciennes lace,* who floated down the endless vistas on expanded fur-belows* very much as angels spread their wings. In front was a gigantic verandah on which an army might have encamped—a vast wooden terrace with a roof as high as the nave of a cathedral. Here our young men enjoyed, as they supposed, a glimpse of American society, which was distributed over the measureless expanse in a variety of sedentary attitudes and appeared to consist largely of pretty young girls, dressed as for a *fête champêtre*,* swaying to and fro in rocking-chairs, fanning themselves with large straw fans and enjoying an enviable exemption from social cares. Lord Lambeth had a theory, which it might be interesting to trace to its origin, that it would be not only agreeable, but easily possible, to enter into relations with one of these young ladies; and his companion found occasion to check his social yearning.

'You had better take care—else you'll have an offended father or brother pulling out a bowie-knife.'*

'I assure you it's all right,' Lord Lambeth replied. 'You know the Americans come to these big hotels to make acquaintances.'

'I know nothing about it, and neither do you,' said his comrade, who, like a clever man, had begun to see that the observation of American society demanded a readjustment of their standard.

'Hang it then, let's find out!' he cried with some impatience. 'You know I don't want to miss anything.'

'We *will* find out,' said Percy Beaumont very reasonably. 'We'll go and see Mrs Westgate and make all the proper enquiries.'

And so the enquiring pair, who had this lady's address inscribed in her husband's hand on a card, descended from the verandah of the big hotel and took their way, according to direction, along a large straight road, past a series of fresh-looking villas, embosomed in shrubs and flowers and enclosed in an ingenious variety of wooden palings. The morning shone and fluttered, the villas stood up bravely in their smartness, and the walk of the young travellers turned all to confidence. Everything looked as if it had received a coat of fresh paint the day before—the red roofs, the green shutters, the clean bright browns and buffs of the house-fronts. The flower-beds on the little lawns sparkled in the radiant air and the gravel in the short carriage-sweeps flashed and twinkled. Along the road came a hundred little basket-phaetons* in which, almost always, a couple of ladies were sitting—ladies in white dresses and long white gloves, holding the reins and looking at the two Englishmen, whose nationality was not elusive, through fine blue veils, tied tightly about their faces as if to guard their complexions.* At last the visitors came within sight of the sea again, and then, having interrogated a gardener over the paling of a villa, turned into an open gate. Here they found themselves face to face with the ocean and with a many-pointed much-balconied structure, resembling a magnified chalet, perched on a green embankment just above it. The house had a verandah of extraordinary width all round, and a great many doors and windows standing open to the verandah. These various apertures had, together, such an accessible hospitable air, such a breezy flutter, within, of light curtains, such expansive thresholds and reassuring interiors, that our friends hardly knew which was the regular entrance and, after hesitating a moment, presented themselves at one of the windows. The room within was indistinct, but in a moment a graceful figure vaguely shaped itself in the rich-looking gloom—a lady came to meet them. Then they saw she had been seated at a table writing, and that, hearing them, she had got up. She stepped out into the light; she wore a frank charming smile, with which she held out her hand to Percy Beaumont.

'Oh you must be Lord Lambeth and Mr Beaumont. I've heard from my husband that you were coming. I make you warmly welcome.' And she shook hands with each of her guests. Her guests were a little shy, but they made a gallant effort; they responded with smiles and exclamations, they apologised for not knowing the front door. The lady returned with vivacity that when she wanted to see people very much she didn't insist on those distinctions, and that Mr Westgate had written to her of his English friends in terms that made her really anxious. 'He says you're so terribly prostrated,' she reported.

'Oh you mean by the heat?'—Percy Beaumont rose to it. 'We were rather knocked up, but we feel wonderfully better. We had such a jolly—a—voyage down here. It's so very good of you to mind.'

'Yes, it's so very kind of you,' murmured Lord Lambeth.

Mrs Westgate stood smiling; Mrs Westgate was pretty. 'Well, I did mind, and I thought of sending for you this morning to the Ocean House.* I'm very glad you're better, and I'm charmed you're really with us. You must come round to the other side of the piazza.' And she led the way, with a light smooth step, looking back at the young men and smiling.

The other side of the piazza was, as Lord Lambeth presently remarked, a very jolly place. It was of the most liberal proportions and, with its awnings, its fanciful chairs, its cushions and rugs, its view of the ocean close at hand and tumbling along the base of the low cliffs whose level tops intervened in lawnlike smoothness, formed a charming complement to the drawing-room. As such it was in course of employment at the present hour; it was occupied by a social circle. There were several ladies and two or three gentlemen, to whom Mrs Westgate proceeded to introduce the distinguished strangers. She mentioned a great many names, very freely and distinctly; the young Englishmen, shuffling about and bowing, were rather bewildered. But at last they were provided with chairs—low wicker chairs, gilded and tied with a great many ribbons—and one of the ladies (a very young person with a little snub nose and several dimples) offered Percy Beaumont a fan. The fan was also adorned with pink love-knots, but the more guarded of our couple declined it, though he was very hot. Presently, however, everything turned to ease; the breeze from the sea was delicious and the view charming; the people sitting about looked fresh and fair. Several of the younger ladies were clearly girls, and the gentlemen slim bright youths such as our friends had seen the day before in New York. The ladies were working on bands of tapestry, and one of the young men had an open book in his lap. Percy afterwards learned from a lady that this young man had been reading aloud—that he was from Boston and was very fond of reading aloud. Percy pronounced it a great pity they had interrupted him; he should like so much (from all he had heard) to listen to a Bostonian read. Couldn't the young man be induced to go on?

'Oh no,' said this informant very freely; 'he wouldn't be able to get the young ladies to attend to him now.'

There was something very friendly, Beaumont saw, in the attitude of the company; they looked at their new recruits with an air of animated sympathy and interest; they smiled, brightly and unanimously, at everything that dropped from either. Lord Lambeth and his companion felt they were indeed made cordially welcome. Mrs Westgate seated herself between them, and while she talked continuously to each they had occasion to observe that she came up to their friend Littledale's promise. She was thirty years old, with the eyes and the smile of a girl of seventeen, and was light and graceful—elegant, exquisite. Mrs Westgate was, further, what she had occasion to describe some person, among her many winged words, as being, all spontaneity. Frank and demonstrative, she appeared always—while she looked at you delightedly with her beautiful young eyes—to be making sudden confessions and concessions, breaking out after momentary wonders.

'We shall expect to see a great deal of you,' she said to Lord Lambeth with her bland intensity. 'We're very fond of Englishmen here; that is there are a great many we've been fond of. After a day or two you must come and stay with us; we hope you'll stay a nice long while. Newport's quite attractive when you come really to know it, when you know plenty of people. Of course you and Mr Beaumont will have no difficulty about that. Englishmen are very well received here; there are almost always two or three of them about. I think they always like it, and I must say I should think they would. They receive particular attention—I must say I think they sometimes get spoiled; but I'm sure you and Mr Beaumont are proof against that. My husband tells

me you're friends of Captain Littledale's; he was such a charming
man. He made himself so agreeable here that I wonder he didn't
stay. That would have carried out his system. It couldn't have
been pleasanter for him in his own country. Though I suppose it's
very pleasant in England too—for English people. I don't know
myself; I've been there very little. I've been a great deal abroad,
but I always cling to the Continent. I must say I'm extremely fond
of Paris; you know we Americans always are; we go there when
we die.* Did you ever hear that before?—it was said by a great
wit. I mean the good Americans; but we're all good—you'll see
that for yourself. All I know of England is London, and all I know
of London is that place—on that little corner, you know—where
you buy jackets, jackets with that coarse braid and those big
buttons. They make very good jackets in London, I'll do you the
justice to say that. And some people like the hats. But about
the hats I was always a heretic; I always got my hats in Paris. You
can't wear an English hat—at least, I never could—unless you
dress your hair à l'anglaise;* and I must say that's a talent I never
possessed. In Paris they'll make things to suit your peculiarities;
but in England I think you like much more to have—how shall
I say it?—one thing for everybody. I mean as regards dress. I don't
know about other things; but I've always supposed that in other
things everything was different. I mean according to the people—
according to the classes and all that. I'm afraid you'll think I don't
take a very favourable view; but you know you can't take a very
favourable view in Dover Street and the month of November.
That has always been my fate. Do you know Jones's Hotel in
Dover Street?* That's all I know of England. Of course every one
admits that the English hotels are your weak point.* There was
always the most frightful fog—I couldn't see to try my things on.
When I got over to America—into the light—I usually found
they were twice too big. The next time I mean to go at the right
season; I guess I'll go next year. I want very much to take my
sister; she has never been to England. I don't know whether you
know what I mean by saying that the Englishmen who come here
sometimes get spoiled. I mean they take things as a matter of
course—things that are done for them. Now naturally anything's

a matter of course only when the Englishmen are very nice. But you'll say—oh yes you will, or you would if some of you ever did say much!—they're almost always very nice. You can't expect this to be nearly such an interesting country as England; there are not nearly so many things to see, and we haven't your country life. I've never seen anything of your country life; when I'm in Europe I'm always on the Continent. But I've heard a great deal about it; I know that when you're among yourselves in the country you have the most beautiful time. Of course we've nothing of that sort, we've nothing on that scale. I don't apologise, Lord Lambeth; some Americans are always apologising; you must have noticed that. We've the reputation of always boasting and 'blowing' and waving the American flag; but I must say that what strikes me is that we're perpetually making excuses and trying to smooth things over. The American flag has quite gone out of fashion; it's very carefully folded up, like a table-cloth the worse for wear. Why should we apologise? The English never apologise—do they? No, I must say *I* never apologise. You must take us as we come— with all our imperfections on our heads.* Of course we haven't your country life and your old ruins and your great estates and your leisure-class and all that—though I don't really know any- thing about them, because when I go over I always cling to the Continent. But if we haven't I should think you might find it a pleasant change—I think any country's pleasant where they have pleasant manners. Captain Littledale told me he had never seen such pleasant manners as at Newport, and he had been a great deal in European society. Hadn't he been in the diplomatic ser- vice? He told me the dream of his life was to get appointed to a diplomatic post in Washington. But he doesn't seem to have succeeded. Perhaps that was only a part of *his* pleasant manners. I suppose at any rate that in England promotion—and all that sort of thing—is fearfully slow. With us, you know, it's a great deal too quick. You see I admit our drawbacks. But I must confess I think Newport an ideal place. I don't know anything like it any- where. Captain Littledale told me *he* didn't know anything like it anywhere. It's entirely different from most watering-places;* it's a much more refined life. I must say I think that when one goes to a foreign country one ought to enjoy the differences. Of course there are differences; otherwise what did one come abroad for? Look for your pleasure in the differences, Lord Lambeth; that's the way to do it; and then I am sure you'll find American society—at least the Newport phase—quite unique. I wish very much Mr Westgate were here; but he's dreadfully confined to New York. I suppose you think that's very strange—for a gentleman. Only you see we haven't any leisure-class.'

Mrs Westgate's discourse was delivered with a mild merciless monotony, a paucity of intonation, an impartial flatness that suggested a flowery mead scrupulously 'done over' by a steam roller that had reduced its texture to that of a drawing-room carpet. Lord Lambeth listened to her with, it must be confessed, a rather ineffectual attention, though he summoned to his aid such a show as he might of discriminating motions and murmurs. He had no great faculty for apprehending generalisations. There were some three or four indeed which, in the play of his own intelligence, he had originated and which had sometimes appeared to meet the case—any case; yet he felt he had never known such a case as Mrs Westgate or as her presentation of *her* cases. But at the present time he could hardly have been said to follow this exponent as she darted fish-like through the sea of speculation. Fortunately she asked for no special rejoinder, since she looked about at the rest of the company as well and smiled at Mr Beaumont on the other side of her as if he too must understand her and agree with her. He was measurably more successful than his companion; for besides being, as we know, cleverer, his attention was not vaguely distracted by close vicinity to a remarkably interesting young person with dark hair and blue eyes. This was the situation of Lord Lambeth, to whom it occurred after a while that the young person with blue eyes and dark hair might be the pretty sister of whom Mrs Westgate had spoken. She presently turned to him with a remark establishing her identity.

'It's a great pity you couldn't have brought my brother-in-law with you. It's a great shame he should be in New York on such days as these.'

'Oh yes—it's very stuffy,' said Lord Lambeth.

'It must be dreadful there,' said the pretty sister.

'I dare say he's immensely taken up,' the young man returned with a sense of conscientiously yearning toward American realities.

'The gentlemen in America work too much,' his friend went on.

'Oh do they? Well, I dare say they like it,' he hopefully threw out.

'*I* don't like it. One never sees them.'

'Don't you really?' asked Lord Lambeth. 'I shouldn't have fancied that.'

'Have you come to study American manners?' the blue eyes and dark hair went on.

'Oh I don't know. I just came over for the joke of it. I haven't got long.' Then occurred a pause, after which he began again. 'But he *will* turn up here, won't he?'

'I certainly hope he will. He must help to entertain you and Mr Beaumont.'

Lord Lambeth looked at her from handsome eyes that were brown. 'Do you suppose he'd have come down with us if we had pressed it?'

The pretty girl treated this as rather an easy conundrum. 'I dare say he would,' she smiled.

'Really!' said the young Englishman. 'Well, he was no end civil.'

His young woman seemed much amused; this at least was in her eyes, which freely met Lord Lambeth's. 'He *would* be. He's a perfect husband. But all Americans are that,' she confidently continued.

'Really!' Lord Lambeth exclaimed again; and wondered whether all American ladies had such a passion for generalising as these two.

III

HE sat there a good while: there was a great deal of talk; it was all pitched in a key of expression and emphasis rather new to him. Every one present, the cool maidens not least, personally addressed him, and seemed to make a particular point of doing so by the friendly repetition of his name. Three or four other persons came in, and there was a shifting of seats, a changing of places; the gentlemen took, individually, an interest in the visitors, putting somehow more imagination and more 'high comedy' into this effort than the latter had ever seen displayed save in a play or a story. These well-wishers feared the two Britons mightn't be comfortable at their hotel—it being, as one of them said, 'not so private as those dear little English inns of yours.' This last gentleman added that as yet perhaps, alas, privacy wasn't quite so easily obtained in America as might be desired; still, he continued, you could generally get it by paying for it; in fact you could get everything in America nowadays by paying for it. The life was really growing more private; it was growing greatly to resemble European—which wasn't to be wondered at when two thirds of the people leading it were so awfully much at home in Europe. Europe, in the course of this conversation, was indeed, as Lord Lambeth afterwards remarked to his compatriot, rather bewilderingly rubbed into them: did they pretend to be European, and when had they ever been entered under that head? Everything at Newport, at all events, was described to them as thoroughly private; they would probably find themselves, when all was said, a good deal struck with that. It was also represented to the strangers that it mattered very little whether their hotel was agreeable, as every one would want them to 'visit round', as somebody called it: they would stay with other people and in any case would be constantly at Mrs Westgate's. They would find that charming; it was the pleasantest house in Newport. It was only a pity Mr Westgate was never there—he being a tremendously fine man, one of the finest they had. He worked like a horse and left his wife to play the social part. Well, she played it all right, if that was all he wanted. He liked her to enjoy herself, and she did know how. She was highly cultivated and a splendid converser—the sort of converser people would come miles to hear. But some preferred her sister, who was in a different style altogether. Some even thought her prettier, but decidedly Miss Alden wasn't so smart. She was more in the Boston style—the *quiet* Boston; she had lived a great deal there and was very highly educated. Boston girls, it was intimated, were more on the English model.

Lord Lambeth had presently a chance to test the truth of this last proposition; for, the company rising in compliance with a suggestion from their hostess that they should walk down to the rocks and look at the sea, the young Englishman again found himself, as they strolled across the grass, in proximity to Mrs Westgate's sister. Though Miss Alden was but a girl of twenty she appeared conscious of the weight of expectation— unless she quite wantonly took on duties she might have let alone; and this was perhaps the more to be noticed as she seemed by habit rather grave and backward, perhaps even proud, with little of the other's free fraternising. She might have been thought too deadly thin, not to say also too deadly pale; but while she moved over the grass, her arms hanging at her sides, and, seriously or absently, forgot expectations, though again brightly to remember them and to look at the summer sea as if that was what she really cared for, her companion judged her at least as pretty as Mrs Westgate and reflected that if this was the Boston style, 'the quiet Boston', it would do very well. He could fancy her very clever, highly educated and all the rest of it; but clearly also there were ways in which she could spare a fellow—could ease him; she wouldn't keep him so long on the stretch at once. For all her cleverness moreover he felt she had to think a little what to say; she didn't say the first thing that came into her head: he had come from a different part of the world, from a different society, and she was trying to adapt her conversation. The others were scattered about the rocks; Mrs Westgate had charge of Percy Beaumont.

'Very jolly place for this sort of thing,' Lord Lambeth said. 'It must do beautifully to sit.'

'It does indeed; there are cosy nooks and there are breezy ones, which I often try—as if they had been made on purpose.'

'Ah I suppose you've had a lot made,' he fell in.

She seemed to wonder. 'Oh no, we've had nothing made. It's all pure nature.'

'I should think you'd have a few little benches—rustic seats and that sort of thing. It might really be so jolly to "develop" the place,' he suggested.

It made her thoughtful—even a little rueful. 'I'm afraid we haven't so many of those things as you.'

'Ah well, if you go in for pure nature, as you were saying, there's nothing like that. Nature, over here, must be awfully grand.' And Lord Lambeth looked about him.

The little coast-line that contributed to the view melted away, but it too much lacked presence and character—a fact Miss Alden appeared to rise to a perception of. 'I'm afraid it seems to you very rough. It's not like the coast-scenery in Kingsley's novels.'*

He wouldn't let her, however, undervalue it. 'Ah the novels always overdo everything, you know. You mustn't go by the novels.'

They wandered a little on the rocks; they stopped to look into a narrow chasm where the rising tide made a curious bellowing sound. It was loud enough to prevent their hearing each other, and they stood for some moments in silence. The girl's eyes took in her companion, observing him attentively but covertly, as those of women even in blinking youth know how to do. Lord Lambeth repaid contemplation; tall straight and strong, he was handsome as certain young Englishmen, and certain young Englishmen almost alone, are handsome; with a perfect finish of feature and a visible repose of mind, an inaccessibility to questions, somehow stamped in by the same strong die and pressure that nature, designing a precious medal, had selected and applied. It was not that he looked stupid; it was only, we assume, that his perceptions didn't show in his face for restless or his imagination for irritable. He was not, as he would himself have said, tremendously clever; but, though there was rather a constant appeal for delay in his waiting, his perfectly patient eye, this registered simplicity had its beauty as well and, whatever it might have appeared to plead for, didn't plead in the name of indifference or inaction. This most searching of his new friends thought him the handsomest young man she had ever seen; and Bessie Alden's imagination, unlike that of her companion, was irritable. He, however, had already made up his mind, quite originally and without aid, that she had a grace exceedingly her own.

'I dare say it's very gay here—that you've lots of balls and parties,' he said; since, though not tremendously clever, he rather prided himself on having with women a strict sufficiency of conversation.

'Oh yes, there's a great deal going on. There are not so many balls, but there are a good many other pleasant things,' Bessie Alden explained. 'You'll see for yourself; we live rather in the midst of it.'

'It will be very kind of you to let us see. But I thought you Americans were always dancing.'

'I suppose we dance a good deal, though I've never seen much of it. We don't do it much at any rate in summer. And I'm sure', she said, 'that we haven't as many balls as you in England.'

He wondered—these so many prompt assumptions about his own country made him gape a little. 'Ah in England it all depends, you know.'

'You'll not think much of our gaieties,' she said—though she seemed to settle it for him with a quaver of interrogation. The interrogation sounded earnest indeed and the decision arch; the mixture, at any rate, was charming. 'Those things with us are much less splendid than in England.'

'I fancy you don't really mean that,' her companion laughed.

'I assure you I really mean everything I say,' she returned. 'Certainly from what I've read about English society it is very different.'

'Ah well, you know,' said Lord Lambeth, who appeared to cling to this general theory, 'those things are often described by fellows who know nothing about them. You mustn't mind what you read.'

'Ah what a blasphemous speech—I *must* mind what I read!' our young woman protested. 'When I read Thackeray and George Eliot* how can I help minding?'

'Oh well, Thackeray and George Eliot'—and her friend pleasantly bethought himself. 'I'm afraid I haven't read much of them.'

'Don't you suppose they knew about society?' asked Bessie Alden.

'Oh I dare say they knew; they must have got up their subject.

Good writers do, don't they? But those fashionable novels are mostly awful rot, you know.'

His companion rested on him a moment her dark blue eyes; after which she looked down into the chasm where the water was tumbling about. 'Do you mean Catherine Grace Gore* for instance?' she then more aspiringly asked.

But at this he broke down—he coloured, laughed, gave up. 'I'm afraid I haven't read that either. I'm afraid you'll think I'm not very intellectual.'

'Reading Mrs Gore is no proof of intellect. But I like reading everything about English life—even poor books. I'm so curious about it,' said Bessie Alden.

'Aren't ladies curious about everything?' he asked with continued hilarity.

'I don't think so. I don't think we're enough so—that we care about many things. So it's all the more of a compliment,' she added, 'that I should want to know so much about England.'

The logic here seemed a little close; but Lord Lambeth, advised of a compliment, found his natural modesty close at hand. 'I'm sure you know a great deal more than I do.'

'I really think I know a great deal—for a person who has never been there.'

'Have you really never been there?' cried he. 'Fancy!'

'Never—except in imagination. And I *have* been to Paris,' she admitted.

'Fancy,' he repeated with gaiety—'fancy taking those brutes first! But you *will* come soon?'

'It's the dream of my life!' Bessie Alden brightly professed.

'Your sister at any rate seems to know a tremendous lot about us,' Lord Lambeth went on.

She appeared to take her view of this. 'My sister and I are two very different persons. She has been a great deal in Europe. She has been in England a little—not intimately. But she has met English people in other countries, and she arrives very quickly at conclusions.'

'Ah I guess she does,' he laughed. 'But you must have known some too.'

'No—I don't think I've ever spoken to one before. You're the first Englishman that—to my knowledge—I've ever talked with.'

Bessie Alden made this statement with a certain gravity—almost, as it seemed to the young man, an impressiveness. The impressive always made him feel awkward, and he now began to laugh and swing his stick: 'Ah you'd have been sure to know!' And then he added after an instant: 'I'm sorry I'm not a better specimen.'

The girl looked away, but taking it more gaily. 'You must remember you're only a beginning.' Then she retraced her steps, leading the way back to the lawn, where they saw Mrs Westgate come toward them with Percy Beaumont still at her side. 'Perhaps I shall go to England next year,' Miss Alden continued; 'I want to immensely. My sister expects to cross about then, and she has asked me to go with her. If I do I shall make her stay as long as possible in London.'

'Ah, you must come early in July,' said Lord Lambeth. 'That's the time when there's most going on.'

'I don't think I can wait even till early in July,' his friend returned. 'By the first of May I shall be very impatient.' They had gone further, and Mrs Westgate and her companion were near. 'Kitty,' said the younger sister, 'I've given out that we go to London next May. So please to conduct yourself accordingly.'

Percy Beaumont wore a somewhat animated—even a slightly irritated—air. He was by no means of so handsome an effect as his comrade, though in the latter's absence he might, with his manly stature and his fair dense beard, his fresh clean skin and his quiet outlook, have pleased by a due affirmation of the best British points. Just now Beaumont's clear eyes had a rather troubled light, which, after glancing at Bessie Alden while she spoke, he turned with some intensity on Lord Lambeth. Mrs Westgate's beautiful radiance of interest and dissent fell meanwhile impartially everywhere.

'You had better wait till the time comes,' she said to her sister. 'Perhaps next May you won't care so much for London. Mr Beaumont and I', she went on, smiling at her companion, 'have had a tremendous discussion. We don't agree about anything. It's perfectly delightful.'

'Oh I say, Percy!' exclaimed Lord Lambeth.

'I disagree,' said Beaumont, raising his eyebrows and stroking down his back hair, 'even to the point of thinking it *not* delightful.'

'Ah you *must* have been getting it!' cried his friend.

'I don't see anything delightful in my disagreeing with Mrs Westgate,' said Percy Beaumont.

'Well, I do!' Mrs Westgate declared as she turned again to her sister. 'You know you've to go to town. There must be something at the door for you. You had better take Lord Lambeth.'

Mr Beaumont, at this point, looked straight at his comrade, trying to catch his eye. But Lord Lambeth wouldn't look at him; his own eyes were better occupied. 'I shall be very happy'—Bessie Alden rose straight to their hostess's suggestion. 'I'm only going to some shops. But I'll drive you about and show you the place.'

'An American woman who respects herself', said Mrs Westgate, turning to the elder man with her bright expository air, 'must buy something every day of her life. If she can't do it herself she must send out some member of her family for the purpose. So Bessie goes forth to fulfil my mission.'

The girl had walked away with Lord Lambeth by her side, to whom she was talking still; and Percy Beaumont watched them as they passed toward the house. 'She fulfils her own mission,' he presently said; 'that of being very attractive.'

But even here Mrs Westgate discriminated. 'I don't know that I should precisely say attractive. She's not so much that as she's charming when you really know her. She's very shy.'

'Oh indeed?' said Percy Beaumont with evident wonder. And then as if to alternate with a certain grace the note of scepticism: 'I guess your shyness, in that case, is different from ours.'

'Everything of ours is different from yours,' Mrs Westgate instantly returned. 'But my poor sister's given over, I hold, to a fine Boston *gaucherie** that has rubbed off on her by being there so much. She's a dear good girl, however; she's a charming type of girl. She is not in the least a flirt; that isn't at all her line; she doesn't know the alphabet of any such vulgarity. She's very simple, very serious, very *true*. She has lived, however, rather too much in Boston with another sister of mine, the eldest of us, who

married a Bostonian. Bessie's very cultivated, not at all like me—
I'm not in the least cultivated and am called so only by those who
don't know what true culture is. But Bessie does; she has studied
Greek; she has read everything; she's what they call in Boston
"thoughtful".'

'Ah well, it only depends on what one thinks *about*,' said
Mr Beaumont, who appeared to find her zeal for distinctions
catching.

'I really believe', Mrs Westgate pursued, 'that the most
charming girl in the world is a Boston superstructure on a New
York *fond*, or perhaps a New York superstructure on a Boston
fond. At any rate it's the mixture,' she declared, continuing to
supply her guest with information and to do him the honours of
the American world with a zeal that left nothing to be desired.

Lord Lambeth got into a light low pony-cart with Bessie Alden,
and she drove him down the long Avenue,* whose extent he had
measured on foot a couple of hours before, into the ancient town,
as it was called in that part of the world, of Newport. The ancient
town was a curious affair—a collection of fresh-looking little
wooden houses, painted white, scattered over a hill-side and clus-
tering about a long straight street paved with huge old cobbles.
There were plenty of shops, a large allowance of which appeared
those of fruit-vendors, with piles of huge water-melons and
pumpkins stacked in front of them; while, drawn up before the
shops or bumping about on the round stones, were innumerable
other like or different carts freighted with ladies of high fashion
who greeted each other from vehicle to vehicle and conversed on
the edge of the pavement in a manner that struck Lord Lambeth
as of the last effusiveness: with a great many 'Oh my dears' and
little quick sounds and motions—obscure native words, shibboleths* and signs. His companion went into seventeen shops—
he amused himself with counting them—and accumulated at
the bottom of the trap a pile of bundles that hardly left the
young Englishman a place for his feet As she had no other attendant he sat in the phaeton to hold the pony; where, though not a
particularly acute observer, he saw much harmlessly to divert
him—especially the ladies just mentioned, who wandered up

and down with an aimless intentness, as if looking for something to buy, and who, tripping in and out of their vehicles, displayed remarkably pretty feet. It all seemed to Lord Lambeth very odd and bright and gay. And he felt by the time they got back to the villa that he had made a stride in intimacy with Miss Alden.

The young Englishmen spent the whole of that day and the whole of many successive days in the cultivation, right and left, far and near, of this celerity of social progress. They agreed that it was all extremely jolly—that they had never known anything more agreeable. It is not proposed to report the detail of their sojourn on this charming shore; though were it convenient I might present a record of impressions none the less soothing that they were not exhaustively analysed. Many of them still linger in the minds of our travellers, attended by a train of harmonious images—images of early breezy shining hours on lawns and piazzas that overlooked the sea; of innumerable pretty girls saying innumerable quaint and familiar things; of infinite lounging and talking and laughing and flirting and lunching and dining; of a confidence that broke down, of a freedom that pulled up, nowhere; of an idyllic ease that was somehow too ordered for a primitive social consciousness and too innocent for a developed; of occasions on which they so knew every one and every thing that they almost ached with reciprocity; of drives and rides in the late afternoon, over gleaming beaches, on long sea-roads, beneath a sky lighted up by marvellous sunsets; of tea-tables, on the return, informal, irregular, agreeable; of evenings at open windows or on the perpetual verandahs, in the summer starlight, above the warm Atlantic and amid irrelevant outbursts of clever minstrelsy. The young Englishmen were introduced to everybody, entertained by everybody, intimate with everybody, and it was all the book of life, of American life, at least; with the chapter of 'complications' bodily omitted. At the end of three days they had removed their luggage from the hotel and had gone to stay with Mrs Westgate— a step as to which Percy Beaumont at first took up an attitude of mistrust apparently founded on some odd and just a little barbaric talk forced on him, he would have been tempted to say, and

very soon after their advent, by Miss Alden. He had indeed been
aware of her occasional approach or appeal, since she wasn't literally always in conversation with Lord Lambeth. He had medi-
tated on Mrs Westgate's account of her sister and discovered for
himself that the young lady was 'sharp' (Percy's critical categories
remained few and simple) and appeared to have read a great deal.
She seemed perfectly well-bred, though he couldn't make out
that, as Mrs Westgate funnily insisted, she was shy. If she was shy
she carried it off with an ease—!

'Mr Beaumont,' she had said, 'please tell me something about
Lord Lambeth's family. How would you say it in England?—
his position.'

'His position?' Percy's instinct was to speak as if he had never
heard of such a matter.

'His rank—or whatever you call it. Unfortunately we haven't
got a "Peerage",* like the people in Thackeray.'

'That's a great pity,' Percy pleaded. 'You'd find the whole
matter in black and white, and upon my honour I know very little
about it.'

The girl seemed to wonder at this innocence. 'You know at
least whether he's what they call a great noble.'

'Oh yes, he's in that line.'

'Is he a "peer of the realm"?'*

'Well, as yet—very nearly.'

'And has he any other title than Lord Lambeth?'

'His title's the Marquis of Lambeth.' With which the fountain
of Bessie's information appeared to run a little dry. She looked at
him, however, with such interest that he presently added: 'He's
the son of the Duke of Bayswater.'

'The eldest —?'

'The only one.'

'And are his parents living?'

'Naturally—as to his father. If *he* weren't living Lambeth
would be a duke.'

'So that when "the old lord" dies'—and the girl smiled with
more simplicity than might have been expected in one so
'sharp'—'he'll become Duke of Bayswater?'

'Of course,' said their common friend. 'But his father's in excellent health.'

'And his mother?'

Percy seemed amused. 'The Duchess is built to last!'

'And has he any sisters?'

'Yes, there are two.'

'And what are they called?'

'One of them's married. She's the Countess of Pimlico.'*

'And the other?'

'The other's unmarried—she's plain Lady Julia.'

Bessie entered into it all. 'Is she very plain?'

He began to laugh again. 'You wouldn't find her so handsome as her brother,' he said; and it was after this that he attempted to dissuade the heir of the Duke of Bayswater from accepting Mrs Westgate's invitation. 'Depend upon it,' he said, 'that girl means to have a go at you.'

'It seems to me you're doing your best to make a fool of me,' the modest young nobleman answered.

'She has been asking me', his friend imperturbably pursued, 'all about your people and your possessions.'

'I'm sure it's very good of her!' Lord Lambeth returned.

'Well then,' said Percy, 'if you go straight into it, if you hurl yourself bang upon the spears, you do so with your eyes open.'

'Damn my eyes!' the young man pronounced. 'If one's to be a dozen times a day at the house it's a great deal more convenient to sleep there. I'm sick of travelling up and down this beastly Avenue.'

Since he had determined to go Percy would of course have been very sorry to allow him to go alone; he was a man of many scruples—in the direction in which he had any at all—and he remembered his promise to the Duchess. It was obviously the memory of this promise that made Mr Beaumont say to his companion a couple of days later that he rather wondered he should be so fond of such a girl.

'In the first place how do you know how fond I am?' asked Lord Lambeth. 'And in the second why shouldn't I be fond of her?'

'I shouldn't think she'd be in your line.'

'What do you call my "line"? You don't set her down, I suppose, as "fast"?'*

'Exactly so. Mrs Westgate tells me that there's no such thing as the fast girl in America; that it's an English invention altogether and that the term has no meaning here.'

'All the better. It's an animal I detest,' said Lord Lambeth.

'You prefer then rather a priggish American *précieuse*?'*

Lord Lambeth took his time. 'Do you call Miss Alden all that?'

'Her sister tells me', said Percy Beaumont, 'that she's tremendously literary.'

'Well, why shouldn't she be? She's certainly very clever and has every appearance of a well-stored mind.'

Percy for an instant watched his young friend, who had turned away. 'I should rather have supposed you'd find her stores oppressive.'

The young man, after this, faced him again. 'Why, do you think me such a dunce?' And then as his friend but vaguely protested: 'The girl's all right,' he said—and quite as if this judgement covered all the ground. It wasn't that there was no ground—but he knew what he was about.

Percy, for a while further, and a little uncomfortably flushed with the sense of his false position—that of presenting culture in a 'mean' light, as they said at Newport—Percy kept his peace; but on August 10th he wrote to the Duchess of Bayswater. His conception of certain special duties and decencies, as I have said, was strong, and this step wholly fell in with it. His companion meanwhile was having much talk with Miss Alden—on the red sea-rocks beyond the lawn; in the course of long island rides, with a slow return in the glowing twilight; on the deep verandah, late in the evening. Lord Lambeth, who had stayed at many houses, had never stayed at one in which it was possible for a young man to converse so freely and frequently with a young lady. This young lady no longer applied to their other guest for information concerning his lordship. She addressed herself directly to the young nobleman. She asked him a great many questions, some of which did, according to Mr Beaumont's term, a little oppress him; for he took no pleasure in talking about himself.

'Lord Lambeth'—this had been one of them—'are you an hereditary legislator?'

'Oh I say,' he returned, 'don't make me call myself such names as that.'

'But you're natural members of Parliament.'

'I don't like the sound of that either.'

'Doesn't your father sit in the House of Lords?' Bessie Alden went on.

'Very seldom,' said Lord Lambeth.

'Is it a very august position?' she asked.

'Oh dear no,' Lord Lambeth smiled.

'I should think it would be very grand'—she serenely kept it up, as the female American, he judged, would always keep anything up—'to possess simply by an accident of birth the right to make laws for a great nation.'

'Ah but one doesn't make laws. There's a lot of humbug about it.'

'I don't believe that,' the girl unconfusedly declared. 'It must be a great privilege, and I should think that if one thought of it in the right way—from a high point of view—it would be very inspiring.'

'The less one thinks of it the better, I guess!' Lord Lambeth after a moment returned.

'I think it's tremendous'—this at least she kept up; and on another occasion she asked him if he had any tenantry. Hereupon it was that, as I have said, he felt a little the burden of her earnestness.

But he took it good-humouredly. 'Do you want to buy up their leases?'

'Well—have you got any "livings"?'* she demanded as if the word were rich and rare.

'Oh I say!' he cried. 'Have *you* got a pet clergyman looking out?' But she made him plead guilty to his having, in prospect, a castle; he confessed to but one. It was the place in which he had been born and brought up, and, as he had an old-time liking for it, he was beguiled into a few pleasant facts about it and into pronouncing it really very jolly. Bessie listened with great interest,

declaring she would give the world to see such a place. To which
he charmingly made answer: 'It would be awfully kind of you to
come and stay there, you know.' It was not inconvenient to him
meanwhile that Percy Beaumont hadn't happened to hear him
make this genial remark.

Mr Westgate, all this time, hadn't, as they said at Newport,
'come on'. His wife more than once announced that she expected
him on the morrow; but on the morrow she wandered about a
little, with a telegram in her jewelled fingers pronouncing it too
'fiendish' he should let his business so dreadfully absorb him
that he could but platonically hope, as she expressed it, his
two Englishmen were having a good time. 'I must say', said
Mrs Westgate, 'that it's no thanks to him if you are!' And she
went on to explain, while she kept up that slow-paced circulation
which enabled her well-adjusted skirts to display themselves
so advantageously, that unfortunately in America there was no
leisure-class and that the universal passionate surrender of the
men to business-questions and business-questions only, as if they
were the all in all of life, was a tide that would have to be stemmed.
It was Lord Lambeth's theory, freely propounded when the young
men were together, that Percy was having a very good time with
Mrs Westgate and that under the pretext of meeting for the purpose of animated discussion they were indulging in practices that
imparted a shade of hypocrisy to the lady's regret for her husband's absence.

'I assure you we're always discussing and differing,'
Mr Beaumont however asseverated. 'She's awfully argumenta-
tive. American ladies certainly don't mind contradicting you flat.
Upon my word I don't think I was ever treated so by a woman
before. We have ours ever so much more in hand. She's so devil-
ish positive.'

The superlative degree so variously affirmed, however, was
evidently a source of attraction in Mrs Westgate, for the elder
man was constantly at his hostess's side. He detached himself one
day to the extent of going to New York to talk over the Tennessee
Central with her husband; but he was absent only forty-eight
hours, during which, with that gentleman's assistance, he

completely settled this piece of business. 'They know how to put things—and put people—"through" in New York,' he subsequently and quite breathlessly observed to his comrade; and he added that Mr Westgate had seemed markedly to fear his wife might suffer for loss of her guest—he had been in such an awful hurry to send him back to her. 'I'm afraid you'll never come up to an American husband—if that's what the wives expect,' he said to Lord Lambeth.

Mrs Westgate, however, was not to enjoy much longer the entertainment with which an indulgent husband had desired to keep her provided. August had still a part of its course to run when his lordship received from his mother the disconcerting news that his father had been taken ill and that he had best at once come home. The young nobleman concealed his chagrin with no great success. 'I left the Duke but the other day absolutely all right—so what the deuce does it mean?' he asked of his comrade. 'What's a fellow to do?'

Percy Beaumont was scarce less annoyed; he had deemed it his duty, as we know, to report faithfully to the Duchess, but had not expected this distinguished woman to act so promptly on his hint. 'It means', he said, 'that your father is somehow, and rather suddenly, laid up. I don't suppose it's anything serious, but you've no option. Take the first steamer, but take it without alarm.'

This really struck Lord Lambeth as meaning that he essentially needn't take it, since alarm would have been his only good motive; yet he nevertheless, after an hour of intenser irritation than he could quite have explained to himself, made his farewells; in the course of which he exchanged a few last words with Bessie Alden that are the only ones making good their place in our record. 'Of course I needn't assure you that if you should come to England next year I expect to be the very first person notified of it.'

She looked at him in that way she had which never quite struck him as straight and clear, yet which always struck him as kind and true. 'Oh if we come to London I should think you'd sufficiently hear of it.'

Percy Beaumont felt it his duty also to embark, and this same rigour compelled him, one windless afternoon, in mid-Atlantic, to say to his friend that he suspected the Duchess's telegram to have been in part the result of something he himself had written her. 'I wrote her—as I distinctly warned you I had promised in general to do—that you were extremely interested in a little American girl.'

The young man, much upset by this avowal, indulged for some moments in the strong and simple language of resentment. But if I have described him as inclined to candour and to reason I can give no better proof of it than the fact of his being ready to face the truth by the end of half an hour. 'You were quite right after all. I'm very much interested in her. Only, to be fair,' he added, 'you should have told my mother also that she's not—at all seriously—interested in poor me.'

Mr Beaumont gave the rein to mirth and mockery. 'There's nothing so charming as modesty in a young man in the position of "poor" you. That speech settles for me the question of what's the matter with you.'

Lord Lambeth's handsome eyes turned rueful and queer. 'Is anything so flagrantly the matter with me?'

'Everything, my dear boy,' laughed his companion, passing a hand into his arm for a walk.

'Well, *she* isn't interested—she isn't!' the young man insisted.

'My poor friend,' said Percy Beaumont rather gravely, 'you're very far gone!'

IV

IN point of fact, as the latter would have said, Mrs Westgate disembarked by the next mid-May on the British coast. She was accompanied by her sister, but unattended by any other member of her family. To the lost comfort of a husband respectably to produce, as she phrased it, she was now habituated; she had made half a dozen journeys to Europe under this drawback of looking ill-temperedly separated and yet of being thanklessly enslaved, and she still decently accounted for her spurious singleness to wondering friends on this side of the Atlantic by formulating the grim truth—the only grimness indeed in all her view—that in America there is no leisure-class. The two ladies came up to London and alighted at Jones's Hotel, where Mrs Westgate, who had made on former occasions the most agreeable impression at this establishment, received an obsequious greeting. Bessie Alden had felt much excited about coming to England; she had expected the 'associations' would carry her away and counted on the joy of treating her eyes and her imagination to all the things she had read of in poets and historians. She was very fond of the poets and historians, of the picturesque, of the past, of associations, of relics and reverberations of greatness; so that on coming into the great English world, where strangeness and familiarity would go hand in hand, she was prepared for a swarm of fresh emotions. They began very promptly—these tender fluttering sensations; they began with the sight of the beautiful English landscape, whose dark richness was quickened and brightened by the season; with the carpeted fields and flowering hedge-rows, as she looked at them from the window of the train; with the spires of the rural churches peeping above the rook-haunted tree-tops; with the oak-studded, deer-peopled parks, the ancient homes, the cloudy light, the speech, the manners, all the significant differences. Mrs Westgate's response was of course less quick and less extravagant, and she gave but a wandering attention to her sister's ejaculations and rhapsodies.

'You know my enjoyment of England's not so intellectual as Bessie's,' she said to several of her friends in the course of her visit to this country. 'And yet if it's not intellectual I can't say it's in the least sensual. I don't think I can quite say what it is, my enjoyment of England.' When once it was settled that the two ladies should come abroad and should spend a few weeks in London and perhaps in other parts of the celebrated island on their way to the Continent, they of course exchanged a good many allusions to their English acquaintance.

'It will certainly be much nicer having friends there,' was a remark that had one day dropped from Bessie while she sat on the sunny deck of the steamer, at her sister's feet, from under which spread conveniently a large soft rug.

'Whom do you mean by friends?' Mrs Westgate had then invited the girl to say.

'All those English gentlemen you've known and entertained. Captain Littledale, for instance. And Lord Lambeth and Mr Beaumont,' the girl further mentioned.

'Do you expect them to give us a very grand reception?'

She reflected a moment; she was addicted, as we know, to fine reflexion. 'Well—to be nice.'

'My poor sweet child!' murmured her sister.

'What have I said that's so silly?' Bessie asked.

'You're a little too simple; just a little. It's very becoming, but it pleases people at your expense.'

'I'm certainly too simple to understand you,' said our young lady.

Mrs Westgate had an ominous pause. 'Shall I tell you a story?'

'If you'd be so good. That's what's frequently done to amuse simple people.'

Mrs Westgate consulted her memory while her companion sat at gaze of the shining sea. 'Did you ever hear of the Duke of Green-Erin?'*

'I think not,' said Bessie.

'Well, it's no matter,' her sister went on.

'It's a proof of my simplicity.'

'My story's meant to illustrate that of some other people,' said Mrs Westgate. 'The Duke of Green-Erin's what they call in England a great swell, and some five years ago he came to America. He spent most of his time in New York, and in New York he spent his days and his nights at the Butterworths'. You've heard at least of the Butterworths. *Bien.* They did everything in the world for him—the poor Butterworths—they turned themselves inside out. They gave him a dozen dinner-parties and balls, and were the means of his being invited to fifty more. At first he used to come into Mrs Butterworth's box at the opera in a tweed travelling-suit, but some one stopped that. At any rate he had a beautiful time and they parted the best friends in the world. Two years elapse and the Butterworths come abroad and go to London. The first thing they see in all the papers—in England those things are in the most prominent place—is that the Duke of Green-Erin has arrived in town for the season. They wait a little, and then Mr Butterworth—as polite as ever—goes and leaves a card. They wait a little more; the visit's not returned; they wait three weeks: *silence de mort*,* the Duke gives no sign. The Butterworths see a lot of other people, put down the Duke of Green-Erin as a rude ungrateful man and forget all about him. One fine day they go to Ascot Races*—where they meet him face to face. He stares a moment and then comes up to Mr Butterworth, taking something from his pocket-book—something which proves to be a banknote. "I'm glad to see you, Mr Butterworth," he says, "so that I pay you that ten pounds I lost to you in New York. I saw the other day you remembered our bet; here are the ten pounds, Mr Butterworth. Good-bye, Mr Butterworth." And off he goes, and that's the last they see of the Duke of Green-Erin.'

'Is that your story?' asked Bessie Alden.

'Don't tell me you don't think it interesting!' her sister replied.

'I don't think I believe it,' said the girl.

'Ah then,' cried Mrs Westgate, 'mademoiselle isn't of such an unspotted *candeur*! Believe it or not as you like. There's at any rate no smoke without fire.'

'Is that the way', asked Bessie after a moment, 'that you expect your friends to treat you?'

'I defy them to treat me very ill, for the simple reason that I shall never give them the opportunity. With the best will in the world, in that case, they can't be very disobliging.'

Our young lady for a time said nothing. 'I don't see what makes you talk that way,' she then resumed. 'The English are a great people.'

'Exactly; and that's just the way they've grown great—by dropping you when you've ceased to be useful. People say they aren't clever, but I find them prodigiously clever.'

'You know you've liked them—all the Englishmen you've seen,' Bessie brought up.

'They've liked *me*,' her sister returned; 'so I think I'd rather put it. And of course one likes that.'

Bessie pursued for some moments her studies in sea-green.

'Well,' she said, 'whether they like me or not, I mean to like them. And happily,' she wound up, 'Lord Lambeth doesn't owe me ten pounds.'

During the first few days after their arrival at Jones's Hotel our charming Americans were much occupied with what they would have called looking about them. They found occasion to make numerous purchases, and their opportunities for enquiry and comment were only those supplied by the deferential London shopmen. Bessie Alden, even in driving from the station, felt to intensity the many-voiced appeal of the capital of the race from which she had sprung, and, at the risk of exhibiting her as a person of vulgar tastes, it must be recorded that for many days she desired no higher pleasure than to roll about the crowded streets in the public conveyances. They presented to her attentive eyes strange pictures and figures, and it's at least beneath the dignity of our historic muse to enumerate the trivial objects and incidents in which the imagination of this simple young lady from Boston lost itself. It may be freely mentioned, however, that whenever, after a round of visits in Bond Street and Regent Street, she was about to return with her sister to Jones's Hotel, she desired they should, at whatever cost to convenience, be driven home by way of Westminster Abbey. She had begun by asking if it wouldn't be possible to take the Tower en route to their lodgings; but it happened that at a more primitive stage of her culture Mrs Westgate had paid a visit to this venerable relic, which she spoke of ever afterwards, vaguely, as a dreadful disappointment. She thus expressed the liveliest disapproval of any attempt to combine historical researches with the purchase of hair-brushes and note-paper. The most she would consent to do in the line of backward brooding was to spend half an hour at Madame Tussaud's,* where she saw several dusty wax effigies of members of the Royal Family. It was made clear to Bessie that if she wished to go to the Tower she must get some one else to take her. Bessie expressed hereupon an earnest disposition to go alone; but in respect to this proposal as well Mrs Westgate had the cold sense of complications.

'Remember', she said, 'that you're not in your innocent

little Boston. It's not a question of walking up and down Beacon Street.'* With which she went on to explain that there were two classes of American girls in Europe—those who walked about alone and those who didn't. 'You happen to belong, my dear,' she said to her sister, 'to the class that doesn't.'

'It's only', laughed Bessie, though all yearningly, 'because you happen quite arbitrarily to place me.' And she devoted much private meditation to this question of effecting a visit to the Tower of London.

Suddenly it seemed as if the problem might be solved; the two ladies at Jones's Hotel received a visit from Willie Woodley. So was familiarly designated a young American who had sailed from New York a few days after their own departure and who, enjoying some freedom of acquaintance with them in that city, had lost no time, on his arrival in London, in coming to pay them his respects. He had in fact gone to see them directly after going to see his tailor; than which there can be no greater exhibition of promptitude on the part of a young American just installed at the Charing Cross Hotel.* He was a slight mild youth, without high colour but with many elegant forms, famous for the authority with which he led the 'German'* in New York. He was indeed, by the young ladies who habitually figured in such evolutions, reckoned 'the best dancer in the world'; it was in those terms he was always spoken of and his pleasant identity indicated. He was the most convenient gentle young man, for almost any casual light purpose, it was possible to meet; he was beautifully dressed—'in the English style'—and knew an immense deal about London. He had been at Newport during the previous summer, at the time of our young Englishmen's visit, and he took extreme pleasure in the society of Bessie Alden, whom he never addressed but as 'Miss Bessie'. She immediately arranged with him, in the presence of her sister, that he should guide her to the scene of Lady Jane Grey's execution.*

'You may do as you please,' said Mrs Westgate. 'Only—if you desire the information—it is not the custom here for young ladies to knock about London with wild young men.'

'Miss Bessie has waltzed with me so often—not to call it so

wildly,' the young man returned, 'that she can surely go out with me in a jog-trot cab.'

'I consider public waltzing', said Mrs Westgate, 'the most innocent, because the most guarded and regulated, pleasure of our time.'

'It's a jolly compliment to our time!' Mr Woodley cried with a laugh of the most candid significance.

'I don't see why I should regard what's done here,' Bessie pursued. 'Why should I suffer the restrictions of a society of which I enjoy none of the privileges?'

'That's very good—very good,' her friend applauded.

'Oh go to the Tower and feel the axe if you like!' said Mrs Westgate. 'I consent to your going with Mr Woodley; but I wouldn't let you go with an Englishman.'

'Miss Bessie wouldn't care to go with an Englishman!' Mr Woodley declared with an asperity doubtless not unnatural in a young man who, dressing in a manner that I have indicated and knowing a great deal, as I have said, about London, saw no reason for drawing these sharp distinctions. He agreed upon a day with Miss Bessie—a day of that same week; while an ingenious mind might perhaps have traced a connexion between the girl's reference to her lack of social privilege or festal initiation and a question she asked on the morrow as she sat with her sister at luncheon.

'Don't you mean to write to—to any one?'

'I wrote this morning to Captain Littledale,' Mrs Westgate replied.

'But Mr Woodley believes Captain Littledale away in India.'

'He said he thought he had heard so; he knows nothing about it.'

For a moment Bessie said nothing more; then at last, 'And don't you intend to write to—to Mr Beaumont?' she enquired.

Her sister waited with a look at her. 'You mean to Lord Lambeth.'

'I said Mr Beaumont because he was—at Newport—so good a friend of yours.'

Mrs Westgate prolonged the attitude of sisterly truth. 'I don't really care two straws for Mr Beaumont.'

'You were certainly very nice to him.'

'I'm very nice to every one,' said Mrs Westgate simply.

Nothing indeed could have been simpler save perhaps the way Bessie smiled back: 'To every one but me.'

Her sister continued to look at her. 'Are you in love with Lord Lambeth?'

Our young woman stared a moment, and the question was too unattended with any train even to make her shy. 'Not that I know of.'

'Because if you are,' Mrs Westgate went on, 'I shall certainly not send for him.'

'That proves what I said,' Bessie gaily insisted—'that you're not really nice to me.'

'It would be a poor service, my dear child,' said her sister.

'In what sense? There's nothing *against* Lord Lambeth that I know of.'

Mrs Westgate seemed to cover much country in a few moments. 'You *are* in love with him then?'

Bessie stared again, but this time blushing a little. 'Ah if you'll not be serious we won't mention him again.'

For some minutes accordingly Lord Lambeth was shrouded in silence, and it was Mrs Westgate who, at the end of this period, removed the ban. 'Of course I shall let him know we're here. I think he'd be hurt—justly enough—if we should go away without seeing him. It's fair to give him a chance to come and thank me for the kindness we showed him. But I don't want to seem eager.'

'Neither do I,' said Bessie very simply.

'Though I confess', her companion added, 'that I'm curious to see how he'll behave.'

'He behaved very well at Newport.'

'Newport isn't London. At Newport he could do as he liked; but here it's another affair. He has to have an eye to consequences.'

'If he had more freedom then at Newport,' argued Bessie, 'it's the more to his credit that he behaved well; and if he has to be so careful here it's possible he'll behave even better.'

'Better, better?' echoed her sister a little impatiently. 'My dear child, what do you mean by better and what's your point of view?'

Bessie wondered. 'What do *you* mean by my point of view?'

'Don't you care for Lord Lambeth—a tiny speck?' Mrs Westgate demanded.

This time Bessie Alden took it with still deeper reserve. She slowly got up from table, turning her face away. 'You'll oblige me by not talking so.'

Mrs Westgate sat watching her for some moments as she moved slowly about the room and went and stood at the window. 'I'll write to him this afternoon,' she said at last.

'Do as you please!' Bessie answered; after which she turned round. 'I'm not afraid to say I like Lord Lambeth. I like him very much.'

Mrs Westgate bethought herself. 'He's not clever.'

'Well, there have been clever people whom I've disliked,' the girl said; 'so I suppose I may like a stupid one. Besides, Lord Lambeth's no stupider than any one else.'

'No stupider than he gives you warning of,' her sister smiled.

'If I were in love with him as you said just now,' Bessie returned, 'it would be bad policy on your part to abuse him.'

'My dear child, don't give me lessons in policy!' cried Mrs Westgate. 'The policy I mean to follow is very deep.'

The girl began once more to walk about; then she stopped before her companion. 'I've never heard in the course of five minutes so many hints and innuendoes. I wish you'd tell me in plain English what you mean.'

'I mean you may be much annoyed.'

'That's still only a hint,' said Bessie.

Her sister just hesitated. 'It will be said of you that you've come after him—that you followed him.'

Bessie threw back her pretty head much as a startled hind, and a look flashed into her face that made Mrs Westgate get up. 'Who says such things as that?'

'People here.'

'I don't believe it.'

'You've a very convenient faculty of doubt. But my policy will be, as I say, very deep. I shall leave you to find out as many things as possible for yourself.'

Bessie fixed her eyes on her sister, and Mrs Westgate could have believed there were tears in them. 'Do they talk that way here?'

'You'll see. I shall let you alone.'

'Don't let me alone,' said Bessie Alden. 'Take me away.'

'No; I want to see what you make of it,' her sister continued.

'I don't understand.'

'You'll understand after Lord Lambeth has come,' said Mrs Westgate with a persistence of private amusement.

The two ladies had arranged that on this afternoon Willie Woodley should go with them to Hyde Park, where Bessie expected it would prove a rich passage to have sat on a little green chair under the great trees and beside Rotten Row.* The want of a suitable escort had hitherto hampered this adventure; but no escort, now, for such an expedition, could have been more suitable than their devoted young countryman, whose mission in life, it might almost be said, was to find chairs for ladies and who appeared on the stroke of half-past five adorned with every superficial grace that could qualify him for the scene.

'I've written to Lord Lambeth, my dear,' Mrs Westgate mentioned on coming into the room where Bessie, drawing on long grey gloves, had given their visitor the impression that she was particularly attuned. Bessie said nothing, but Willie Woodley exclaimed that his lordship was in town; he had seen his name in the *Morning Post*.* 'Do you read the *Morning Post*?' Mrs Westgate thereupon asked.

'Oh yes; it's great fun.' Mr Woodley almost spoke as if the pleasure were attended with physical risk.

'I want so to see it,' said Bessie, 'there's so much about it in Thackeray.'*

'I'll send it to you every morning!' cried the young man with elation.

He found them what Bessie thought excellent places under the great trees and beside the famous avenue the humours of which had been made familiar to the girl's childhood by the pictures in *Punch*.* The day was bright and warm and the crowd of riders and spectators, as well as the great procession of carriages, proportionately dense and many-coloured. The scene bore the stamp of the London social pressure at its highest, and it made our young woman think of more things than she could easily express to her companions. She sat silent, under her parasol, while her imagination, according to its wont, kept pace with the deep strong tide of the exhibition. Old impressions and preconceptions became living things before the show, and she found herself, amid the crowd of images, fitting a history to this person and a theory to that, and making a place for them all in her small private museum of types. But if she said little her sister on one side and Willie Woodley on the other delivered themselves in lively alternation.

'Look at that green dress with blue flounces. Quelle toilette!' said Mrs Westgate.

'That's the Marquis of Blackborough,' the young man was able to contribute—'the one in the queer white coat. I heard him speak the other night in the House of Lords; it was something about ramrods; he called them *wamwods*. He's an awful swell.'

'Did you ever see anything like the way they're pinned back?' Mrs Westgate resumed. 'They never know where to stop.'

'They do nothing but stop,' said Willie Woodley. 'It prevents them from walking. Here comes a great celebrity—Lady Beatrice Bellevue. She's awfully fast; see what little steps she takes.'

'Well, my dear,' Mrs Westgate pursued to Bessie, 'I hope you're getting some ideas for your couturière?'*

'I'm getting plenty of ideas,' said Bessie, 'but I don't know that my couturière would particularly appreciate them.'

Their companion presently perceived a mounted friend who drew up beside the barrier of the Row and beckoned to him. He went forward and the crowd of pedestrians closed about him, so that for some minutes he was hidden from sight. At last he reappeared, bringing a gentleman with him—a gentleman whom Bessie at first supposed to be his friend dismounted. But at a second glance she found herself looking at Lord Lambeth, who was shaking hands with her sister.

'I found him over there,' said Willie Woodley, 'and I told him you were here.'

And then Lord Lambeth, raising his hat afresh, shook hands with Bessie—'Fancy your being here!' He was blushing and smiling; he looked very handsome and he had a note of splendour he had not had in America. The girl's free fancy, as we know, was just then in marked exercise; so that the tall young Englishman, as he stood there looking down at her, had the benefit of it. 'He's handsomer and more splendid than anything I've ever seen,' she said to herself. And then she remembered he was a Marquis and she thought he somehow looked a Marquis. 'Really, you know,' he cried, 'you ought to have let a fellow know you've come!'

'I wrote to you an hour ago,' said Mrs Westgate.

'Doesn't all the world know it?' smiled Bessie.

'I assure you I didn't know it!' he insisted. 'Upon my honour I hadn't heard of it. Ask Woodley now; had I, Woodley?'

'Well, I think you're rather a humbug,' this gentleman brought forth.

'You don't believe that—do you, Miss Alden?' asked his lordship. 'You don't believe I'm rather a humbug, eh?'

'No,' said Bessie after an instant, but choosing and conferring a grace on the literal—'I don't.'

'You're too tall to stand up, Lord Lambeth,' Mrs Westgate pronounced 'You approach the normal only when you sit down. Be so good as to get a chair.'

He found one and placed it sidewise, close to the two ladies. 'If I hadn't met Woodley I should never have found you,' he went on. 'Should I, Woodley?'

'Well, I guess not,' said the young American.

'Not even with my letter?' asked Mrs Westgate.

'Ah well, I haven't got your letter yet; I suppose I shall get it this evening. It was awfully kind of you to write.'

'So I said to Bessie,' the elder lady observed.

'*Did* she say so, Miss Alden?' Lord Lambeth a little pointlessly enquired. 'I dare say you've been here a month.'

'We've been here three,' mocked Mrs Westgate.

'*Have* you been here three months?' the young man asked again of Bessie.

'It seems a long time,' Bessie answered.

He had but a brief wonder—he found something. 'I say, after that you had better not call me a humbug! I've only been in town three weeks, but you must have been hiding away. I haven't seen you anywhere.'

'Where should you have seen us—where should we have gone?' Mrs Westgate fairly put to him.

It found Willie Woodley at least ready. 'You should have gone to Hurlingham.'*

'No, let Lord Lambeth tell us,' Mrs Westgate insisted.

'There are plenty of places to go to,' he said—'each one stupider than the other. I mean people's houses. They send you cards.'

'No one has sent us a scrap of a card,' Bessie laughed.

Mrs Westgate attenuated. 'We're very quiet. We're here as travellers.'

'We've been to Madame Tussaud's,' Bessie further mentioned.

'Oh I say!' cried Lord Lambeth.

'We thought we should find your image there,' said Mrs Westgate—'yours and Mr Beaumont's.'

'In the Chamber of Horrors?'* laughed the young man.

'It did duty very well for a party,' said Mrs Westgate. 'All the women were *décolletées*,* and many of the figures looked as if they could almost speak.'

'Upon my word,' his lordship returned, 'you see people at London parties who look a long way from that!'

'Do you think Mr Woodley could find us Mr Beaumont?' asked the elder of the ladies.

He stared and looked about. 'I dare say he could. Percy sometimes comes here. Don't you think you could find him, Woodley? Make a dive or a dash for it.'

'Thank you; I've had enough of violent movement,' said Willie Woodley. 'I'll wait till Mr Beaumont comes to the surface.'

'I'll bring him to see you,' said Lord Lambeth. 'Where are you staying?'

'You'll find the address in my letter—Jones's Hotel.'

'Oh one of those places just out of Piccadilly? Beastly hole, isn't it?' Lord Lambeth enquired.

'I believe it's the best hotel in London,' said Mrs Westgate.

'But they give you awful rubbish to eat, don't they?' his lordship went on.

Mrs Westgate practised the same serenity. 'Awful.'

'I always feel so sorry for people who come up to town and go to live in those dens,' continued the young man. 'They eat nothing but filth.'

'Oh I say!' cried Willie Woodley.

'Well, and how do you like London, Miss Alden?' Lord Lambeth asked, unperturbed by this ejaculation.

The girl was prompt. 'I think it grand.'

'My sister likes it, in spite of the "filth"!' Mrs Westgate recorded.

'I hope then you're going to stop a long time.'

'As long as I can,' Bessie replied.

'And where's wonderful Mr Westgate?' asked Lord Lambeth of this gentleman's wife.

'He's where he always is—in that tiresome New York.'

'He must have staying power,' said the young man.

She appeared to consider. 'Well, he stays ahead of every one else.'

Lord Lambeth sat nearly an hour with his American friends; but it is not our purpose to relate their conversation in full. He addressed a great many remarks to the younger lady and finally turned toward her altogether, while Willie Woodley wasted a certain amount of effort to regale Mrs Westgate. Bessie herself was sparing of effusion; she thought, on her guard, of what her sister had said to her at luncheon. Little by little, however, she interested herself again in her English friend very much as she had done at Newport; only it seemed to her he might here become more interesting. He would be an unconscious part of the antiquity, the impressiveness, the picturesqueness of England; of all of which things poor Bessie Alden, like most familiars of the overciphered *tabula rasa*, was terribly at the mercy.

'I've often wished I were back at Newport,' the young man candidly stated. 'Those days I spent at your sister's were awfully jolly.'

'We enjoyed them very much; I hope your father's better.'

'Oh dear yes. When I got to England the old humbug was out grouse-shooting. It was what you call in America a gigantic fraud. My mother had got nervous. My three weeks at Newport seemed a happy dream.'

'America certainly is very different from England,' said Bessie.

'I hope you like England better, eh?' he returned almost persuasively.

'No Englishman can ask that seriously of a person of another country.'

He turned his cheerful brown eyes on her. 'You mean it's a matter of course?'

'If I were English,' said Bessie, 'it would certainly seem to me a matter of course that every one should be a good patriot.'

'Oh dear, yes; patriotism's everything.' He appeared not quite to follow, but was clearly contented. 'Now what are you going to do here?'

'On Thursday I'm going to the Tower.'

'The Tower?'

'The Tower of London. Did you never hear of it?'

'Oh yes, I've been there,' said Lord Lambeth. 'I was taken there by my governess when I was six years old. It's a rum idea your going there.'

'Do give me a few more rum ideas then. I want to see everything of that sort. I'm going to Hampton Court and to Windsor and to the Dulwich Gallery.'*

He seemed greatly amused. 'I wonder you don't go to Rosherville Gardens.'*

Bessie yearned. 'Are they interesting?'

'Oh wonderful!'

'Are they weirdly old? That's all I care for,' she said.

'They're tremendously old; they're all falling to ruins.'

The girl rose to it. 'I think there's nothing so charming as an old ruinous garden. We must certainly go there.'

Her friend broke out into mirth. 'I say, Woodley, here's Miss Alden wants to go down to Rosherville Gardens! Hang it, they *are* "weird"!'

Willie Woodley looked a little blank; he was caught in the fact of ignorance of an apparently conspicuous feature of London life. But in a moment he turned it off. 'Very well,' he said, 'I'll write for a permit.'

Lord Lambeth's exhilaration increased. "Gad, I believe that, to get your money's worth over here, you Americans would go anywhere!'

'We wish to go to Parliament,' said Bessie. 'That's one of the first things.'

'Ah it would bore you to death!' he returned.

'We wish to hear you speak.'

'I never speak—except to young ladies.'

She looked at him from under the shade of her parasol. 'You're very strange,' she then quietly concluded. 'I don't think I approve of you.'

'Ah now don't be severe, Miss Alden!' he cried with the note of sincerity. 'Please don't be severe. I want you to like me—awfully.'

'To like you awfully? You mustn't laugh at me then when I make mistakes. I regard it as my right—as a free-born American— to make as many mistakes as I choose.'

'Upon my word I didn't laugh at you,' the young man pleaded.

'And not only that,' Bessie went on; 'but I hold that all my mistakes should be set down to my credit. You must think the better of me for them.'

'I can't think better of you than I do,' he declared.

Again, shadily, she took him in. 'You certainly speak very well to young ladies. But why don't you address the House?—isn't that what they call it?'

'Because I've nothing to say.'

'Haven't you a great position?' she demanded.

He looked a moment at the back of his glove. 'I'll set that down as one of your mistakes—to your credit.' And as if he disliked talking about his position he changed the subject. 'I wish you'd let me go with you to the Tower and to Hampton Court and to all those other places.'

'We shall be most happy,' said Bessie.

'And of course I shall be delighted to show you the Houses of

Parliament—some day that suits you. There are a lot of things I want to do for you. I want you to have a good time. And I should like very much to present some of my friends to you if it wouldn't bore you. Then it would be awfully kind of you to come down to Branches.'

'We're much obliged to you, Lord Lambeth,' said Bessie. 'And what may Branches be?'

'It's a house in the country. I think you might like it.'

Willie Woodley and Mrs Westgate were at this moment sitting in silence, and the young man's ear caught these last words of the other pair. 'He's inviting Miss Bessie to one of his castles,' he murmured to his companion.

Mrs Westgate hereupon, foreseeing what she mentally called 'complications', immediately got up; and the two ladies, taking leave of their English friend, returned, under conduct of their American, to Jones's Hotel.

V

LORD LAMBETH came to see them on the morrow, bringing Percy Beaumont with him—the latter having at once declared his intention of neglecting none of the usual offices of civility. This declaration, however, on his kinsman's informing him of the advent of the two ladies, had been preceded by another exchange.

'Here they are then and you're in for it.'

'And what am I in for?' the younger man had enquired.

'I'll let your mother give it a name. With all respect to whom,' Percy had added, 'I must decline on this occasion to do any more police duty. The Duchess must look after you herself.'

'I'll give her a chance,' the Duchess's son had returned a trifle grimly. 'I shall make her go and see them.'

'She won't do it, my boy.'

'We'll see if she doesn't,' said Lord Lambeth.

But if Mr Beaumont took a subtle view of the arrival of the fair strangers at Jones's Hotel he was sufficiently capable of a still deeper refinement to offer them a smiling countenance. He fell into animated conversation—conversation animated at least on *her* side—with Mrs Westgate, while his companion appealed more confusedly to the younger lady. Mrs Westgate began confessing and protesting, declaring and discriminating.

'I must say London's a great deal brighter and prettier just now than it was when I was here last—in the month of November. There's evidently a great deal going on, and you seem to have a good many flowers. I've no doubt it's very charming for all you people and that you amuse yourselves immensely. It's very good of you to let Bessie and me come and sit and look at you. I suppose you'll think I'm very satirical, but I must confess that that's the feeling I have in London.'

'I'm afraid I don't quite understand to what feeling you allude,' said Percy Beaumont.

'The feeling that it's all very well for you English people. Everything's beautifully arranged for you.'

'It seems to me it's very well arranged here for some Americans sometimes,' Percy plucked up spirit to answer.

'For some of them, yes—if they like to be patronised. But I must say I don't like to be patronised. I may be very eccentric and undisciplined and unreasonable, but I confess I never was fond of patronage. I like to associate with people on the same terms as I do in my own country; that's a peculiar taste that I have. But here people seem to expect something else—really I can't make out quite what. I'm afraid you'll think I'm very ungrateful, for I certainly have received in one way and another a great deal of attention. The last time I was here a lady sent me a message that I was at liberty to come and pay her my respects.'

'Dear me, I hope you didn't go,' Mr Beaumont cried.

'You're deliriously naïf, I must say that for you!' Mrs Westgate promptly pursued. 'It must be a great advantage to you here in London. I suppose that if I myself had a little more naïveté—of your blessed national lack of any approach to a sense for shades—I should enjoy it more. I should be content to sit on a chair in the Park and see the people pass, to be told that this is the Duchess of Suffolk and that the Lord Chamberlain, and that I must be thankful for the privilege of beholding them. I dare say it's very peevish and critical of me to ask for anything else. But I was always critical—it's the joy of my life—and I freely confess to the sin of being fastidious. I'm told there's some remarkably superior second-rate society provided here for strangers. *Merci!* I don't want any superior second-rate society. I want the society I've been accustomed to.'

Percy mustered a rueful gaiety. 'I hope you don't call Lambeth and me second-rate!'

'Oh I'm accustomed to you!' said Mrs Westgate. 'Do you know you English sometimes make the most wonderful speeches? The first time I came to London I went out to dine—as I told you, I've received a great deal of attention. After dinner, in the drawing-room, I had some conversation with an old lady—no, you mustn't look that way: I assure you I had! I forget what we talked about, but she presently said, in allusion to something we were discussing: "Oh, you know, the aristocracy do so-and-so, but in one's own class of life it's very different." In one's own class of life! What's a poor unprotected American woman to do in a country where she is liable to have that sort of thing said to her?'

'I should say she's not to mind, not a rap—though you seem to get hold of some very queer old ladies. I compliment you on your acquaintance!' Percy pursued. 'If you're trying to bring me to admit that London's an odious place you'll not succeed. I'm extremely fond of it and think it the jolliest place in the world.'

'Pour vous autres—I never said the contrary,' Mrs Westgate retorted—an expression made use of, this last, because both inter-locutors had begun to raise their voices. Mr Beaumont natur-ally didn't like to hear the seat of his existence abused, and Mrs Westgate, no less naturally, didn't like a stubborn debater.

'Hallo!' said Lord Lambeth; 'what are they up to now?' And he came away from the window, where he had been standing with Bessie.

'I quite agree with a very clever countrywoman of mine,' the elder lady continued with charming ardour even if with imperfect relevancy. She smiled at the two gentlemen for a moment with terrible brightness, as if to toss at their feet—upon their native heath—the gauntlet of defiance. 'For me there are only two social positions worth speaking of—that of an American lady and that of the Emperor of Russia.'

'And what do you do with the American gentlemen?' asked Lord Lambeth.

'She leaves them in America!' said his comrade.

On the departure of their visitors Bessie mentioned that Lord Lambeth would come the next day, to go with them to the Tower, and that he had kindly offered to bring his 'trap'* and drive them all through the city. Mrs Westgate listened in silence to this news and for some time afterwards also said nothing. But at last, 'If you hadn't requested me the other day not to speak of it,' she began, 'there's something I'd make bold to ask you.' Bessie frowned a little; her dark blue eyes grew more dark than blue. But her sister went on. 'As it is I'll take the risk. You're not in love with Lord Lambeth: I believe it perfectly. Very good. But is there by chance any danger of your becoming so? It's a very simple question—don't take offence. I've a particular reason', said Mrs Westgate, 'for wanting to know.'

Bessie for some moments said nothing; she only looked displeased. 'No; there's no danger,' she at last answered with a certain dryness.

'Then I should like to frighten them!' cried her sister, clasping jewelled hands.

'To frighten whom?'

'All these people. Lord Lambeth's family and friends.'

The girl wondered. 'How should you frighten them?'

'It wouldn't be I—it would be you. It would frighten them to suppose you holding in thrall his lordship's young affections.'

Our young lady, her clear eyes still overshadowed by her dark brows, continued to examine it. 'Why should that frighten them?'

Mrs Westgate winged her shaft with a smile before launching it. 'Because they think you're not good enough. You're a charming girl, beautiful and amiable, intelligent and clever, and as *bien-élevée* as it is possible to be; but you're not a fit match for Lord Lambeth.'

Bessie showed again a coldness. 'Where do you get such

extraordinary ideas? You've said some such odd things lately. My dear Kitty, where do you collect them?'

But Kitty, unabashed, held to her idea. 'Yes, it would put them on pins and needles, and it wouldn't hurt *you*. Mr Beaumont's already most uneasy. I could soon see that.'

The girl turned it over. 'Do you mean they spy on him, that they interfere with him?'

'I don't know what power they have to interfere, but I know that a British *materfamilias*—and when she's a Duchess into the bargain—is often a force to be reckoned with.'

It has already been intimated that before certain appearances of strange or sinister cast our young woman was apt to shy off into scepticism. She abstained on the present occasion from expressing disbelief, for she wished not to irritate her sister. But she said to herself that Kitty had been misinformed—that this was a traveller's tale. Though she was a girl of quick imagination there could in the nature of things be no truth for her in the attribution to her of a vulgar identity. Only the form she gave her doubt was: 'I must say that in that case I'm very sorry for Lord Lambeth.'

Mrs Westgate, more and more exhilarated by her own scheme, irradiated interest. 'If I could only believe it was safe! But when you begin to pity him I, on my side, am afraid.'

'Afraid of what?'

'Of your pitying him too much.'

Bessie turned impatiently off—then at the end of a minute faced about. 'What if I *should* pity him too much?'

Mrs Westgate hereupon averted herself, but after a moment's reflexion met the case. 'It would come, after all, to the same thing.'

Lord Lambeth came the next day with his trap, when the two ladies, attended by Willie Woodley, placed themselves under his guidance and were conveyed eastward, through some of the most fascinating, as Bessie called them, even though the duskiest districts, to the great turreted donjon that overlooks the London shipping. They alighted together to enter the famous fortress, where they secured the services of a venerable beef-eater,* who, ignoring the presence of other dependants on his leisure, made a fine exclusive party of them and marched them through courts and corridors, through armouries and prisons. He delivered his usual peripatetic discourse, and they stopped and stared and peeped and stooped according as he marshalled and directed them. Bessie appealed to this worthy—even on more heads than he seemed aware of; she overtaxed, in her earnestness, his learnt lesson and found the place, as she more than once mentioned to him, quite delirious. Lord Lambeth was in high good-humour; his delirium at least was gay and he betrayed afresh that aptitude for the simpler forms of ironic comment that the girl had noted in him. Willie Woodley kept looking at the ceilings and tapping the walls with the knuckle of a pearl-grey glove; and Mrs Westgate, asking at frequent intervals to be allowed to sit down and wait till they came back, was as frequently informed that they would never do anything so weak. When it befell that Bessie's glowing appeals, chiefly on collateral points of English history, but left the warder gaping she resorted straight to Lord Lambeth. His lordship then pleaded gross incompetence, declaring he knew nothing about that sort of thing and greatly diverted, to all appearance, at being treated as an authority.

'You can't honestly expect people to know as awfully much as you,' he said.

'I should expect you to know a great deal more,' Bessie Alden returned.

'Well, women always know more than men about names and dates and historical characters,' he said. 'There was Lady Jane Grey we've just been hearing about, who went in for Latin and Greek and all the learning of her age.'

'*You* have no right to be ignorant at all events,' Bessie argued with all her freedom.

'Why haven't I as good a right as any one else?'

'Because you've lived in the midst of all these things.'

'What things do you mean? Axes and blocks and thumbscrews?'

'All these historical things. You belong to an historical family.'

'Bessie really harks back too much to the dead past—she makes too much of it,' Mrs Westgate opined, catching the sense of this colloquy.

'Yes, you hark back,' the young man laughed, thankful for a formula. 'You do make too much of the dead past.'

He went with the ladies a couple of days later to Hampton Court, Willie Woodley being also of the party. The afternoon was charming, the famous horse-chestnuts blossomed to admiration, and Lord Lambeth, who found in Miss Alden the improving governess, he declared, of his later immaturity, as Mademoiselle Boquet, dragging him by the hand to view all lions, had been that of his earliest, pronounced the old red palace not half so beastly as he had supposed. Bessie herself rose to raptures; she went about murmuring and "raving". 'It's too lovely; it's too enchanting; it's too exactly what it ought to be!'

At Hampton Court the tinkling flocks are not provided with an official bellwether, but are left to browse at discretion on the tough herbage of History. It happened in this manner that, in default of another informant, our young woman, who on doubtful questions was able to suggest a great many alternatives, found herself again apply for judicious support to Lord Lambeth. He, however, could but once more declare himself a broken reed and that his education, in such matters, had been sadly neglected.

'And I'm sorry it makes you so wretched,' he further professed.

'You're so disappointing, you know,' she returned; but more in pity—pity for herself—than in anger.

'Ah now don't say that! That's the worst thing you could possibly say.'

'No'—she spoke with a sad lucidity—'it's not so bad as to say that I had expected nothing of you.'

'I don't know'—and he seemed to rejoice in a chance to demur. 'Give me a notion of the sort of thing you expected.'

'Well, that you'd be more what I should like to be—what I should try to be—in your place.'

'Ah my place!' he groaned. 'You're always talking about my place.'

The girl gave him a look; he might have thought she coloured; and for a little she made no rejoinder. 'Does it strike you that I'm always talking about your place?'

'I'm sure you do it a great honour,' he said as if fearing he had sounded uncivil.

'I've often thought about it,' she went on after a moment.

'I've often thought of your future as an hereditary legislator. An hereditary legislator ought to know so many things, oughtn't he?'

'Not if he doesn't legislate.'

'But you *will* legislate one of these days—you may have to at any time; it's absurd your saying you won't. You're very much looked up to here—I'm assured of that.'

'I don't know that I ever noticed it.'

'It's because you're used to it then. You ought to fill the place.'

'How do you mean, fill it?' asked Lord Lambeth.

'You ought to be very clever and brilliant—to be "up" in almost everything.'

He turned on her his handsome young face of profane wonder. 'Shall I tell you something? A young man in my position, as you call it —'

'I didn't invent the term,' she interposed. 'I've seen it in a great many books.'

'Hang it, you're always at your books! A fellow in my position then does well enough at the worst—he muddles along whatever he does. That's about what I mean to say.'

'Well, if your own people are content with you,' Bessie laughed, 'it's not for me to complain. But I shall always think that properly you should have a great mind—a great character.'

'Ah that's very theoretic!' the young man promptly brought out. 'Depend upon it, that's a Yankee prejudice.'

'Happy the country then,' she as eagerly declared, 'where people's prejudices make so for light.'*

He stopped short, with his slightly strained gaiety, as for the pleasantness of high argument. 'What it comes to then is that we're all here a pack of fools and me the biggest of the lot?'

'I said nothing so rude of a great people—and a great person. But I must repeat that you personally are—in your representative capacity that's to be—disappointing.'

'My dear Miss Alden,' he simply cried at this, 'I'm the best fellow in the world!'

'Ah if it were not for that!' she beautifully smiled.

Mrs Westgate had many more friends in London than she pretended, and before long had renewed acquaintance with most of them. Their hospitality was prompt, so that, one thing leading to another, she began, as the phrase is, to go out. Bessie Alden, in this way, saw a good deal of what she took great pleasure in calling to herself English society. She went to balls and danced, she went to dinners and talked, she went to concerts and listened—at concerts Bessie always listened—she went to exhibitions and wondered. Her enjoyment was keen and her curiosity insatiable, and, grateful in general for all her opportunities, she especially prized the privilege of meeting certain celebrated persons, authors and artists, philosophers and statesmen, of whose renown she had been a humble and distant beholder and who now, as part of the frequent furniture of London drawing-rooms, struck her as stars fallen from the firmament and become palpable—revealing also sometimes on contact qualities not to have been predicted of bodies sidereal. Bessie, who knew so many of her contemporaries by reputation, lost in this way certain fond illusions; but on the other hand she had innumerable satisfactions and enthusiasms, and she laid bare the wealth of her emotions to a dear friend of her own sex in Boston, with whom she was in voluminous correspondence. Some of her sentiments indeed she sought mildly to flash upon Lord Lambeth, who came almost every day to Jones's Hotel and whom Mrs Westgate admitted to be really devoted. Captain Littledale, it appeared, had gone to India; and of several others of this lady's ex-pensioners—gentlemen who, as she said, had made, in New York, a club-house of her drawing-room—no tidings were to be obtained; but this particular friend of other days was certainly attentive enough to make up for the accidental absences, the short memories, the remarked lapses, of every one else. He drove the sisters in the Park, took them to visit private collections of pictures and, having a house of his own, invited them to luncheon, to tea, to dinner, to supper even after the arduous German opera. Mrs Westgate, following the fashion of many of her countrywomen, caused herself and her companion to be presented at the English Court by her diplomatic representative— for it was in this manner that she alluded to the American Minister to England,* enquiring what on earth he was put there for if not to make the proper arrangements for her reception at Court.

Lord Lambeth expressed a hatred of Courts, but he had social privileges or exercised some court function—these undiscriminated attributes, dim backgrounds where old gold seemed to shine through transparent conventions, were romantically rich to our young heroine—that involved his support of his sovereign on the day on which the two ladies at Jones's Hotel repaired to Buckingham Palace in a remarkable coach sent by his lordship to fetch them. He appeared in a gorgeous uniform, and Bessie Alden was particularly struck with his glory—especially when on her asking him, rather foolishly as she felt, if he were a loyal subject, he replied that he was a loyal subject to herself. This pronouncement was emphasised by his dancing with her at a royal ball to which the two ladies afterwards went, and was not impaired by the fact that she thought he danced very ill. He struck her as wonderfully kind; she asked herself with growing vivacity why he should be so kind. It was just his character—that seemed the natural reply. She had told her relative how much she liked him, and now that she liked him more she wondered at her excess. She liked him for his clear nature; to this question as well that seemed the natural answer. The truth was that when once the impressions of London life began to crowd thickly upon her she completely forgot her subtle sister's warning on the cynicism of public opinion. It had given her great pain at the moment; but there was no particular reason why she should remember it: it corresponded too little with any sensible reality. Besides which there was her habit, her beautiful system, of consenting to know nothing of human baseness or of the vulgar side. There were things, just as there were people, that were as nought from the moment one ignored them. She was accordingly not haunted with the sense of a low imputation. She wasn't in love with Lord Lambeth—she assured herself of that. It will immediately be observed that when such assurances become necessary the state of a young lady's affections is already ambiguous; and indeed the girl made no attempt to dissimulate (to her finer intelligence) that 'appeal of type'—she had a ready name for it—to which her gallant hovering gentleman caused her wonderingly to respond. She was fully aware that she liked it, this so unalloyed image of the simple candid manly healthy English temperament. She spoke to herself of it as if she liked the man for it instead of her liking it for the man. She cherished the thought of his bravery, which she had never in the least seen tested, enjoyed a fond view in him of the free and instinctive range of the 'gentlemanly' character, and was as familiar with his good looks as if she habitually handed him out his neckties. She was perfectly conscious moreover of privately dilating on his more adventitious merits—of the effect on her imagination of the large opportunities of so splendid a person; opportunities she hardly knew for what, but, as she supposed, for doing great things, for setting an example, for exerting an influence, for conferring happiness, for encouraging the arts. She had an ideal of conduct for a young man who should find himself in this grand position, and she tried to adapt it to her friend's behaviour as you might attempt to fit a silhouette in cut paper over a shadow projected on a wall. Bessie Alden's silhouette, however, refused to coincide at all points with his lordship's figure; a want of harmony that she sometimes deplored beyond discretion. It was his own affair she at moments told herself—it wasn't *her* concern the least in the world. When he was absent it was of course less striking—then he might have seemed sufficiently to unite high responsibilities with high braveries. But when he sat there within sight, laughing and talking with his usual effect of natural salubrity and mental mediocrity, she took the measure of his shortcoming and felt acutely that if his position was, so to speak, heroic, there was little of that large line in the young man himself. Then her imagination wandered away from him—very far away; for it was an incontestable fact that at these moments he lagged ever so much behind it. He affected her as on occasion, dreadful to say, almost *actively* stupid. It may have been that while she so curiously enquired and so critically brooded *her* personal wit, her presence of mind, made no great show—though it is also possible that she sometimes positively charmed, or at least interested, her friend by this very betrayal of the frequent, the distant and unreported, excursion. So it would have hung together that a part of her unconscious appeal to him from the first had been in his feeling her judge and appraise him more freely and irresponsibly—more at her ease and her leisure, as it were—than several young ladies with whom he had passed for adventurously intimate. To be convinced of her 'cleverness' and yet also to be aware of her appreciation—when the cleverness might have been after all but dangerous and complicating—all made, to Lord Lambeth's sense, for convenience and cheer. Hadn't he compassed the satisfaction, that high aim of young men greatly placed and greatly moneyed, of being liked for himself? It was true a cynical counsellor might have whispered to him: 'Liked for yourself? Ah not so very awfully *much*!' He had at any rate the constant hope of adding to that quantity.

It may not seem to fit in—but the truth was strange—that Bessie Alden, when he struck her as 'deficient', found herself aspiring by that very reason to some finer way of liking him. This was fairly indeed on grounds of conscience—because she felt he had been thoroughly 'nice' to her sister and so deemed it no more than fair that she should think as well of him as he thought of her. The effort in question was possibly sometimes not so successful as it might have been, the result being at moments an irritation, which, though consciously vague, was yet, with inconsequence, acute enough to express itself in hostile criticism of several British institutions. Bessie went to entertainments at which she met Lord Lambeth, but also to others at which he was neither actually nor imaginably present; and it was chiefly at these latter that she encountered those literary and artistic celebrities of whom mention has been made. After a while she reduced the matter to a principle. If he should appear anywhere she might take it for a flat sign that there would be neither poets nor philosophers; and as a result—for it was almost a direct result—she used to enumerate to the young man these objects of her admiration.

'You seem to be awfully fond of that sort of people,' he said one day as if the idea had just occurred to him.

'They're the people in England I'm most curious to see,' she promptly replied.

'I suppose that's because you've read so much,' Lord Lambeth gallantly threw off.

'I've *not* read so much. It's because we think so much of them at home.'

'Oh I see! In your so awfully clever Boston.'

'Not only in our awfully clever Boston, but in our just commonly clever everywhere. We hold them in great honour,' said Bessie. 'It's they who go to the best dinner-parties.'

'I dare say you're right. I can't say I know many of them.'

'It's a pity you don't,' she returned. 'It would do you some good.'

'I dare say it would,' said the young man very humbly. 'But I must say I don't like the looks of some of them.'

'Neither do I—of some of them. But there are all kinds, and many of them are charming.'

'I've talked with two or three of them,' Lord Lambeth went on, 'and I thought they had a kind of fawning manner.'

'Why should they fawn?' Bessie demanded.

'I'm sure I don't know. Why indeed?'

'Perhaps you only thought so,' she suggested.

'Well, of course,' her companion allowed, 'that's a kind of thing that can't be proved.'

'In America they don't fawn,' she went on.

'Don't they? Ah well then they must be better company.'

She had a pause. 'That's one of the few things I don't like about England,—your keeping the distinguished people apart.'

'How do you mean, apart?'

'Why letting them come only to certain places. You never see them.'

All his pleasant face wondered—he seemed to take it as another of her rather stiff riddles. 'What people do you mean?'

'The eminent people; the authors and artists; the clever people.'

'Oh there are other eminent people besides those!' said Lord Lambeth.

'Well, you certainly keep them apart,' Bessie earnestly contended.

'And there are plenty of other clever people.'

It was spoken with a fine simple faith, yet the tone of it made her laugh. '"Plenty"? How many?'

On another occasion—just after a dinner-party—she mentioned something else in England she didn't like.

'Oh I say!' he cried; 'haven't you abused us enough?'

'I've never abused you at all,' said Bessie; 'but I don't like your "precedence".'

She was to feel relieved at his not taking it solemnly. 'It isn't *my* precedence!'

'Yes, it's yours—just exactly yours; and I think it's odious,' she insisted.

'I never saw such a young lady for discussing things! Has some one had the impudence to go before you?' Lord Lambeth asked.

'It's not the going before me I object to,' said Bessie; 'it's their pretending they've a right to do it—a right I should grovellingly recognise.'

'I never saw such a person, either, for not "recognising", let alone for not "grovelling". Every one here has to grovel to somebody or to something—and no doubt it's all beastly. But one takes the thick with the thin, and it saves a lot of trouble.'

'It *makes* a lot of trouble, by which I mean a lot of ugliness. It's horrid!' Bessie maintained.

'But how would you have the first people go?' the young man asked. 'They can't go last, you know.'

'Whom do you mean by the first people?'

'Ah if you mean to question first principles!' said Lord Lambeth.

'If those are your first principles no wonder some of your arrangements are horrid!' she cried with a charming but not wholly sincere ferocity. 'I'm a silly chit, no doubt, so of course I go last; but imagine what Kitty must feel on being informed that she's not at liberty to budge till certain other ladies have passed out!'

'Oh I say, she's not "informed"'!' he protested. 'No one would do such a thing as that.'

'She's made to feel it—as if they were afraid she'd make a rush for the door. No, you've a lovely country'—she clung as for consistency to her discrimination—'but your precedence is horrid.'

'I certainly shouldn't think your sister would like it,' Lord Lambeth said with even exaggerated gravity. But she couldn't induce him—amused as he almost always was at the effect of giving her, as he called it, her head—to join her in more formal reprobation of this repulsive custom, which he spoke of as a convenience she would destroy without offering a better in its place.

VI

PERCY BEAUMONT had all this time been a very much less frequent visitor at Jones's Hotel than his former fellow traveller; he had in fact called but twice on the two American ladies. Lord Lambeth, who often saw him, reproached him with his neglect and declared that though Mrs Westgate had said nothing about it he made no doubt she was secretly wounded by it. 'She suffers too much to speak,' said his comrade.

'That's all gammon,' Percy returned; 'there's a limit to what people can suffer!' And though sending no apologies to Jones's Hotel he undertook in a manner to explain his absence. 'You're always there yourself, confound you, and that's reason enough for my not going.'

'I don't see why. There's enough for both of us.'

'Well, I don't care to be a witness of your reckless passion,' said Percy Beaumont.

His friend turned on him a cold eye and for a moment said nothing, presently, however, speaking a little stiffly. 'My passion doesn't make such a show as you might suppose, considering what a demonstrative beggar I am.'

'I don't want to know anything about it—anything whatever,' said Beaumont. 'Your mother asks me every time she sees me whether I believe you're really lost—and Lady Pimlico does the same. I prefer to be able to answer that I'm in complete ignorance, that I never go there. I stay away for consistency's sake. As I said the other day they must look after you themselves.'

'Well, you're wonderfully considerate,' the young man returned. 'They never question *me*.'

'They're afraid of you. They're afraid of annoying you and making you worse. So they go to work very cautiously, and, somewhere or other, they get their information. They know a great deal about you. They know you've been with those ladies to the dome of Saint Paul's and—where was the other place?—to the Thames Tunnel.'*

'If all their knowledge is as accurate as that it must be very valuable,' said Lord Lambeth.

'Well, at any rate, they know you've been visiting the "sights of the metropolis". They think—very naturally, as it seems to me—that when you take to visiting the sights of the metropolis with a little nobody of an American girl something may be supposed to be "up".' The young man met this remark with scornful laughter, but his companion continued after a pause: 'I told you just now that I cultivate my ignorance, but I find I can no longer stand my suspense. I confess I do want to know whether you propose to marry Miss Alden.'

On this point Lord Lambeth gave his questioner no prompt satisfaction; he only mused—frowningly, portentously. 'By Jove they go rather too far. They *shall* have cause to worry—I promise them.'

Percy Beaumont, however, continued to aim at lucidity. 'You don't, it's true, quite redeem your threats. You said the other day you'd make your mother call.'

Lord Lambeth just hung fire. 'Well, I asked her to.'

'And she declined?'

'Yes, but she shall do it yet.'

'Upon my word,' said Percy, 'if she gets much more scared I verily believe she will.' His friend watched him on this, and he went on. 'She'll go to the girl herself.'

'How do you mean "go" to her?'

'She'll try to get "at" her—to square her. She won't care what she does.'

Lord Lambeth turned away in silence; he took twenty steps and slowly returned. 'She had better take care what she does. I've invited Mrs Westgate and Miss Alden to Branches, and this evening I shall name a day.'

'And shall you invite your mother and your sisters to meet them?'

Lord Lambeth indulged in one of his rare discriminations. 'I shall give them the opportunity.'

'That will touch the Duchess up,' said Percy Beaumont. 'I "guess" she'll come.'

'She may do as she pleases.'

'Then do you really propose to marry the little sister?'

'I like the way you talk about it!' the young man cried. 'She won't gobble me down. Don't be afraid.'

'She won't leave you on your knees,' Percy declared. 'What the devil's the inducement?'

'You talk about proposing—wait till I *have* proposed,' Lord Lambeth went on.

His friend looked at him harder. 'That's right, my dear chap. Think of *all* the bearings.'

'She's a charming girl,' pursued his lordship.

'Of course she's a charming girl. I don't know a girl more charming—in a very quiet way. But there are other charming girls—charming in all sorts of ways—nearer home.'

'I particularly like her spirit,' said Bessie's admirer—almost as on a policy of aggravation.

'What's the peculiarity of her spirit?'

'She's not afraid, and she says things out and thinks herself as good as any one. She's the only girl I've ever seen,' Lord Lambeth explained, 'who hasn't seemed to me dying to marry me.'

Mr Beaumont considered it. 'How do you know she isn't dying if you haven't felt her pulse? I mean if you haven't asked her?'

'I don't know how; but I know it.'

'I'm sure she asked *me*—over there—questions enough about your property and your titles,' Percy declared.

'She has done that to me too—again and again,' his friend returned. 'But she wants to know about everything.'

'Everything? Ah I'll warrant she wants to know. Depend upon it she's dying to marry you just as much, and just by the same law, as all the rest of them.'

It appeared to give the young man, for a moment, something rather special to think of. 'I shouldn't like her to refuse me— I shouldn't like that.'

'If the thing would be so disagreeable then, both to you and to her, in heaven's name leave it alone.' Such was the moral drawn by Mr Beaumont; which left him practically the last word in the discussion.

Mrs Westgate, on her side, had plenty to say to her sister about the rarity of the latter's visits and the non-appearance at their own door of the Duchess of Bayswater. She confessed, however, to taking more pleasure in this hush of symptoms than she could have taken in the most lavish attentions on the part of that great lady. 'It's unmistakeable,' she said, 'delightfully unmistakeable; a most interesting sign that we've made them wretched. The day we dined with him I was really sorry for the poor boy.' It will have been gathered that the entertainment offered by Lord Lambeth to his American friends had been graced by the presence of no near relation. He had invited several choice spirits to meet them, but the ladies of his immediate family were to Mrs Westgate's sense—a sense perhaps morbidly acute—conspicuous by their hostile absence.

'I don't want to work you up any further,' Bessie at last ventured to remark, 'but I don't know why you should have so many theories about Lord Lambeth's poor mother. You know a great many young men in New York without knowing their mothers.'

Mrs Westgate rested deep eyes on her sister and then turned away. 'My dear Bessie, you're superb!'

'One thing's certain'—the girl continued not to blench at her irony. 'If I believed I were a cause of annoyance, however unwitting, to Lord Lambeth's family I should insist —'

'Insist on my leaving England?' Mrs Westgate broke in.

'No, not that. I want to go to the National Gallery again; I want to see Stratford-on-Avon and Canterbury Cathedral. But I should insist on his ceasing relations with us.'

'That would be very modest and very pretty of you—but you wouldn't do it at this point.'

'Why do you say "at this point"?' Bessie asked. 'Have I ceased to be modest?'

'You care for him too much. A month ago, when you said you didn't, I believe it was quite true. But at present, my dear child,' said Mrs Westgate, 'you wouldn't find it quite so simple a matter never to see Lord Lambeth again. I've watched it come on.'

'You're mistaken,' Bessie declared. 'You don't understand.'

'Ah you poor proud thing, don't be perverse!' her companion returned.

The girl gave the matter, thus admonished, some visible thought. 'I know him better certainly, if you mean that. And I like him very much. But I don't like him enough to make trouble for him with his family. However, I don't believe in that.'

'I like the way you say "however"!' Mrs Westgate commented. 'Do you pretend you wouldn't be glad to marry him?'

Again Bessie calmly considered. 'It would take a great deal more than is at all imaginable to make me marry him.'

Her relative showed an impatience. 'And what's the great difficulty?'

'The great difficulty is that I shouldn't care to,' said Bessie Alden.

The morning after Lord Lambeth had had with his own frankest critic that exchange of ideas which has just been narrated, the ladies at Jones's Hotel received from him a written invitation to pay their projected visit to Branches Castle on the following Tuesday. 'I think I've made up a very pleasant party,' his lordship went on. 'Several people whom you know, and my mother and sisters, who have been accidentally prevented from making your acquaintance sooner.' Bessie at this lost no time in calling her sister's attention to the injustice she had done the Duchess of Bayswater, whose hostility was now proved to be a vain illusion.

'Wait till you see if she comes,' said Mrs Westgate. 'And if she's to meet us at her son's house the obligation's all the greater for her to call on us.'

Bessie hadn't to wait long, for it appeared that her friend's parent now descried the direction in which, according to her companion's observation, courtesy pointed. On the morrow, early in the afternoon, two cards were brought to the apartment of the American ladies—one of them bearing the name of the Duchess of Bayswater and the other that of the Countess of Pimlico. Mrs Westgate glanced at the clock. 'It isn't yet four,' she said; 'they've come early; they want really to find us. We'll receive them.' And she gave orders that her visitors should be admitted. A few moments later they were introduced and a solemn exchange of amenities took place. The Duchess was a large lady with a fine fresh colour; the Countess of Pimlico was very pretty and elegant.

The Duchess looked about her as she sat down—looked not especially at Mrs Westgate. 'I dare say my son has told you that I've been wanting to come to see you,' she dropped—and from no towering nor inconvenient height.

'You're very kind,' said Mrs Westgate vaguely—her conscience not allowing her to assent to this proposition, and indeed not permitting her to enunciate her own with any appreciable emphasis.

'He tells us you were so kind to him in America,' said the Duchess.

'We're very glad', Mrs Westgate replied, 'to have been able to make him feel a little more—a little less—a little at home.'

'I think he stayed at your house,' the visitor more heavily breathed, but as an overture, across to Bessie Alden.

Mrs Westgate intercepted the remark. 'A very short time indeed.'

'Oh!' said the Duchess; and she continued to address her interest to Bessie, who was engaged in conversation with her daughter.

'Do you like London?' Lady Pimlico had asked of Bessie, after looking at her a good deal—at her face and her hands, her dress and her hair.

The girl was prompt and clear. 'Very much indeed.'

'Do you like this hotel?'

'It's very comfortable.'

'Do you like stopping at hotels?' Lady Pimlico asked after a pause.

'I'm very fond of travelling, and I suppose hotels are a necessary part of it. But they're not the part I'm fondest of,' Bessie without difficulty admitted.

'Oh I hate travelling!' said Lord Lambeth's sister, who transferred her attention to Mrs Westgate.

'My son tells me you're going to Branches,' the Duchess presently resumed.

'Lord Lambeth has been so good as to ask us,' said Mrs Westgate, who felt herself now under the eyes of both visitors

and who had her customary happy consciousness of a distinguished appearance. The only mitigation of her felicity on this
point was that, having taken in every item of that of the Duchess,
she said to herself: 'She won't know how well I'm dressed!'

'He has been so good as to tell me he expects me, but I'm not
quite sure of what I can do,' the noble lady exhaled.

'He had offered us the p— the prospect of meeting you,'
Mrs Westgate further contributed.

'I hate the country at this season,' the Duchess went on.

Her hostess melted to sweetness. 'I delight in it at all seasons.
And I think it now above all pleasanter than London.'

But the Duchess's eyes were absent again; she was looking very
fixedly at Bessie. In a minute she slowly rose, passed across the
room with a great rustle and an effect of momentous displace-
ment, reached a chair that stood empty at the girl's right hand and
silently seated herself. As she was a majestic voluminous woman
this little transaction had inevitably an air of somewhat impressive
intention. It diffused a certain awkwardness, which Lady Pimlico,
as a sympathetic daughter, perhaps desired to rectify in turning to
Mrs Westgate. 'I suppose you go out immensely.'

'No, very little. We're strangers, and we didn't come for the
local society.'

'I see,' said Lady Pimlico. 'It's rather nice in town just now.'

'I've known it of course duskier and dingier. But we only go to
see a few people,' Mrs Westgate added—'old friends or persons
we particularly like.'

'Of course one can't like every one,' Lady Pimlico conceded.

'It depends on one's society,' Mrs Westgate returned.

The Duchess meanwhile had addressed herself to Bessie. 'My
son tells me the young ladies in America are so clever.'

'I'm glad they made so good an impression on him,' our heroine
smiled.

The Duchess took the case, clearly, as no matter for grimacing; there reigned in her large pink face a meridian calm. 'He's
very susceptible. He thinks every one clever—and sometimes
they are.'

'Sometimes,' Bessie cheerfully assented.

The Duchess continued all serenely and publicly to appraise her. 'Lambeth's very susceptible, but he's very volatile too.'

'Volatile?' Bessie echoed.

'He's very inconstant. It won't do to depend on him.'

'Ah,' the girl returned, 'I don't recognise that description. We've depended on him greatly, my sister and I, and have found him so faithful. He has never disappointed us.'

'He'll disappoint you yet,' said her Grace with a certain rich force.

Bessie gave a laugh of amusement as at such a contention from such a quarter. 'I suppose it will depend on what we expect of him.'

'The less you expect the better,' said her massive monitress.

'Well, we expect nothing unreasonable.'

The Duchess had a fine contemplative pause—evidently with more to say. She made, in the quantity, her next selection. 'Lambeth says he has seen so much of you.'

'He has been with us very often—he has been a ministering angel,' Bessie hastened to put on record.

'I dare say you're used to that. I'm told there's a great deal of that in America.'

'A great deal of angelic ministering?' the girl laughed again.

'Is that what you call it? I know you've different expressions.'

'We certainly don't always understand each other,' said Mrs Westgate, the termination of whose interview with Lady Pimlico had allowed her to revert to their elder visitor.

'I'm speaking of the young men calling so much on the young ladies,' the Duchess explained.

'But surely in England,' Mrs Westgate appealed, 'the young ladies don't call on the young men?'

'Some of them do—almost!' Lady Pimlico declared. 'When a young man's a great *parti*.'*

'Bessie, you must make a note of that,' said Mrs Westgate. 'My sister'—she gave their friends the benefit of the knowledge—'is a model traveller. She writes down all the curious facts she hears in a little book she keeps for the purpose.'

The Duchess took it, with a noble art of her own, as if she

hadn't heard it; and while she was so occupied—for this involved a large deliberation—her daughter turned to Bessie. 'My brother has told us of your being so clever.'

'He should have said my sister,' Bessie returned—'when she treats you to such flights as that.'

'Shall you be long at Branches?' the Duchess abruptly asked of her.

Bessie was to have afterwards a vivid remembrance of wondering what her Grace (she was so glad Duchesses had that predicate) would mean by 'long'. But she might as well somehow have wondered what the occupants of the planet Mars would. 'He has invited us for three days.'

'I think I must really manage it,' the Duchess declared—'and my daughter too.'

'That will be charming!'

'Delightful!' cried Mrs Westgate.

'I shall expect to see a deal of you,' the Duchess continued. 'When I go to Branches I monopolise my son's guests.'

'They must give themselves up to you,' said Mrs Westgate all graciously.

'I quite yearn to see it—to see the Castle,' Bessie went on to the larger lady. 'I've never seen one—in England at least; and you know we've none in America.'

'Ah you're fond of castles?'—her Grace quite took it up.

'Of the idea of them—which is all I know—immensely.' And the girl's pale light deepened for the assurance. 'It has been the dream of my life to live in one.'

The Duchess looked at her as if hardly knowing how to take such words, which, from the ducal point of view, had either to be very artless or very aggressive. 'Well,' she said, rising, 'I'll show you Branches myself.' And upon this the noble ladies took their departure.

'What did they mean by it?' Mrs Westgate sought to know when they had gone.

'They meant to do the friendly thing,' Bessie surmised, 'because we're going to meet them.'

'It's too late to do the friendly thing,' Mrs Westgate replied almost grimly. 'They meant to overawe us by their fine manners and their grandeur; they meant to make you *lâcher prise*.'*

'*Lâcher prise*? What strange things you say!' the girl sighed as fairly for pain.

'They meant to snub us so that we shouldn't dare to go to Branches,' Mrs Westgate substituted with confidence.

'On the contrary,' said Bessie, 'the Duchess offered to show me the place herself.'

'Yes, you may depend upon it she won't let you out of her sight. She'll show you the place from morning till night.'

'You've a theory for everything,' our young woman a little more helplessly allowed.

'And you apparently have none for anything.'

'I saw no attempt to "overawe" us,' Bessie nevertheless persisted. 'Their manners weren't fine.'

'They were not even good!' Mrs Westgate declared.

Her sister had a pause, but in a few moments claimed the possession of an excellent theory. 'They just came to look at me!' she brought out as with much ingenuity. Mrs Westgate did the idea justice; she greeted it with a smile and pronounced it a credit to a fresh young mind; while in reality she felt that the girl's scepticism, or her charity, or, as she had sometimes called it appropriately, her idealism, was proof against irony. Bessie, however, remained meditative all the rest of that day and well on into the morrow. She privately ached—almost as under a dishonour—with the aftersense of having been inspected in that particular way.

On the morrow before luncheon Mrs Westgate, having occasion to go out for an hour, left her sister writing a letter. When she came back she met Lord Lambeth at the door of the hotel and in the act of leaving it. She thought he looked considerably embarrassed; he certainly, she said to herself, had no spring. 'I'm sorry to have missed you. Won't you come back?' she asked.

'No—I can't. I've seen your sister. I can never come back.' Then he looked at her a moment and took her hand. 'Good-bye, Mrs Westgate—you've been very kind to me.' And with what she thought a strange sad air on his handsome young face he turned away.

She went in only to find Bessie still writing her letter; find her, that is, seated at the table with the arrested pen in her hand. She put her question after a moment. 'Lord Lambeth has been here?'

Then Bessie got up and showed her a pale serious face—bending it on her for some time, confessing silently and, a little, pleading. 'I told him', the girl said at last, 'that we couldn't go to Branches.'

Mrs Westgate gave a gasp of temporary disappointment. 'He might have waited', she nevertheless smiled, 'till one had seen the Castle.' An hour afterwards she spoke again. 'I do wish, you know, you might have accepted him.'

'I couldn't,' said Bessie with the slowest gravest gentlest of headshakes.

'He's really such a dear,' Mrs Westgate pursued.

'I couldn't,' Bessie repeated.

'If it's only', her sister added, 'because those women will think they succeeded—that they paralysed us!'

Our young lady turned away, but presently added: 'They were interesting. I should have liked to see them again.'

'So should I!' cried Mrs Westgate with much point.

'And I should have liked to see the Castle,' said Bessie. 'But now we must leave England.'

Her sister's eyes studied her. 'You won't wait to go to the National Gallery?'

'Not now.'

'Nor to Canterbury Cathedral?'

Bessie lost herself for a little in this. 'We can stop there on our way to Paris,' she then said.

Lord Lambeth didn't tell Percy Beaumont that the contingency he was not prepared at all to like had occurred; but that gentleman, on hearing that the two ladies had left London, wondered with some intensity what had happened; wondered, that is, till the Duchess of Bayswater came a little to his assistance. The two ladies went to Paris—when Mrs Westgate beguiled the journey by repeating several times: 'That's what I regret; they'll think they petrified us.' But Bessie Alden, strange and charming girl, seemed to regret nothing.

APPENDIX 1

EXTRACTS FROM JAMES'S PREFACES TO THE NEW YORK EDITION

THE following extracts are the relevant passages from the Prefaces to vols. xviii and xiv of the New York Edition of *The Novels and Tales of Henry James*, 1907–9.

Daisy Miller

It was in Rome during the autumn of 1877; a friend then living there* but settled now in a South less weighted with appeals and memories happened to mention—which she might perfectly not have done—some simple and uninformed American lady of the previous winter, whose young daughter, a child of nature and of freedom, accompanying her from hotel to hotel, had 'picked up' by the wayside, with the best conscience in the world, a good-looking Roman, of vague identity, astonished at his luck, yet (so far as might be, by the pair) all innocently, all serenely exhibited and introduced: this at least till the occurrence of some small social check, some interrupting incident, of no great gravity or dignity, and which I forget. I had never heard, save on this showing, of the amiable but not otherwise eminent ladies, who weren't in fact named,* I think, and whose case had merely served to point a familiar moral; and it must have been just their want of salience that left a margin for the small pencil-mark inveterately signifying, in such connexions, 'Dramatise, dramatise!' The result of my recognising a few months later the sense of my pencil-mark was the short chronicle of 'Daisy Miller', which I indited in London the following spring and then addressed, with no conditions attached, as I remember, to the editor of a magazine* that had its seat of publication at Philadelphia and had lately appeared to appreciate my contributions. That gentleman however (an historian of some repute) promptly returned me my missive, and with an absence of comment that struck me at the time as rather grim—as, given the circumstances, requiring indeed some explanation: till a friend to whom I appealed for light, giving him the thing to read, declared it could only have passed with the Philadelphian critic for 'an outrage on American girlhood'. This was verily a light, and of bewildering intensity; though I was presently to read into the matter a further helpful inference. To the fault of being outrageous this little composition added that of being essentially and pre-eminently a *nouvelle*; a signal example in fact of that type, foredoomed at the best, in more cases than not, to editorial disfavour. If accordingly I was afterwards to be cradled, almost blissfully, in the conception that 'Daisy' at least, among my productions, might approach 'success', such success for example, on her eventual appearance, as the state of being promptly pirated in Boston*—a sweet tribute I hadn't yet received and was never again to know—the irony of things yet claimed its rights, I couldn't but long continue to feel, in the circumstance that quite a special reprobation had waited on the first appearance in the world of the ultimately most prosperous child of my invention. So doubly discredited, at all events, this bantling met indulgence, with no great delay, in the eyes of my admirable friend the late Leslie Stephen* and was published in two numbers of *The Cornhill Magazine* (1878).

It qualified itself in that publication and afterwards as 'a Study'; for reasons which I confess I fail to recapture unless they may have taken account simply of a certain flatness in my poor little heroine's literal denomination. Flatness indeed, one must have felt, was the very sum of her story; so that perhaps after all the attached epithet was meant but as a deprecation, addressed to the reader, of any great critical hope of stirring scenes. It provided for mere concentration, and on an object scant and superficially vulgar—from which, however, a sufficiently brooding tenderness might eventually extract a shy incongruous charm. I suppress at all events here the appended qualification—in view of the simple truth, which ought from the first to have been apparent to me, that my little exhibition is made to no degree whatever in critical but, quite inordinately and extravagantly, in poetical terms. It comes back to me that I was at a certain hour long afterwards to have reflected, in this connexion, on the characteristic free play of the whirligig of time.* It was in Italy again—in Venice and in the prized society of an interesting friend, now dead,* with whom I happened to wait, on the Grand Canal, at the animated water-steps of one of the hotels. The considerable little terrace there was so disposed as to make a salient stage for certain demonstrations on the part of two young girls, children *they*, if ever, of nature and of freedom, whose use of those resources, in the general public eye, and under our own as we sat in the gondola, drew from the lips of a second companion, sociably afloat with us, the remark that there before us, with no sign absent, were a couple of attesting Daisy Millers. Then it was that, in my charming hostess's prompt protest, the whirligig, as I have called it, at once betrayed itself.

'How can you liken *those* creatures to a figure of which the only fault is touchingly to have transmuted so sorry a type and to have, by a poetic artifice, not only led our judgement of it astray, but made *any* judgement quite impossible?' With which this gentle lady and admirable critic turned on the author himself. 'You *know* you quite falsified, by the turn you gave it, the thing you had begun with having in mind, the thing you had had, to satiety, the chance of "observing": your pretty perversion of it, or your unprincipled mystification of our sense of it, does it really too much honour—in spite of which, none the less, as anything charming or touching always to that extent justifies itself, we after a fashion forgive and understand you. But why *waste* your romance? There are cases, too many, in which you've done it again; in which, provoked by a spirit of observation at first no doubt sufficiently sincere, and with the measured and felt truth fairly twitching your sleeve, you have yielded to your incurable prejudice in favour of grace—to whatever it is in you that makes so inordinately for form and prettiness and pathos; not to say sometimes for misplaced drolling. Is it that you've after all too much imagination? Those awful young women capering at the hotel-door, *they* are the real little Daisy Millers that were; whereas yours in the tale is such a one, more's the pity, as—for pitch of the ingenuous, for quality of the artless—couldn't possibly have been at all.' My answer to all which bristled of course with more professions than I can or need report here; the chief of them inevitably to the effect that my supposedly typical little figure was of course pure poetry, and had never been anything else; since this is what helpful imagination, in however slight a dose, ever directly makes for. As for the original grossness of readers, I daresay I added, that was another matter—but one which at any rate had then quite ceased to signify.

An International Episode

I have gathered into this volume several short fictions of the type I have already found it convenient to refer to as 'international'*—though I freely recognise, before the array of my productions, of whatever length and whatever brevity, the general applicability of that term. On the interest of *contrasted* things any painter of life and manners inevitably much depends, and contrast, fortunately for him, is easy to seek and to recognise; the only difficulty is in presenting it again with effect, in extracting from it its sense and its lesson. The reader of these volumes will certainly see it offered in no form so frequent or so salient as that of the opposition of aspects from country to country. Their author,

I am quite aware, would seem struck with no possibility of contrast in the human lot so great as that encountered as we turn back and forth between the distinctively American and the distinctively European outlook. He might even perhaps on such a showing be represented as scarce aware, before the human scene, of any other sharp antithesis at all. He is far from denying that this one has always been vivid for him; yet there are cases in which, however obvious and however contributive, its office for the particular demonstration, has been quite secondary, and in which the work is by no means merely addressed to the illustration of it. These things have had in the latter case their proper subject: as, for instance, the subject of 'The Wings of the Dove', or that of 'The Golden Bowl', has not been the exhibited behaviour of certain Americans as Americans, of certain English persons as English, of certain Romans as Romans. Americans, Englishmen, Romans are, in the whole matter, agents or victims; but this is in virtue of an association nowadays so developed, so easily to be taken for granted, as to have created a new scale of relations altogether, a state of things from which *emphasised* internationalism has either quite dropped or is well on its way to drop. The dramatic side of human situations subsists of course on contrast; and when we come to the two novels I have just named we shall see, for example, just how they positively provide themselves with that source of interest. We shall see nevertheless at the same time that the subject could in each case have been perfectly expressed had *all* the persons concerned been only American or only English or only Roman or whatever.

If it be asked then, in this light, why they deviate from that natural harmony, why the author resorts to the greater extravagance when the less would serve, the answer is simply that the course taken has been, on reflexion, the course of the greater amusement. That is an explanation adequate, I admit, only when itself a little explained—but I shall have due occasion to explain it. Let me for the moment merely note that the very condition I here glance at—that of the achieved social fusion, say, without the sense and experience of which neither 'The Wings of the Dove', nor 'The Golden Bowl', nor 'The Portrait of a Lady', nor even, after all, I think, 'The Ambassadors', would have been written—represents a series of facts of the highest interest and one that, at this time of day, the late-coming observer and painter, the novelist sometimes depressed by all the drawbacks of a literary form overworked and relaxed, can only rejoice to meet in his path and to measure more and more as a portent and an opportunity. In proportion as he intelligently meets it, and more especially in proportion as he may happen to have 'assisted'* from far back at so many of the odd and fresh phenomena involved, must he see a vast new province, infinitely peopled and infinitely elastic—by which I mean with incalculable power to grow—annexed to the kingdom of the dramatist. On this point, however, much more is to be said than I can touch on by the way—so that I return to my minor contention; which is that in a whole group of tales I here collect* the principle of illustration has on the other hand quite definitely been that the idea could *not* have expressed itself without the narrower application of international terms. . . .

Nothing appeals to me more, I confess, as a 'critic of life' in any sense worthy of the name, than the finer—if indeed thereby the less easily formulated—group of the conquests of civilisation, the multiplied symptoms among educated people, from wherever drawn, of a common intelligence and a social fusion tending to abridge old rigours of separation. This too, I must admit, in spite of the many-coloured sanctity of such rigours in general, which have hitherto made countries smaller but kept the globe larger, and by which immediate strangeness, immediate beauty, immediate curiosity were so much fostered. . . . Behind all the small comedies and tragedies of the international, in a word, has exquisitely lurked for me the idea of some eventual sublime consensus of the educated; the exquisite conceivabilities of which, intellectual, moral, emotional, sensual, social, political—all, I mean, in the face of felt difficulty and danger—constitute stuff for such 'situations' as may easily make many of those of a more familiar type turn pale. *There*, if one will—in the dauntless fusions to come—is the personal drama of the future.

APPENDIX 2

STAGE AND SCREEN VERSIONS
OF 'DAISY MILLER'

IN 1882 James made his own version of 'Daisy Miller' for the theatre, and the tale has continued to attract adaptations for the stage, screen, radio, and television. Of these the most significant and the most durable is the 1974 film directed by Peter Bogdanovich, starring Cybill Shepherd in the title role, Barry Brown as Winterbourne, and a strong supporting cast.

Daisy Miller: A Comedy in Three Acts was the fourth of the surprisingly large number of plays James wrote, of which the best known, for the high hopes it inspired and the correspondingly deep disappointment of its failure in 1895, is *Guy Domville*.[1] Passionately as he felt about the theatre, and zealously as he pursued the prospect of its financial rewards, James never mastered its arts and crafts, and there is no more of a case for mounting a production of his *Daisy Miller* now than there was back in the 1880s when theatre managers in New York and London gave it as cold a shoulder as Mrs Walker turns on young Daisy. James introduces some new characters, especially the intriguing Madame de Katkoff, the Russian princess with a shady past, inflates the role of the courier Eugenio, and banishes Mrs Miller entirely from view. He translates with startling crudity Winterbourne's unspoken thoughts and feelings into direct speech ('She's simply amazing!'), and gives similarly blatant lines to Daisy herself ('He can do with me what he will').[2] Daisy recovers from the malaria just in time for Winterbourne to realize what a fool he has been. 'Vile idiot! Impenetrable fool!' he exclaims, burying his head in her lap.[3] The ruling dramatic conventions of the 'well-made' play restrict the use of space to three venues: the garden and terrace of the Hotel at Vevey, the promenade of the Pincian in Rome, and a public parlour in a Rome hotel. This makes one realize how richly James's original tale deployed its imagined settings, both indoor and out, including of course the excursion to Chillon and

---

[1] *The Complete Plays of Henry James*, ed. Edel. Unless noted otherwise, full details of references in this appendix may be found in the Select Bibliography.

[2] Ibid. 131, 156.

[3] Ibid. 175.

all the historic locations in Rome. The loss of these settings is scarcely
compensated for by giving Daisy some lines from Byron's *Childe
Harold* to quote, though it does reduce the cultural distance separating
her from Winterbourne.

Nevertheless, there is still a real interest in reading the play, as a
significant number of people appear to have done from its first publication in the *Atlantic Monthly* in the spring of 1883 and in book form a
few months later. It remained in print up until the 1920s, selling more
than 3,000 copies over thirty-three years.[4] The intensity of James's
involvement in its composition and its possibilities, however chimeri-
cal, is also intriguing. Some of this must derive from the moment of its
writing, in Boston, shortly after his mother's death in January 1882.
Back in London the following August, James reflected on this emotional epoch: 'My work at this time interested me, too, and I look back
upon the whole three months with a kind of religious veneration.'
Not that the immediate results were encouraging. His experience with
theatre managers on both sides of the Atlantic left James with few illusions about 'the conditions of production on our unhappy English
stage', he confessed to himself. 'I have learned, very vividly, that if one
attempts to work for it one must be prepared for *disgust*, deep and
unspeakable disgust. But though I am disgusted, I do not think I am
discouraged. . . . The dramatic form seems to me the most beautiful
thing possible; the misery of the thing is that the baseness of the
English-speaking stage affords no setting for it.'[5] This contrast between
the most beautiful thing possible and the degrading baseness of its settings is itself one of James's great fictional subjects. Indeed it is a way
of thinking about Daisy Miller and her tale.[6]

The fate of Bogdanovich's film resonates curiously with this vision
of a beautiful thing unjustly demeaned. For reasons ably described
by Peggy McCormack, this movie received on its release in 1974
an extravagantly hostile reception from critics and reviewers. Up
until then Bogdanovich had been something of a golden boy; *The
Last Picture Show* (1971) in particular was hailed as a masterpiece.

[4] William A. Wortman, 'The "Interminable Dramatic Daisy Miller"', 284.
[5] *The Complete Notebooks of Henry James*, ed. Edel and Powers, 232.
[6] For critical commentary on James's comedy, in addition to Wortman, 'The
"Interminable Dramatic Daisy Miller"', and the introduction by Edel to his edition of
the plays, see Susan Carlson, *Women of Grace: James's Plays and the Comedy of Manners*
(Ann Arbor, 1985); Christopher Greenwood, *Adapting to the Stage: Theatre and the Work
of Henry James* (Aldershot, 2000); and William T. Stafford (ed.), *James's Daisy Miller:
The Story, the Play, the Critics* (New York, 1963).

Together with two other still rising stars, Francis Ford Coppola
(the two *Godfather* films) and William Friedkin (*The French Connection*
and *The Exorcist*), Bogdanovich set up the Directors Company to guarantee the trio a measure of artistic freedom. The knives however were
ready and waiting. Bogdanovich and Shepherd had a very public affair
and paraded their 'romance' with a shamelessness still something
of a novelty in the 1970s. Commentators at the time seem to have
missed the irony that Shepherd was provoking reactions comparable to
those Daisy arouses amongst her compatriots. In hindsight one can see
the partial alignment and contrast between Daisy and Winterbourne
within the fiction and Shepherd and Bogdanovich outside it—as if the
jubilant off-screen affair were reparation or antidote for the failed
on-screen romance. Bogdanovich was probably wise to reject the idea
of playing the role of Winterbourne in his own movie, but their joint
performance on the celebrity platform excited reactions that could
scarcely have been more viciously punitive. Added to this were charges
against each of them on grounds more closely associated with their
professional pretensions. Bogdanovich was convicted of arrogance in
his pronouncements 'as the self-appointed intellectual historian of
American cinema'.[7] And Shepherd, the former model, came in for a lot
of abuse about her acting talents, or their paucity. For a couple of
decades the general consensus was that the film was a failure, and it
marked an immediate decline in the professional fortunes of its two
leading figures.

   With the passage of time it has received a more balanced hearing and
viewing. Bogdanovich's talents as a director have been more generously assessed, and other fine elements in the film's making properly
honoured, including the well-crafted screenplay co-authored with
Frederic Raphael, the gorgeous cinematography by Vittorio Sorao, and
the excellent casting of the secondary roles.[8] So too, no less interest-
ingly, has Shepherd's performance as Daisy, even if—or because—hers
is not James's Daisy but a substantial revision of it. Shepherd's strong
physique gives her, precisely, real substance (one commentator remarks
on her challenging *chin*). And the breathless monotony with which she
speaks many of her lines makes the moment at which she gets to
sing—'When You and I Were Young, Maggie', a song popular in the
1870s—all the more effective. Like a number of other such scenes this

   [7] Peggy McCormack, 'Reexamining Bogdanovich's *Daisy Miller*', 38.
   [8] See David Cross, 'Framing the "Sketch": Bogdanovich's *Daisy Miller*', 127–42, and
McCormack, 'Reexamining Bogdanovich's *Daisy Miller*'.

represents an intelligently purposive departure from the source text in James's tale.

Two aspects of the film demonstrate the possibilities inherent in the transposition of a literary text into this new medium, one of which is shared with the theatre and the other of which is not. The first is the effect of losing the narrative voice controlling James's tale and of gaining independent physical presence for the characters' voices and bodies. We get to see and hear Daisy for ourselves, rather than through Winterbourne's eyes or over his shoulder. We can make up our own minds and feelings about her, or try to. Also of course about Winterbourne (who emerges as a more sympathetic figure than in James's tale), and all the other characters. In this respect film and theatre come closer together. But from another point of view film draws closer to written narrative in the freedom with which it can reorganize space and time and endow its settings with phenomenal force and vividness. Bogdanovich does this to excellent effect, with the same real public locations as in James's tale—in Switzerland and Rome—but also freely finding new venues such as the baths at Vevey in which Mrs Costello and her nephew exchange views on the Millers, and a Punch and Judy show in Rome enjoyed by Daisy and Winterbourne. These serve to give body to many issues—the manners, morals, emotions, reflections—that are invested in verbal form in James's prose. David Cross comments that 'His concise realisation of abstract social forces in visual images serves Bogdanovich well throughout the film'.[9] This suggests that as an art form film provides a more satisfactory means of reimagining the rich possibilities of James's verbal art—of providing a 'setting' for 'the most beautiful thing possible'—than has appeared feasible in the theatre, at least so far.

[9] Cross, 'Framing the "Sketch": Bogdanovich's *Daisy Miller*', 136.

APPENDIX 3

VARIANT READINGS

THE following pages offer a brief analysis and some examples of the numerous changes between the texts first published in book form and the text of the New York Edition adopted in the current volume. The New York edition text is given first, followed by the text of the first British edition in book form (Macmillan, 1879: see Note on the Texts, p. xxxi), by page and line number in the present volume. Variants between the *Cornhill* serial versions and the texts of the first edition in book form are few in number, save for one lengthy passage in 'An International Episode', indicated below at the head of the sample variants to that tale, as recorded by Aziz in the Textual Variants to his edition of the *Tales*, iii. 438, 440 (which prints the original *Cornhill* versions). Readers who wish to pursue the topic of James's revisions in depth are referred to Philip Horne's indispensable *Henry James and Revision: The New York Edition* (Oxford, 1990), which includes a close study of the revisions of 'Daisy Miller' (pp. 228–64), though not of 'An International Episode'.

In both tales the most prominent feature of the revisions is the heightened attention to the characters' speech, to qualities of tone, intonation, intention, and implication, and to their effects on the hearer. The act of speaking becomes more dramatic in the sense we are given of both participants, of what passes (or fails to pass) between them. We are asked to imagine in far more detail the physical gestures and attitudes that accompany the uttering of words and their reception. And the pauses, hesitations, and silences that punctuate speech are much more fully characterized.

At the simplest level this means that the bare speech-tags with which the early versions are content ('he said', 'she said') are nuanced and elaborated: 'Winterbourne was emboldened to reply', 'Daisy imperturbably laughed', and 'she then quite colourlessly remarked'. Qualifying adverbs such as 'undiscourageably' (Daisy), 'resentfully' (Winterbourne), and 'unconfusedly' (Bessie) are frequently inserted to characterize the quality of a remark, question or answer. 'Winterbourne rejoined' is transformed into 'the young man permitted himself to growl'. Other vocal sounds are similarly nuanced, so that 'a little laugh' of Mrs Miller's becomes 'a sound that partook for Winterbourne of an odd strain between mirth and woe'. Her children raise their voices higher: where before he 'responded', now Randolph 'shouted'; where once she 'murmured', Daisy now 'piped from a considerable distance'. Whole new sentences introduce an utterance: 'She [Daisy] met it with a vivacity that could only flatter him', or describe its effect: 'Mrs Costello made a wondrous face'; 'The girl seemed to wonder at this innocence'. Silences that were once blank become coloured: instead of 'Winterbourne was silent', we read that 'He had to make the best of it'; instead of 'Beaumont was silent a moment', that 'The same influences appeared, however, with Mr Beaumont to make rather for anxiety'; instead of 'Mrs Westgate was silent a moment', that 'Mrs Westgate seemed to cover much country in a few moments'. Most strikingly, when Daisy demands to know if Winterbourne believes that she is engaged, in 1879 we are told that 'He was silent a moment', whereas in 1909, 'He asked himself, and it was for a moment like testing a heart-beat'.

As this last example suggests, the Winterbourne of the later version is more self-conscious than his earlier avatar, more susceptible to shame at his failure to intercept and control the ambivalent feelings that Daisy arouses in him: whereas he was once 'vexed with himself', his later incarnation finds that 'it vexed, it even a little humiliated' that he could not 'appreciate her justly'. Some of the lengthier extracts below will repay close examination for the difference in the depth and nature of the impression she makes on him. But although we largely see Daisy through his eyes, she too is credited with more depth and weight, and the conflict intensified between the values and manners of the Miller family and those of Geneva and Rome. In 'An International Episode', neither Bessie Alden nor Lord Lambeth monopolize the tale's point of view to the extent that Winterbourne does in 'Daisy Miller'; if the first half dwells on his view of Bessie, in the second it's the other way round. As in the earlier tale, however, revision intensifies the impression they make on each other, and their quandary over the relation between 'nature' and 'habit' in each other's personality and conduct. In the earlier version for instance the young American woman strikes her English admirer as 'by nature a reserved and retiring person', whereas in the later she seems to him 'by habit rather grave and backward, perhaps even proud'.

Both tales, in revision, take pains to accentuate cultural differences—between the Millers and their 'European' hosts, between the English and Americans—through an increased quantity of idiomatic expression and contemporary slang, especially on the part of the outsiders, the less initiated. The Millers no longer say 'isn't' but 'ain't', 'he doesn't' but 'he don't', 'the Italian' but 'just the finest kind of Italian', while the Englishmen now say 'trust him for the right kick-off' instead of 'trust to him for putting you into circulation', 'we shall muddle through' instead of 'we shall do very well', and 'They know how to put things—and put people—"through" in New York' instead of 'They certainly do things quickly in New York'. What are in themselves light, slight shifts gather a cumulative force and contribute significantly to these tales' enduring drama.

Daisy Miller

4.20 he had been put to school there as a boy and had afterwards even gone, on trial—trial of the grey old 'Academy' on the steep and stony hillside—to college there] he had been put to school there as a boy, and he had afterwards gone to college there

7.4 coming to stand in front of you in a garden with all the confidence in life] standing in front of you in a garden

7.11 the young lady turned again to the little boy, whom she addressed quite as if they were alone together] the young lady turned to the little boy again

8.8 she was really not in the least embarrassed. She might be cold, she might be austere, she might even be prim; for that was apparently—he had already so generalised—what the most 'distant' American girls did: they came and planted themselves straight in front of you to show how rigidly unapproachable they were. There hadn't been the slightest flush in her fresh fairness however; so that she was clearly neither offended nor fluttered. Only she was composed—he had seen that before too—of charming little parts that didn't match and that made no *ensemble*; and if she looked another way when he spoke to her, and seemed not particularly to hear him, this was simply her habit, her manner, the result of her having no idea whatever of 'form' (with such a tell-tale appendage as Randolph where in the world would she have got it?) in any such connexion. As he talked a little more and pointed out some of the objects of interest in the view, with which she appeared wholly unacquainted, she gradually, none the less, gave him more of the benefit of her attention; and then he saw that act unqualified by the faintest shadow of reserve. It wasn't however what would have been called a 'bold' front that she presented, for her expression was as decently limpid as the very cleanest water. Her eyes were the very prettiest conceivable, and indeed Winterbourne hadn't for a long time seen anything prettier than his fair country-woman's various features—her complexion, her nose, her ears, her teeth. He took a great interest generally in that range of effects and was addicted to noting and, as it were, recording them; so that in regard to this young lady's face he made several observations. It wasn't at all insipid, yet at the same time wasn't pointedly—what point, on earth, could she ever make?—expressive; and though it offered such a collection of small finenesses and neatnesses he mentally accused it—very forgivingly—of a want of finish. He thought nothing more likely than that its wearer would have had her own experience of the action of her charms, as she would certainly have acquired a resulting confidence; but even should she depend on this for her main amusement her bright sweet superficial little visage gave out neither mockery nor irony. Before long it became clear that, however these things might be, she was much disposed to conversation.]

she was not in the least embarrassed herself. There had not been the slightest alteration in her charming complexion; she was evidently neither offended nor fluttered. If she looked another way when he spoke to her, and seemed not particularly to hear him, this was simply her habit, her manner. Yet, as he talked a little more, and pointed out some of the objects of interest in the view, with which she appeared quite unacquainted, she gradually gave him more of the benefit of her glance; and then he saw that this glance was perfectly direct and unshrinking. It was not, however, what would have been called an immodest glance, for the young girl's eyes were singularly honest and fresh. They were wonderfully pretty eyes; and, indeed, Winterbourne had not seen for a long time anything prettier than his fair countrywoman's various features—her complexion, her nose, her ears, her teeth. He had a great relish for feminine beauty; he was addicted to observing and analysing it; and as regards this young lady's face he made several observations. It was not at all insipid, but it was not exactly expressive; and though it was eminently delicate Winterbourne mentally accused it—very forgivingly—of a want of finish. He thought it very possible that Master Randolph's sister was a coquette; he was sure she had a spirit of her own; but in her bright, sweet, superficial little visage there was no mockery,

no irony. Before long it became obvious that she was much
disposed towards conversation.

12.14 never at least save in cases where to say such things was to have
       at the same time some rather complicated consciousness about
       them.] never, at least, save in cases where to say such things
       seemed a kind of demonstrative evidence of a certain laxity of
       deportment.

12.17 of an actual or a potential *arrière-pensée*] of actual or potential
       inconduite

12.22 Certainly she was very charming, but how extraordinarily com-
       municative and how tremendously easy!] Certainly she was very
       charming; but how deucedly sociable!

12.26 Or was she also a designing, an audacious, in short an expert
       young person?] Or was she also a designing, an audacious, an
       unscrupulous young person?

15.21 as she moved away, drawing her muslin furbelows over the walk,
       he spoke to himself of her natural elegance.] as she moved away,
       drawing her muslin furbelows over the gravel, said to himself
       that she had the *tournure* of a princess.

15.30 'An obstreperous little boy and a preposterous big courier?']
       'And a courier?'

16.11   one must be irreproachable in all such forms.] one must always
        be attentive to one's aunt.

17.10 I think he smokes in their faces.] I think he smokes.

17.26 'She's a very innocent girl.'] 'She's a very nice girl.'

17.37 'Then she's just what I supposed.'
          'And what did you suppose?'
          'Why that she's a horror.']
       'Dear me!' cried Mrs Costello. 'What a dreadful girl!'

18.34 it was probable she did go even by the American allowance rather
       far.] it was probable that anything might be expected of her.

19.22 The soft impartiality of her *constatations*, as Winterbourne
       would have termed them, was a thing by itself—exquisite little
       fatalist as they seemed to make her. 'Let us hope she'll persuade
       him,' he encouragingly said.] 'Let us hope she will persuade
       him,' observed Winterbourne.

20.24 And she quite crowed for the fun of it.] And she gave a little
       laugh.

20.34 Daisy Miller looked out at these great lights and shades and
       again proclaimed a gay indifference—] Daisy Miller looked out

upon the mysterious prospect, and then she gave another little
laugh.

21.29 She gave him, he thought, the oddest glance.] Miss Miller gave
him a serious glance.

22.6 'Mr Frederick Forsyth Winterbourne,' said the latter's
young friend, repeating his lesson of a moment before and
introducing him very frankly and prettily.] 'Mr Winterbourne,'
said Miss Daisy Miller, introducing the young man very frankly
and prettily.

26.6 she only remained an elegant image of free light irony.] she only
stood there laughing.

27.10 Her daughter turned away from their friend, all lighted with her
odd perversity.] Daisy turned away from Winterbourne, looking
at him, smiling and fanning herself.

27.28 dressed exactly in the way that consorted best, to his fancy, with
their adventure. He was a man of imagination and, as our ancestors used to say, of sensibility; as he took in her charming air and
caught from the great staircase her impatient confiding step the
note of some small sweet strain of romance, not intense but clear
and sweet, seemed to sound for their start. He could have
believed he was *really* going 'off' with her. He led her out
through all the idle people assembled—they all looked at her
straight and hard.]
dressed in the perfection of a soberly elegant travelling-costume.
Winterbourne was a man of imagination and, as our ancestors
used to say, of sensibility; as he looked at her dress and, on the
great staircase, her little rapid, confiding step, he felt as if there
were something romantic going forward. He could have believed
he was going to elope with her. He passed out with her among all
the idle people that were assembled there; they were all looking
at her very hard;

28.5 Winterbourne's companion found time for many characteristic
remarks and other demonstrations, not a few of which were,
from the extremity of their candour, slightly disconcerting. To
the young man himself their small excursion showed so far
delightfully irregular and incongruously intimate that, even
allowing for her habitual sense of freedom, he had some expectation of seeing her appear to find in it the same savour. But it
must be confessed that he was in this particular rather disappointed. Miss Miller was highly animated, she was in the brightest

spirits; but she was clearly not at all in a nervous flutter—as she should have been to match *his* tension; she avoided neither his eyes nor those of any one else; she neither coloured from an awkward consciousness when she looked at him nor when she saw that people were looking at herself.]

Winterbourne's companion found time to say a great many things. To the young man himself their little excursion was so much of an escapade—an adventure—that, even allowing for her habitual sense of freedom, he had some expectation of seeing her regard it in the same way. But it must be confessed that, in this particular, he was disappointed. Daisy Miller was extremely animated, she was in charming spirits; but she was apparently not at all excited; she was not fluttered; she avoided neither his eyes nor those of anyone else; she blushed neither when she looked at him nor when she saw that people were looking at her.

28.25 It was the most charming innocent prattle he had ever heard, for, by his own experience hitherto, when young persons were so ingenuous they were less articulate and when they were so confident were more sophisticated. If he had assented to the idea that she was 'common', at any rate, *was* she proving so, after all, or was he simply getting used to her commonness? Her discourse was for the most part of what immediately and superficially surrounded them, but there were moments when it threw out a longer look or took a sudden straight plunge.]

It was the most charming garrulity he had ever heard. He had assented to the idea that she was 'common'; but was she so, after all, or was he simply getting used to her commonness? Her conversation was chiefly of what metaphysicians term the objective cast; but every now and then it took a subjective turn.

31.18 the girl at his side, her animation a little spent, was now quite distractingly passive.] the young girl was very quiet.

31.27 the little abomination] the young person

36.2 simply because of a certain sweet appeal to his fond fancy, not to say to his finest curiosity.] simply because of a certain sentimental impatience.

36.12 have I come all the way to Rome only to be riddled with your silver shafts?] have I come all the way to Rome to encounter your reproaches?

37.17 Daisy peacefully smiled, while the way that she 'condoned' these things almost melted Winterbourne's heart.] said Daisy, smiling.

38.11 I don't want to do anything that's going to affect my health—or my character, either!] I don't want to do anything improper.

40.11 her charming eyes, her charming teeth and her happy dimples.] her charming eyes and her happy dimples.

40.27 he seemed to shine, in his coxcombical way, with the desire to please and the fact of his own intelligent joy] he had a brilliant smile, an intelligent eye

40.31 she mentioned with the easiest grace the name of each of her companions to the other.] she mentioned the name of each of her companions to the other.

41.12 Mr Giovanelli had indeed great advantages; but it was deeply disgusting to Daisy's other friend that something in her shouldn't have instinctively discriminated against such a type.] Mr Giovanelli had certainly a very pretty face; but Winterbourne felt a superior indignation at his own lovely fellow-countrywoman's not knowing the difference between a spurious gentleman and a real one.

41.23 wasn't it possible to regard the choice of these very circumstances as a proof more of vulgarity than of anything else?] was it not impossible to regard the choice of these very circumstances as a proof of extreme cynicism?

42.13 Winterbourne—suddenly and rather oddly rubbed the wrong way by this—raised his grave eyebrows.] Winterbourne raised his eyebrows.

44.18 Daisy gave rein to her amusement.] Daisy gave a violent laugh.

44.25 She was evidently wound up. He accordingly hastened to overtake Daisy and her more faithful ally, and, offering her his hand, told her that Mrs Walker had made a stringent claim on his presence. He had expected her to answer with something rather free, something still more significant of the perversity from which the voice of society, through the lips of their distressed friend, had so earnestly endeavoured to dissuade her. But she only let her hand slip, as she scarce looked at him, through his slightly awkward grasp; while Mr Giovanelli, to make it worse, bade him farewell with too emphatic a flourish of the hat.]
She was evidently in earnest. Winterbourne overtook Daisy and her companion and, offering the young girl his hand, told her that Mrs Walker had made an imperious claim upon his society.

He expected that in answer she would say something rather free, something to commit herself farther to that 'recklessness' from which Mrs Walker had so charitably endeavoured to dissuade her. But she only shook his hand, hardly looking at him, while Mr Giovanelli bade him farewell with a too emphatic flourish of his hat.

45.25 'Ah we needn't mind the servants!' Winterbourne compassionately signified. 'The poor girl's only fault', he presently added, 'is her complete lack of education.'] 'The servants be hanged!' said Winterbourne angrily. 'The poor girl's only fault', he presently added, 'is that she is very uncultivated.'

49.8 'I'm not sorry we can't dance,' he candidly returned. 'I'm incapable of a step.'

'Of course you're incapable of a step,' the girl assented. 'I should think your legs *would* be stiff cooped in there so much of the time in that victoria.'

'Well, they were very restless these three days ago,' he amicably laughed; 'all they really wanted was to dance attendance on you.'

'Oh my other friend—my friend in need—stuck to me; he seems more at one with his limbs than you are—I'll say that for him.']

'I am not sorry we can't dance,' Winterbourne answered. 'I don't dance.'

'Of course you don't dance; you're too stiff,' said Miss Daisy. 'I hope you enjoyed your drive with Mrs Walker.'

'No I didn't enjoy it; I preferred walking with you.'

'We paired off, that was much better,' said Daisy

49.32 'I'm afraid your habits are those of a ruthless flirt,' said Winterbourne with studied severity.

'Of course they are!'—and she hoped, evidently, by the manner of it, to take his breath away.]

'I am afraid your habits are those of a flirt,' said Winterbourne gravely.

'Of course they are,' she cried, giving him her little smiling stare again.

50.35 She had allowed him up to this point to speak so frankly that he had no thought of shocking her by the force of his logic; yet she now none the less immediately rose, blushing visibly and leaving him mentally to exclaim that the name of little American flirts was incoherence. 'Mr Giovanelli at least,' she answered, sparing but a single small queer glance for it, a queerer small glance, he felt, than he had ever yet had from her, 'Mr Giovanelli never says to me such very disagreeable things.']

She had allowed him up to this point to talk so frankly that he had no expectation of shocking her by his ejaculation; but she immediately got up, blushing visibly, and leaving him to exclaim mentally that little American flirts were the queerest creatures in the world. 'Mr Giovanelli, at least,' she said, giving her interlocutor a single glance, 'never says such very disagreeable things to me.'

51.6   The subject of their contention had finished singing; he left the piano, and his recognition of what—a little awkwardly—didn't take place in celebration of this might nevertheless have been an acclaimed operatic tenor's series of repeated ducks before the curtain. So he bowed himself over Daisy. 'Won't you come to the other room and have some tea?' he asked—offering Mrs Walker's slightly thin refreshment as he might have done all the kingdoms of the earth.]

Mr Giovanelli had finished singing; he left the piano and came over to Daisy. 'Won't you come into the other room and have some tea?' he asked, bending before her with his decorative smile.

51.19 with her finest little intention of torment and triumph.] with her little tormenting manner.

52.2   looking with a small white prettiness] looking with a pale, grave face

52.7   But this lady's face was also as a stone. 'She never enters my drawing-room again.'] 'She never enters my drawing-room again,' replied his hostess.

52.34 It pleased him to believe that even were twenty other things different and Daisy should love him and he should know it and like it, he would still never be afraid of Daisy. It must be added that this conviction was not altogether flattering to her; it represented that she was nothing every way if not light.] He had a pleasant sense that he should never be afraid of Daisy Miller. It must be added that this sentiment was not altogether flattering to Daisy; it was part of his conviction, or rather of his apprehension, that she would prove a very light young person.

53.30 'They're certainly thick as thieves,' our embarrassed young man
       allowed.] 'They are certainly very intimate,' said Winterbourne.

54.15 The shiny—but, to do him justice, not greasy—little Roman.]
       The little Italian.

54.28 a possibly explosive Mr Miller in that mysterious land of dollars
       and six-shooters.] a substantial Mr Miller in that mysterious
       land of dollars.

55.26 that little American who's so much more a work of nature than
       of art] that pretty American girl

56.29 He set her down as hopelessly childish and shallow, as such mere
       giddiness and ignorance incarnate as was powerless either to
       heed or to suffer.] He said to himself that she was too light and
       childish, too uncultivated and unreasoning, too provincial, to
       have reflected upon her ostracism or even to have perceived it.

59.26 Above was a moon half-developed] There was a waning moon

59.29 the sense of the romantic in him] as a lover of the picturesque

60.5   The air of other ages surrounded one; but the air of other ages,
       coldly analysed, was no better than a villainous miasma.] The
       historic atmosphere was there, certainly; but the historic atmos-
       phere, scientifically considered, was no better than a villainous
       miasma.

60.17 These words were winged with their accent, so that they flut-
       tered and settled about him in the darkness like vague white
       doves. It was Miss Daisy Miller who had released them for
       flight.] These were the words he heard, in the familiar accent of
       Miss Daisy Miller.

60.21 Winterbourne found himself pulled up with final horror
       now—and, it must be added, with final relief. It was as if a
       sudden clearance had taken place in the ambiguity of the poor
       girl's appearances and the whole riddle of her contradictions
       had grown easy to read. She was a young lady about the *shades* of
       whose perversity a foolish puzzled gentleman need no longer
       trouble his head or his heart. That once questionable quantity
       had no shades—it was a mere black little blot.]
       Winterbourne stopped, with a sort of horror; and, it must be
       added, with a sort of relief. It was as if a sudden illumination had
       been flashed upon the ambiguity of Daisy's behaviour and the
       riddle had become easy to read. She was a young lady whom a
       gentleman need no longer be at pains to respect.

60.24 He felt angry at all his shiftings of view—he felt ashamed of all his tender little scruples and all his witless little mercies.] He felt angry with himself that he had bothered so much about the right way of regarding Miss Daisy Miller.

61.5   What a clever little reprobate she was, he was amply able to reflect at this, and how smartly she feigned, how promptly she sought to play off on him, a surprised and injured innocence! But nothing would induce him to cut her either 'dead' or to within any measurable distance even of the famous 'inch' of her life.] What a clever little reprobate she was, and how smartly she played an injured innocence! But he wouldn't cut her.

61.17 Daisy, lovely in the sinister silver radiance, appraised him a moment, roughness and all. 'Well, I guess all the evening.' She answered with spirit and, he could see even then, with exaggeration. 'I never saw anything so quaint.'] Daisy, lovely in the flattering moonlight, looked at him a moment. Then—'All the evening,' she answered gently. . . 'I never saw anything so pretty.'

62.6   He tried to deny himself the small fine anguish of looking at her, but his eyes themselves refused to spare him, and she seemed moreover not in the least embarrassed.] He kept looking at her; she seemed not in the least embarrassed.

62.11 Then noticing her companion's silence she asked him why he was so stiff—it had always been her great word. He made no answer, but he felt his laugh an immense negation of stiffness.] Then, noticing Winterbourne's silence, she asked him why he didn't speak. He made no answer; he only began to laugh.

62.24 He felt her lighted eyes fairly penetrate the thick gloom of the vaulted passage—as if to seek some access to him she hadn't yet compassed. But Giovanelli, with a graceful inconsequence, was at present all for retreat.] He felt the young girl's pretty eyes fixed upon him through the thick gloom of the archway; she was apparently going to answer. But Giovanelli hurried her forward.

63.20 'You can't see anything over here without the moon's right up. In America they don't go round by the moon!' Mrs Miller meanwhile wholly surrendered to her genius for unapparent uses; her salon knew her less than ever,] 'You can't see anything here at night, except when there's a moon. In America there's always a moon!' Mrs Miller was invisible;

63.27 Winterbourne constantly attended for news from the sick-room, which reached him, however, but with worrying indirectness, though he once had speech, for a moment, of the poor girl's physician and once saw Mrs Miller, who, sharply alarmed, struck him as thereby more happily inspired than he could have conceived and indeed as the most noiseless and light-handed of nurses. She invoked a good deal the remote shade of Dr Davis]

Winterbourne went often to ask for news of her, and once he saw Mrs Miller, who, though deeply alarmed, was—rather to his surprise—perfectly composed, and, as it appeared, a most efficient and judicious nurse. She talked a good deal about Dr Davis

64.27 Giovanelli, in decorous mourning, showed but a whiter face; his button-hole lacked its nosegay and he had visibly something urgent—and even to distress—to say, which he scarce knew how to 'place'. He decided at last to confide it with a pale convulsion to Winterbourne. 'She was the most beautiful young lady I ever saw, and the most amiable.' To which he added in a moment: 'Also—naturally!—the most innocent.'

Winterbourne sounded him with hard dry eyes, but presently repeated his words, 'The most innocent?']

Giovanelli was very pale; on this occasion he had no flower in his button-hole; he seemed to wish to say something. At last he said, 'She was the most beautiful young lady I ever saw, and the most amiable.' And then he added in a moment, 'And she was the most innocent.'

Winterbourne looked at him, and presently repeated his words, 'And the most innocent?'

64.37 It came somehow so much too late that our friend could only glare at its having come at all.] Winterbourne felt sore and angry.

65.3 Giovanelli raised his neat shoulders and eyebrows to within suspicion of a shrug. 'For myself I had no fear; and *she*—she did what she liked.'

Winterbourne's eyes attached themselves to the ground. 'She did what she liked!'

It determined on the part of poor Giovanelli a further pious, a further candid, confidence.]

Mr Giovanelli's urbanity was apparently imperturbable. He looked on the ground a moment, and then he said, 'For myself, I had no fear; and she wanted to go.'

'That was no reason!' Winterbourne declared.

The subtle Roman again dropped his eyes.

65.21 Mrs Costello extracted from the charming old hotel there a value that the Miller family hadn't mastered the secret of. In the interval Winterbourne had often thought of the most interesting member of that trio—of her mystifying manners and her queer adventure.] Mrs Costello was fond of Vevey. In the interval Winterbourne had often thought of Daisy Miller and her mystifying manners.

65.33 'She took an odd way to gain it! But do you mean by what you say', Mrs Costello asked, 'that she would have reciprocated one's affection?'

As he made no answer to this she after a little looked round at him—he hadn't been directly within sight; but the effect of that wasn't to make her repeat her question. He spoke, however, after a while. 'You were right in that remark that you made last summer. I was booked to make a mistake. I've lived too long in foreign parts.' And this time she herself said nothing.]

'Is that a modest way', asked Mrs Costello, 'of saying that she would have reciprocated one's affection?'

Winterbourne offered no answer to this question; but he presently said, 'You were right in that remark that you made last summer. I was booked to make a mistake. I have lived too long in foreign parts.'

An International Episode

One substantial passage not present in the *Cornhill* serial version is added to the 1879 Macmillan text and retained (with revisions) in the New York text, beginning ' "I'm glad he didn't tell us to go there," ' to 'apparently more of a moralist', on pp. 72–3 of the current edition.

69.8 The midsummer aspect of New York is doubtless not the most engaging, though nothing perhaps could well more solicit an alarmed attention. Of quite other sense and sound from those of any typical English street was the endless rude channel, rich in incongruities] The midsummer aspect of New York is not perhaps the most favourable one; still, it is not without its picturesque and even brilliant side. Nothing could well resemble less a typical English street than the interminable avenue, rich in incongruities

69.13 the rough animation of the sidewalks] the comfortable animation of the sidewalks

70.23 They were formed for good spirits and addicted and appointed to hilarity; they were more observant than they appeared; they were, in an inarticulate accidentally dissimulative fashion, capable of high appreciation.] They were extremely good-natured young men; they were more observant than they appeared; in a sort of inarticulate, accidentally dissimulative fashion, they were highly appreciative.

72.15 before a vast marble altar of sacrifice, a thing shaped like the counter of a huge shop.] before a brilliantly-illuminated counter, of vast extent.

73.37 trust him for the right kick-off.] trust to him for putting you into circulation.

75.11 the seventh heaven, as it were, of the edifice.] the seventh horizontal compartment of the edifice.

75.21 a face suggesting one of the ingenious modern objects with alternative uses, good as a blade or as a hammer, good for the deeps and for the shallows. His forehead was high but expressive, his eyes sharp but amused] with an expression that was at one and the same time sociable and business-like, a quick, intelligent eye

77.9 with his face of toil, his voice of leisure and his general intention, apparently, of everything] in his slow, humorous voice, with a distinctness of utterance which appeared to his visitors to be part of a facetious intention—a strangely leisurely, speculative voice for a man evidently so busy and, as they felt, so professional

77.28 Mr Westgate's amused eyes grew almost tender.] Mr Westgate gave one of his slow, keen looks again.

78.17 'It's a regular old city—don't you let them hear you call it a village or a hamlet or anything of that kind. They'd half-kill you. Only it's a city of pleasure—of lawns and gardens and verandahs and views and, above all, of good Samaritans,' Mr Westgate developed.] 'It isn't a town,' said Mr Westgate, laughing. 'It's a—well, what shall I call it? It's a watering-place. In short, it's Newport. You'll see what it is.'

79.8 Lord Lambeth flushed himself, in his charming way, with wonder, though his friend glanced to make sure he wasn't looking too credulous—they had heard so much about American practices. He decided in time, at any rate, to take a safe middle course.] Lord Lambeth stared, blushing a little; and Percy Beaumont stared a little also—but only with his fine natural complexion; glancing aside after a moment to see that his com-

panion was not looking too credulous, for he had heard a great
deal about American humour.

80.27 Take it as it's meant. Renounce your own personality. I'll come
down by and by and enjoy what's left of you.] I'll come down
by-and-by and look after you.

80.30 a monstrous floating hotel or even as a semi-submerged
kindergarten.] an extraordinary mixture of a ship and a hotel.

82.30 'For God's sake keep free of her.'
 'How do you mean, "free"?'
 'Depend upon it she'll try to land you.'
 'Oh rot!' said Lord Lambeth.
 'American girls are very "cute",' the other urged.
 'So much the better,' said the young man.]
 'For God's sake, don't get entangled with her.'
 'How do you mean, entangled?'
 'Depend upon it she will try to hook you.'
 'Oh, bother!' said Lord Lambeth.
 'American girls are very clever,' urged his companion.
 'So much the better,' the young man declared.

85.3 The morning shone and fluttered, the villas stood up bravely in
their smartness, and the walk of the young travellers turned all
to confidence.] The morning was brilliant and cool, the villas
were smart and snug, and the walk of the young travellers was
very entertaining.

87.27 with her bland intensity.] with a kind of joyous earnestness.

89.1 But you'll say—oh yes you will, or you would if some of you ever
did say much!—they're almost always very nice. You can't
expect this to be nearly such an interesting country as England]
But, of course, they are almost always very nice. Of course, this
isn't nearly such an interesting country as England

90.9 Mrs Westgate's discourse was delivered with a mild merciless
monotony, a paucity of intonation, an impartial flatness that
suggested a flowery mead scrupulously 'done over' by a steam
roller that had reduced its texture to that of a drawing-room
carpet.] Mrs Westgate's discourse, delivered in a soft, sweet
voice, flowed on like a miniature torrent and was interrupted by
a hundred little smiles, glances and gestures, which might have
figured the irregularities and obstructions of such a stream.

90.14 though he summoned to his aid such a show as he might of discriminating motions and murmurs.] although he indulged in a

good many little murmurs and ejaculations of assent and deprecation.

90.18 which had sometimes appeared to meet the case—any case; yet he felt he had never known such a case as Mrs Westgate or as her presentation of *her* cases. But at the present time he could hardly have been said to follow this exponent as she darted fish-like through the sea of speculation.] which had seemed convenient at the moment; but at the present time he could hardly have been said to follow Mrs Westgate as she darted gracefully about in a sea of speculation.

91.2 'I dare say he's immensely taken up,' the young man returned with a sense of conscientiously yearning toward American realities.] 'I daresay he is very busy,' Lord Lambeth observed.

91.24 His young woman seemed much amused; this at least was in her eyes, which freely met Lord Lambeth's.] the young lady rejoined.

91.31 it was all pitched in a key of expression and emphasis rather new to him. Every one present, the cool maidens not least, personally addressed him, and seemed to make a point of doing so by the friendly repetition of his name. Three or four other persons came in, and there was a shifting of seats, a changing of places; the gentlemen took, individually, an interest in the visitors, putting somehow more imagination and more 'high comedy' into this effort than the latter had ever seen displayed save in a play or a story.]
it was all very friendly and lively and jolly. Every one present, sooner or later, said something to him, and seemed to make a particular point of addressing him by name. Two or three other persons came in, and there was a shifting of seats and changing of places; the gentlemen all entered into intimate conversation with the two Englishmen, made them urgent offers of hospitality, and hoped they might frequently be of service to them.

92.13 The life was really growing more private; it was growing greatly to resemble European—which wasn't to be wondered at when two thirds of the people leading it were so awfully much at home in Europe. Europe, in the course of this conversation, was indeed, as Lord Lambeth afterwards remarked to his compatriot, rather bewilderingly rubbed into them: did they pretend to be European, and when had they ever been entered under that head?]

American life was certainly growing a great deal more private; it was growing very much like England.

92.30 left his wife to play the social part.] left his wife—well, to do about as she liked.

93.9 she appeared conscious of the weight of expectation—unless she quite wantonly took on duties she might have let alone; and this was perhaps the more to be noticed as she seemed by habit rather grave and backward, perhaps even proud, with little of the other's free fraternising. She might have been thought too deadly thin, not to say also too deadly pale; but while she moved over the grass, her arms hanging at her sides, and, seriously or absently, forgot expectations, though again brightly to remember them and to look at the summer sea as if that was what she really cared for, her companion judged her at least as pretty as Mrs Westgate and reflected that if this was the Boston style, 'the quiet Boston', it would do very well. He could fancy her very clever, highly educated and all the rest of it; but clearly also there were ways in which she could spare a fellow— could ease him; she wouldn't keep him so long on the stretch at once.]

she appeared to feel the obligation to exert an active hospitality; and this was perhaps the more to be noticed as she seemed by nature a reserved and retiring person, and had little of her sister's fraternising quality. She was perhaps rather too thin, and she was a little pale; but as she moved slowly over the grass, with her arms hanging at her sides, looking gravely for a moment at the sea and then brightly, for all her gravity, at him, Lord Lambeth thought her at least as pretty as Mrs Westgate, and reflected that if this was the Boston style the Boston style was very charming. He thought she looked very clever; he could imagine that she was highly educated; but at the same time she seemed gentle and graceful.

94.23 a visible repose of mind, an inaccessibility to questions, somehow stamped in by the same strong die and pressure that nature, designing a precious medal, had selected and applied. It was not that he looked stupid; it was only, we assume, that his perceptions didn't show in his face for restless or his imagination for irritable.] a look of intellectual repose and gentle good temper which seemed somehow to be consequent upon his well-cut nose and chin. And to speak of Lord Lambeth's expression of intellectual repose is not simply a civil way of saying that he looked stupid. He was evidently not a young man of an irritable imagination;

94.29 but, though there was rather a constant appeal for delay in his waiting, his perfectly patient eye, this registered simplicity had its beauty as well and, whatever it might have appeared to plead for, didn't plead in the name of indifference or inaction. This most searching of his new friends thought him the handsomest young man she had ever seen;] but, though there was a kind of appealing dullness in his eye he looked thoroughly reasonable and competent, and his appearance proclaimed that to be a nobleman, an athlete, and an excellent fellow, was a sufficiently brilliant combination of qualities. The young girl beside him, it may be attested without farther delay, thought him the handsomest young man she had ever seen.

94.35 He, however, had already made up his mind, quite originally and without aid, that she had a grace exceedingly her own.] He, however, was also making up his mind that she was uncommonly pretty.

97.26 he might, with his manly stature and his fair dense beard, his fresh clean skin and his quiet outlook, have pleased by a due affirmation of the best British points.] he might have passed for a striking specimen of the tall, muscular, fair-bearded, clear-eyed Englishman.

97.30 Mrs Westgate's beautiful radiance of interest and dissent fell meanwhile impartially everywhere.] Mrs Westgate meanwhile, with her superfluously pretty gaze, looked at every one alike.

98.27 'Oh indeed?' said Percy Beaumont with evident wonder. And then as if to alternate with a certain grace the note of scepticism: 'I guess your shyness, in that case, is different from ours.'
'Everything of ours is different from yours,' Mrs Westgate returned. 'But my poor sister's given over, I hold, to a fine Boston *gaucherie* that has rubbed off on her by being there so much.]
'Oh indeed?' said Percy Beaumont.
'Extremely shy,' Mrs Westgate repeated.

98.36 She has lived, however, rather too much in Boston] She has lived a great deal in Boston

99.12 continuing to supply her guest with information and to do him the honours of the American world with a zeal that left nothing to be desired.] continued to give Percy Beaumont a great deal of information.

99.30 little quick sounds and motions—obscure native words, shibboleths and signs.] little quick exclamations and caresses.

100.5 he had made a stride in intimacy with Miss Alden.] he had had a great deal of desultory conversation with Bessie Alden.

100.19 of a confidence that broke down, of a freedom that pulled up, nowhere; of an idyllic ease that was somehow too ordered for a primitive social consciousness and too innocent for a developed; of occasions on which they so knew every one and every thing that they almost ached with reciprocity] of universal friendliness and frankness; of occasions on which they knew every one and everything and had an extraordinary sense of ease

100.31 it was all the book of life, of American life, at least; with the chapter of 'complications' bodily omitted.] [. . .]

100.35 took up an attitude of mistrust apparently founded on some odd and just a little barbaric talk forced on him, he would have been tempted to say, and very soon after their advent, by Miss Alden. He had indeed been aware of her occasional approach or appeal] offered some conscientious opposition. I call his opposition conscientious because it was founded upon some talk that he had had, on the second day, with Bessie Alden. He had indeed had a good deal of talk with her

102.22 if you go straight into it, if you hurl yourself bang upon the spears, you do so with your eyes open.] if you go, you go with your eyes open.

102.29 he was a man of many scruples—in the direction in which he had any at all] he was a man of conscience

103.16 The young man, after this, faced him again. 'Why, do you think me such a dunce?' And then as his friend but vaguely protested: 'The girl's all right,' he said—and quite as if this judgement covered all the ground. It wasn't that there was no ground— but he knew what he was about.

Percy, for a while further, and a little uncomfortably flushed with the sense of his false position—that of presenting culture in a 'mean' light, as they said at Newport—Percy kept his peace;] 'In point of fact,' Lord Lambeth rejoined, 'I find it uncommonly lively.'

After this, Percy Beaumont held his tongue;

104.30 'Well—have you got any "livings"?' she demanded as if the

word were rich and rare.] 'Well—have you got any "livings"?'
she demanded.

105.9 pronouncing it too 'fiendish' he should let his business so
dreadfully absorb him that he could but platonically hope]
declaring it was very tiresome that his business detained him in
New York; that he could only hope

106.24 This really struck Lord Lambeth as meaning that he essentially
needn't take it, since alarm would have been his only good
motive; yet he nevertheless, after an hour of intenser irritation
than he could quite have explained to himself, made his farewells; in the course of which he exchanged a few last words
with Bessie Alden that are the only ones making good their
place in our record.] Lord Lambeth made his farewells; but the
few last words that he exchanged with Bessie Alden are the only
ones that have a place in our record.

106.32 She looked at him in that way she had which never quite struck
him as straight and clear, yet which always struck him as kind
and true.] Bessie Alden looked at him a little and she smiled.

107.14 Mr Beaumont gave the rein to mirth and mockery. 'There's
nothing so charming as modesty in a young man in the position
of "poor" you. That speech settles for me the question of
what's the matter with you.'

Lord Lambeth's handsome eyes turned rueful and queer. 'Is
anything so flagrantly the matter with me?'

'Everything, my dear boy,' laughed his companion, passing
a hand into his arm for a walk.]

Percy Beaumont gave a little laugh. 'There is nothing so
charming as modesty in a young man in your position. That
speech is a capital proof that you are sweet on her.'

108.27 I can't say it's in the least sensual.] I can't say it is physical.

111.9 felt to intensity the many-voiced appeal of the capital of the
race from which she had sprung] took an immense fancy to the
British metropolis

111.35 had the cold sense of complications.] sprinkled cold water.

112.24 He was the most convenient gentle young man, for almost any
casual light purpose] He was the gentlest, softest young man

113.3 'I consider public waltzing', said Mrs Westgate, 'the most innocent
because the most guarded and regulated, pleasure of our time.'

'It's a jolly compliment to our time!' Mr Woodley cried with
a laugh of the most candid significance.]

'I consider waltzing', said Mrs Westgate, 'the most innocent pleasure of our time.'

'It's a compliment to our time!' exclaimed the young man, with a little laugh, in spite of himself.

115.4 This time Bessie Alden took it with still deeper reserve.] This time Bessie Alden was displeased;

116.27 Mr Woodley almost spoke as if the pleasure were attended with physical risk.] Willie Woodley affirmed.

117.5 kept pace with the deep strong tide of the exhibition. Old impressions and preconceptions became living things before the show] let itself loose into the great changing assemblage of striking and suggestive figures. They stirred up a host of old impressions and preconceptions

118.19 'No,' said Bessie after an instant, but choosing and conferring a grace on the literal—'I don't.'] 'No,' said Bessie, 'I don't.'

120.33 like most familiars of the overciphered *tabula rasa*] like many a Yankee maiden

123.31 But if Mr Beaumont took a subtle view of the arrival of the fair strangers at Jones's hotel he was sufficiently capable of a still deeper refinement to offer them a smiling countenance.] But if Percy Beaumont took a sombre view of the arrival of the two ladies at Jones's Hotel, he was sufficiently a man of the world to offer them a smiling countenance.

124.32 I suppose that if I myself had a little more naïveté—of your blessed national lack of any approach to a sense for shades— I should enjoy it more.] I suppose that if I myself had a little more *naïveté*, I should enjoy it more.

126.32 Mrs Westgate winged her shaft with a smile before launching it.] Mrs Westgate poised her answer with a smile before delivering it.

127.8 I know that a British *materfamilias*—and when she's a Duchess into the bargain—is often a force to be reckoned with.] I know that a British mamma may worry her son's life out.

128.3 Bessie appealed to this worthy—even on more heads than he seemed aware of; she overtaxed, in her earnestness, his learnt lesson and found the place, as she more than once mentioned to him, quite delirious.] Bessie Alden asked the old man in the crimson doublet a great many questions; she thought it a most fascinating place.

128.7 his delirium at least was gay and he betrayed afresh that aptitude for the simpler forms of ironic comment that the girl had

noted in him.] he was constantly laughing; he enjoyed what he
would have called the lark.

129.4 Lord Lambeth, who found in Miss Alden the improving governess, he declared, of his later immaturity, as Mademoiselle
Boquet, dragging him by the hand to view all lions, had been
that of his earliest, pronounced the old red palace not half so
beastly as he had supposed. Bessie herself rose to raptures; she
went about murmuring and 'raving'.] Lord Lambeth, who
quite entered into the spirit of the cockney excursionist,
declared that it was a jolly old place. Bessie Alden was in ecsta-
sies; she went about murmuring and exclaiming.

129.20 'You're so disappointing, you know,' she returned: but more in
pity—pity for herself—than in anger.] 'You are very disappointing, Lord Lambeth,' she said.

130.25 where people's prejudices make so for light.] where even
people's prejudices are so elevated.

130.27 He stopped short, with his slightly strained gaiety, as for the
pleasantness of high argument. 'What it comes to then is
that we're all here a pack of fools and me the biggest of the
lot?'
    'I said nothing so rude of a great people—and a great person.
But I must repeat that you personally are—in your representative capacity that's to be—disappointing.']
    'Well, after all,' observed Lord Lambeth, 'I don't know that
I am such a fool as you are trying to make me out.'
    'I said nothing so rude as that; but I must repeat that you are
disappointing.'

131.30 invited them to luncheon, to tea, to dinner, to supper, even
after the arduous German opera.] invited them to dinner.

132.1 Lord Lambeth expressed a hatred of Courts, but he had
social privileges or exercised some court function—these
undiscriminated attributes, dim backgrounds where old gold
seemed to shine through transparent conventions, were romantically rich to our young heroine—that involved his support of
his sovereign] Lord Lambeth declared that he hated Drawing
Rooms, but he participated in the ceremony

132.25 Besides which there was her habit, her beautiful system, of
consenting to know nothing of human baseness or of the vulgar
side. There were things, just as there were people, that were as
nought from the moment one ignored them. She was accord-

ingly not haunted with the sense of a low imputation.] And it was disagreeable to Bessie to remember disagreeable things. So she was not haunted with the sense of a vulgar imputation.

132.33 made no attempt to dissimulate (to her finer intelligence) that 'appeal of type'—she had a ready name for it—to which her gallant hovering gentleman caused her wonderingly to respond. She was fully aware that she liked it, this so unalloyed image of the simple candid manly healthy English temperament. She spoke to herself of it as if she liked the man for it instead of liking it for the man.] made no attempt to dissimulate—to herself, of course—a certain tenderness that she felt for the young nobleman. She said to herself that she liked the type to which he belonged—the simple, candid, manly, healthy English temperament.

133.23 with his usual effect of natural salubrity and mental mediocrity, she took the measure of his shortcoming] with his customary good-humour and simplicity, she measured it more accurately

133.29 He affected her as on occasion, dreadful to say, almost *actively* stupid. It may have been that while she so curiously enquired and so critically brooded *her* personal wit, her presence of mind, made no great show—though it is also possible that she sometimes positively charmed, or at least interested, her friend by this very betrayal of the frequent, the distant and unreported, excursion. So it would have hung together that a part of her unconscious appeal to him from the first had been in his feeling her judge and appraise him more freely and irresponsibly—more at her ease and her leisure, as it were—than several young ladies with whom he had passed for adventurously intimate. To be convinced of her 'cleverness' and yet also to be aware of her appreciation—when the cleverness might have been after all but dangerous and complicating—all made, to Lord Lambeth's sense, for convenience and cheer. Hadn't he compassed the satisfaction, that high aim of young men greatly placed and greatly moneyed, of being liked for himself?]
I am afraid that while Bessie's imagination was thus invidiously roaming, she cannot have been herself a very lively companion; but it may well have been that these occasional fits of indifference seemed to Lord Lambeth a part of the young girl's personal charm. It had been a part of this charm from the first that he felt that she judged him and measured him more freely and

irresponsibly—more at her ease and her leisure, as it were—
than several young ladies with whom he had been on the whole
about as intimate. To feel this, and yet to feel that she also liked
him, was very agreeable to Lord Lambeth. He fancied he had
compassed that gratification so desirable to young men of title
and fortune—being liked for himself.

135.26   All his pleasant face wondered—he seemed to take it as another
of her rather stiff riddles.] Lord Lambeth looked at her a
moment.

136.35   But she couldn't induce him—amused as he almost always was
at the effect of giving her, as he called it, her head—to join her
in more formal reprobation of this repulsive custom, which he
spoke of as a convenience she would destroy without offering a
better in its place.] But Bessie Alden could induce him to enter
no formal protest against this repulsive custom, which he
seemed to think an extreme convenience.

138.18   Percy Beaumont, however, continued to aim at lucidity.] Percy
Beaumont began to laugh.

138.28   She'll try to get 'at' her—to square her. She won't care what
she does.] She will beg her off, or she will bribe her. She will
take strong measures.

141.9   'Do you pretend you wouldn't be glad to marry him?'
         Again Bessie calmly considered. 'It would take a great deal
more than is at all imaginable to make me marry him.'
         Her relative showed an impatience.]
         'Come, you would not marry him?'
         'Oh no,' said the young girl.
         Mrs Westgate, for a moment, seemed vexed.

143.10   Her hostess melted to sweetness.] Mrs Westgate gave a little
shrug.

143.13   passed across the room with a great rustle and an effect of
momentous displacement] walked to a chair

143.23   I've known it of course duskier and dingier.] It's charming

143.33   The Duchess took the case, clearly, as no matter for grimacing;
there reigned in her large pink face a meridian calm.] The
Duchess was not smiling; her large fresh face was very tranquil.

144.13   her massive monitress] Lord Lambeth's mother

145.8   Bessie was to have afterwards a vivid remembrance of wondering what her Grace (she was so glad Duchesses had that
predicate) would mean by 'long'. But she might as well some-

how have wondered what the occupants of the planet Mars would.] [. . .]

146.3 the girl sighed as fairly for pain.] murmured Bessie Alden.

146.25 She privately ached—almost as under a dishonour—with the aftersense of having been inspected in that particular way.] [. . .]

147.12 said Bessie with the slowest gravest gentlest of headshakes.] said Bessie gently.

147.36 But Bessie Alden, strange and charming girl, seemed to regret nothing.] But Bessie Alden seemed to regret nothing.

EXPLANATORY NOTES

IF not provided here, full details of works referred to can be found in the Select Bibliography. References to Shakespeare are to the *Complete Works*, 2nd edn., ed. Stanley Wells, Gary Taylor, John Jowett, and William Montgomery (Oxford: Oxford University Press, 2005). References to Byron are to *The Complete Poetical Works*, 7 vols., ed. Jerome J. McGann (Oxford: Clarendon Press, 1980–93).

I must acknowledge a debt to Jean Gooder for her notes to 'Daisy Miller' in the preceding Oxford World's Classics edition (1985), and to Adeline R. Tintner for her article ' "An International Episode" '. These items are abbreviated as Gooder and Tintner respectively in the notes.

DAISY MILLER

3 *the little town of Vevey*: a stylish resort on the eastern shore of Lake Geneva. In 1879 Baedeker described it as the second town in the Canton de Vaud, advising tourists that 'The Lake has for centuries been a favourite theme with writers of all countries. Its connection with some of the greatest names of modern times is universally known; Voltaire and Goethe speak of it with enthusiasm; Rousseau makes it the scene of his impassioned romance, the "Nouvelle Héloïse"; the exquisite stanzas of Byron, who spent some time on its shores, describe its varied beauties; and Alexander Dumas deems it worthy of comparison with the bay of Naples' (K. Baedeker, *Switzerland: Handbook for Travellers* (Leipzig, 1879), 197). Baedeker further described the fine views in various directions including Chillon to the south-east, and to the south the Alps of Valais, the Dent du Midi, Mont Velan (adjoining the Great St Bernard), and Mont Catogne (the 'Sugar-loaf'). It listed the Hôtel des Trois Couronnes as one of three grand hotels on the lake, all 'spacious and comfortable'. ' "Daisy Miller" is a story about, and for, tourists,' writes Roslyn Jolly ('Travel and Tourism', 346). See also James Buzard, *The Beaten Track*, and Motley F. Deakin, 'Two Studies in Daisy Miller'. Kristin Boudreau notes that first readers of James's tale could also have been familiar with Vevey and Lake Geneva from Louisa May Alcott's *Little Women* (1868), where they feature significantly in the chapter 'Learning to Forget' (introduction to the Broadview Press edition of James's tale, ed. Kristin Boudreau and Megan Stoner Morgan (Peterborough, Ont., 2011), 28–9).

Newport and Saratoga: Newport, Rhode Island, and Saratoga in upstate New York were markedly different resorts, as James's essays of 1870 make clear ('Saratoga' and 'Newport', *Collected Travel Writings: Great Britain and America*, 750–66). In Saratoga his fellow citizens suggested to James 'the swarming vastness—the multifarious possibilities and activities of our young civilisation. . . . They are not the mellow fruit of a society which has walked hand-in-hand with tradition and culture; they are hard nuts, which have grown and ripened as they could. When they talk among themselves, I seem to hear the cracking of the shells.' And yet the stylishness of the women's dress presented 'a quite momentous spectacle; the democratisation of elegance. . . . many of these sumptuous persons have enjoyed neither the advantages of a careful education nor the privileges of an introduction to society. She walks more or less of a queen, however, each uninitiated nobody' (ibid. 752–3). Indeed when he expresses regret that 'a figure so exquisite should have so vulgar a setting', one may see the setting he provides for Daisy in Switzerland and Rome as reparation, a 'poetic artifice' of the kind acknowledged in his Preface. As for Newport, it seemed by comparison 'really substantial and civilised. Æsthetically speaking, you may remain at Newport with a fairly good conscience; at Saratoga, you linger under passionate protest. At Newport life is public, if you will; at Saratoga it is absolutely common. The difference, in a word, is the difference between a group of undiscriminating hotels and a series of organised homes. Saratoga perhaps deserves our greater homage, as being characteristically democratic and American; let us, then, make Saratoga the heaven of our aspiration, but let us yet a while content ourselves with Newport as the lowly earth of our residence' (ibid. 761). See further, note to p. 89.

3 *Ocean House . . . Congress Hall*: fashionable hotels in Newport, Rhode Island (featuring also in 'An International Episode'), and Saratoga.

Dent du Midi . . . Castle of Chillon: two spectacular tourist landmarks noted by all the guidebooks, a spectacular peak across the lake from Vevey, and a chateau with massive walls and towers to the east, between Montreux and Villeneuve, on an isolated rock just offshore. This latter was made famous by Byron's poem 'The Prisoner of Chillon' (1816), based (not with entire accuracy, as the author conceded) on the story of François de Bonnivard (1496–1570), who championed the revolt of the Genevese against the tyrannous Duke of Savoy and for his pains spent six years imprisoned in this chateau. The sonnet before the main body of the poem is a ringing invocation of 'Liberty'—'Eternal Spirit of the chainless Mind!'

> Chillon! thy prison is a holy place,
> And thy sad floor an altar,—for 'twas trod,
> Until his very steps have left a trace,
> Worn, as if thy cold pavement were a sod,
> By Bonnivard!—May none those marks efface!
> For they appeal from tyranny to God.
>
> (*Poetical Works*, iv. 3)

Baedeker informed tourists that 'The steps of Bonivard [*sic*] and other illustrious captives have left their traces on the pavement. A fine effect is produced by the beams of the setting sun streaming through the narrow loopholes into these sombre precincts. Among the thousands of names inscribed on the pillars are those of Byron, Eugène Sue, and Victor Hugo' (*Switzerland*, 206). Jolly notes that the excursion shows 'how much James was able to "work" the phenomenon of tourism for comedy, for criticism, for poetry and for pathos' ('Travel and Tourism', 348).

4 *little capital of Calvinism*: in the earlier version, it was the 'metropolis'. In 'Swiss Notes' (1872) James had described it as 'the Presbyterian mother-city' (*Collected Travel Writings: The Continent*, 627). Baedeker warned tourists there was more to think about than to see. 'The principles which since the sixteenth century have shaken Europe to its foundation, have emanated chiefly from Geneva.' The city was famous for Calvin and Rousseau, 'the great advocates, one of religious, the other of social reform' (*Switzerland*, 193).

grey old 'Academy': Henry's elder brother William James had attended this college in 1859–60, and Henry too, though officially enrolled elsewhere, had sat in on courses in French literature and natural philosophy.

6 *dressed in white muslin, with a hundred frills and flounces*: commentators on the significance of the visual arts to James have noted the similarity of this description to his review of James Tissot's painting of 1877, *The Deck of the H.M.S. Calcutta* (*Henry James: The Painter's Eye*, ed. John L. Sweeney (London, 1956), 140–1): 'M. Tissot's taste is highly remarkable; what I care less for is his sentiment, which seems sterile and disagreeable'; 'realism' such as this struck James as 'vulgar and *banal*' (ibid. 141). Hughes suggests a closer resemblance to Tissot's portrait of Miss Lloyd (1876), which features the same dress as the later work, with the addition of a parasol. Whatever James thought of Tissot's painting, Hughes rightly notes: 'James makes it clear that if Daisy's dresses are frivolous, they are not vulgar' (*James and the Art of Dress*, 18); 'The puzzle of the novella is that Daisy's taste in clothes may reflect a genuine aesthetic sensibility as much as it does the despised New Money of *post-bellum* America' (ibid. 21).

7 *the Simplon*: the Simplon Pass across the mountains from Switzerland into Italy, subject of some famous lines included in William Wordsworth's *The Prelude*, Book VI (1850).

10 *Schenectady*: a city in upstate New York, fifteen miles north-east of Albany, the state capital. An industrial centre best known at the time of the tale's setting for building railway locomotives, it had been a focus for abolitionist activities before the Civil War; by the time of the New York Edition it had grown in importance as the headquarters, since 1892, of the General Electric Company.

the cars: railway carriages, in modern British parlance. 'In the United States the term has become restricted almost entirely to vehicles designed for travelling on railways' (*OED*). Railway transport was essential to the expansion and democratization of tourist travel in the last decades of the nineteenth century.

12 *an actual or a potential arrière-pensée*: in the earlier version it had been *inconduite* ('misbehaviour') of which Winterbourne thought Daisy might be accused, whereas now it is, more suspiciously, 'an ulterior motive' (see Horne, *James and Revision*, 238–9).

15 *muslin furbelows*: 'A piece of stuff pleated and puckered on a gown or petticoat; a flounce; the pleated border of a petticoat or gown' (*OED*). See also 'An International Episode', p. 84.

16 *Forty-Second Street*: a fashionable address in the late nineteenth century, in the district known as Murray Hill, home to the city's social elite, now changed beyond recognition. Gooder recommends Edith Wharton's *Old New York* (1924).

   a Comanche savage: Native American Indians were much in the news in the 1870s as the threats to their traditional way of life reached a climax.

19 *constatations*: 'statements' or 'findings', in a forensic sense.

20 *comme il faut*: 'proper', 'correct'.

   she wore white puffs: to me these 'puffs' suggest sleeves, as in the *OED*'s citation, from Beatrix Potter's 1884 *Journal*, of 'Tight long sleeves with puffs to put on over them', rather than the hairstyle, then fashionable in Paris, proposed by Gooder.

27 *as our ancestors used to say, of sensibility*: that is, in the sense of 'Quickness and acuteness of apprehension or feeling; the quality of being easily and strongly affected by emotional influences; sensitiveness' (*OED*), especially prominent in the latter half of the eighteenth and early nineteenth centuries, as for example in the title of Jane Austen's novel *Sense and Sensibility* (1811).

29 *oubliettes*: secret dungeons, so called because anyone consigned to them could be 'forgotten'.

   without other society than that of their guide: a 'romantic' variation on the experience of most tourists, like James himself who, Gooder notes, had found it impossible to escape from the crush and was told it was always like this ('Swiss Notes', *Collected Travel Writings: The Continent*, 632).

   the unhappy Bonnivard: see note to p.3. The historical Bonnivard was twice imprisoned by the Duke of Savoy, from 1519 to 1521 and 1530 to 1536, on the second occasion at Chillon, until the Bernese stormed the castle. On his release he lived as a highly respected citizen of the Genevese Republic until his death at the age of 75.

31 *Rome toward the end of January*: many of the tourist sights and venues in the second half of this tale had already featured in James's writing, in his first full-length novel, *Roderick Hudson* (1875), and the five essays that made their debut in American periodicals in 1873, were gathered for the concerted volume of *Transatlantic Sketches* (1875), and many years later

revised for reissue in *Italian Hours* (1909). Of these, it is particularly valuable to read alongside this tale 'A Roman Holiday' and 'From a Roman Note-Book'.

32 *Cherbuliez*: born in Geneva, Victor Cherbuliez (1829–99) wrote many popular works of fiction which often first appeared in the *Revue des deux mondes*, including the one referred to here, *Paule Méré* (1864). In 1873 James described it as 'an attempted exposure, rather youthful in its unsparing ardour, of the narrowness and intolerance of Genevese society', and its author as 'an old friend' (*Literary Criticism*, ii. 185–6, 184). Two years later he was deploring the old friend's decline—'the most striking example of the eclipse of a great talent that we have ever encountered' (*Literary Criticism*, ii. 195), and shortly after writing 'Daisy Miller', he described Cherbuliez as 'that pitiful prostitute', quite the opposite of his admired Turgenev, who by contrast had not 'a gram of coquetry' (*James Letters*, ed. Edel, ii. 183). ('Coquetry' is one of the charges levelled against Daisy.) And yet as several scholars have shown, the explicit reference here to *Paule Méré* points directly to a literary source for his own tale. The irony at Mrs Costello's expense is that she wants to read a novel in which her own repressive attitudes are frankly presented and roundly condemned. Edward Stone describes some of the similarities between James's tale and its French-Swiss model: 'In both, the action opens in a provincial Swiss pension and closes in Italy; in both, a young leisured idler half representing, half resenting, Genevan propriety irresolutely opposes a close female relative in his affection for a young woman who does not "belong" there; in both, this young woman is ostensibly immodest, yet actually quite chaste. Finally, in both an apparently compromising situation destroys the hero's faith; and both heroes learn of their mistake too late' (Stone, *Battle and the Books*, 89). Angus Wrenn considers some of the changes of emphasis James effects, as for example by moving the heroine's death from Venice to Rome (Wrenn, *James and the Second Empire*, 75–81), as well as James's further debts to Cherbuliez, general and particular (ibid. 62–98).

the American banker's: Murray's *Handbook of Rome and Its Environs*, 12th edn. (London, 1875), 23 noted that Messrs. Macquay, Hooker and Co., 20, Piazza di Spagna 'conduct a large portion of the American business'.

33 *Via Gregoriana*: one of the most prestigious streets in Rome, starting from Trinità dei Monti and the Spanish Steps.

35 *the infant Hannibal*: legend has it that the Carthaginian leader famous for marching his army over the Alps into Italy and winning several dramatic victories, vowed, as a child, eternal enmity to Rome.

the City of Richmond: built in 1873 at Glasgow by Tod & McGregor and owned by the Inman Line, this steamship sailed between Liverpool and New York from 1874 to 1890, making the crossing in about eight days.

37 *the hotel*: in the dramatic version of the tale, the hotel is named as the Hôtel de Paris, overlooking the Corso. But there was no shortage of

expensive fashionable hotels such as the Hôtel Londres on the Piazza di
Spagna, or Hôtel de Rome on the Corso, 'much frequented by ambassadors and distinguished persons travelling with numerous suites', Murray
noted (*Handbook*, 13).

37 *the Pincio*: in 1875 Murray observed that Rome's places of public resort
had been much improved and were now second to none except, perhaps,
those of London and Paris. 'The most beautiful and frequented is that on
the Monte Pincio, occupying all the level space between the Muro Torto
and the garden of the Villa Medicis' (*Handbook*, 112). Baedeker noted that
'This is a fashionable drive in the evening, when the Italians frequently
pay and receive visits in their carriages, presenting a gay and characteristic
scene. . . . The projecting terrace at the summit commands a magnificent
view of modern Rome' (K. Baedeker, *Central Italy and Rome* (Leipzig,
1886), 143). James was struck by the theatricality of the female figure
centre stage, the object of intense scrutiny: 'Such a staring, lounging, dan-
dified, amiable crowd! . . . Europe is certainly the continent of the practised stare. The ladies on the Pincio have to run the gauntlet; but they
seem to do so complacently enough. The European woman is brought up
to the sense of having a definite part in the way of manners or manner to
play in public. To lie back in a barouche alone, balancing a parasol and
seeming to ignore the extremely immediate gaze of two serried ranks of
male creatures on each side of her path, save here or there to recognise one
of them with an imperceptible nod, is one of her daily duties' ('From a
Roman Note-Book', *Collected Travel Writings: The Continent*, 475–6).

'condoned': James puts this in inverted commas because it was just
entering everyday discourse in its modern sense of 'tolerate, approve or
sanction', having previously held a technical legal sense relating to viola-
tion of the marriage vow. The *OED* suggests that it was after the 1857
Divorce Act that the more relaxed modern usage began to pass into
ordinary parlance.

41 *a penny-a-liner*: a demeaning term for a 'hack' writer, especially a journal-
ist, paid a penny a line.

her amoroso: lover, admirer.

43 *the victoria*: 'A light, low, four-wheeled carriage having a collapsible hood,
with seats (usually) for two persons and an elevated seat in front for the
driver' (*OED*).

46 *the Villa Borghese*: this large public park dates back to the early seventeenth century, when Cardinal Scipione Borghese began turning a vine-
yard into the most extensive formal gardens in Rome since antiquity. In
the nineteenth century it was relandscaped in the naturalistic English
style, and became, Murray says, 'one of the favourite resorts of the Roman
people in summer, and the most convenient promenade for the upper
classes and foreign residents at all seasons' (*Handbook*, 360–1). Baedeker
notes that the north side of the Pincio is supported by lofty walls, opposite

which are 'the well-planted grounds' of the Villa Borghese' (*Central Italy and Rome*, 143).

48 *Elle s'affiche, la malheureuse*: 'She's making a spectacle of herself, poor girl' (Gooder).

52 *discretion is the better part of solicitude*: a variation on or even a perversion of the conventional wisdom that discretion is the better part of valour (in 1879 discretion had been 'the better part of surveillance').

53 *Saint Peter's*: Murray encouraged tourists at every opportunity to view Rome through Byron's poetry, as for example on St Peter's, some lines from *Childe Harold*. The *Handbook* also reminds readers 'to conform to the usages of the people of the country where they are residing, and not to consider, as we are ashamed to confess is too often the case, the ceremonies of the Church almost as theatrical representations' (p. 136).

the Corso: 'the principal street of Rome . . . [it] contains numerous shops and is enlivened, especially towards evening, by crowds of carriages and foot-passengers' (Baedeker, *Central Italy and Rome*, 147).

54 *scarcely went on all fours*: the *OED* says that 'to run on all fours' is to move 'fairly, evenly', rather than 'to limp like a lame dog', and so, figuratively 'to present an exact analogy or comparison (with)'; presumably it is the infelicity of the word 'romps' that tickles the narrator, when you would expect of 'the Golden Age' more elegant verbs of movement.

a cavaliere avvocato: 'gentleman lawyer'. In 1877 James lodged in Rome 'in the bosom of a Roman family; that of the Cavaliere Avvocato Spinetti—a rather ragged and besmirched establishment. But I pay little and have lots of sun' (*James Letters*, ed. Edel, ii. 142).

a marchese: an Italian marquis.

qui se passe ses fantaisies!: 'who is indulging her fantasies', 'doing what she likes'.

55 *the Doria Palace*: the Palazzo Doria-Pamphilj in the Corso is 'the most magnificent perhaps of all the Roman palaces' (Murray, *Handbook*, 317); it houses a large gallery of paintings.

the great portrait of Innocent X, by Velasquez: seeing this painting for the first time in 1869 James described it as a 'really great picture' (*Life in Letters*, ed. Horne, 30). The Spanish artist Velásquez painted Pope Innocent X, founder of the Pamphilj family, on a visit to Rome in 1651. See Adeline R. Tintner, 'The Masterpiece as Verbal Pun: "Daisy Miller" and Innocent X', in *The Museum World of Henry James* (Ann Arbor, 1986), 63–8.

du meilleur monde: 'of the best society'.

57 *the Palace of the Caesars*: on the Palatine Hill, the supposed residence of Rome's founding heroes, of Augustus and subsequent emperors, a site as charged with imperial power—its zenith, decline, and fall—as anywhere in the Western world.

57 *deep interfusion*: see Introduction, pp. xviii–xix.

59 *the Cælian hill . . . the Arch of Constantine . . . the Forum*: classic tourist attractions. As noted above, Murray quotes Byron freely to induce the appropriately 'romantic' response to the ruins of empire, as here for example from *Childe Harold*, Canto the Fourth, in the section on 'Forums' (*Handbook*, 21):

> Yes; and in yon field below,
> A thousand years of silenced factions sleep—
> The Forum, where the immortal accents glow,
> And still the eloquent air breathes—burns with Cicero!
>
> The field of freedom, faction, fame, and blood:
> Here a proud people's passions were exhaled,
> From the first hour of empire in the bud
> To that when further worlds to conquer fail'd; . . .
> (*Poetical Works*, ii. 161–2)

the Colosseum: an amphitheatre begun by the Emperor Vespasian in AD 72, dedicated by Titus, completed by Domitian, and altered up until the sixth century. Murray commented: 'The gladiatorial spectacles of which it was the scene for nearly 400 years are matters of history, and it is not necessary to dwell upon them further than to state that, at the dedication of the building by Titus, 5000 wild beasts were slaughtered in the arena, and the games in honour of the event lasted for nearly 100 days . . . During the persecution of the Christians the amphitheatre was the scene of fearful barbarities . . . the traditions of the Church are filled with the names of martyrs who perished in the arena' (*Handbook*, 54). In 'A Roman Holiday', James noted that 'One of course never passes the Colosseum without paying it one's respects—without going in under one of the hundred portals and crossing the long oval and sitting down awhile, generally at the foot of the cross in the centre' (*Collected Travel Writings: The Continent*, 421).

60 *Byron's famous lines out of 'Manfred'*: few tourists failed to do as Winterbourne does here, Murray commented (*Handbook*, 59), beginning at the lines in the long monologue spoken by Byron's protagonist at the start of Act III, sc. 4:

> I do remember me, that in my youth,
> When I was wandering,—upon such a night
> I stood within the Colosseum's wall
> 'Midst the chief relics of almighty Rome

and culminating thus:

> And thou didst shine, thou rolling moon, upon
> All this, and cast a wide and tender light,
> Which soften'd down the hoar austerity

> Of rugged desolation, and fill'd up,
> As 'twere, anew, the gaps of centuries;
> Leaving that beautiful which still was so,
> And making that which was not, till the place
> Became religion, and the heart ran o'er
> With silent worship of the great of old!—
> The dead, but sceptred sovereigns, who still rule
> Our spirits from their urns.—
>
> (*Poetical Works*, ii. 97–8)

like vague white doves: Horne suggests that these white doves (the simile is an addition in the New York text) derive from Hawthorne's *The Marble Faun* (ch. 6), where they are associated with the innocence of Hilda. He further proposes that Daisy is touched, at least in Winterbourne's imagination, by the corruption associated with Hilda's antitype in that novel, Miriam, especially at the point where he sees Daisy and her accomplice 'roll away through the cynical streets of Rome' (p. 55). Horne concludes that 'the spectral presence in the story of Hawthorne's "guilty couple" puts a pressure of analogy on Daisy and Giovanelli in the Coliseum . . . —a pressure which the image of the white doves resists' (*James and Revision*, 250–1, n. 15).

61 *the perniciosa*: Murray quotes an eminent Italian physician to this effect: 'The real Roman fever is nothing else than the ordinary intermittent fever or ague, the same which exists in all marshy countries of temperate and Southern Europe. This fever, however, at Rome, assumes sometimes, though in rare cases, a very malignant character, then called the *Febbre Perniciosa*, and if not attended to, or cut short in time, is very likely to prove fatal' (*Handbook*, 347).

62 *He felt her lighted eyes . . . hadn't yet compassed*: Horne points out the Shakespearean echoes introduced to the New York Edition text by addition of the words 'passage' and 'access', which conjure up Lady Macbeth's determination to harden her heart: 'Make thick my blood, | Stop up th'access and passage to remorse, . . .' (*Macbeth*, I. v. 42–3; Horne, *James and Revision*, 242–3).

64 *the little Protestant cemetery*: Murray calls this burial ground, resting place of the poets Shelley and Keats, the sculptors Richard Wyatt and John Gibson, and the surgeon John Bell, 'one of those objects which all foreign travellers will regard with melancholy interest. . . . The silence and seclusion of the spot, and the inscriptions which tell the British traveller in his native tongue of those who have found their last resting-place beneath the bright skies of the Eternal City, appeal irresistibly to the heart. The cemetery has an air of romantic beauty which forms a striking contrast with the tomb of the ancient Roman and with the massive city walls and towers which overlook it' (*Handbook*, 342). In 1873 James writes more than one fine passage about this spot, 'where the ancient and modern world are insidiously contrasted. They make between them one of the solemn places

of Rome—although indeed when funereal things are so interfused it seems ungrateful to call them sad. Here is a mixture of tears and smiles, of stones and flowers, of mourning cypresses and radiant sky, which gives us the impression of our looking back at death from the brighter side of the grave' ('The After-Season in Rome', *Collected Travel Writings: The Continent*, 467–8). And again: 'Bathed in the clear Roman light the place is heart-breaking for what it asks you—in such a world as *this*—to renounce. If it should "make one in love with death to lie there," that's only if death should be conscious. As the case stands the weight of a tremendous past presses upon the flowery sod, and the sleeper's mortality feels the contact of all the mortality with which the brilliant air is tainted' ('From a Roman Note-Book', ibid. 471).

65 *'She did what she liked!'*: an addition in the New York Edition text, this phrase echoes a famous warning of Matthew Arnold's against the 'anarchy' that results in 'doing as one likes', a misunderstanding of the nature of 'freedom' for which 'culture' is the proper and only remedy (*Culture and Anarchy* (1869), ch. 2, 'Doing as One Likes'). James wrote essays on Arnold in 1865 and 1884, the latter while Arnold was on a tour of 'the great country of the Philistines', James noted with some amusement (*Literary Criticism*, i. 720). As the embodiment of 'the cultivated man', Arnold would be greeted with particular curiosity in the land where 'The curiosity with regard to culture is extreme . . .; if there is in some quarters a considerable uncertainty as to what it may consist of, there is everywhere a great wish to get hold of it, at least on trial' (ibid. 730). In 'An International Episode' Mrs Westgate reflects on the difference between Newport and London, at least for Lord Lambeth, when she tells her young sister that 'At Newport he could do as he liked; but here [in London] it's another affair' (p. 114).

AN INTERNATIONAL EPISODE

69 *in 1874*: Adeline Tintner argues that James's choice of date characterizes the tale as a 'Centennial story'. In its second half the American women set foot in England in May 1875, almost exactly a hundred years after the first shots were fired in the American War of Independence.

Broadway: the oldest thoroughfare on Manhattan, running north–south almost the whole length of the island. Looking back in old age, James associated Broadway with his own early schooling in the early 1850s at the Institution Vergnès and a school run by 'Mr Pulling Jenks': 'Broadway must have been then as one of the alleys of Eden, for any sinister contact or consequence involved for us' (*A Small Boy and Others*, ed. Collister, 164).

Union Square: a public square in downtown Manhattan, well known to James from childhood years when his family lived, from 1847 to 1855, at 58 West Fourteenth Street, just east of Sixth Avenue (*A Small Boy and Others*, ed. Collister, 81–2). A prosperous residential area in the 1840s and 1850s, it would in the years after the Civil War become increasingly commercialized, and by 1874 the English visitors would have seen one of New York's earliest skyscrapers, built by the Domestic Sewing Machine Company (ibid. 81 n. 171).

the monument to Washington: an equestrian statue of George Washington (first president of the United States, 1789–97), erected in 1856.

70 *an air of capacious hospitality*: so restless and itinerant was the childhood of the James children that Henry described himself and his four siblings as 'hotel children', and throughout his life he took a keen interest in the phenomenon and experience of hotel life, culminating in some remarkable passages in *The American Scene* (1907) on the Waldorf-Astoria (ch. 2, 'New York Revisited), and 'the Hotel World' (ch. 14, 'Florida').

71 *Pompadour-looking dresses*: so named after the Marquise de Pompadour, lover of Louis XV, this is a style of dress cut square and low in the neck.

the thingumbob: a colloquialism (also 'thingummy', or 'thingummybob') that has been around in Britain since the late eighteenth century, though now beginning to pass out of currency, it indicates something for which you can't remember the name, what Americans would be more likely to call a 'whatcha-m'-callit' (Eric Partridge, *A Dictionary of Slang and Unconventional English*, 8th edn., ed. Paul Beale (London, 2002), 1220, 1322).

72 *Grosvenor Square*: a large garden square in the wealthy district of Mayfair in London. At the time, the central garden was reserved exclusively for the use of residents of the surrounding houses. The comparison is interesting in the context of this tale; Grosvenor Square came to be identified with an American presence after John Adams, one of the 'founding fathers' of the United States, established in 1785 the first American mission to the Court of St James.

the Fifth Avenue: by the late 1800s Fifth Avenue was already a prime New York tourist attraction, famed for its high society and culture: exclusive clubs, luxurious hotels, and elegant shops. Visitors could take designated stagecoach tours up and down it to view at first hand the opulent residences of the wealthiest New Yorkers. The Brevoorts were the first family to live on Fifth Avenue, and were soon joined by the Vanderbilts and the Astors. James remembers 'the Old Fifth Avenue' in ch. 2 of *The American Scene*, 'New York Revisited'.

73 *The cave of Æolus*: in Greek mythology Aeolus is god of the four winds. James's tale is much concerned with hospitality, so the role played by this minor deity in Homer is worth recalling. A good host, Aeolus provides Odysseus with a bag containing all the adverse winds so the hero can reach Ithaca in safety, but curiosity ensures that the gift is abused and the bag opened, with catastrophic results (*Odyssey*, Book 10).

Percy Beaumont Esq.: Adeline Tintner points out that Alexis de Tocqueville's travelling companion to America in 1831 was Gustave de

Beaumont (1802–66), eminent magistrate and prison reformer, co-author
of their study of the American prison system, *Du système pénitentiare aux
États-Unis, et de son application en France* (1833), but subsequently overshadowed by the author of *Democracy in America* (1835, 1840). Tintner
suggests that Percy Beaumont's name helps to imply a general ironic reference to de Tocqueville's famous analysis of American manners.

74 *hackney-coach*: a popular late-nineteenth-century mode of city transport
available for hire. Hackney coaches could be distinguished from hackney
carriages by being drawn by two horses, and having four wheels and six
seats.

75 *hydraulic elevator*: the earliest powered elevators appeared in America in
1850; by the 1870s the technology had advanced with fast and efficient
roped-hydraulic elevators supplied by the Otis Elevator Company.

76 *sherry-cobblers*: a drink popular in the nineteenth century on both sides of
the Atlantic, a sherry cobbler is a mixture of dry sherry, sugar, citrus, and
ice, garnished with late summer fruits. In Albert Smith et al., *Sketches of
London Life and Character* (1849), 29, the cocktail is described as being
'the one in greatest request' in London clubs: 'nectar, whatever it was,
could not have been more delicious to the gods of old . . . It is not strong
to be sure; but this is an advantage, in addition to that of the corresponding modesty of price'.

Newport: James knew the town well, having lived there in 1858–9, and
again, after a year's absence in Europe, until the family settled in Boston
in 1864. James wrote essays on 'Newport' (1870) and on 'The Sense of
Newport' (1906, repr. in *The American Scene*, 1907). Newport features
largely in his autobiographical writing in *Notes of a Son and Brother*
(1914), and as the setting for one of his last, unfinished novels, *The Ivory
Tower* (1917). His 1870 essay conjures up the vision of an idyllic existence
similar to the one over which Mrs Westgate presides: 'Here you find a
solution of the insoluble problem—to combine an abundance of society
with an abundance of solitude. In their charming broad-windowed drawing-rooms, on their great seaward piazzas, within sight of the serious
Atlantic horizon, which is so familiar to the eye and so mysterious to the
heart, caressed by the gentle breeze which makes all but simple, social,
delightful *now* and *here* seem unreal and untasteful—the sweet fruit of the
lotus grows more than ever succulent and magical. How sensible they
ought to be, the denizens of these pleasant places, of their peculiar felicity
and distinction! How it should purify their temper and refine their tastes!'
(*Collected Travel Writings: Great Britain and America*, 766).

the Russia: a Cunard Line steamship built in Glasgow in 1867, by J. & G.
Thomson & Co., that sailed between Liverpool and New York.

77 *The Tennessee Central*: James is picking up on business opportunities
much in the air in the late 1870s. The Tennessee and Pacific Railroad had
operated between Lebanon and Nashville from 1871 before its finances
collapsed in 1877. Perhaps this accounts for the 'grievance' of Percy

Beaumont's friends. The company that would become the Tennessee Central was only founded by Alexander S. Crawford as the Nashville and Knoxville Railroad in 1884; a service from Lebanon was opened in 1888, and in 1893 it was chartered as the Tennessee Central Railroad. At its height it extended from Harriman, Tennessee, on the east to Hopkinsville, Kentucky, on the west, a distance of 248 miles.

78 *Boston*: the contrast between Boston and New York was of massive significance to James personally, in his life and his writing, and to the development of the US more generally in the second half of the nineteenth century. If it was the 'intellectual centre', or believed itself to be so, then New York was certainly its 'business centre', as the cameo portrait of Mr Westgate suggests. Boston—and Cambridge—feature with particular prominence in *The Europeans* (1878), *The Bostonians* (1886), *The American Scene* (ch. 7, 'Boston'), and *Notes of a Son and Brother* (where he describes it as 'the Puritan capital', 275).

80 *a big boat*: Tintner comments that this would have been the same steamer taken by de Tocqueville and de Beaumont forty-three years earlier in the other direction, from Newport to New York, though by the time of James's story it seems to have been better equipped, with private cabins (p. 30).

mirrors en pied: full-length mirrors.

84 *Valenciennes lace*: named after the city of Valenciennes in northern France where it was first produced, characterized by the openness of the mesh and a flat, even texture; by the mid-nineteenth century, it was mainly machine-made.

furbelows: see note to p. 15.

a fête champêtre: an elegant and lavish form of garden party, popularized in France, especially in the court at Versailles, during the eighteenth century.

a bowie-knife: a fixed-blade fighting knife, which came to prominence after the 1827 Sandbar Fight in Kentucky, Louisiana, in which James Bowie killed the sheriff of Rapides Parish.

85 *basket-phaetons*: open carriages with wickerwork body, drawn by one or two horses, phaetons could be distinguished by their lightness, speed, and four ostentatiously large wheels.

fine blue veils . . . to guard their complexions: nineteenth-century fashion favoured pale skin for women with any pretensions to gentility. This dictated the protection of the complexion with parasols (so effectively wielded by Daisy Miller), bonnets, hats, and hats with veils.

86 *the Ocean House*: fashionable luxury hotel built in 1868 in Watch Hill to cater for the moneyed and leisured in the post-Civil War years. Rebuilt in the early twenty-first century, in 2012 its website proclaimed: 'one of the last remaining grand oceanfront hotels and resorts in New England, the

Ocean House is a celebration of the golden age of leisure and beachfront hospitality': http://www.fivestaralliance.com/4star-hotels/newport-ri/ ocean-house (accessed 24 June 2012).

88 *we go there when we die*: in 'The Sense of Newport' (1906), James wistfully recalls the brief, 'sacred' period in Newport's history when Europeanized Americans like himself and his family, 'mild, oh delightfully mild, cosmopolites', took up longer residence in the town. He wonders about the reasons for their departure, and concludes that it was to escape the encroaching 'grossness', the 'white elephants' of modernization and development. Or perhaps they simply died out: 'They must have died, some of them, in order to "go back"—to go back, that is, to Paris' (*Collected Travel Writings: Great Britain and America*, 538–40).

hair à l'anglaise: a style first popularized in the 1830s when hair was arranged in a chignon at the nape of the neck with long sausage curls. In America the fashion may have been sustained by keepsakes, gift books given to women and girls at New Year's, featuring images of fashionably attired women with long, 'anglaises' curls. By the 1870s and 1880s, 'anglaises' were most often worn as part of elaborate evening hairstyles amid braids and smaller curls were left to flow down the back.

Jones's Hotel in Dover Street: a flimsily concealed reference to Brown's Hotel, the best-known hotel in Dover Street, Mayfair. Brown's was opened in 1837 and proved popular with American visitors, including Theodore Roosevelt, who spent two honeymoons here.

English hotels are your weak point: less true in 1908 than some thirty years earlier in 1879, given the number of fashionable hotels that had gone up to meet the rising tide of wealthy tourists in the interim. But James would have been loth to amend Mrs Westgate's characteristically chauvinistic judgement.

89 *with all our imperfections on our heads*: an echo of the Ghost's description of his murder in *Hamlet*, 'No reck'ning made, but sent to my account | With all my imperfections on my head.' (I. v. 78–9)

different from most watering-places: Saratoga, for example. See note to p. 3.

94 *the coast-scenery in Kingsley's novels*: author, Anglican priest, and professor, Charles Kingsley (1819–75) appeared to the young James in 1866 as 'a consummate Englishman'. On his death James described him as 'the apostle of English pluck, English arms and legs, and the English sporting and fighting temper generally', but thought that *Westward Ho!* (1855) would be one of the half-dozen modern English novels worth saving for posterity (*Literary Criticism*, i. 1101, 1104–5). Kingsley's fiction contained some lyrical descriptions of natural scenery, notably of Hampshire and the West Country.

95 *Thackeray and George Eliot*: like her author, young Bessie will discover that her preconceptions of England have been powerfully shaped by her

reading, though for her author in the 1850s it had been Thackeray and
Dickens (plus more ephemeral fare). Though Thackeray died in 1863, a
Bostonian like Bessie growing up in the 1870s would still have been reading him, but the author of *Middlemarch* (1871–2) and *Daniel Deronda*
(1874–6) would have been more to her earnest young taste than Dickens.

96 *Catherine Grace Gore*: an English writer (1799–1861), celebrated in her
time for over seventy novels depicting the manners of high society,
including *Mothers and Daughters* (1830), *Mrs Armytage: or Female
Domination* (1836), and *Cecil, or the Adventures of a Coxcomb* (1841). She
has been preserved for posterity by Thackeray's parody in 'Lords and
Liveries', in *Mr Punch's Prize Novelists* (1847).

98 *gaucherie*: 'awkwardness'.

99 *the long Avenue*: Newport's chief thoroughfare, where summer residents
and visitors went to see and be seen, forming a 'heterogeneous procession', as James describes it in his early essay on the town. 'The peculiar
charm of this great westward expanse is very difficult to define. It is in an
especial degree the charm of Newport in general—the combined lowness
of tone, as painters call it, in all the elements of *terra firma*, and the extraordinary elevation of tone in the air' (*Collected Travel Writings: Great Britain
and America*, 760, 765).

shibboleths: words, gestures, manners only intelligible to those of your own
sect, party, or people.

101 *a "Peerage"*: a reference book, such as Burke's or Debrett's *Peerage*, listing
the nobility, their genealogy, history, connections, and titles.

"peer of the realm": member of a rank of hereditary nobility, as distinct
from someone raised to the nobility for his or her own lifetime, a 'life
peer'.

102 *Countess of Pimlico*: commenting on the shadow cast by Thackeray on
James's tale, Tintner notes that one of his parodies contains a Lady
Pimlico (mother-in-law of Lady Fanny Flummery, author of forty-five
novels in fifteen years, very like Mrs Gore), that elsewhere he has a character named 'Amethyst Pimlico' and a little Lord Pimlico, and a tale
entitled *The Orphan of Pimlico: A Moral Tale of Belgravian Life*, posthu-
mously published in 1876. Outside of Thackeray's parodic and satiric
writing, the districts of London represented by Pimlico, Bayswater, and
Lambeth were unlikely to yield countesses, dukes, and duchesses, but to
be 'Lord Lambeth' has particularly dishonourable associations, Tintner
contends, since the area 'has always represented the lowest possible living
conditions in London'. She concludes that 'it seems reasonable to see "An
International Episode" as James's Book of Snobs' (p. 33).

103 *"fast"*: that is, 'careless of propriety of decorum'.

a priggish American précieuse: in 1879 Bessie was accused of being 'a blue-
stocking', a term of disdain dating from the eighteenth century for women
with intellectual or literary pretensions. But the equivalent French term,

précieuse, goes back further to the seventeenth century, to the circle of refined and learned women in the salon of Madame de Rambouillet and others, mocked for alleged pedantry and affectation by Boileau, Racine, and Molière (whose comedy *Les Précieuses ridicules* was produced in 1659).

104 *"livings"*: a church office, normally the charge of a parish, in the gift of a nobleman, landowner, or institution.

109 *the Duke of Green-Erin*: another fake title, 'Erin' being a romantic name for Ireland, popular in the nineteenth century.

110 *silence de mort*: 'a deathly silence'.

Ascot Races: ancient racecourse famous for its four-day Royal Meeting, patronized by royalty and fashionable society, a fixture of the London 'season'.

111 *Bond Street ... Regent Street ... Westminster Abbey ... the Tower ... Madame Tussaud's*: the two sisters are following a conventional route around the major shopping streets and tourist sites. Bond Street came to prominence as a shopping promenade in the early decades of the nineteenth century with the influx of French goods and fashions; by the end of the century the shops in Regent Street included Peter Robinson's, Jay's, and Dickins & Jones. Madame Marie Gresholtz (later Tussaud) brought the famous waxwork exhibition over from Paris to London in 1802, where they were installed first at the Lyceum Theatre, before moving in 1833 to Baker Street. Madame Tussaud's was well established in James's lifetime as a prime tourist attraction, along with Westminster Abbey, the Houses of Parliament, Hyde Park, St Paul's Cathedral, and the Tower of London.

112 *Beacon Street*: historic street in the centre of Boston.

Charing Cross Hotel: at the time of the tale's setting this was a modern hotel, opened in 1865, a year after the railway station, with an imposing façade in the French Renaissance style.

the 'German': the full name for this dance was the German cotillion, 'an elaborate form of quadrille' (*OED*).

the scene of Lady Jane Grey's execution: Lady Jane Grey (1536/7–54), great-granddaughter of Henry VII and cousin of Edward VI, nominated as the latter's successor. She reigned for a mere nine days in July 1553 before being superseded by Mary. Executed at a tender age the following year, she was celebrated as a Protestant martyr.

116 *Hyde Park ... Rotten Row*: large park in central London, opened to the public by Charles I in 1637, and avenue on the south side of Hyde Park where the fashionable world displayed itself, in horse-drawn carriages or on horseback.

the Morning Post: daily London newspaper of conservative stance and deferential attitude to the wealthy, powerful, and fashionable; it ran from 1772 to 1937, when it was acquired by the *Daily Telegraph*.

so much about it in Thackeray: the *Morning Post* was the object of

Thackeray's satire in *Punch* and elsewhere, especially its social reporter, whom he recreated as the footman, 'Jeames'.

Punch: humorous weekly magazine founded in 1841, particularly famous for its cartoons, a staple feature of British culture life for the next 150 years.

117 *couturière*: dressmaker.

119 *Hurlingham*: Tintner comments that 'Hurlingham, part of the borough of Fulham in London, has had a special place in English aristocratic sporting life since 1869, when the then lessee of a property of many acres decided to found a shooting club. The Prince of Wales, later Edward VII, became an honorary member, and, just at the time James was writing his story, the club became very fashionable. Polo was established four years before the story was written, and lacrosse and tennis followed in 1877' (p. 38). The club continues to enjoy royal patronage but no longer commands quite the same social prestige.

the Chamber of Horrors: one of the main attractions of Madame Tussaud's, originally featuring victims of the French Revolution, then murderers and other criminals.

décolletées: 'wearing low-cut dresses, with bare neck and shoulders'.

121 *Hampton Court . . . Windsor . . . Dulwich Gallery*: standard destinations on the tourist route. Over 900 years old, Windsor Castle is an official residence of the reigning monarch; Hampton Court, strongly associated with Henry VIII, was opened to the public by the young Queen Victoria in 1838; the Dulwich Picture Gallery in Dulwich, south London, was designed by Sir John Soane and opened to the public in 1817.

Rosherville Gardens: pleasure gardens in Gravesend, Kent, once owned by Jeremiah Rosher, pleasantly accessible by paddle steamer down the Thames, a popular resort for Londoners through the middle of the century, though closed by 1901. *Not* a normal destination for tourists, and certainly too vulgar for Lord Lambeth and the circles he moves in. They get a mention in Thackeray's *The Newcomes* (1853–5), vol. ii, ch. 6.

126 *his 'trap'*: colloquial term for a 'small carriage on springs; usually, a two-wheeled spring carriage, a gig, a spring-cart' (*OED*).

127 *a venerable beef-eater*: one of the ceremonial guards of the Tower of London, popularly known as 'Beefeaters', for reasons that remain obscure.

130 *'Happy the country . . . where people's prejudices make so for light'*: Tintner comments that Bessie is inventing a saying on the model of 'a quotation that had passed down from the classical historians Lucan and Virgil to Montesquieu, finally reaching Carlyle in his famous aphorism, "Happy the people whose annals are blank in history-books." Bessie has invented her own aphorism based on one handed down from traditional historians, and thereby allies herself with the great historians' (p. 28).

131 *the American Minister to England*: title of the official known since 1893 as

the United States ambassador to the United Kingdom. At the time of the tale's first writing and publication, the post was held by John Welsh (1877–9); he was succeeded by James Russell Lowell, of whom James wrote a warm appreciation on his death in 1891, and a further essay in 1896 (*Literary Criticism*, i. 516–50). When the New York edition was published, the ambassador was Whitelaw Reid, the former newspaper editor who had failed to appreciate the letters James had written from Paris for his New York *Tribune* in 1875–6.

138 *Saint Paul's . . . the Thames Tunnel*: two major landmarks, Sir Christopher Wren's late-seventeenth-century cathedral, and the Tunnel beneath the Thames, a triumph of modern engineering by the Brunels, Marc and his more famous son Isambard Kingdom, constructed between 1825 and 1843.

144 *a great parti*: a great 'match', marriageable prospect.

146 *lâcher prise*: 'let go'.

APPENDIX 1

149 *a friend then living there*: the best candidate seems to be Alice Bartlett, with whom James had gone riding in the Roman *campagna* in 1873, and read Tasso's poetry twice a week (see *Life in Letters*, ed. Horne, 90 n.1). In 1902 he remembered Alice (Warren, as she now was) in a letter to another friend of the old Roman days, now living in the American South, Sarah Butler Wister (*James Letters*, ed. Edel, iv. 260). James got the hint for the tale while staying in Rome in the autumn of 1877.

ladies, who weren't in fact named: Julia Newberry, her mother and sister, had travelled round Europe in 1872–4, and they were familiar figures in the expatriate American community in Rome when Julia died there, aged 22, on 4 April 1876, and was buried in the Protestant cemetery. A wealthy Chicago family, the Newberrys have been claimed as models for the Millers, the correspondence between Julia and Daisy 'difficult to ignore' (Aziz, 'Introduction', *Tales*, iii. 16).

the editor of a magazine: John Foster Kirk was editor of the Philadelphian *Lippincott's Magazine*, in which several travel sketches and a review by James had appeared in 1877. The following year Kirk published the tale 'Théodolinde' and an essay on 'The British Soldier'. But he did not want 'Daisy Miller' (see *Life in Letters*, ed. Horne, 92–3, n. 4).

150 *promptly pirated in Boston*: by *Littell's Living Age*, 6 and 27 July 1878, and the *Home Journal* (New York), 31 July, 7 and 14 August 1878 (see *Bibliography*, ed. Edel and Laurence, 39).

the late Leslie Stephen: the eminent man of letters and mountaineer, first editor of the *Dictionary of National Biography*, father of Virginia Woolf and Vanessa Bell, had died in 1904 at the age of 71.

the whirligig of time: a phrase lifted from the *coup de grâce* Feste delivers to

Malvolio at the end of Shakespeare's *Twelfth Night*: 'thus the whirligig of time brings in his revenges' (V. i. 373)

an interesting friend, now dead: interesting friends of James's associated with Venice, now dead, included the wealthy American hostess Katherine de Kay Bronson (1834–1901).

151 *I have already found it convenient to refer to as 'international'*: James ends his Preface to *The Portrait of a Lady* (vols. iii and iv) with the memory of settling in London a few years previously, when 'the "international" light lay, in those days, thick and rich upon the scene' (*Literary Criticism*, ii. 1085). In his Preface to *The Reverberator* and other tales (vol. xiii), he picks this reference up and reflects that 'everything that possibly could . . . managed at that time (as it had done before and was undiscourageably to continue to do) to *be* international for me' (*Literary Criticism*, ii. 1197). The *OED* credits the philosopher, jurist and reformer Jeremy Bentham with coining the word 'international' in 1789 as a term in jurisprudence to describe the branch of law commonly known as 'the law of nations'. It established itself and diversified its application throughout the nineteenth century, especially the later decades, in which James's career came to fruition.

153 *to have 'assisted' . . . at*: an anglicization of the French *assister à*, 'to attend, be present at'.

a whole group of tales I here collect: the other short fictions gathered in this volume of the New York Edition are 'Lady Barbarina', 'The Siege of London', 'The Pension Beaurepas', 'A Bundle of Letters', and 'The Point of View'.

American Literature

British and Irish Literature

Children's Literature

Classics and Ancient Literature

Colonial Literature

Eastern Literature

European Literature

Gothic Literature

History

Medieval Literature

Oxford English Drama

Poetry

Philosophy

Politics

Religion

The Oxford Shakespeare

	Late Victorian Gothic Tales
JANE AUSTEN	Emma
	Mansfield Park
	Persuasion
	Pride and Prejudice
	Selected Letters
	Sense and Sensibility
MRS BEETON	Book of Household Management
MARY ELIZABETH BRADDON	Lady Audley's Secret
ANNE BRONTË	The Tenant of Wildfell Hall
CHARLOTTE BRONTË	Jane Eyre
	Shirley
	Villette
EMILY BRONTË	Wuthering Heights
ROBERT BROWNING	The Major Works
JOHN CLARE	The Major Works
SAMUEL TAYLOR COLERIDGE	The Major Works
WILKIE COLLINS	The Moonstone
	No Name
	The Woman in White
CHARLES DARWIN	The Origin of Species
THOMAS DE QUINCEY	The Confessions of an English Opium-Eater
	On Murder
CHARLES DICKENS	The Adventures of Oliver Twist
	Barnaby Rudge
	Bleak House
	David Copperfield
	Great Expectations
	Nicholas Nickleby
	The Old Curiosity Shop
	Our Mutual Friend
	The Pickwick Papers

A SELECTION OF   **OXFORD WORLD'S CLASSICS**

JOHN BUCHAN

Greenmantle
Huntingtower
The Thirty-Nine Steps

JOSEPH CONRAD

Chance
Heart of Darkness and Other Tales
Lord Jim
Nostromo
An Outcast of the Islands
The Secret Agent
Typhoon and Other Tales
Under Western Eyes

ARTHUR CONAN DOYLE

The Adventures of Sherlock Holmes
The Case-Book of Sherlock Holmes
The Hound of the Baskervilles
The Lost World
The Memoirs of Sherlock Holmes
A Study in Scarlet

FORD MADOX FORD

The Good Soldier

JOHN GALSWORTHY

The Forsyte Saga

JAMES JOYCE

A Portrait of the Artist as a Young Man
Dubliners
Occasional, Critical, and Political Writing
Ulysses

RUDYARD KIPLING

Captains Courageous
The Complete Stalky & Co
The Jungle Books
Just So Stories
Kim
The Man Who Would Be King
Plain Tales from the Hills
War Stories and Poems